CAUG
BILLIO
EMBRACE
BY
ELIZABETH BEVARLY

AND

THE TYCOON'S
TEMPORARY BABY
BY
EMILY McKAY

As chivalrous as a fairy-tale paladin...

He slipped off his tuxedo jacket and draped it over her shoulders.

"You don't have to do that," Della protested. The garment fairly swallowed her, but it was redolent with both his scent and his warmth, and she was helpless not to pull it more closely around herself.

"Now you'll get cold," she told him.

Marcus shook his head. "I haven't been cold since the moment I laid eyes on you. A little thing like snow and a subfreezing temperature isn't going to change that."

Della wasn't feeling cold, either. Not that that would make her return his jacket to him. It felt too nice being enveloped in it. Almost as if she were being enveloped by Marcus himself.

Almost.

Dear Reader,

It's time for another visit to Talk of the Town, Chicago's most famous haute couture rental boutique. (All right, *my* most famous haute couture rental boutique. In fact, my only haute couture rental boutique.) This time around, it's Della Hannan who's looking to spiff herself up, and for a very special occasion. See, Della made a promise to herself when she was a kid that, for her thirtieth birthday, she'd celebrate in major style. She also promised herself as a kid that she'd be a millionaire by the time she turned thirty, but we can't have everything, can we?

So even if the millionaire thing will be pretend, the style will be quite real—even if it is rented.

The only problem is, Della can't afford to be noticed out and about because she has a little secret. Okay, okay, a *huge* secret. But it's hard to go unnoticed when one is arrayed from head to toe in the likes of Carolina Herrera and Dolce&Gabbana. And notice her Marcus Fallon does. Big-time. The last thing that guy wants to do, however, is be kept a secret. Go big or go home, that's Marcus. But when he and Della get snowed in for a weekend, he doesn't want her to go anywhere…

I hope you have as much fun reading about Della and Marcus as I had writing them. And may all your dreams be stylish ones.

Happy reading!

Elizabeth Bevarly

CAUGHT IN THE BILLIONAIRE'S EMBRACE

BY
ELIZABETH BEVARLY

Published in Great Britain 2012
by Mills & Boon, an imprint of Harlequin (UK) Limited,
Eton House, 18-24 Paradise Road, Richmond, Surrey TW9 1SR

© Elizabeth Bevarly 2011

ISBN: 978 0 263 89115 7

51-0212

Harlequin (UK) policy is to use papers that are natural, renewable and
recyclable products and made from wood grown in sustainable forests. The
logging and manufacturing processes conform to the legal environmental
regulations of the country of origin.

Printed and bound in Spain
by Blackprint CPI, Barcelona

Elizabeth Bevarly is the RITA® Award-nominated, nationally bestselling author of more than five dozen books. When she's not writing, she's watching *Project Runway* and *What Not to Wear*, but only for research purposes. She's also confident that she'll someday find a story in *House Hunters International*, so she watches that religiously, too. In the meantime, she makes do with her real life of ready-to-wear from Macy's and college exploratory trips around the Midwest with her husband and soon-to-be-a-senior son.

For everyone who's ever worked in women's fashion,
especially employees of The Limited stores
in Cherry Hill and Echelon Malls,
where I got my start in writing by penning pages
in the stockroom during lunch.
I miss you guys. A lot.

One

There was only one thing that could make Della Hannan's thirtieth birthday better than she'd already planned for it to be, and it was a thing she hadn't even planned. That was saying something, since she'd been fine-tuning the details for the celebration since she was a little girl growing up in the kind of neighborhood where birthdays were pretty much unaffordable and therefore pretty much ignored. Where a lot of things were unaffordable and therefore ignored. Things like, well…Della, for instance. But that was why she had promised herself such a festive event. Because, even as a little girl, she'd known she had only herself to count on.

Of course, the past eleven months had rather thrown a wrench in that line of thinking, because since meeting Geoffrey, she'd had no choice but to count on him. Geoffrey wasn't here tonight, though, and she wasn't going to let herself think about him or anything else from that world. Tonight was special. Tonight was for her. And it would be everything an underprivileged kid from one of New York's roughest neighborhoods could have imagined.

Back then, Della had sworn that by the time she turned thirty, she would have escaped the mean streets of her borough and become a self-made millionaire living park-side uptown. And she'd vowed to mark the big three-oh in the style of the rich and famous, that she had imagined she'd become accustomed as this point in life. She wasn't about to renege on that promise, even if she was celebrating in Chicago instead of New York. She would begin with dinner at a five-star restaurant, follow that with a box seat at the opera and top it off with a nightcap at the sort of club that allowed entrée to only the crème de la crème of society. She was outfitted in thousands of dollars worth of haute couture, dripping in rubies and diamonds, and she had been coiffed and manicured at the city's finest salon.

She sighed with much contentment as she enjoyed the first part of her evening. Palumbo's on State Street was the sort of restaurant where prices rivaled the budgets of some sovereign nations. She had, it went without saying, ordered the most expensive items on the menu—four courses, all of which bore European names she'd had to practice all week to pronounce correctly. (Thank goodness the menu had been posted online so she could check in advance and not appear as some kind of philistine when she ordered. And how lovely to have the opportunity to use the word *philistine,* even if it was only in her head.) Because ordering the most expensive items on one's birthday was what anyone who was sophisticated and chic and rich would do, right?

The thought made her surreptitiously survey her surroundings, to make sure the other diners—sophisticated, chic and rich, every last one of them—were also enjoying the most expensive bounty. And, okay, okay, to also make sure Geoffrey hadn't somehow followed her, even though she'd done an excellent job sneaking out—she always did—and even though she wasn't scheduled to check in with him until her daily call tomorrow. He couldn't know where she was going, anyway, even if he did discover she'd slipped out when she wasn't supposed to. She'd planned tonight's escape even more meticulously than she'd planned her thirtieth birthday celebration.

For all anyone here knew, she was just as blue-blooded as they were and belonged in this society every bit as much. And, thankfully, there was no sign of Geoffrey anywhere. Check and check.

And Della did feel as if she belonged here, sipping champagne as she anticipated the arrival of her calamari appetizer. She'd been moving in environments like this for years, despite not having been born into a wealthy family. She'd clawed her way out of the slum and into the upper echelons of society—even if she'd only been a fringe member—and she'd studied and emulated everyone in this world until she'd had no trouble passing herself off as a pure-blooded member.

Tonight was no exception. She'd paid a not-so-small fortune to rent the crimson velvet Carolina Herrera gown and Dolce & Gabbana shoes, not to mention the Bulgari earrings and pendant and the black silk Valentino opera coat necessitated by the frigid December temperatures. The red hues, she knew, complemented her gray eyes and the dark blond hair that was long enough now to have been swept up into a French twist, held in place by a single hidden comb.

She lifted a hand to make sure every hair was in place, smiling at how much she enjoyed having it long. She'd worn it boyishly short all her life, until earlier this year, and hadn't sported her natural color since high school, when she'd dyed her hair black during her grunge phase and liked it enough to keep it that way. She hadn't even realized how it had deepened to such a beautiful honey-infused blond over the years. Between her natural color and the new length—not to mention her rented duds—no one from the old neighborhood would recognize her tonight.

But she wasn't thinking about any of that, either, she reminded herself. Tonight really was going to be perfect. It really was going to be everything she had planned all those years ago.

Except maybe for the handsome, elegantly attired man the hostess had seated at a table near hers a few moments ago, and whom she hadn't been able to resist sneaking peeks at during each of those moments. When Della was a kid, she'd never entertained the idea of having a companion for her special evening. She wasn't sure why not. Maybe because of the aforementioned knowing she would always have only herself to count on. Or maybe because, as a kid, she couldn't even imagine a guy like him. In her neighborhood, *elegantly attired* had meant one's shirt was buttoned. And *handsome* had meant a guy had all his teeth.

Without warning, the man glanced up, his gaze connecting with hers. Something between the two of them…clicked. Or something. The man dipped his dark head toward Della in silent acknowledgment, one corner of his mouth lifting in something vaguely resembling a smile. After only a moment's hesitation, she lifted her glass in a silent toast to him. Swathed in a tuxedo that had been tailored to emphasize every magnificent inch of him, he was framed by billows of amber silk that edged the window behind him. His dark eyes were warmed by the dreamy light of the candle flickering in a crystal holder in front of him, and his little half smile sent a shudder of something hot and electric skittering down Della's spine. Because it was the kind of smile that told a woman he was not just undressing her with his eyes, but he was also considering using a lot of his other body parts on her, too.

When she felt the heat of a blush creep into her cheeks, she hastily glanced away. Lifting her champagne to her mouth for a cooling sip, she did her best to focus on something else—the crisp white tablecloths, the sparkling china, the glittering crowd. Inescapably, however, her attention wandered back to the man at the table opposite hers.

Who was still gazing at her with much interest.

"So what do you think?" he asked her, raising his voice enough to be heard two small tables away from his own.

Della blinked at him, nonplussed. Understanding, for the first time in her life, what *nonplussed* actually meant: confusion mixed with a funny little buzz in the belly that wasn't altogether unpleasant. A million different possible replies to his question ricocheted around in her brain. *I think you're the most beautiful man I've ever seen,* for example. And, *what are you doing New Year's Eve?* Even a smooth, *hey, lover.* And of course—it went without saying—*oh,* bay-*bee!*

"For dinner," he added, holding up the menu. "What do you recommend?"

Ooooh, what did Della think about *that?* Well, that was a totally different question from the one she'd been thinking he asked, wasn't it? Good thing she'd been too nonplussed to answer.

"Um, I'm not sure," she said. "This is the first time I've dined here." Somehow, she didn't think a man like him would be too impressed if she told him to order whatever was most expensive, because it would make him appear chic, sophisticated and rich. He was all those things simply by existing on the planet.

Her answer seemed to surprise him. "But how can this be your first time? Palumbo's has been a Chicago institution for nearly a hundred years. Are you not from Chicago originally?"

There was no way Della was going to answer that question. Mostly because no one other than Geoffrey knew she was here, and he was keeping much too close an eye on her. Even if he didn't know exactly where she was at the moment, she wasn't about to risk his discovery of her little escape by breathing a word of it to anyone.

So she wouldn't—couldn't—tell this man that. Either she'd have to lie—which Della never did, even though her honesty had gotten her into trouble more than once, as evidenced by her having to rely on Geoffrey at the moment—or else her reply would lead to the kind of small talk that might make her talk about her past. Or, even worse, her present. And she wanted to be as far removed from both of those tonight as she could be, on account of nothing in her past or present lent itself to Carolina Herrera gowns or diamonds and rubies or box seats to *La Bohème.*

So she replied instead to the first question he'd asked. "I ordered the special. I adore seafood."

He said nothing for a moment, and Della wondered if it was because he was pondering her answer to his first question or trying to decide whether or not to press the fact that she hadn't replied to the second. Finally, he said, "I'll remember that."

For some reason, though, he made it sound as if it were the fact that she loved seafood that he would remember, and not that she had recommended it for dinner.

He opened his mouth to say something else, but his server arrived to place a short, amber-colored cocktail in front of him and a dewy pink cosmopolitan on the table at the place directly next to his.

He was expecting someone to join him, Della realized. A woman, judging by the color and daintiness of the drink. Couples didn't dine in places like Palumbo's unless their relationship went beyond casual—or one of them was looking to make it more than casual. This guy was throwing steamy glances her way, even flirting with her, despite the fact that there would be a woman joining him momentarily. That meant the guy was a complete jerk.

Okay, so maybe her thirtieth birthday celebration wasn't going to go *quite* as perfectly as she had planned, since she was going to have to be seated near a jerk. And—*oh, all right*—maybe it wasn't only because of the jerk that the celebration wouldn't be exactly what she'd had in mind. Maybe it wasn't even because her gown and accessories were rentals from a Michigan Avenue boutique instead of pulled casually from her own closet.

Maybe, just maybe, it was because, in addition to not being the life of a millionaire, Della's current life wasn't even her own. Everything about her life these days—every thing she did, every place she went, every word she spoke—had to be vetted and controlled by Geoffrey. Her life would never be normal again. Or, at least, it would never be the life she had made for herself or the one she had planned. It would be a life manufactured and orchestrated by someone else.

As soon as the thought formed, she pushed it to the furthest, darkest recesses of her brain. She wouldn't think about any of that tonight, she reminded herself again, wondering why she was finding it all so hard to forget. Because tonight, she didn't want to be Della anyway. Tonight, for one night, she wanted to be the woman she had envisioned herself to be two decades and two thousand miles ago: CinderDella, toast of the town and belle of the ball. Nothing was going to mar this evening. Not even Prince Less-Than-Charming over there who was still making bedroom eyes at her while waiting on a girlfriend who could do a helluva lot better.

As if cued by the thought, the hostess seated a boisterous party of four at the table between them, completely blocking the man from her view. For that Della was grateful and not disappointed, even if some twisted part of her made her think that was what she was feeling.

Well, even if he was a jerk, he was still the most beautiful man she'd ever seen.

And she saw him again an hour and a half later—at the Lyric Opera when she was trying to locate her seat. After realizing she was in the wrong part of the auditorium, Della asked an usher for directions, then found herself gazing at a box across the room that afforded an amazing view of the stage…and where sat the handsome stranger she'd seen at dinner. Just as he'd been at the restaurant, he was surrounded by gold, this time a cascade of engraved gilt that encrusted the walls and ensconced the stage. Likewise as he'd been at the restaurant, he was seated alone.

Okay, so maybe as she'd left Palumbo's, Della had happened to notice that his date still hadn't shown up. Not that she'd been *trying* to notice that. She just had, that was all. Though whether the woman had gotten waylaid somewhere and been unable to make their rendezvous, or she'd wised up about what kind of man he was, Della couldn't have said.

Not that she cared either way. Hey, she'd barely noticed. In case she hadn't mentioned that.

Now as she strode down the aisle to her seat, she similarly barely noticed that it was not only in the same box the man was occupying, but also in the same row, as well—a small one at the front that contained only three chairs. She also barely noticed that he had placed both a program and a long-stemmed rose on the seat beside his own, as if the chair would soon be occupied. So evidently his girlfriend had indeed been waylaid earlier and was intending to catch up to him here.

Butterflies head-butted Della's midsection at the prospect of having to sit in such close proximity to the man. Once she squeezed past him to get to her seat, there would be no escaping him—unless she wanted to pull a Groucho Marx maneuver from *A Night at the Opera* and swing across the auditorium on a cable.

She inhaled a single, fortifying breath and forced her feet to move forward until she stood at the edge of the row beside him. His head snapped up, and, when he recognized her, he grinned that shudders-down-the-spine grin again. Heat flared in her belly, her brain turned to mush, and the *excuse me* Della had been about to utter evaporated in her mouth.

He murmured a greeting as he stood, but she barely heard it, because she was too busy trying not to swoon. Not only did he smell delectable—a luscious mix of spice and wood smoke—but he was also much taller than she'd realized, forcing her to tip back her head to meet his gaze. It was an action to which she was unaccustomed, since she pushed the six-foot mark herself in the two-inch heels she was wearing. Even without heels, she was accustomed to being at eye level with virtually everyone. With this man, however, eye level meant gazing at shoulders that spanned a distance roughly the size of Montana.

But it was his face that drew her attention. His jawline was resolute, his nose was straight and refined, his cheekbones looked as if they'd been hewn from marble, and his eyes… Oh, his eyes. His eyes were the color of bittersweet chocolate, a brown so dark and so compelling that Della couldn't tear her gaze away. Then she realized it wasn't the depth or color of his eyes that so captivated her. It was her recognition of something in them that was at odds with his dazzling smile. A somberness, even sadness, that was unmistakable.

The moment she identified it, however, a shadow fell over his eyes, almost as if he was aware of her understanding and didn't want her to see too deeply into him.

"We've got to stop meeting like this," he said, his smile broadening.

The humor in his tone surprised her, coming as it did on the heels of the shadows in his eyes. Even so, she couldn't quite keep herself from smiling back. "It is a little odd, isn't it?"

"Actually, I'm thinking of a different word."

Not sure that she wanted to know what it was, she heard herself ask anyway, "Oh?"

"*Lucky*," he said immediately. "I was thinking it was *lucky*."

She wasn't sure what to say in response to that, so she held up her ticket and gestured toward her seat. She made sure to give the rose-laden chair between hers and his a meaningful inspection before saying, "If you don't mind? That's my seat."

For a minute, he only continued to gaze at her, his eyes revealing nothing now of what might be going through his head. Then, "Not at all," he replied, sidestepping into the aisle to give her room to pass.

When he did, she hastened to take her seat, immediately opening her program to read it before he had a chance to say anything that might start a conversation.

He didn't take the hint, however, and said as he returned to his seat, "How was your dinner?"

Not looking up from the program, Della replied, "Lovely."

Her one-word response did nothing to dissuade him, either. "I ended up ordering the pheasant. It was amazing."

When Della only nodded silently without looking up from her program, he added, "You should try it next time you're at Palumbo's. I highly recommend it."

He was fishing. Trying to find out if she lived here in town the same way he had when he'd asked her why she'd never been to Palumbo's. He was trying to gauge whether or not there was a chance the two of them might run into each other again, either by accident or by design. Even with a long-stemmed rose and mystery woman between them.

"I'll take it under advisement," she told him. And returned to reading her program.

But still, he didn't take the hint. "You know, I don't meet many people of my own generation who enjoy opera," he said, trying a new tack. "Especially not enough to see it performed live. Or spring for box seats. You must really love it."

Della sighed inwardly, silently cursing him for the change of subject. That was a low blow. There was no way she could resist a conversation about her most favorite thing in the world.

"I adore it, actually," she said helplessly, letting the program fall open onto her lap.

When she turned to look at him again, his expression made clear he was as delighted to be here as she was and that he felt every bit as passionately about opera. So passionately that his love for the medium had chased away the darkness that had clouded his eyes earlier. She realized now that they weren't entirely brown. Flecks of gold wreathed the irises, making his eyes appear more faceted somehow, drawing her in even more deeply.

"I've loved opera since I was a little girl," she told him. "Our next-door neighbor was a huge fan and introduced me to all the classics." She didn't add that that was only because she could hear Mrs. Klosterman's radio through the paper-thin walls of their tenement, or how Della had hung on every word of the announcer's analysis of each opera once it had concluded. "The first time I saw one performed live," she continued, not bothering to mention that it was live on PBS, not live on stage, "I was enchanted."

She actually would have loved to major in music and

make the study of opera her life's work. But college had been beyond the means of an average student from her economic stratum, so she'd gone directly to work after graduating from high school, as a gofer in the offices of one of Wall Street's most noted and respected brokerage houses. And even though she'd worked her way up the corporate ladder to become an executive assistant, Della had never made the time to go for the degree. She'd been supporting herself fairly well on her salary—certainly better than she'd ever imagined she would growing up in the sort of neighborhood she had—and she'd been happy with the way her life was going. At least until that life had shattered into a million pieces, and she'd been left with nothing but Geoffrey, who'd offered her a dubious sort of refuge—and not without a price.

Almost as if that thought had cued the orchestra, the music swelled, and the lights dimmed. Della couldn't resist one last look at her companion as the room grew dark, but when she saw him gazing at her—and noted the seat between them still empty—she quickly turned her attention to the stage.

After that, she fell into the world of Mimi and Rodolfo and their bohemian friends, leaving her own reality behind. So much so, that when the lights came up for intermission, it took Della a moment to return from nineteenth century Paris to twenty-first century Chicago. She blinked a few times and inhaled a deep breath and, before she could stop herself, looked over at her companion—who was looking at her in the same way he had been when the lights had dimmed, almost as if he'd spent the entire first half of the opera watching her instead.

That strange buzz erupted in her belly again, so she

quickly glanced at the crowd. The myriad splendor of the women's gowns made them look like brightly colored gems amid the gilt of the auditorium, the sparkle of their jewelry only enhancing the image. Della watched many of the ladies link arms with their companions as they left for intermission, and noted how the men bent their heads affectionately toward them as they laughed or chatted.

For a moment, she felt a keen regret that this night couldn't last forever. Wouldn't it be lovely to enjoy evenings like this whenever she wanted, without regard for their cost or the risk of being seen in a place where she shouldn't be? She couldn't remember the last time she'd had a night out at all, never mind one like this. Geoffrey kept her locked away like Rapunzel. She spent her time reading books, watching downloaded movies and staring at the walls that were, for all intents and purposes, her cell. Even if the place Geoffrey had provided lacked bars and held sufficient creature comforts, Della still felt like a prisoner. Hell, she was a prisoner. And she would be until Geoffrey told her she could go.

But even that thought brought little comfort, because she had no idea *where* she would go, or what she would do, once Geoffrey decided she was no longer necessary. She would have to start all over again with virtually nothing. The same way she had when she left the old neighborhood behind.

It was all the more reason to enjoy tonight to the fullest, Della told herself. Who knew what the future held beyond even the next few hours?

"So what do you think so far?"

She turned at the sound of the rich, velvety baritone, and her pulse rippled when she saw the smoky look he was giving her. Truly, she had to get a grip. Not only did the guy show evidence of being a class-A heel, flirting with one woman when he was supposed to be out with another, but he was also way out of Della's league.

"I have to confess that *La Bohème* isn't one of my favorites," she admitted. "I think Puccini was a bit reserved when he scored it, especially when you compare it to the exhilaration of something like *Manon Lescaut*. But I am enjoying it. Very much."

Of course, some of that might have had to do with the company seated in her box. Not that she had to tell him that. Not that she had to admit it to herself.

"How about you?" she asked. "What's your verdict?"

"I think I've seen it too many times to be objective anymore," he said. "But it's interesting you say that about Puccini's being too reserved with it. I've always kind of thought the same thing. I actually like Leoncavallo's interpretation of Murger's book much better."

She grinned. "I do, too."

He grinned back. "That puts us in the minority, you know."

"I know."

"In fact," he added, "I like Leoncavallo's *La Bohème* even better than his *Pagliacci,* an opinion that will get you tossed out of some opera houses."

She laughed at that. "I like it better than *Pagliacci,* too. Looks like we'll be kicked to the curb together."

He chuckled lightly, both of them quieting at the same time, neither seeming to know what to say next. After a couple of awkward seconds, Della ventured, "Well, if you've already seen *La Bohème* too many times, and you don't care for it as much as you do other operas, then why are you here tonight?"

He shrugged, but there was something in the gesture that was in no way careless, and the warmth that had eased his expression fled. "I have season tickets."

Tickets, she repeated to herself. Not *ticket.* Plural, not singular. Meaning he was indeed the owner of the empty seat beside his and had been expecting someone to occupy it tonight. Someone who might very well be with him all the other nights of the season. A wife, perhaps?

She hastily glanced at his left hand but saw no ring. Still, there were plenty of married people who eschewed the ring thing these days. Della wondered who normally joined him and why she wasn't here tonight. She waited to see if he would add something about the mysteriously empty chair. Something that might clarify the sudden drop in temperature that seemed to shimmer between them. Because she sensed that that vacant chair was what had generated the faint chill.

Instead, he shook off his odd, momentary funk and said, "That is how I know you don't normally attend Lyric Opera performances. At least not on opening night, and not in the seat you're sitting in tonight." He smiled again, and the chill abated some. "I would have noticed."

She did her best to ignore the butterflies doing the rumba in her stomach. "This is my first time coming here," she confessed.

His inspection of her grew ponderous. "Your first time at Palumbo's. Your first time at the Lyric. So you have just moved to Chicago recently, haven't you?"

She was saved from having to reply, because the opera gods and goddesses—Wagnerian, she'd bet, every one of them—smiled down on her. Her companion was beckoned from below by a couple who had recognized him and wanted to say hello—and who addressed him as Marcus, giving Della his first name, at least. Then they proceeded to say way more than hello to him, chatting until the lights flickered once, twice, three times, indicating that the performance was about to resume. At that, the couple scurried off, and he—Marcus—turned to look at Della again.

"Can you see all right from where you are?" he asked. He patted the chair next to him that still contained the unopened program and rose. "You might have a better vantage point from this seat. You want to have the best angle for 'Addio Dolce Svegliare Alla Mattina.'"

The Italian rolled off his tongue as if he spoke it fluently, and a ribbon of something warm and gooey unfurled in her. Even though the vantage point would be no different from the one she had now—which he must realize, too—Della was surprised by how much she wanted to accept his offer. Whoever usually sat there obviously wasn't coming. And he didn't seem to be as bothered by that as a man involved in a romantic relationship should be. So maybe his relationship with the usual occupant of the chair wasn't romantic, in spite of the red, red rose.

Or maybe he was just a big ol' hound dog with whom she'd be better off not sharing anything more than opera chitchat. Maybe he should only be another lovely, momentary memory to go along with all the other lovely, momentary memories she was storing from this evening.

"Thank you, but the view from here is fine," she said. And it was, she told herself. For now. For tonight. But not, unfortunately, forever.

Two

Marcus Fallon sat in his usual seat at his usual table drinking his usual nightcap in his usual club, thinking the most unusual thoughts. Or, at least, thoughts about a most unusual woman. A woman unlike any he'd ever met before. And not only because she shared his passion for, and opinions about, opera, either. Unfortunately, the moment the curtain had fallen on *La Bohème,* she'd hurried past him with a breathlessly uttered *good night,* scurried up the aisle ahead of everyone else in the box and he'd lost her in the crowd before he'd been able to say a word. He'd experienced a moment of whimsy as he'd scanned the stairs on his way out looking for a glass slipper, but even that small fairy-tale clue had eluded him. She was gone. Just like that. Almost as if she'd never been there at all. And he had no idea how to find her.

He lifted his Scotch to his lips again, filling his

mouth with the smooth, smoky liquor, scanning the crowd here as if he were looking for her again. Strangely, he realized he was. But all he saw was the usual crowd milling around the dark-paneled, richly appointed, sumptuously decorated room. Bernie Stegman was, as usual, sitting in an oxblood leather wingback near the fireplace, chatting up Lucas Whidmore, who sat in an identical chair on the other side. Delores and Marion Hagemann were having a late dinner with Edith and Lawrence Byck at their usual table in the corner, the quartet framed by heavy velvet drapes the color of old money. Cynthia Harrison was doing her usual flirting with Stu, the usual Saturday bartender, who was sidestepping her advances with his usual aplomb. He would lose his job if he were caught canoodling with the patrons.

Thoughts of canoodling brought Marcus's ruminations back to the mysterious lady in red. Not that that was entirely surprising, since the minute he'd seen her sitting opposite him at Palumbo's, canoodling had been at the forefront of his brain. She'd simply been that stunning. What was really strange, though, was that once he'd started talking to her at the Lyric, canoodling had fallen by the wayside, and what he'd really wanted to do with her was talk more about opera. And not only because she shared his unconventional opinions, either. But because of the way she'd lit up while talking about it. As beautiful as she'd been, seated alone at her table in the restaurant, she'd become radiant during their conversation.

Radiant, he repeated to himself, frowning. Now there was a word he'd never used to describe a woman before. Then again, that could be because he'd seldom moved past the stage with a woman where he found her beautiful. Meaning he'd seldom reached a stage where he actually talked to one. Once he bedded a woman—and that usually came pretty early after meeting one—he lost interest. But that was because few women were worth knowing beyond the biblical sense.

Unbidden, a reproving voice erupted in his brain, taking him to task for his less-than-stellar commentary, but it wasn't his own. It was Charlotte's sandpaper rasp, made that way by too many cigarettes over the course of her eighty-two years. More than once over the past two decades since making her acquaintance, he'd let slip some politically incorrect comment about the opposite sex, only to have her haul him up by his metaphorical collar—and sometimes by his not-so-metaphorical collar—to set him straight.

God, he missed her.

He glanced at the pink cosmopolitan sitting opposite his single malt on the table, the glass dewy with condensation since it had been sitting there for so long. The rose, too, had begun to wilt, its petals blackening at their edges. Even the opera program looked limp and tattered already. All of them were at the end of their lives. Just as Charlotte had been the last time he'd sat at this table looking in the same direction.

She'd died two days after closing night at the Lyric. It had been seven months since her funeral, and Marcus still felt her loss keenly. He wondered, not for the first time, what happened after a soul left this world to enter the next. Was Charlotte still able to enjoy her occasional cosmo? Did they have performances of Verdi and Bizet where she was now? And was she able to enjoy the rare prime rib she'd loved to order at Palumbo's?

Marcus hoped so. Charlotte deserved only the best,

wherever she was. Because the best was what she had always given him.

A flash of red caught his eye, and Marcus glanced up. But it was only Emma Stegman, heading from the bar toward her father. Marcus scanned the room again for good measure but saw only more of the usual suspects. He knew everyone here, he thought. So why was he sitting alone? Hell, Stu the bartender wasn't the only guy Cynthia Harrison had tried canoodling with. If Marcus wanted to, he could sidle up next to her and be headed to the Ambassador Hotel, which was adjacent to the club, in no time. And he sure wouldn't lose his job for it. All he'd lose would be the empty feeling inside that had been with him since Charlotte's death. Of course, the feeling would come back tomorrow, when he was alone again....

He lifted his glass and downed what was left of his Scotch, then, for good measure, downed Charlotte's cosmopolitan, too, in one long gulp. He squeezed his eyes shut for a moment as he waited for the taste to leave his mouth—how had she stood those things?—then opened them again...

...to see a vision in red seated at a table on the other side of the room. He could not believe his good fortune. Seeing her one time had been chance. Seeing her twice had been lucky. Seeing her a third time...

That could only be fate.

Forgetting, for now, that he didn't believe in such a thing, and before he risked losing her again, he immediately rose and crossed to where she was seated, signaling for Stu at the same time and gesturing toward her table. Without waiting to be invited, he pulled out the chair across from hers and seated himself.

She glanced up at his appearance, surprise etched

on her features. But her lips curled into the faintest of smiles, reassuring him. That was another new experience for him. He'd never had to be reassured of anything. On the contrary, he'd taken everything in life for granted. That was what happened when you were born into one of the Gold Coast's oldest and most illustrious families. You got everything you wanted, often without even having to ask for it. In fact, you even got the things you didn't ask for. Usually handed to you on a silver platter. Sometimes literally.

"We have got to stop meeting like this."

This time it was she, not Marcus, who spoke the words he had said to her at the Lyric.

"On the contrary," he replied. "I'm beginning to like meeting you like this."

A hint of pink bloomed on her cheeks at his remark, and delight wound through his belly at seeing her blush. He couldn't remember the last time he'd made a woman blush. Not shyly, anyway. Not becomingly. Usually, if he made a woman blush, it was because he'd suggested they do something in the bedroom that most of society considered shameful. It was all the more reason, in his opinion, why it should be enjoyed.

But he was getting way ahead of himself. Anything in the bedroom with this woman was still, oh…hours away.

"Mind if I join you?" he asked.

"I think you already have."

He feigned surprise. "So I have. Then you'll have to let me buy you a drink."

She opened her mouth to reply and, for a moment, he feared she would decline his offer. Another new experience for Marcus. Not only fearing a woman would turn him down—since that almost never happened—but also feeling a knot of disappointment in his chest at the possibility. On those rare occasions when a woman did turn him down, he simply shrugged it off and moved to the next one. Because, inevitably, there was always a next one. With this woman, however…

Well, he couldn't imagine a next one. Not even with Cynthia Harrison falling out of her dress less than ten feet away.

"All right," she finally said, as Stu arrived at their table. She looked at the bartender. "I'll have a glass of champagne, please."

"Bring a bottle," Marcus instructed before the bartender had a chance to get away. "The Perrier-Jouët Cuvée Belle Epoque. 2002."

"Really, that's not necessary…." she began, her voice trailing off on the last word.

Deciding it was because she didn't know how to address him—and because he wanted to give her his name so that he could get hers in return—he finished for her, "Marcus. Marcus—"

"Don't tell me your last name."

He halted before revealing it, less because she asked him not to than because he found her command curious.

"Why not?"

"Just don't, that's all."

He started to give it to her anyway—never let it be said that Marcus Fallon ever did as he was told—but for some reason decided to honor her request. That was even stranger, since never let it be said that Marcus Fallon did the honorable thing, either. "All right." He lifted his right hand for her to shake. "And you are…?"

She hesitated before taking his hand, then gingerly

placed her own lightly against his. Her fingers were slender and delicate against his large, blunt ones and, unable to help himself, he closed his hand possessively over hers. Her skin was soft and warm, as creamy as ivory, and he found himself wondering if that was true of the rest of her. The blush on her cheeks deepened as he covered her hand with his, but she didn't pull hers away.

His appeal for her name hung in the air between them without a response. "Della," she told him finally. "My name is Della."

No last name from her, either, then. Fine, he thought. He wouldn't push it. But before the night was over, he'd know not only her last name, but everything else about her, too. Especially where each and every one of her erogenous zones were and what kind of erotic sounds she uttered whenever he located a new one.

Neither of them said anything more, only studied each other's faces as their hands remained joined. She had amazing eyes. Pale, clear gray, the kind of eyes a man could lose himself in forever. The kind that hid nothing and said much. Honest eyes, he finally decided. Noble. The eyes of a person who would always do the right thing.

Damn.

Stu cleared his throat a little too obviously beside them, and she gave a soft tug to free her fingers. Reluctantly, he let them go. She lowered her hand to the table near his, however, resting it palm down on the white linen. So he did likewise, flattening his hand until his fingers almost—almost—touched hers.

"Will there be anything else, Mr.—?" Stu stopped before revealing Marcus's last name, obviously having overheard the exchange. Quickly, he amended, "Will there be anything else, sir?"

Marcus waved a hand airily in his direction, muttering that Stu should bring some kind of appetizer, too, but didn't specify what. He honestly didn't care about anything, other than the intriguing woman who sat across from him.

"Well," he began, trying to jump-start the conversation again. "If you're sitting here in the Windsor Club, you can't be too new to Chicago. They have a waiting list to get in, and last I heard, it was two years, at least, before anyone added to it could even expect an application. Unless you're here as a guest of another member?" That would be just his luck. That he'd meet a woman like this, and she'd be involved with someone else.

"I'm on my own," she told him. Then, after a small hesitation, she added, "Tonight."

Suggesting she wasn't on her own on other nights, Marcus thought. For the first time, it occurred to him to glance down at her left hand. Not that a wedding ring had ever stopped him from seducing a woman before. But she sported only one ring, and it was on her right hand. The left bore no sign of ever having had one. So she wasn't even engaged. At least not to a man who had the decency to buy her a ring.

"Or maybe," he continued thoughtfully, "you're a member of one of the Windsor's original charter families who earn and keep their membership by a simple accident of birth." He grinned. "Like me. As many times as they've tried to throw me out of this place, they can't."

She grinned back. "And why on earth would they

throw out a paragon of formality and decency like you?"

His eyebrows shot up at that. "You really are new in town if no one's warned you about me yet. That's usually the first thing they tell beautiful young socialites. In fact, ninety percent of the tourist brochures for the city say something like, 'Welcome to Chicago. While you're here, be sure to visit Navy Pier, the Hancock Tower, the Field Museum and the Shedd Aquarium. And whatever you do, stay away from Marcus—" Again he halted before saying his last name. "Well, stay away from Marcus-Whose-Last-Name-You-Don't-Want-To-Know. That guy's nothing but trouble.'"

She laughed at that. She had a really great laugh. Uninhibited, unrestrained, genuinely happy. "And what do the other ten percent of the travel brochures say?"

"Well, those would be the ones they give out to conventioneers looking for a good time while they're away from the ball and chain. Those are the ones that list all the, ah, less seemly places in town." He smiled again. "I'm actually featured very prominently in those. Not by name, mind you, but..." He shrugged. "Those damned photographers don't care who they take pictures of."

She laughed again, stirring something warm and fizzy inside Marcus unlike anything he'd ever felt before. "I don't believe you," she said. "I find it hard to jibe *The Bartered Bride* with bump and grind."

"There's more to me than opera, you know." He met her gaze levelly. "A lot more."

The blush blossomed in her cheeks again, making him chuckle more softly. She was saved from having to respond to his comment, however, when Stu arrived with their champagne and a tray of fruit and cheese. The bartender went a little overboard with the presentation and opening of the bottle, but it was probably because he, too, recognized that Della—yes, Marcus did like that name—wasn't a usual customer. In fact, there was nothing usual about her. She was, in a word, extraordinary.

After receiving approval for the champagne, Stu poured a glass for each of them. As he did, Marcus told Della, "I am notorious in this town. Ask anyone."

She turned to the bartender, who was nestling the champagne in a silver bucket of ice. "Is he really notorious?" she asked.

The bartender glanced first at Marcus, who nodded imperceptibly to let Stu know his tip wouldn't be compromised by his honesty, then at Della. "Oh, yes, ma'am. And not just in Chicago. He makes the society pages all over the country, wherever he goes, and he's a regular feature on a lot of those celebrity websites. If you're seen with him, it's a good bet you'll wind up there yourself. He's infamous."

Della turned to Marcus, her eyes no longer full of laughter, but now brimming with something akin to… fear? Oh, surely not. What would she have to be afraid of?

"Is that true?" she asked.

Still puzzled by her reaction, but not wanting to lie to her—especially since it would be easy enough for her to find out with a simple internet search—he told her, "I'm afraid so."

Her lips parted fractionally, and her expression became almost panicked. Deciding she must be feigning fear as a joke, he played along, telling her, "Don't worry. They never let riffraff like the paparazzi into the club.

You're perfectly safe with me here. No one will see you with me."

It occurred to him as he said it that that was exactly what she feared—being seen with him. Not just by the paparazzi, but by some individual in particular. An individual who might not like seeing her out with Marcus. Or anyone else, for that matter.

She did have that look about her, he decided as he considered her again. Pampered, well tended to, cared for—at least on the surface. The kind of woman who made her way in the world by making herself available to men who could afford her. There were still a surprising number of such women in society, even in this day and age when a woman shouldn't have to rely on her sexuality to make her way in the world. Beautiful, elegant, reserved, they tended to be. At least on the surface.

Not that he'd ever seen Della among such women in the level of society in which he traveled. That only fueled his suspicion that she was merely visiting the city. Dammit.

It took a moment for her expression to clear, but she finally emitted a single—albeit a tad humorless—chuckle. "Of course," she said. "I mean...I knew that. I was only kidding."

He nodded, but there was a part of him that wasn't quite convinced. Maybe she really was attached to someone else. Maybe she even *belonged* to that someone. Maybe that someone wouldn't be too happy about her being here tonight alone. Or anywhere alone. Maybe that someone would be even more unhappy to find her with another man. Maybe she really was afraid her photo would show up somewhere with Marcus at her side, and she'd be in big, big trouble with that someone.

Just who was she, this mysterious lady in red? And why did Marcus want so badly to find out?

In an effort to dispel the odd tension that had erupted between them, he lifted his glass of champagne and said, softly, "Cheers."

There was another small hesitation on her part before, she, too, lifted her glass. "Cheers," she echoed even more softly.

The toast didn't put an end to the frisson of uneasiness that still hovered over the table, but it did put a bit of the bloom back in her cheeks. It was enough, he decided. For now.

But certainly not forever.

Della gazed at the man seated across the table from her as she sipped her champagne, and she wondered exactly when the evening had jumped the track and started screeching headlong into a dark, scary tunnel. One minute, she'd been about to embark on the last leg of her evening by enjoying a final glass of champagne at Chicago's celebrated Windsor Club—which she'd gotten into only by bribing the doorman with another small fortune—and the next minute, she'd found herself gazing once again into the gold-flecked, chocolate-brown eyes that had so intrigued her at the opera.

Marcus. His name fit him. Stoic and classic, commanding and uncompromising. How strange that she should run into him at every destination she'd visited tonight. Then again, she'd gone out of her way to choose destinations that were magnets for the rich and powerful, and he certainly fit that bill. Of course, now she was learning he was part of that other adjective that went along with rich—*famous*—and that was a condition she most definitely had to avoid.

So what was she afraid of? He was right. There was no one in the club who didn't belong here. Other than herself, she meant. Nobody had even seemed to notice the two of them. Not to mention it was late and, even if it was Saturday, ninety percent of the city's population had gone home. There was snow in the forecast for later, even if it wasn't anything a city like Chicago couldn't handle. Most people were probably hunkered down in their living rooms and bedrooms, having stocked up on provisions earlier, and were looking forward to a Sunday being snowed in with nothing to do.

Della wished she could enjoy something like that, but she felt as though she'd been snowed in with nothing to do for the past eleven months. At least when she wasn't at Geoffrey's beck and call.

But tonight that wasn't the case. Tonight she was having fun. She should look at the opportunity to share the last couple of hours of her celebration with a man like Marcus as the icing on her birthday cake.

"So…" she began, trying to recapture the flirtatiousness of their earlier exchange. Still trying to figure out when, exactly, she'd decided to return his flirtations. "What kinds of things have you done to make yourself so notorious?"

He savored another sip of his champagne, then placed the glass on the table between them. But instead of releasing it, he dragged his fingers up over the stem and along the bowl of the flute, then up farther along the elegant line of its sides. Della found herself mesmerized by the voyage of those fingers, especially when he began to idly trace the rim with the pad of his middle finger. Around and around it went, slowly, slowly…oh, so slowly…until a coil of heat began to unwrap in her belly and purl into parts beyond.

She found herself wondering what it would be like to have him drawing idle circles like that elsewhere, someplace like, oh…she didn't know. Herself maybe. Along her shoulder, perhaps. Or down her thigh. Touching her in other places, too—places where such caresses might drive her to the brink of madness.

Her eyes fluttered closed as the thought formed in her brain, as if by not watching what he was doing, she might better dispel the visions dancing around in her head. But closing her eyes only made those images more vivid. More earthy. More erotic. More…*oh*. So much more *more*. She snapped her eyes open again in an effort to squash the visions completely. But that left her looking at Marcus, who was gazing at her with faint amusement, as if he'd seen where her attention had settled and knew exactly what she was thinking about.

As he studied her, he stilled his finger on the rim of the glass and settled his index finger beside it. Della watched helplessly as he scissored them along the rim, first opening, then closing, then opening again. With great deliberation, he curled them into the glass until they touched the top of the champagne, then he dampened each finger with the effervescent wine. Then he carefully pulled them out and lifted them to her lips, brushing lightly over her mouth with the dew of champagne.

Heat swamped her, making her stomach simmer, her breasts tingle and her heart rate quadruple, and dampening her between her legs. Without even thinking about what she was doing, she parted her lips enough to allow him to tuck one finger inside. She tasted the champagne then, along with the faint essence of Marcus. And Marcus was, by far, the most intoxicating.

Quickly, she drew her head back and licked the remnants of his touch from her lips. Not that that did anything to quell her arousal. What had come over her? How could she be this attracted to a man this quickly? She knew almost nothing about him, save his name and the fact that he loved opera and good champagne and had bought a rose for someone earlier in the evening who—

The rose. How could she have forgotten about that? She might very well be sitting here enjoying the advances of a married man! Or, at the very least, one who belonged to someone else. And the last thing she wanted to be was part of a triangle.

Where was the rose now? Had he thrown it resentfully into the trash or pressed it between the pages of the neglected opera program as a keepsake? Involuntarily, she scanned the other tables in the club until she saw an empty one not far away with a rose and opera program lying atop it. And another martini glass—though this time it was empty. Had the woman he was expecting finally caught up with him? Had he only moments ago been sharing a moment like this with someone else? Could he really be that big a heel?

"Who were you expecting tonight?"

The question was out of her mouth before Della even realized it had formed in her brain. It obviously surprised Marcus as much as it had her, because his dark eyebrows shot up again.

"No one," he told her. And then, almost as if he couldn't stop himself, he added, "Not even you. I could never have anticipated someone like you."

"But the rose... The pink drink..."

He turned to follow the track of her gaze, saw the table where he must have been sitting when she came in. His shoulders drooped a little, and his head dipped forward, as if in defeat. Or perhaps melancholy? When he looked at her, the shadows she'd noted before were back in his eyes. Definitely the latter.

"I did buy the rose and order the drink for someone else," he said. "And yes, she was someone special."

"Was?" Della echoed. "Then you and she aren't..."

"What?"

"Together?"

His expression revealed nothing of what he might be feeling or thinking. "No."

She wanted to ask more about the woman, but something in his demeanor told her not to. It was none of her business, she reminded herself. It was bad enough she'd brought up memories for him that clearly weren't happy. Whoever the woman was, it was obvious she wasn't a part of his life anymore. Even if it was likewise obvious that he still wanted her to be.

And why did that realization prick her insides so much? Della wouldn't even see Marcus again after tonight. It didn't matter if he cared deeply for someone else, and the less she knew about him, the better. That way, he would be easier to forget.

Even if he was the kind of man a woman never forgot.

In spite of her relinquishing the subject, he added, "I knew she wouldn't be coming tonight, but it felt strange not to buy the rose and order her a drink the way I always did before. She always ran late," he added parenthetically and, Della couldn't help but note, affectionately. "It felt almost as if I were betraying her somehow not ordering for her, when really she was the one who—" He halted abruptly and met Della's gaze again. But now he didn't look quite so grim. "An uncharacteristic bout of sentimentality on my part, I guess. But no, Della. I'm not with anyone." He hesitated a telling moment before asking, "Are you?"

Well, now, there was a loaded question if ever there was one. Della wasn't with anyone—not the way Marcus meant it, anyway. She hadn't been with anyone that way for nearly a year. And that one had been someone she never should have been with in the first place. Not just because of the sort of man Egan Collingwood turned out to be, either. But Della was indeed with someone—in a different way. She was with Geoffrey. For now, anyway. And as long as she was with Geoffrey, there was no way she could be with anyone else.

She didn't want to tell Marcus that, though, so she only lifted her champagne to her lips for another sip. When he continued to study her in that inquisitive way, she enjoyed another sip. And another. And another. Until—would you look at that?—the glass was completely empty. The moment she set it on the table, however, Marcus poured her a refill, allowing the champagne to almost reach to the brim before lowering the bottle.

She grinned at the ridiculously full glass. "Marcus, are you trying to get me drunk?"

"Yes," he replied immediately.

His frankness surprised her, and she laughed. Honestly, she couldn't remember the last time she'd laughed so much in one evening. Even before Egan, she hadn't been so prone to jollity. She'd never even used a word like *jollity* before.

"Well, it won't work," she said, even as she carefully

lifted the glass to her mouth. "I have a remarkable metabolism."

Now his smile turned faintly predatory. "I'm counting on that, actually."

Yikes.

Well, the joke was on him. Because Mr. Marcus Notorious might think he had the evening mapped out with the quickest route from chance dinner meeting to white-hot marathon of sex, but there was no way that was going to happen. Della had to have her rented clothes back tomorrow when Talk of the Town opened at noon or she'd lose her deposit. Even the promise of a white-hot marathon of sex with a maddeningly irresistible guy wasn't going to keep her from forgetting that.

She looked at Marcus, at his smoldering eyes and sizzling grin. At the brutally strong jaw and ruthless cheekbones. As if trying to counter the ruggedness of his features, an unruly lock of dark hair had tumbled carelessly over his forehead, begging for the gentling of a woman's fingers.

Well. Probably that wasn't going to keep her from getting her deposit. Hmm. Actually, that was kind of a tough call....

But then, Della couldn't spend the night doing anything anywhere, anyway. As it was, if Geoffrey called the house tonight and she didn't answer, he'd be hopping mad. Of course, he'd only have to call her on her cell phone to know she was okay, but he'd be furious that she wasn't cloistered where she was supposed to be. She'd been lucky enough so far that he hadn't ever called the house when she'd snuck out on those handful of occasions when she became bored to the point of lunacy. But she wasn't sure how much longer her luck would hold. If Geoffrey ever got wind of her excursions, he'd want to wring her neck. Then he'd become even more determined to keep her hidden.

Still looking at Marcus, but trying not to think about the way he was making her feel, she leaned back in her chair and said, "So you get women drunk and then take advantage of them. Now I know the kinds of things you've done to make yourself so notorious."

"Oh, I never have to get women drunk to take advantage, Della," he said with complete confidence and without an ounce of arrogance. "In fact, I never have to take advantage."

She had no doubt that was true. She'd just met the man, and she was already having thoughts about him and inclinations toward him she shouldn't be having. Too many thoughts. And *way* too many inclinations.

"Then what does make you so notorious?"

He leaned forward, bracing his elbows on the table as he invaded her space, effectively erasing what meager distance she'd put between them. "Where do I begin?" he asked. "And, more important, do you have all night?"

Double yikes.

Having no idea what to say to that, she lifted her champagne for another idle sip…only to enjoy a healthy quaff instead. Well, it was very good. And she was starting to feel a lovely little buzz that was buffing the rough edges off…oh, everything.

As if he realized the turn her thoughts had taken, Marcus pushed his hand across the table until his fingertips were touching hers. A spark shot through Della, even at that simple, innocent touch. And when his hand crept up over hers, that spark leaped into a flame.

"Because if you *do* have all night," he added, "I'd be more than happy to give you a *very* thorough illustration."

Triple yikes. And another quaff, for good measure.

Ah, that was better. Now, what was it she had been about to say? Something about needing to get home because it was approaching midnight and, any minute now, she was going to turn into a bumpkin. Um, she meant pumpkin. Not that that was much better.

She searched for something to say that would extricate her from her predicament, but no words came. Probably because no ideas came. And probably no ideas came because they were all being crowded out by the visions featuring her and Marcus that kept jumping to the forefront of her brain. He really was incredibly sexy. And it had been such a long time since she'd been with anyone who turned her on the way he did. And it would probably be even longer before she found someone she wanted to be with again. She had no idea what would happen once Geoffrey was done with her. All she had that was certain was right now. This place. This moment. This man. This sexy, notorious, willing man. This man she should in no way allow herself to succumb to. This man who would haunt her for the rest of her life.

This man who, for some reason, she couldn't bring herself to leave quite yet....

Three

Della tore her gaze from his, forcing herself to look at something—anything—other than Marcus. Gazing past him, she found herself looking at the windows of two French doors not far from their table. The snow the forecasters had promised earlier in the day had begun to fall—delicate, dazzling flecks of white shimmering in the lamplight outside. As a native New Yorker, Della was no stranger to snow. And Chicago had seen snow more than once already this season. But there was something as magical to her about snow today as there had been when she was a child. When it had snowed then, at least for a little while, her neighborhood ceased to be a broken landscape of grimy concrete and asphalt and would transform into an enchanted world of sparkling white. The rusty fire escape outside her bedroom window morphed into a diamond-covered staircase that led to the top of an imprisoned princess's turret. The piles of garbage at the curb turned into pillows of glittering fairy-dust. The corroded cars became pearly silver coaches. Snow drove the gangs and dealers inside, who preyed on the neighborhood like wicked witches and evil sorcerers, so that all Della could see for block after block were radiant castles of white.

At least for a little while.

How appropriate that it should snow tonight, when she was actually enjoying the sort of enchanted adventure she'd had to invent as a child. How strangely right it felt to see those fat, fantastic flakes falling behind the man who had been such a bewitching Prince Charming this evening.

"It's snowing," she said softly.

Marcus turned to follow her gaze, then looked at Della again. His expression indicated that snow didn't hold the same fascination or whimsical appeal for him that it did for her.

"They're predicting four or five inches," he said, sounding disappointed at the change of subject.

He looked down at their hands, at how his rested atop hers and how hers just lay there. With clear reluctance, he pulled his toward himself. It was what she wanted, Della told herself. A change in subject to change her feelings instead of changing her mind. So why did his withdrawal have the opposite effect? Why did she want him to take her hand again, only this time turn it so their palms were flat against each other and their fingers entwined?

Still, he didn't retreat completely. His fingertips still brushed hers, and she could feel the warmth of his skin clinging to her own. It was all she could do not to reach for him and arrange their hands the way they'd been before.

It was for the best, she told herself again. This was a momentary encounter. A momentary exchange. A momentary everything. Especially now that the snow had begun, she really should be leaving. She'd told the driver of her hired car that she would be at the club only until midnight. It was nearing that now. She definitely needed to wind down this...whatever it was...with Marcus. Then she needed to be on her way.

So why wasn't she?

"It will be just enough snow to turn everything into an ungodly mess," Marcus said distastefully, giving her the perfect segue she needed to say her farewells. Unfortunately, he added, "At least no one will have to battle rush hour to get to work," reminding her that tomorrow was Sunday, so it wasn't as though she had to get up *that* early. She could squeeze in another moment or two....

"By afternoon," he continued, "the city will be one big pile of black slush. Snow is nothing but a pain in the—"

"I love snow. I think it's beautiful."

Marcus smiled indulgently. "Spoken like someone who's never had to maneuver in it," he replied. Then he brightened. "But with that clue, I can add to my knowledge of you. I now know that, not only have you only arrived in Chicago recently, but you came here from some hot, sunny place that never has to worry about the hassle of snow."

She said nothing to contradict him. It wasn't lying when you didn't say anything. And the more misconceptions he had about her, the better.

At her silence, he grinned with much satisfaction.

"I'm right, aren't I? You came here from someplace where it's hot all the time, didn't you?"

Oh, if he only knew. It had certainly been "hot" for her in New York when she left. Just not the way he meant. So she only smiled and said, "Guilty."

And not only of being from a "hot" place. She was guilty of twisting the truth in an effort to stay honest with him. Guilty of letting him believe she was someone she wasn't. Guilty of leading him on...

But she wasn't doing that last, she tried to reassure herself. Neither of them was making any promises to the other. If anything, promises were exactly what the two of them were trying to avoid. And, truth be told, she still wasn't sure what her intentions were where Marcus was concerned. He was clearly interested in sharing more than champagne and an assortment of fruit and cheese with her. He was waiting for her to give him some sign that she was interested in more than that, too. And although there was a not-so-small part of her that was definitely interested, there was another part of her still clinging to rationality, to sanity, to fidelity.

Because even though succumbing to Marcus's seduction wouldn't make her unfaithful to another man, it would make her unfaithful to herself. She hadn't scrabbled her way out of the soul-swallowing slums and into one of Wall Street's most powerful, most dynamic investing firms by believing in fairy tales and capitulating to whimsy. She'd done it by being pragmatic, hardworking and focused.

Then again, being those things was also what had forced her to flee the very life she'd toiled in and fought so hard to build.

She sighed inwardly. There it was again. More thinking about things she wasn't supposed to be thinking about tonight. Recalling the dissolution of her old life and fretting over the irresolution of her new one didn't belong in the fantasy life she was living *now*. It was her birthday. The one day of the year where it was okay for a person to be selfish and self-indulgent. It was the perfect time for her to be thinking about the moment. The moment was all that mattered for now. The moment was all she had that was certain. The moment was all she had that she could control. With another glance at Marcus—whose place in this night, in this moment, she still hadn't determined—she rose from her chair and moved to the French doors to watch the snow.

There was a small terrace beyond them, dark because of the late hour and frigid season. Della could just discern the outline of a handful of tables and chairs— all covered for the winter—and some potted topiaries that lay dormant. A layer of white covered all of it, so it must have been snowing harder and for longer than either of them had realized. Then again, when a woman was preoccupied by a man such as Marcus, it was hard to recognize that there was anything else out in the world at all.

As if conjured by the thought, she felt him slip up behind her, close enough that his body was flush against her own. She told herself she was only imagining the way she could feel the heat from his body mingling with hers, but the scent of him... That was all too real. All too wonderful. All too exhilarating.

"It was barely flurrying when I came in," she said. "I'm surprised how much has already fallen."

He said nothing for a moment, only continued to exude warmth and his intoxicatingly spicy fragrance.

Finally, quietly, he said, "The snow isn't the only thing that's been surprising tonight."

She couldn't disagree. Yet as unexpected as Marcus had been, his presence somehow felt perfectly right. Prince Charming was the only thing that had been missing from Della's fairy-tale plan for the evening, even if he was a complete stranger. Then again, he wasn't a stranger, not really. They'd known each other for hours now. They'd shared, in a way, a lovely dinner, a spectacular opera, some quiet conversation and gentle touches. They'd made each other smile. They'd made each other laugh. They'd made each other…feel things.

Della liked Marcus. He liked her. That made them something more than strangers, surely. She just wasn't quite certain what.

Impulsively, she tested the handle of the door and found it unlocked. Another surprise. Or perhaps more magic. Unable to help herself, she pushed open the door and strode quickly out onto the terrace, turning around slowly in the falling snow.

"Della," Marcus objected from inside, "what are you doing? It's freezing out there."

Funny, but she didn't feel cold. On the contrary, being with him made her hot to her core.

"I can't help it," she said as she halted her rotation to face him. "It's so beautiful. And so quiet. Listen."

As happened with snow, the sounds of the city beyond the terrace were muffled and silent, but the snow itself seemed to make a soft, supple sound as it fell. Reluctantly, Marcus shoved his hands into his trouser pockets and walked onto the terrace, shaking his head at her.

"You're worse than a little kid," he said. But he was smiling that delicious smile again.

As he drew nearer, Della moved farther away, until she'd backed herself into the far corner of the terrace, away from the door. When her back bumped the wall, the motion unsettled a small bundle of snow from somewhere above her, sending it cascading down around over her. She laughed as she shook her head to scatter the flakes, then the comb that had been holding her hair came loose, making it fall around her shoulders. He came to her immediately, slipping a little on his way, grabbing the railing to steady himself as his laughter joined her own.

"Well, aren't we a mess?" she said.

Not that she cared. Her life had been a mess for a year now. At least this mess was a fun one. She extended her hand over the balcony to let the snowflakes collect in her palm one by one. As soon as they landed, they melted, but the moisture still sparkled against her skin. "Look at it, Marcus," she said. "How can you think it's not lovely?"

He tucked himself into the corner of the darkened terrace as snugly as she was. "It's cold," he corrected her. "And you left your coat inside."

As chivalrously as a paladin, he slipped off his tuxedo jacket and reached around her to drape it over her shoulders. The garment fairly swallowed her, but it was redolent with both his scent and his warmth, and she was helpless not to pull it more closely around herself.

"Now you'll get cold," she told him.

"I haven't been cold since the moment I laid eyes on you. A little thing like snow and subfreezing temperature isn't going to change that."

Della wasn't feeling cold, either. Not that that would make her return his jacket to him. It felt too nice being enveloped in it. Almost as if she were being enveloped by Marcus himself.

Almost.

As if reading her mind—again—he started to lean forward, dipping his head toward hers. Knowing he intended to kiss her, Della turned quickly away. Why, she had no idea. She wanted him to kiss her. She wanted to kiss him, too. But she still couldn't quite bring herself to allow it. She wasn't the woman he thought she was. She was beginning to wonder if she was even the woman *she* thought she was. Soon, she *would* be someone else—entirely and literally. And in a couple of hours, she and Marcus would be nothing but a fond memory lodged in each other's brains. What kind of memory did she want to be for him? What kind of memory did she want him to be for her?

Marcus didn't give her time to think about it, because the moment she had her back to him, he coiled both arms around her waist to pull her against himself. His broad chest more than spanned her shoulders, but his long torso aligned perfectly with hers. It was at the small of her back where she felt him most, however, because as he drew her closer, rubbing their bodies together, he stirred to life against her.

Della's heart rate quickened at the realization that he was becoming as aroused as she. Heat coursed through her when he dipped his head to hers, his mouth hovering just over her ear. His breath was warm and damp against her skin, at odds with the snow, clouding her senses until she was dizzy not knowing what was what.

"I can say the snow isn't lovely," he murmured, his

voice as hot and demanding as the rest of him, "because I've seen something much lovelier this evening. In fact, you, my intriguing Della, are absolutely electrifying."

Instead of replying to that—mostly because she was afraid of what she might say...and even more afraid of what she might do—Della leaned further over the railing and into the falling snow. She turned her face to the caress of cold air, hoping it would be the antidote she needed to quell the swirling, simmering sensations inside her. Instead, her new position pushed her backside even more intimately against Marcus, and she felt him swell to even greater life against her.

She swallowed hard at the recognition of his condition, curling her fingers tightly over the metal railing, afraid of where her hands might wander otherwise. She wasn't so lucky with her thoughts, though, because they wandered plenty, telling her things she didn't want to hear. Things about how she would never meet another man like Marcus, and how he could be out of her life in a matter of moments, and how there was nothing sadder in life than a missed opportunity. So she tipped her face upward, welcoming the soft cascade of snowflakes, hoping they would numb her brain and make her forget...

...everything. Every ugly memory of where she'd grown up. Every miserable feeling she'd had since discovering the truth about Egan Collingwood. Every anxious moment she'd experienced since discovering even worse truths at work. Every terrible shudder of loneliness that had plagued her over the past eleven months. Every reason why she shouldn't do exactly what she wanted to do with Marcus. He was the surprise birthday gift that fate had presented her, sporting a big, satin bow.

Again, as if he'd read her mind, he covered her hands with his and gently urged them apart, opening his jacket over the front of her dress so that he could slip his fingers between the two garments. They went immediately to her rib cage, strumming it as if fine-tuning a delicate instrument. Ripples of pleasure wound through Della as he touched her, and she sighed her delight, her breath a puff of fog in the frigid air. Unable to help herself, she leaned against him, reaching behind herself with both hands to curl her fingers into his hair. Marcus used her new position to plunder her at will, covering her breasts with sure fingers.

"Oh," she murmured at his touch. "Oh, Marcus."

He said nothing in response, only dipped his head to her neck to drag kisses along the column of her throat. One hand gently kneaded her breast, while the other began to venture lower, moving along the elegant curves of her waist and hip and thigh, where he bunched the fabric of her dress in his fist. Slowly, slowly, oh... so slowly, he drew the garment upward, until Della could feel the cold and snow on her stocking-clad legs. Because of the gown's length, and because of the cold, she'd worn tights that rolled just above the knee, leaving her thighs bare. When she felt the whip of cold on her naked skin, she gasped, not only because of the frosty air, but also because she realized how far, how fast, things had progressed between them.

"Marcus," she began to protest. But the words sounded halfhearted, even to her own ears.

"Shh," he told her. "I just want to touch you. I just want to feel your skin beneath my fingertips."

She told herself to tell him he'd done that by holding her hand, but the words stilled before emerging. It had been so long since she'd felt a man's touch. Too long.

She'd forgotten how delicious it felt to be this close to another human being. Had forgotten how essential it was to share physical intimacy with another person. Had forgotten how exquisite it could be, how alive it could make her feel. Had forgotten—

Marcus found the leg of her panties and pushed it aside, threading his fingers into the damp, molten core of her.

Oh...oh, Marcus... She'd forgotten how that could feel, too.

"You're so wet," he murmured against her ear, obviously surprised by her response to him. "Della... oh, sweetheart...it's like... It's like you're already ready for me to—"

He moved his fingers against her again, eliciting a groan from deep inside her. Her fingers fell to the railing again, convulsing on it, then relaxed, then gripped the fixture again. Hard. She turned her fists first one way, then the other, then began to move them up and down along the length of the railing, the way she would touch a man's—

Marcus stroked her again, and somehow, she knew he was watching the movement of her hands and thinking the same thing she was thinking. Feeling the same thing she felt. Wanting the same thing she wanted.

He nuzzled her neck again, this time nipping her lightly with his teeth, an action she found unbelievably erotic. In response, she moved a hand behind herself and fumbled for his belt, working both it and the fly of his trousers open with trembling fingers.

Well, why shouldn't she? It was her birthday. She was celebrating. She'd already given herself so many gifts tonight. Why not one more? Why not enjoy this man the way they both wanted to enjoy each other?

When Marcus realized what she was doing, he moved away from her long enough to help her complete the action. She started to turn around, but he placed both hands firmly on her waist and held her in place with her back to him. So she reached behind herself and thrust her hand into his trousers, finding him naked and hard and ready. He gasped at what must have been the coldness of her hand, but she quickly warmed them both. Cupping the heavy head of his shaft in one hand, she palmed him over the satiny balm of his anticipated release before moving her fingers lower along his length. And lower. And lower. Until she caught her breath at just how magnificent he was.

She honestly wasn't sure what she had been thinking she would do next, and in that moment, Marcus's thoughts seemed to mirror her own. Dropping one hand from her waist, he fisted the fabric of her skirt again. Only this time, it was in the back, and this time he hiked it over her waist. As Della clung to the damp railing, Marcus pulled down her panties, pushing them past her knees. Della did the rest, stepping completely out of them.

And then he was moving behind her again, deftly rolling on a condom he must have had at the ready. But then, he was notorious, wasn't he? She had only a scant second to marvel at how he was sexually indiscriminate enough to be so prepared for sex, yet responsible enough to take such a precaution. Then, as the snow cascaded around her, Marcus thrust himself into her from behind, burying himself deeply.

When she cried out at the depth of his penetration, he gently covered her mouth with his hand. Then he began to move inside her, pulling himself out almost completely before bucking against her again, going even deeper. She had to bite her lip to keep herself silent, but he rewarded her by moving his hand between her legs and fingering the damp folds of her flesh. Of course, that only made her want to cry out again…

But she didn't cry out. She only felt. Felt the tight coil of heat in her belly pull tighter still, until her entire body seemed ready to explode. She felt the man behind her fill her again and again and again, felt the dizzying sensations of hunger and desire and need mingling and twining until they all became one. And then she felt the white-hot release of her climax shaking her, followed immediately by his.

And then he was removing himself from inside her and wrapping up the spent condom, rearranging their clothes as best he could before he spun her around and covered her mouth with his. For a long time, he only kissed her and kissed her and kissed her. Then, finally, he pulled back enough so that he could frame her face with both hands. It was snowing harder now, swirls of powder blowing up onto the terrace, surrounding them in a virtual tornado of white. Marcus's breath was coming in gasps, puffs of white against the sparkle of snow that merged with her own hitched breathing.

He dipped his head until his forehead was pressed against hers. "Nothing like that has ever happened to me before," he said between breaths. "Della, my God. You're a narcotic."

She wasn't sure how to reply to that, so she said nothing. She only curled her fingers in the front of his shirt and clung to him. They stood that way for long moments, neither seeming to know what to say or do. Della was confident no one inside the club had seen what had happened. Not only was the place deserted by now, but the two of them had also been obscured by both the darkness and the blowing snow. She also noted with a smile that they'd managed to fog up the windows behind them to opacity.

Finally, Marcus pulled away from her. But only far enough that he could gaze into her face. She'd expected him to demand the return of his jacket and say something like, "Holy cow, would you look at the time? I gotta get outta here."

Instead, he threaded his fingers gently into her hair and, very softly, asked, "Do you know what my favorite thing is about the Windsor Club?"

Still not trusting her voice, Della only shook her head.

"My favorite thing is that it's connected to the Ambassador Hotel. On nights like this, when driving could be dangerous due to a mix of weather, darkness and extremely good champagne, you can just...spend the night there. You don't have to set foot outside to get there. You can walk down the hall and through a breezeway and be at the registration desk in a matter of minutes. And, thanks to your platinum club status, within minutes of that, you can be in a luxury suite ordering another bottle of champagne from their twenty-four-hour room service."

Finally finding her voice, Della told him, "But I don't have platinum club status at the Ambassador Hotel."

He feigned forgetfulness. "That's right. You just came to Chicago recently, didn't you? So I guess you'll have to be with someone else who has platinum club status."

She smiled. "And who could I possibly know who might have that?"

"So it wouldn't be a problem for you spending the

night at the Ambassador? With me? You don't have any…obligations waiting for you anywhere?"

Only the obligation of returning her clothes by noon and checking in with Geoffrey by nine, as she did every morning. And she always woke by five, even without an alarm, even after a sleepless night. It was ingrained in her because Mr. Nathanson, her boss, had always insisted she be at her desk the same time he was—at 7:00 a.m. sharp, before anyone else showed up for work. At the time, Della had thought it was because the man was a workaholic. Had she known it was actually because he was corrupt…

She turned her attention to Marcus again, where it belonged. He was a gift, she reminded herself. One night with him would be the most amazing birthday present she'd ever received—from herself to herself. It would be terrible not to accept a gift like him.

"No," she finally said. "I don't have any…obligations." She lifted a hand to thread her fingers through his hair, loving the way the snow had dampened it and their encounter had warmed it. "Not until tomorrow. One night, Marcus," she made herself say, because it was very, very important that he realize that was all it would be. It was even more important that she realize it. "One night is all I can promise you."

"One night is all I'm asking for, Della."

It was probably all he wanted from any woman, she thought. Because it was probably all a man like him could promise in return.

She told herself that made her feel better. They both wanted the same thing. They both needed the same thing. They were both willing to give and take equally. Tonight would be exactly what she had planned it to be all those years ago: One night. Of magic. Her gift to herself.

Marcus lifted his hand to trace a finger lightly over her cheek. "Well, then, my sweet, intriguing Della," he said softly, "why don't you and I take a little walk and find out where it leads?"

Four

Marcus stood at the broad window of the hotel suite dressed in the plush royal blue robe the hotel so thoughtfully provided for all its guests and watched the snow fall. And fall. And fall. And fall. Fat, furious flakes coming down so thick and so fast, he could barely make out the buildings on the other side of Michigan Avenue.

Unbelievable. What was supposed to have been a manageable snowfall of three to five inches had turned into a blizzard during the night. The entire city was on hold until the snowplows could get out and do their thing, but since everyone had been caught by surprise, they couldn't do anything until the snow let up. A lot.

And the snow didn't show any sign of letting up. At all.

The situation was going to be untenable for a while. No one would be going anywhere until tomorrow at the earliest. Not that Marcus cared. Because it meant that the one night Della had promised was all she could give him would now, by necessity, become two.

That was something he should definitely care about. The last thing he looked for in a one-night stand was for it to last more than one night. Hell, half the time he was safely back at his place before the night was even over. Once he was sexually satisfied by a woman, there was never any reason to hang around. Even the prospect of being sexually satisfied a second time rarely kept him from leaving.

But with Della, even being satisfied a third time hadn't quelled his appetite for more. Once he'd regained enough strength to manage it. They'd both been insatiable last night, to the point where they'd slept only long enough to recover from their previous coupling, then come together even more fiercely than before. That third time, they'd had to rely on oral gratification alone to bring each other to climax, since the second time had been so rough. Not that either of them had seemed to mind. Della had been as demanding and wild as a tigress, and Marcus had mounted her the way a jungle cat would have claimed his mate.

And even that hadn't been enough to satisfy him. In fact, that had only made him want her more. When he'd awoken that morning beside her, their bodies had been so intricately entwined, he'd barely been able to tell where hers ended and his began. Marcus never slept with a woman after having sex with her. Never. And he'd certainly never gathered one close that way and held her with such possessiveness. For a long time after waking, he'd only lain silently beside her, holding her, listening to her soft respiration, inhaling her scent. It was different now. Last night she'd smelled soft and flowery. This morning she smelled musky and dark. And, God help him, Marcus had grown hard against her as he lay there, and it had been all he could do not to take her again in her sleep. Instead, he'd eased his way out of the bed without waking her, donned the robe and called for room service.

Even its arrival hadn't woken Della. But that might be because Marcus had intercepted the steward in the hallway when he'd heard the rattle of the approaching cart and brought it in himself. He hadn't wanted to wake her before she was ready. Strangely, however, that hadn't been because he wanted her rested up for another night like last night—and, hey, maybe a day like last night, too—but because he simply liked watching her sleep.

He turned away from the window and let go of the sheer curtains, throwing the room into an otherworldly dusk created by the thickly falling snow. He loved the understated luxury of the Ambassador, loved the taupe walls and buff-colored, cleanly tailored furnishings with the dashes of blues and greens in the form of throw pillows and abstract artwork. He'd wanted a suite, of course, but there hadn't been one available. At the time, it hadn't seemed a problem, since he'd known he and Della would only need the place for a few hours. Now that their stay was looking to be for most of the weekend, it would have been nice to have a little more room to spread out.

He looked over at the bed, where she still slept, and smiled. Then again, there was a lot to be said for close quarters. Even if those quarters were still five-star hotel roomy.

Della lay on her stomach, the ivory sheets tangled over her lower half, her creamy back and shoulders laid bare. Silently, he neared the bed, pausing beside it.

Her hair flowed like a honey river above her head and down the side of the pillow, and her hand was curled into a loose fist near her mouth. Her lips were swollen from the ferocity of their kisses, and her cheek was pink where his beard had abraded her. He remembered wrapping fistfuls of that hair around his fingers as he'd ridden her last night, then stroking it back into place as the two of them had gentled their movements in the afterglow. Even in the furiousness of their actions, he'd noted how thick and silky the strands were, and he'd loved the feel of her soft tresses tumbling through his fingers.

He was about to turn away to pour two cups of coffee—maybe the aroma of Jamaica Blue Mountain would rouse her—when she began to stir. Slowly, murmuring soft sounds of wakefulness, she inhaled a deep, satisfied breath and released it slowly. Her eyes still closed, she rolled over and arched her arms over her head for an idle stretch. The action displayed her full breasts to their best advantage, stiffening her rosy nipples. Then she straightened her legs to stretch them, too, the sheet falling away as she spread them open, making visible the dark blond nest between her legs.

Again, Marcus stirred to life simply looking at her. She was utter perfection, beauty so unflawed and pure that he almost wished he hadn't sullied her.

Almost.

Instead, unable to help himself, he leaned over and traced the pad of his middle finger along her calf.

She moaned softly in response to his touch, smiling a very tempting smile, but she still didn't open her eyes. So Marcus drew his finger higher, up over her knee and along her thigh. She gasped a little this time, then uttered a low, erotic sound that seemed to come from deep inside her. But she still didn't open her eyes.

So Marcus leaned over the bed, moving his finger to the inside of her thigh, closer to the juncture of her legs. Della, in turn, opened her legs wider. Now Marcus smiled, too, and drove his hand into the silky thatch of curls hiding the feminine core of her. For long seconds, he furrowed her with light, slow, measured movements, pushing his fingers through the hot, damp folds of flesh. Deliberately, he avoided the sweet little spot that would drive her over the edge, but he skirted close a time or two, just to hear her swift intake of breath and ensuing groan of pleasure. When he pulled away again, he slipped a finger inside her, gently, since he knew she must still be tender from the night before. When she lifted her hips from the mattress to pull him deeper, he withdrew his finger, then inserted it slowly again. And again. And again.

When he knew she was at the verge of coming apart, he brought his thumb into the action, this time settling it resolutely on her now-drenched skin. It was easy for him to rub the pad of his thumb over her sweet spot, even when she began bucking her hips wildly at the onslaught. His fingers were covered with her essence now, making his manipulations come more quickly, more insistently. With one final push, he brought her to climax, making her cry out at the sensations that rocked her. She arched one last time, then slowly came back down to the bed. Marcus drew his hand up along her naked torso, leaving a trail of her own satisfaction in his wake, circling first one nipple, then the other, before moving his hand to the delicate lines of her neck.

"Good morning," he said softly, as if the last few minutes hadn't happened.

She was still breathing raggedly and trembling from his touch, but she managed to whisper, "Oh, yes. It is a *very* good morning. I could wake up that way every morning."

The words should have had panic racing through Marcus. The last thing he wanted to hear was a woman including him in her everyday life. Instead, he found himself warming to the idea of waking her that way each day. Doubtless because any man who started his day knowing he'd brought a woman to climax took with him a sense of power and well-being. Not to mention smugness. It made a man feel as if he could do just about anything.

It had nothing to do with simply enjoying an intimate moment with an exceptional woman.

"There's coffee," he said. "And breakfast. I didn't know what you'd like, so I ordered some of everything."

"Coffee," she said, still a little breathless. "Black," she added as he was about to ask how she took it— almost as if she were reading his mind.

That, too, should have made him bristle. He didn't want women understanding the workings of his brain. Mostly because few of them would approve of his thoughts, since they generally consisted of: A) women other than the one he was with, B) work, C) women other than the one he was with, D) how well the Cubs, Bears or Blackhawks were performing, depending on the season or E) women other than the one he was with.

But he kind of liked the connection with Della and, strangely, didn't want to think of anyone or anything other than her. So he only said, "Coming right up."

By the time he finished pouring two cups and

removing the lids from the cold dishes the steward had brought up, Della was out of bed and wrapped in a robe identical to his own—except that hers swallowed her—and was standing at the window the same way he had been earlier. The snow was still coming down as opaquely as it had been then, and he thought he saw her shake her head.

"It's like a blizzard out there," she murmured incredulously.

"No, it *is* a blizzard out there," Marcus corrected as he came to a halt beside her and extended a cup of coffee, black like his own, toward her.

She took it automatically with one hand, still holding open the curtain with the other. "How are we going to get...home?"

He noted her hesitation on the last word, as if home for her were a somewhat tentative state. Another clue that she really was only visiting here. Nevertheless, she'd assured Marcus that no one would miss her—at least not until today. Both thoughts bothered him a lot more than they should. For one thing, it shouldn't matter if Della was tied to another man, since Marcus didn't want to stake a claim on her anyway. For another thing, they'd both only wanted and promised one night, that should have been more than enough to satisfy their desire to enjoy each other for a little while. The fact that she was only in Chicago temporarily or might be involved with someone else should be of no consequence. In fact, it should reassure him that there would indeed be no strings attached.

For some reason, though, Marcus didn't like the idea of her being only a visitor to Chicago. He liked even less that she might be involved with someone else.

Too much thinking, he told himself, and way too

early in the day for it. It was the weekend. He was snowbound with a gorgeous, incredibly sexy woman. Why was he thinking at all?

"No one is going anywhere today," he said before sipping his coffee. "Not even the snowplows will be able to get out until this lets up."

Della turned to look at him, and that strange, panicked look he'd seen for a few moments last night was back in her eyes. "But I can't stay here all day," she told him, the panic present in her voice now, too. "I have to get...home."

Again the hesitation before the final word, he noted. Again, he didn't like it.

"Is there someplace you absolutely have to be today?" When she didn't reply right away, only arrowed her eyebrows in even more concern, he amended, "Or should I ask, is there some*one* who's expecting you to be someplace today?"

She dropped her gaze at that. Pretty much the only reaction he needed. So there was indeed someone else in her life. Someone she'd have to answer to for any kind of prolonged absence.

"Is it a husband?" he asked, amazed at how casual the question sounded, when he was suddenly feeling anything but.

Her gaze snapped up to his, flashing with anger. Good. Anger was better than panic. Anger stemmed from passion, not fear. "I wouldn't be here with you if I had a husband waiting for me."

Marcus had no idea why he liked that answer so much.

"What about you?" she countered. "Is there a wife somewhere waiting for you? Or has she come to expect this kind of behavior from you?"

He chuckled at that. "The day I have a wife waiting for me somewhere is the day they put me in a padded cell." When she still didn't seem satisfied by the answer—he couldn't imagine why not—he told her bluntly, "I'm not married, Della." Not sure why he bothered to add it, he said, "There's no one waiting anywhere for me." Then, after only a small hesitation, he added, "But there is someone who will be worried about you if you don't come…home…today, isn't there?" He deliberately paused before the word *home,* too, to let her know he'd noticed her own hesitation.

She inhaled a deep breath and released it slowly, then dropped the curtain and curled both hands around the white china coffee cup. She gazed into its depths instead of at Marcus when she spoke. "Home is something of a fluid concept for me at the moment."

Fluid. Interesting word choice. "And by that you mean…?"

Still staring at her coffee, she said, "I can't really explain it to you."

"Can't or won't?"

Now she did meet his gaze. But her expression was void of anything. No panic, no anger, nothing. "Both."

"Why?"

She only shook her head. She brought the cup to her mouth, blew softly on its surface and enjoyed a careful sip. Then she strode to the breakfast cart to inspect its choices. But he couldn't help noting how she looked at the clock as she went, or how her eyes went wide in surprise when she saw the time. It wasn't even eight o'clock yet. On a Sunday, no less. It seemed too early for anyone to have missed her if she had been able to surrender an entire night.

"You really did order a little of everything," she said as she began lifting lids. "Pastries, bacon, sausage, eggs, fruit..."

He thought about saying something about how they both needed to regain their strength after last night, but for some reason, it felt crass to make a comment like that. Another strange turn of events, since Marcus had never worried about being crass before. Besides, what else was there for the two of them to talk about after the kind of night they'd had? Their response to each other had been sexual from the get-go. They'd barely exchanged a dozen words between the time they left the club and awoke this morning—save the earthy, arousing ones they'd uttered about what they wanted done and were going to do to each other. Ninety percent of their time together had been spent copulating. Nine percent had been spent flirting and making known the fact that they wanted to copulate. What were they supposed to say to each other that didn't involve sex? Other than, how do you take your coffee or what did you think of *La Bohème?* And they'd already covered both.

She plucked a sticky pastry from the pile and set it on one of the empty plates. Then, after a small pause, she added another. Then a third. Then she added some strawberries and a couple of slices of cantaloupe. Guess she, too, thought they needed to rebuild their strength after the night they'd had. But, like him, she didn't want to say it out loud.

"Sweet tooth, huh?" he asked as she licked a bit of frosting from the pad of her thumb.

"Just a little," she agreed. Balancing both the plate and cup, she moved to the bed and set them on the nightstand beside it. Then she climbed into bed.

Well, that was certainly promising.

Marcus filled the other plate with eggs, bacon and a bagel, then retrieved his coffee and joined her, placing his breakfast on the opposite nightstand. Where she had seated herself with her legs crossed pretzel-fashion facing him, he leaned against the headboard with his legs extended before him. Noting the way her robe gaped open enough to reveal the upper swells of her breasts, it occurred to him that neither of them had a stitch of clothing to wear except for last night's evening attire, that wasn't exactly the kind of thing a person wanted to wear during the day when a person was trying to make him- or herself comfortable.

Oh, well.

He watched her nibble a strawberry and wondered how he could find such an innocent action so arousing. Then he wondered why he was even asking himself that. Della could make changing a tire arousing.

"Well, since you won't tell me why home is so fluid," he said, "will you at least tell me where you're making it at the moment?"

"No," she replied immediately.

He thought about pressing her on the matter, then decided to try a different tack. "Then will you tell me what brings you to Chicago?"

"No," she responded as quickly.

He tried again. "Will you tell me where you're from originally?"

"No."

"How long you're going to be here?"

"No."

"Where you're going next?"

"No."

"How old you are?"

"Certainly not."

"Do you like piña coladas and getting caught in the rain?"

He wasn't sure, but he thought she may have smiled at that. "Not particularly."

"How about fuzzy gray kittens, volunteering for public television, long walks on the beach, cuddling by firelight and the novels of Philip Roth?"

At that, she only arrowed her eyebrows down in confusion.

"Oh, right. Sorry. That was Miss November. My bad."

Her expression cleared, but she said nothing.

"What's your sign?" Marcus tried again.

That, finally, did make her smile. It wasn't a big smile, but it wasn't bad. It was something they could work on.

"Sagittarius," she told him.

Now that said a lot about her, Marcus thought. Or, at least, it would. If he knew a damned thing about astrology. Still, it was something. Sagittariuses were born in June, weren't they? Or was it October? March?

All right, all right. So he knew as much about her now as he had when he started his interrogation. Which was nothing. Hell, he didn't even know if she was telling the truth about being a Sagittarius or not liking piña coladas and getting caught in the rain.

Immediately, however, he knew she was telling the truth about those things. He had no idea why, but he was confident Della wasn't a liar. She was just a woman who wouldn't reveal anything meaningful about herself and who was sneaking around on a lover. Had she been a liar, she would have had a phony answer for every question he asked, and she would have painted herself as someone she wasn't. Instead, he was left with a blank slate of a woman who could be anyone.

But that, too, wasn't right, he thought. There were a lot of things he knew about Della. He knew she loved an esoteric art form that most people her age had never even tried to expose themselves to. He knew she cried at all the sad parts of an opera, and that she was awed by the intricacies of the music. He'd seen all those reactions on her face when he'd watched her last night instead of *La Bohème*. He knew she liked champagne. He knew she was enchanted by a snowfall. He knew she laughed easily. He knew she was comfortable in red, red, red. All of those things spoke volumes about a person.

And he knew she came from a moneyed background, even if she was currently making her way by having someone else pay for it. It hadn't taken an inspection of her jewelry or a look at the labels in her clothing— even though he had as he'd picked up their things from the floor while she slept—to know that. She was smart, confident and articulate, and had clearly been educated at excellent schools. She carried herself with sophistication and elegance, obviously having been raised by parents for whom such things were important. She'd been perfectly at ease last night in every venue he'd encountered her. If she wasn't the product of wealth and refinement, Marcus was a bloated yak.

Not that wealth and refinement necessarily manufactured a product that was all the things Della was. He need only point to himself to prove that. He'd been kicked out of every tony private school his parents had enrolled him in, until his father finally bought off the director of the last one with a massive contribution for the construction of a new multimedia center. The same contribution had bought Marcus's diploma, since his grades hadn't come close to winning him that. Not because he hadn't been smart, but because he hadn't given a damn. As for sophistication and elegance, he had gone out of his way as a teenager to be neither and had embarrassed his family at every society function he'd attended. He'd raided liquor cabinets, ransacked cars and ruined debutantes—often in the same evening—and he'd earned an arrest record before he even turned sixteen. If it hadn't had been for Charlotte…

He pushed the memories away and instead focused on Della. If it hadn't had been for Charlotte, Marcus wouldn't be sitting here with her right now. And not only because Charlotte's absence last night had allowed him to strike up a conversation with Della, not once, but three times. But because if it hadn't had been for Charlotte, Marcus would now either be in a minimum security prison for wreaking havoc and general mischief past the age of eighteen, or he'd be lolling about on skid row, having been finally disowned by his family.

"What are you thinking about?"

Della's question brought him completely to the present. But it wasn't a question he wanted to answer. Hey, why should he, when she wouldn't answer any of his?

At his silence, she added, "You looked so far away there for a minute."

"I was far away."

"Where?"

He sipped his coffee and met her gaze levelly. "I'm not telling."

"Why not?"

"You won't tell me anything about you, so I'm not telling you anything about me."

For a minute, he thought maybe she'd backpedal and

offer up some answers to his questions in order to get answers to some of her own. Instead, she nodded and said, "It's for the best that way."

Damn. So much for reverse psychology.

"For you or for me?" he asked.

"For both of us."

The more she said, the more puzzled and curious Marcus grew. Just who the hell was she? Where had she come from? Where was she going? Why wouldn't she tell him anything about herself? And why, dammit, did he want so desperately to know everything there was to know about her?

"All right, if you really want to know, I was thinking about something at work," he lied.

She said nothing in response, only picked up one of the pastries and enjoyed a healthy bite.

"Don't you want to at least know what I do for a living?"

"No."

There was that word again. He was really beginning to hate it.

"I work for a brokerage house," he told her, deliberately being vague about his position there, since he still wasn't sure how much to say. Actually, that wasn't quite true. He wanted to say a lot about himself. But not for the usual reasons. Usually, he only opened up to a woman by saying things designed to impress her, in order to get her more quickly into bed. But he'd already gotten Della into bed and still wanted to impress her. That was strange enough in itself. Even stranger was how he suspected that the best way to impress her was to *not* brag about himself. Well, not just yet, anyway.

She was swallowing when he told her about his job,

but it must have gone down the wrong way, because she immediately began to cough. A lot. Marcus was about to reach over to pat her on the back—or administer the Heimlich if necessary—but she held up a hand to stop him and reached for her coffee instead. After a couple of sips, she was okay. Though her face still looked a little pale.

"I'm fine," she said before he could ask. "That swallow went down the wrong way."

He nodded. And once he knew she really was fine, he picked up the conversation where he'd left off. "I work at—"

"Stop," she said, holding up a hand as if trying to physically stop the information from coming. "Don't tell me what you do or where you work. Please, Marcus. We agreed. No background information. No last names. No strings. No past, no present, no future."

"We also agreed only one night, " he reminded her, "but that's obviously not going to be the case. We're stuck here for at least another twenty-four hours. There's no harm in getting to know each other a little better. Unless you can tell me one."

He could see by her expression she could think of at least one. Maybe two. Maybe ten. Never in his life had he met a woman whose face was such an open book. Forget mind reading. A man could discover a lot about Della just by looking at her face. And what Marcus discovered now was that there was no way she was going to open up about herself to him.

Still, that didn't mean he couldn't open himself up to her.

"I work at Fallon Brothers," he said before she could stop him. He didn't add that the Fallons in the name of the multibillion-dollar company that employed him were his great-great grandfather and great-great uncle or that he was the fourth generation of the Fallon empire that would someday be running the company, along with his cousin Jonathan. Except that Marcus was the one who would become CEO upon his father's retirement next year, that meant he would be doing even less work than he was now as a VP, and then the partying would *really* begin. If Marcus was a fixture of the tabloid rags and websites now, he intended to be a permanent, cemented, superglued fixture once he didn't have to answer to his father anymore.

"Marcus, please," Della said again, her voice laced with warning. "Don't say another—"

"My permanent residence is on Lakeshore Drive," he continued, ignoring her. He picked up the pad and pen labeled with the hotel's logo that lay on the nightstand near his breakfast. "Here. I'll write it down for you," he continued, and proceeded to do just that. "But I also have places in London, Hong Kong, Tokyo and Aruba. All the big financial capitals, in fact."

When he looked up after finishing the last digit of his cell number—he'd given her the numbers of the office and his penthouse, too—she was gazing at him with much consternation.

Damn, she was cute when she was consternated.

"Since when is Aruba a big financial capital?" she asked.

"Since I spent a fortune on a house there and spend another fortune on rum every time I go down there."

"I see."

"I'm thirty-eight years old and a Chicago native," he added as he dropped the pad with his address and phone numbers onto the mattress between them. Not that Della even glanced at them. "As an undergrad, I majored in business at Stanford, then got my MBA from Harvard. Yes, I am that clichéd businessman you always hear about, except that I didn't graduate anywhere near the top of my class either time. Doesn't mean I'm not good at what I do," he hastened to add, "it just means I'm not an overachiever—that's where the cliché ends—and that I make time for more than work." He threw her his most lascivious look, just in case she didn't get that part. Which he was pretty sure she did, because she blushed that becoming shade of pink she had last night.

"Marcus, I really wish you wouldn't—"

"Let's see, what else is worth mentioning?" he interrupted, ignoring her. "I broke my arm in a skiing accident when I was eight and broke my ankle in a riding accident when I was ten. I have two sisters—both older and married to men my parents chose for them… not that either of them would ever admit that—along with two nieces and three nephews. My favorite color is red." He hoped she got the significance of that, too, and was more than a little delighted when color bloomed on her cheeks again. "My favorite food is Mediterranean in general and Greek in particular. I usually drive a black Bentley, but I also have a vintage Jaguar roadster—it goes without saying that it's British racing green—and a red Maserati. You already know about the opera thing, but my second greatest passion is port wine. My sign is Leo. And," he finally concluded, "I don't like piña coladas or getting caught in the rain, either."

By the time he finished, Della's irritation at him was an almost palpable thing. He'd sensed it growing as he'd spoken, until he'd halfway expected her to cover her ears with her hands and start humming, then say something like, "La la la la la. I can't hear you. I have my fingers in my ears and I'm humming. La la la la la."

Instead, she'd spent the time nervously breaking her pastry into little pieces and dropping them onto her plate. Now that he was finished, she shifted her gaze from his to those little broken pieces and said, "I really wish you hadn't told me those things."

"Why not?"

"Because every time I discover something else about you, it makes you that much more difficult to forget."

Something stirred to life inside him at her words, but he couldn't say exactly what that something was. It wasn't an unpleasant sensation, but neither was it exactly agreeable. It was just…different. Something he'd never felt before. Something it would take some time to explore.

"That's interesting," he told her. "Because I don't know one tenth that much about you, and I know you're going to be impossible to forget."

Still studying the broken pastry, she made a face, as if she hadn't realized what a mess she'd made of it. She placed the plate on the mattress on top of the pad of paper with the information he'd written down, though he was pretty sure she'd given it a quick glance before covering it. With any luck, she had a photographic memory. With even more luck, he'd notice later that the slip of paper had moved from the bed into her purse.

Her purse, he thought. Women's purses were notorious for storing information—probably more than a computer's hard drive. Not that Marcus could vouch for such a thing. He'd never had the inclination to search a woman's purse before. It was actually a pretty despicable thing for a man to even consider doing.

He couldn't wait to get into Della's.

"All right," she said. "I'll tell you a few things about myself."

Finally, they were getting somewhere. Just where, exactly, he wasn't sure he could say. But it was farther down the road than they'd been a few minutes ago. He wished he could see farther still, to find out if the road was a long and winding one with hills and valleys and magnificent vistas, or if it ended abruptly in a dead end where a bridge had washed out, and where there were burning flares and warning sirens and pylons strung with yellow tape that read Caution!

Then again, did he really care? It wasn't as if anything as minor as cataclysmic disaster had ever stopped him from going after what he wanted before. And he did want Della. He wanted her a lot.

Five

Della tried not to notice how Marcus seemed to have moved closer to her during their exchange. She couldn't help noting other things, however. Such as how love-tousled his dark hair was and how the shadow of beard covered the lower half of his face, both qualities evoking an air of danger about him. Or maybe it was just that she realized now how very dangerous he was. How dangerous her behavior last night had been. How dangerous it was to still be with him this morning with no way to get home. Not only because she was at greater risk of Geoffrey discovering her absence, but also because she was beginning to feel things for Marcus that she had no business feeling. Things that would make it more difficult to leave him when the time came.

She never, ever, should have allowed herself to succumb to her desires last night. Hadn't she learned the hard way how doing that led to trouble? The last time she'd yielded so easily to a man, her life had been left in a shambles. And Egan had been nowhere near as compelling or unforgettable as Marcus.

"I'm originally from the East Coast," she said, hoping that small snippet of information—even if it was a hugely broad one that could mean anything— would appease him.

She should have known better.

"Where on the east coast?" he asked.

She frowned at him and repeated stubbornly, "The east coast."

"North or south?"

"That's all I'm giving you, Marcus. Don't push or that's the only thing you'll learn about me."

He opened his mouth to say more, then shut it again. He was probably recalling how she'd told him she came from someplace hot, and he was assuming it was the latter. But he was clearly not happy about having to acquiesce to her demand.

She wasn't sure whether or not to confess anything about her family, mostly because she hadn't seen any of them for years. Even when they'd all lived under one roof, they hadn't really been much of a family. It was a sad thing to admit, but Della really didn't have feelings for any of them one way or another. Still, if Marcus wanted information, maybe that would be the kind to give him because it wouldn't cost her anything emotionally. It would also potentially be misleading, since most people stayed in touch with their blood relations, so he might think she hadn't traveled too far from her own.

"I have an older brother," she admitted. "And a younger brother, as well." The first had taken off when he was sixteen and Della was fourteen, and she hadn't seen him since. The other, last time she'd heard—which had been about ten years ago—had joined a gang. At the tender age of fifteen. No telling where he was now, either.

On the few occasions when Della thought about her brothers, she tried to convince herself that they'd been motivated by the same things she had, and in the same way. She told herself they'd gotten out of the old neighborhood and found better lives, just as she had. Sometimes she even believed herself. But more often, she feared they had screwed up everything in their lives, too, the same way she had.

"Nieces and nephews?" Marcus asked.

She only shook her head in response to that. To her, the gesture meant *I don't know.* To Marcus, let it mean whatever he wanted it to.

"Any injuries sustained as a child?" he asked, referring to his own.

She supposed she could tell him about the time she cut her foot on a broken beer bottle in a vacant lot during a game of stickball and had to get stitches, but that didn't quite compare to skiing and riding accidents. So she only said, "None worth mentioning."

"Schooling?" he asked.

The School of Hard Knocks, she wanted to say. It was either that, or her infamously crime-ridden high school or disgracefully underachieving elementary school. But neither of those would be the answer he was looking for.

Della knew he was looking for specific answers. He wanted her to be a specific kind of woman. The kind of woman who came from the same society he did and who lived and moved there as easily as he. She wasn't sure if he was the sort of blue blood who would turn his nose up in disgust at her if he knew her true origins, but he would, without question, be disappointed. She was glamorous to him. He'd made that clear. She was intriguing. A woman of mystery and erotica. The last thing he wanted to hear her say was that she'd grown up in a slum, had no formal education, had clawed and fought to win every scrap she ever had, and had taught herself everything she knew by emulating others.

So she said, "Yes. I had schooling."

He smiled at that. "No. I meant where did you go to—"

"My favorite color is blue," she told him. "And my favorite food is *fruits de mer.*" Her French, she was proud to say, sounded as good as his Italian had last night. Unfortunately, *fruits de mer* was about the only thing she could say in French, and only because she'd practiced it for her menu lesson.

"After opera," she continued, "my greatest passion is—"

She halted abruptly. Now here was a problem. Because other than opera, Della really had no passions. She'd never really had an opportunity to find any. After landing the job at Whitworth and Stone when she was eighteen, she'd focused entirely on it in order to stay employed there. She'd worked overtime whenever she could for the money, and she'd spent the rest of her time trying to better herself in whatever ways she could. Reading classic novels from the library. Emulating the speech of actors in movies. Swiping magazines she found in the apartment's recycling bin to educate herself about fashion and etiquette and how to act like a refined human being. Opera had been the only indulgence she'd allowed herself, both because she loved it and it contributed to the kind of person she wanted to be. Beyond that…

Beyond that, she'd never had much of anything else to love.

"After opera…" Marcus prodded her now.

She looked at him, biting back another surge of panic. Never had she felt like a greater impostor than she did in that moment. She really did have nothing. Not a thing in the world. For the first time since leaving her life—such as it was—in New York, she realized how utterly empty her life had been and how absolutely alone she was.

"After opera…" She felt the prickle of tears sting her eyes. No, please. Anything but that. Not here. Not now. Not in front of Marcus. She hadn't cried since she was a child. Not once. Not when things had fallen apart in New York. Not when Geoffrey had told her she had to leave with him. Not during the eleven months since, when she'd had to turn her entire life over to someone else. Why now? Why here? Why in front of the last person on earth she wanted to see her cry?

She lifted a hand to shield her face and jumped up from the bed. "Excuse me," she said hastily as she headed for the bathroom. "I think I have an eyelash in my eye." As she was closing the door, she said over her shoulder, "If you don't mind, I'll take the first shower." Without awaiting a reply, she pushed the door closed and locked it, then turned on the shower full blast. Then she grabbed a towel and dropped to the floor, shoving it hard against her mouth.

I will not cry. I will not cry. I will not cry. I will not cry.

Her eyes grew damp, so she squeezed them shut.

I will not cry. I will not cry. I will not cry. I will not cry.

And somehow, by some miracle, Della kept the tears at bay.

The moment Marcus heard the rattle of the shower curtain closing in the bathroom, he crossed to the dresser where Della had laid her purse the night before. Okay, so maybe this one couldn't hold as much as a computer's hard drive, since it was one of those tiny purses women carried to formal events that was roughly the size of a negative ion. But it was large enough to hold a driver's license, cash and a cell phone, all of which he found inside, along with a tube of lipstick, a collapsible hairbrush, a plain metal keychain from which dangled a single key—house key, not car key— and, curiously, a computer USB drive. But no credit card, he noted, thinking it odd. Meaning she'd paid for her dinner and whatever else last night—a not inconsiderable sum—with cash. Interesting. He just wasn't sure exactly how.

He looked at the driver's license first and saw that it was from New York State. So she had been honest with him about being from the East Coast, but hadn't dissuaded him of his assumption that she came from a hot climate. Also interesting. But again, he wasn't sure how. Looking closer at the license, he saw that her full name was Della Louise Hannan and that she was thirty years old. In fact, she'd turned thirty yesterday. So last night was her celebration of reaching that milestone. The fact that she'd celebrated it alone heartened him— more than it really should have.

He glanced at her address, but it was on one of the higher numbered streets, outside the part of Manhattan with which he was familiar. He knew the better parts of New York like the back of his hand and had expected he would be able to pinpoint Della's address with little effort—doubtless somewhere near or on Fifth Avenue or Central Park. But this was nowhere close to either of those. He memorized it for future investigation, stuck the license in her purse and withdrew her cell phone, flipping it open.

Unfortunately, it was one of those not-particularly-smart phones, a bare-bones model that didn't contain an easy-access menu. So he had to poke around a bit to find what he was looking for, namely her calls received and sent. After a moment, he found both and discovered that every single one had been to and from one person. A person identified simply as Geoffrey.

Any optimism Marcus had begun to feel dissolved at that. Geoffrey could be a first or last name, but somehow he knew that it was definitely a man's name. He fumbled through more screens until he found her contact list and began to scroll to *G*. It took a while to get there. She had dozens of contacts, most listed by last name, but a handful—mostly women—were identified by their first names and, when the names were duplicates, by a last initial. Finally, he came to Geoffrey and clicked on it. There were two numbers listed for him, one designated a work number, the other a cell. The work number was a three one two area code—the man worked in Chicago. The cell number, however, was eight four seven, that was in the suburbs. It was a revelation that revealed nothing to Marcus. A lot of people lived in the 'burbs and worked in the city. And eight four seven covered a lot of 'burbs.

He reminded himself that Geoffrey could be a brother or a cousin or some guy she knew from high school. There was no reason to think he was necessarily a love interest or the man who kept her. Except for the fact that he was clearly the only person she was in touch with, in spite of her knowing a lot more.

But that was what men like that did, didn't they? They isolated the woman they wanted to own from her friends and family until she had no one but the guy to rely on. Whoever this Geoffrey was, Marcus was liking him less and less. That was saying something, because Marcus had begun to really loathe the faceless, nameless man in Della's life without even knowing for sure one existed.

He scrolled through more screens until he found the one that contained her photographs and clicked on those. There weren't a lot, but there were enough to tell him more about her. Several of the photos were pictures of Della with a trio of other women, all about her age. But it took him a few moments to realize one of the women in the pictures *was* Della, since she looked different than she did now—her hair was short and black, not the shoulder-length deep gold it was now. But why would she cover up a color like that? Or wear it so short?

Women.

Judging by the length of her hair now, the photos on her phone must be at least a year old. In a few of them, Della and the other women were dressed in business attire and seated at a table with girly-looking drinks sitting in front of them, appearing as if they were blowing off steam at the end of a workday. Okay, so Della had a job and wasn't necessarily the idle socialite he'd thought her to be. It didn't mean she hadn't come from money. She might have even been a client of some kind of one or more of the other women.

Scrolling further down through the pictures, Marcus finally found what he was looking for. Photos of Della, still with short, dark hair, seated with a man on a beach somewhere. A man who looked old enough to be her father, but who was good-looking and fit. Obviously very rich. Obviously very powerful. Obviously very married.

Marcus knew those things about the guy because he knew the guy's type. Too well. He worked and dealt with men like him every day. A lot of them were his friends. This had to be Geoffrey. Who else would it be? No one else in Della's contact list was identified informally by first name except for her girlfriends.

He navigated to her call list and saw that the last time Geoffrey had called Della was three nights ago. The last time Della had called him was yesterday morning. And the morning before that. And the morning before that. He kept scrolling. She'd called Geoffrey every single morning, weekday or weekend, always either at nine o'clock or within minutes before or after that hour.

Whoever Geoffrey was, he was keeping tabs on her. And he was making sure she was the one who called him, not the other way around. Another way to exert his control over her. Della hadn't made or received phone calls from anyone else for more than three months, at least, that was how far back her call log went. Whoever this guy was, he'd had her disconnected from her friends and family for a long time.

Was that why she had come to Chicago? To escape an abusive lover? But she'd told Marcus last night that one night was all she could give him, and she'd phoned Geoffrey yesterday, so obviously this guy wasn't out of her life yet.

He glanced at the clock on the nightstand. It was

approaching 8:45 a.m. In fifteen minutes, Della would have to make her obligatory daily call. But it was a safe bet she wouldn't do it unless Marcus was out of the room—not if she didn't want him to overhear her. He'd been planning to take a shower after she was finished, but now he was thinking maybe he'd wait a bit. 'Til, say, well after nine o'clock. It would be interesting to see how Geoffrey—whoever the hell he was—would react to Della's lack of cooperation. Maybe he'd call her instead. And that, Marcus thought, was something he definitely wanted to be around for.

It wasn't so much that he wanted to confirm his suspicions that Della was attached to another man in some way—a thought that made the breakfast he'd consumed rebel on him. It was because if someone *was* mistreating her, whether emotionally or mentally or physically, Marcus wanted to know about it. Then he wanted to know the guy's full name. And address. So he could hop in his car the minute the roads were clear, and beat the holy hell out of the guy.

When the shower cut off, Marcus hastily closed the phone and returned it to Della's purse with her other belongings. Then he placed it on the dresser in exactly the same position it had been before. Quickly, he grabbed the newspaper that had been brought up with breakfast and returned to the bed, picked up his coffee and pretended to read.

By the time Della emerged from the shower wrapped in her blue robe again and scrubbing her damp hair with a towel, he'd managed to stow the rage he'd begun to feel for that son of a bitch Geoffrey—at least for the time being.

"The shower is all yours," she said as she drew nearer to the bed.

"Thanks," Marcus replied without looking up from the paper.

From the corner of his eye, he saw her glance at the clock. Mere minutes away from nine. He kept his gaze fixed blindly on the newspaper.

Della's agitation at his tepid response was an almost palpable thing. "You, ah, you might want to hurry. You wouldn't want them to run out of hot water." He looked up long enough to see her shift her weight nervously from one foot to the other. "Since it looks like no one will be checking out today. There are probably quite a few people using the shower."

He turned his attention back to the paper. "I don't think a hotel like the Ambassador got to be a hotel like the Ambassador by running out of hot water on its guests. It'll be fine."

"But still…"

"First I want to finish this article about—" Just what was he pretending to read, anyway? Damn. He'd picked up the Style section. "This article about the return of the, uh, the chunky metallic necklace," he said, somehow without losing a drop of testosterone. "Wow, did those ever go out of style in the first place? And then," he continued, "there were a couple of pieces in the Business section that looked even more interesting." He looked at Della again and saw that panicked look from last night creeping into her expression. "It's not like I have anywhere to go," he said. "And it's been a while since I've been able to take my time with the Sunday *Tribune*."

"But…" Her voice trailed off without her finishing. "Okay. Then I'll, ah, I'll dry my hair." She pointed halfheartedly over her shoulder. "I have a hairbrush in my purse."

Marcus nodded, pretending to be absorbed by the fashion icon that was the chunky metallic necklace.

The moment her back was turned, though, he looked up in time to see her withdraw both her brush and phone from the purse, then stash the cell in her robe pocket. When she started to spin around again, he quickly moved his gaze to the paper.

"You know what?" she said suddenly. "I love ice in my orange juice, so I'm going to run down the hall and see if there's an ice machine on this floor."

And then, Marcus thought, she would duck into a stairwell to check in with the man who was trying to control her life.

"Call room service to bring some up," he told her, still looking at the paper.

"I don't want to trouble them with something like that. They must be busy getting everyone's breakfast to them."

Now Marcus put down the paper. "Then I'll get some ice for you."

"*No,*" she said, a little too quickly and a little too adamantly. She seemed to realize she'd overreacted, because she forced a smile and said, "I'm, ah, I'm starting to feel a bit of cabin fever. A little walk down the hall will be nice."

"In your robe and bare feet?" he asked, dipping his head toward her attire—or lack thereof.

"No one will see," she said as she began to sidestep toward the door. "Everyone else is probably sleeping in."

"Not if they're keeping room service hopping and using up all the hot water the way you say."

"You know what I mean."

"We're not sleeping in," he pointed out.

"Yes, but we—" She stopped abruptly, obviously not wanting to bring up the reason they'd woken early. Or maybe it was just that she wasn't any more certain about what the two of them were doing than Marcus was. "I mean…even if someone does see me," she said, trying a different tack, "what difference does it make? It's a hotel. It's Sunday morning. There must be plenty of people still in their robes and bare feet."

Not when there was a blizzard raging outside, Marcus wanted to say. The only reason he and Della weren't dressed was because they didn't have anything to change into. But he didn't point out any of those things. If he kept trying to prevent her from leaving the room, she would come up with more reasons why she needed to get out. And if he pressed her, she was only going to get suspicious of him.

"Fine," he said, looking at the paper again…and seeing nothing but red. "Don't forget to take the key."

"Of course," she said as she collected that from the dresser, too. "I won't be but a minute."

If she was able to make that promise, Marcus thought, then her conversations with Geoffrey must not involve much. Just enough for the guy to make sure she did what she was told.

He waited only until the door clicked shut behind her, then hurried over to silently open it, enough that he could see her making her way down the hall. She'd already withdrawn the phone from her pocket and was dialing one-handed, meaning she'd still be in sight when her conversation began, so Marcus was bound to miss some of it. Impatiently, he waited until she rounded a corner at the end of the hall, then he slipped the metal rod of the chain lock between it and the jamb and stole after her at twice her pace.

When he peered around the corner, he saw her duck through another door that led to the stairwell and heard her speaking into the phone. But she was speaking softly enough that he couldn't distinguish a word. So he raced after her and halted by the door through which she'd exited and cocked his head close. Unfortunately, he could still only hear incomprehensible murmuring. So, as quietly as he could, he turned the knob and pushed the door open a crack, to see that she had seated herself on the top step with her back to him. So he opened it a little bit more.

"Really, Geoffrey, I'm fine," he heard her say. "There's no reason for you to come over. You'd get stuck in the snow if you tried."

He tried to discern something in her voice that sounded fearful or cowering, but, really, she did sound fine.

"I mean, yeah, the snow is kind of a drag," she continued, "but it's not like you ever let me go anywhere anyway."

So she wasn't supposed to be out and about, Marcus thought. His suspicions were confirmed.

"I had groceries delivered this week," she said, "and I downloaded a couple of books. Thanks for the Kindle and the Netflix subscription, by the way. It's helped a lot."

It was the least the son of a bitch could do, since he wouldn't let her go anywhere.

"What?" he heard Della ask. Then she laughed lightly. "No, nothing like that. That's the last thing I need. Mostly romantic comedies. I need something light and escapist, all things considered."

She paused, though whether it was because Geoffrey was talking or because she was looking for something else to say, Marcus didn't know. Finally, though, she began to speak again. "Okay, if you must know, *Bridget Jones's Diary, Love, Actually* and *Pride and Prejudice*." There was another pause, then she laughed again. "Yes. I love Colin Firth. So does your wife, if you'll recall."

It really wasn't the kind of conversation Marcus had expected to hear her having with a married man who was keeping her a virtual prisoner. But neither did it quite dispel his suspicions that Della was being controlled. What really bothered him, though, was that there was something different in her voice when she spoke to Geoffrey that wasn't there when she was talking to him. A casualness and easiness, a lack of formality, that she hadn't exhibited with Marcus. As if she were actually more comfortable with the other man than she was with him. As if she and Geoffrey shared a relationship that was based less on control and more on trust.

Just what the hell was this guy to her?

Then Marcus heard her say something that chilled him.

"Look, Geoffrey, how much longer am I going to have to live this way? You told me I'd only have to do this for six months. That was eleven months ago. You promised me that if I did everything you guys told me to—"

Guys? So Geoffrey wasn't the only one? She was being passed around among a group? Had he really heard that right?

"—that then I'd be free," she continued. "But I'm still—"

The other man must have cut her off before she could finish, because Della stopped talking and listened obediently without saying a word for several minutes.

He saw her lift a hand to her head and push back her hair with a jerky motion that suggested she was anxious. She murmured a few uh-huhs, then slumped forward with her free hand braced on her knee and her forehead pressed to her palm.

Finally, with clear dejection—and maybe a little fear?—she replied, "Two weeks? That's all the time I have left?"

Until what? Marcus wanted to yell. What the hell was she talking about? What the hell did the man expect her to do that made her sound so unwilling to do it?

"Then it's really going to happen," she said with clear resignation, sounding more reserved than ever. "I'm really going to have to do it."

Do what, for God's sake?

"No, I understand," she said. "I'll go through with it. I mean, it's not like I have much choice, do I?" There was another pause, then she continued, "I know I promised. And I'll hold up my end of the bargain. I just...I didn't think it would be like this, Geoffrey. I didn't think I'd feel like this about everything." More softly, she added, "I didn't think I'd feel like this about myself." Then, because Geoffrey must not have heard that last, she said with unmistakable melancholy. "It was nothing important. Never mind."

Nothing important. Marcus felt a little sick to his stomach. The way she felt about herself wasn't important. This guy had her so wound around his finger that Della didn't even realize how unbalanced and unhealthy the relationship was.

Relationship, hell. What she had with this guy was a bargain. She'd said so herself. And it was obviously a bad one. A least on her end.

"So two weeks then," she said again. "I have two

weeks to get myself ready and in the right frame of mind."

Marcus hated to think what that getting ready would involve. He hated more to think about what the *right frame of mind* for such a thing would be.

He heard her answer a few more yes-and-no questions—with little more than a yes or no, sounding more and more like a child with each one—then heard her promise she would call tomorrow morning at the usual time. Then he heard the sound of her phone flipping closed.

He was about to pull the door to and hurry to the room before she caught him eavesdropping, but he heard something else that stopped him short—the very soft sound of muffled crying.

Something twisted inside him. He wasn't accustomed to hearing a woman cry. Mostly because he made sure he got involved with women who were as shallow as he was. At least where things like emotional involvement were concerned. Obviously, Della wasn't shallow. Obviously, she cared a lot about things like involvement. Even if she was currently involved with the wrong man.

Putting aside, for now, the fact that that word probably applied to himself as much as it did Geoffrey, Marcus pushed open the door and silently moved through it. He didn't know why. It would have been best for him and Della both if he went back to the room and pretended he knew nothing of her conversation. It would have been best if they spent the rest of the weekend pretending there was nothing beyond that room until the two of them had to leave it.

But when he saw her sitting on the stair landing with her feet propped on the carpeted step below her, her arms crossed over her knees, her head rested on her arms, her shoulders shaking lightly, he knew he could never go back to pretending anything. She still had the cell phone clasped in one hand, but it fell, landing with a dull thud when she began to cry harder, and she didn't bother to retrieve it. Instead, she surrendered to her sobs, muffling them by pressing her mouth to the sleeve of her robe. She was so lost in her despair that she had no idea Marcus stood behind her.

He didn't know what to do or say, could only stand there feeling helpless. It was an alien concept, this helplessness, and he didn't like it at all. His instincts told him to flee before she saw him, but his conscience— and he was surprised to discover he actually had one— dictated he do something to make her feel better. He let the two war with each other, to see who would win, but when instinct and conscience kept bickering, he stepped in and made the decision himself. He took a tentative step forward, then another.

As he was reaching down to curl his fingers over her shoulder, she whirled her head quickly around. When she saw him there, her eyes went wide with panic, and she stood so quickly, she almost pitched backward down the stairs. He wrapped his fingers around her wrist as she managed to right herself, but neither seemed to know what to say or do after that. For a long moment, they only stood silently looking at each other. Then, finally, Della stepped onto the landing with Marcus. He released her wrist, but brushed away a tear from her cheek with the pad of his thumb.

He had no idea what to say. He, Marcus Fallon, who had never been at a loss for words in his life. The man who could find a quip—whether appropriate or not—to alleviate any tense situation, who could make light of even the most difficult circumstances, couldn't scrape up one word that would ease the tension in this one. Some knight in shining armor he was turning out to be. But then, he'd never wanted to be a knight in shining armor.

Not until now.

"Are you okay?" he asked softly, threading his fingers into her damp hair.

Her eyes were huge, seeming larger thanks to the presence of her tears, making her look vulnerable and fragile. He knew she was neither of those things, and realizing that one conversation with Geoffrey could make her feel that way made him despise the man even more.

She nodded, but said nothing, only swiped at her wet eyes with both hands before shoving them into the pockets of her robe.

"You don't look okay," Marcus said. He lifted his other hand and wove those fingers through her hair, too, until he found the nape of her neck and cradled it in his palm.

"I'm fine," she assured him quietly, sounding anything but.

Knowing it would be pointless to pretend he hadn't heard her on the phone, he asked, "Who were you talking to?"

She looked at the phone on the floor, then up at Marcus. "How much of that did you hear?"

He thought about telling her he'd heard enough to know she was mixed up with someone she shouldn't be who was obliging her to do something she obviously didn't want to do, but that was kind of like the pot calling the kettle black. She shouldn't be mixed up with Marcus, either. Not being the kind of woman she was.

Namely, the kind whose emotions ran deeper than a sheaf of paper.

"Not very much," he lied. "I got worried when you didn't come back, so I came looking for you."

"Was I gone that long?"

He smiled, unable to help himself. "A few seconds was too long to be away from you."

When she didn't smile back, his own fell. "So who were you talking to, Della?"

"No one," she said. "No one important."

"He's the one you were worried about missing you today, isn't he?"

She hesitated for a moment, then nodded. "But not the way—" She expelled an irritated sound.

"Not the way what?" Marcus asked.

"Nothing." She pulled away from him, then bent down to scoop up her phone and the still-empty ice bucket. She looked at his face, but her gaze immediately ricocheted to the door. "Look, Marcus, can we go back to the room and forget this happened?"

When he said nothing, she looked at him again, her eyebrows arrowed downward. "Can we? Please?"

He crossed his arms over his chest, telling himself the gesture was *not* defensive. Marcus Fallon didn't get defensive. Marcus Fallon was the most offensive human being on the planet. "I don't know, Della. Can we?"

She glanced away again. "I can if you can."

Somehow, he doubted that. Because in addition to being the man who currently claimed Della as his own, Geoffrey seemed like the kind of man who wouldn't let her forget about anything.

In spite of that, Marcus nodded. Once. "Fine. Let's just forget it happened."

Still not looking at him, she replied, "You promise?"

"I do."

When she looked at him again, all traces of her former sadness were gone. She looked matter-of-fact and a little blank. She sounded that way, too, when she said, "Thank you. I appreciate it."

It was only then, when she sounded so formal, that Marcus realized she had, for a few moments, been as familiar with him as she had been with the man on the phone. But now the reserve was in her voice again. When he looked at her, he realized it was in her posture, too. They were indeed back to pretending. He should be relieved about that.

Instead, for some reason, now Marcus kind of wanted to cry.

Six

The mood in the room was considerably darker when they returned, Della couldn't help noticing. As was the room itself. She strode directly to the window and pulled back the curtains to find her worst fears confirmed. She wouldn't have thought it possible, but the snow was coming down even thicker and faster now than it had been when she'd first awoken.

She was never going to get out of here.

But then, what did she care? It wasn't as though she had anything waiting for her out there. Nothing but a nondescript house full of nondescript furnishings in a nondescript Chicago suburb populated by nondescript families. Middle-class, middle-income, middle America. The area had been chosen specifically because it was so unremarkable and unmemorable. Della had been living there for eleven months now, and even she would have been hard-pressed to describe from memory what any of her neighbors or their houses looked like. It was the last place she wanted to be, the last place she should be living, the last place anyone would think to look for her.

That, of course, was the whole point.

What made it worse was that she'd been expressly forbidden to interact with anyone or set foot outside unless absolutely unavoidable, and never without asking Geoffrey for permission first. So far, he hadn't considered a single one of her reasons to be absolutely unavoidable. Hence the sneaking around on those occasions when staying in the house would have driven her unavoidably insane.

As disconcerting as it was to be stuck here with Marcus until tomorrow—at least—a part of her thrilled at the prospect. She'd never felt as free or unencumbered—or uninhibited—as she did with him. She scarcely recognized herself this morning. Never in her life had she behaved with a man the way she had behaved with him. Not only the part about having sex with someone she'd just met, but also the sheer volume of sex they'd had. And the earthiness of it. The carnality of it. She'd *never* done things with other men that she'd done with Marcus last night. But with him, she'd felt no reticence or self-consciousness at all. Probably because he hadn't had any himself. On the contrary—he'd been demanding and exacting when it came to what he wanted. But he'd been every bit as generous when giving himself to her.

Something warm and fizzy bubbled inside, an unfamiliar percolation of both desire and contentment, of want and satisfaction. She'd felt it on and off throughout the night, usually between bouts of lovemaking when their bodies had been damp and entwined. But Marcus was on the other side of the room now, and their exchange in the stairwell had been a less than satisfying one. Even so, she could still feel this way, simply by being in the same room with him, knowing he wasn't leaving her. Not yet.

So really, why was she so eager to leave?

Maybe, she answered herself, it was because a part of her still knew this couldn't last forever and saw no point in prolonging it. The longer it went on, the harder it would be when it came time for the two of them to part. And they would have to part. Soon. The fantasy she and Marcus had carved out last night should have been over already. They should have separated before dawn, before the harsh light of day cast shadows over what they had created together.

They both had obligations that didn't involve the other—Della to Geoffrey and Marcus to the faceless woman for whom he obviously still had deep feelings. Even if he was no longer "with" her, as he claimed, it was clear he still cared very much for her. Too much for the possibility of including someone new in his life. Even if Della was in a position to become that someone new, which she definitely was not. Not here. Not now. Not ever.

How much *had* he heard of her conversation with Geoffrey? she wondered as she turned from the window and saw Marcus pouring himself another cup of coffee. She tried to remember if she'd said anything that might have offered a hint of what her life had become, but she was confident he would never suspect the truth. Because the truth was like something straight out of fiction.

He glanced up suddenly, and when he saw her looking at him, lifted the coffee carafe and asked, "Would you like some?"

It was a mundane question from a man who looked as if this was just another typical morning in his life. But Della could practically feel a vibe emanating from him that reached all the way across the room, and it was neither mundane nor typical. It was cool and distant, and it was, she was certain, a remnant of their exchange in the stairwell.

Was this how it would be for the rest of their time together? Strained and difficult? Please, no, she immediately answered herself. Somehow, they had to recapture their earlier magic. If only for a little while.

"Yes," she said, even though her stomach was roiling too much for her to consume anything. She only wanted some kind of conversation with him that wasn't anxious. "Please."

She strode to the breakfast cart, standing as close to Marcus as she dared, watching him pour. He had magnificent hands, strong with sturdy fingers and no adornments. Looking at his hands, she would never have guessed he worked for a brokerage house. He had the hands of someone who used them for something other than pushing the keys of a computer or cell phone all day.

"Do you play any sports?" she asked impulsively.

His expression was surprised as he handed her her coffee. "I thought you didn't want to know anything about me."

Oh, yeah. She didn't. She already knew more than she wanted to. So maybe it wouldn't hurt to know a little bit more. Ignoring the convoluted logic in that, she said, "I changed my mind."

He handed her her coffee with a resigned sigh. "Squash," he told her. "Three times a week. With another one of the—" He halted, as if he'd been about to reveal something else about himself, but this time it was something he *didn't* want her to know. "With a coworker," he finally finished. He sipped his coffee, then met her gaze levelly. "Why do you ask?"

"Your hands," she said before she could stop herself. "You have good hands, Marcus. They're not the hands of an office worker."

His eyes seemed to go a little darker at that, and she remembered that there were other ways his hands were good, too. Lots and lots of other ways. She spun around, striding away on slightly shaky legs. But when she realized she was walking straight toward the bed, she quickly sidetracked toward two chairs arranged on each side of a table near the window.

"It's still snowing," she said as she sat. "Maybe even harder than before."

Marcus strode to the window, lifted one curtain for a scant moment, then let it drop. "I guess we could turn on the TV to see what the weather guys are saying about how much longer this will last."

"I suppose we could."

But neither of them did. They only looked at each other expectantly, almost as if they were daring the other to do it. Della knew why she didn't. She wondered if Marcus's reason mirrored her own.

Finally, he folded himself into the other chair, setting his cup on the table beside hers. He crossed his legs with deceptive casualness, propped an elbow on the chair arm to rest his chin in his hand and, looking her right in the eye, asked, "Who's Geoffrey?"

Della felt as if someone punched her right in the stomach. Obviously he'd heard more of the phone conversation than he'd let on. She wondered how much. She wondered even harder about how she was supposed to explain her relationship with Geoffrey to Marcus. It wasn't as though she could be vague about something like that.

She reminded herself she didn't have to tell Marcus anything. Not the truth, not a fabrication, nothing. She could say it was none of his business, repeat their agreement not to disclose any personal details about each other—which he'd already breached a number of times, one of which had been at her own encouragement—and change the subject.

But she was surprised to discover there was a part of herself that wanted to tell him about Geoffrey. And not just Geoffrey, but about everything that had led to her meeting him. She wanted to tell Marcus everything about the mess that had started on New Year's Day to herald the beginning of the worst year of her life, about the months of fear and uncertainty that had followed, right up until her encounter with him at Palumbo's. She wanted to tell him about how she hadn't felt safe or contented for eleven months. About how lonely she'd been. About how hopeless and scared she'd felt.

At least until her encounter with him at Palumbo's. It was only now that Della realized she hadn't experienced any of those feelings since meeting Marcus. For the first time in eleven months—maybe for the first time in her life—she'd been free of anxiety and pleasantly at ease. She'd spent the past twelve hours ensconced in a perfect bubble of completeness, where nothing intruded that could cause her harm or pain. All because of a man whose last name she didn't even know.

But she couldn't tell him any of that, either.

She couldn't say a word. She'd taken a virtual vow of silence about what had happened in New York, and she'd been told that if she revealed anything to anyone, it could compromise everything. And then the last eleven months of living in hiding and being so relentlessly alone would have been for nothing.

Two weeks, she reminded herself. That was how long Geoffrey had told her she had to wait. Only two more weeks. In sixteen days, everything would be revealed, everything would come to light, and Della would be free of all of them. Of Geoffrey, of Egan Collingwood, of her boss Mr. Nathanson and everyone else at Whitworth and Stone. And even if that freedom meant losing everything she had now and starting all over somewhere else, even if it meant becoming an entirely new person, at least she would be done with all of it. She would be safe. She would be free. She would be *done*. She just had to hold on for two more weeks.

She opened her mouth to tell Marcus that Geoffrey was none of his business and then change the subject, but instead she hedged, "Well. So much for forgetting about the episode in the stairwell. And you promised."

"I've made a lot of promises since meeting you," he reminded her. "And I haven't kept many of them. You should probably know that about me. I'm great at making promises. Terrible at keeping them."

She nodded. "Good to know."

"Doesn't make me a terrible person," he told her. "It just makes me more human."

It also made him an excellent reminder, Della thought. His assertion that he couldn't keep promises illustrated more clearly why she couldn't tell him anything more about herself. She might very well become the topic of his next cocktail party anecdote or an inadvertently shared story with a colleague who had some connection to the very life she was trying to escape. Not because he was a bad person, as he had said. But because he was human. And humanity was something Della had learned not to trust.

"So who is he, Della?"

She hesitated, trying to remind herself again of all the reasons why she couldn't tell Marcus the truth—or anything else. Then, very softly, she heard herself say, "Geoffrey is a man who…who kind of…" She sighed again. "He kind of takes care of me."

Marcus said nothing for a moment, then nodded slowly. His expression cleared some, and he looked as if he completely understood. That was impossible, because there was still a lot of it that even Della didn't understand.

"You're his mistress, you mean," Marcus said in a remarkably matter-of-fact way. "It's all right, Della. I'm a big boy. You can spell it out for me."

It took a moment for what he was saying to sink in. And not only because the word *mistress* was so old-fashioned, either. Marcus thought she and Geoffrey had a sexual relationship. That he was a wealthy benefactor who was giving her money and gifts in exchange for sexual favors. That she, Della Hannan, the only girl in her neighborhood who had been determined to claw her way out of the slum *not* using sex as the means to get there, was now making her way in the world by renting herself out sexually to the highest bidder.

She should have been insulted. Instead, she wanted to laugh. Because compared to the reality of her situation, his assumption, as tawdry as it sounded, was just so… so… So adorably innocent.

Wow. If she *were* Geoffrey's mistress, that would make her life a million times easier. But number one, the guy was married. Number two, he was old enough to be her father. Number three, he looked like a sixty-something version of Dwight Schrute. And number four, there was no way he could afford a mistress when he had two kids in college and a daughter getting married in six months. After all, federal marshals weren't exactly the highest paid people on the government payroll.

Marcus must have mistaken her lack of response as being offended instead of off guard, because he hastily continued, "Look, Della, it doesn't matter to me. I'm the last person who should, or would, judge the way another person lives their life. I don't consider your situation to be appalling or bad or cheap or dirty or embarrassing or—" He seemed to realize how badly he was belaboring his objections—and he'd barely made a dent if he was going to be all alphabetical about it—something that made them sound even less convincing than they already did. He gave his head a single shake, as if he were trying to clear it. "Besides, it's not like I haven't, ah, kept a woman myself in the past."

Della wasn't sure, but he almost sounded as if he were about to offer her such a job now.

He tried again, holding out one hand as if he were literally groping for the right words. "What I'm trying to say is that I don't think any less of you for it. Sometimes, in order to survive in this world, people have to resort to unconventional methods. It doesn't make them any less a human being than anyone else. In a lot of ways, it makes them better than the people who don't have to struggle to make their way. Because they're…they're survivors, Della. That's what they do. They…they survive. That's what you are, too. You're a survivor. You're unconventional and you're… you're making your way in the world, and you're… You're surviving. You're—"

"No man's mistress," she finished for him, interrupting him before he broke into song. Or broke a blood vessel in his brain trying to cope. Whatever. "That's not how Geoffrey takes care of me, Marcus. We don't have a sexual relationship *at all*. I mean, Geoffrey is his last name. I don't even call him by his first name." It was Winston, and probably why he asked everyone to call him by his last name.

Marcus's relief was almost palpable. So much for not thinking less of anyone who survived in the world through unconventional methods. She might have laughed if he hadn't been right about one thing: She was surviving. And she did depend on Geoffrey's presence in her life to accomplish that.

Della couldn't give Marcus any details about what had happened in New York or the fact that she was a material witness in a federal case that involved her former Wall Street employer, Whitworth and Stone, and her former boss, Donald Nathanson. Especially knowing as she did now that Marcus worked for the equally illustrious Fallon Brothers. It wasn't unlikely that he knew people at Whitworth and Stone and moved in the same circles. Not that she feared he would report her to anyone, since no one there even knew—yet—about the case the feds were building. As far as anyone at Whitworth and Stone was concerned, the reason Della had stopped showing up for work without giving notice was because of personal reasons that would make performing her job intolerable. After all, Egan had been one of Whitworth and Stone's up-and-coming executives.

She had no way of knowing how Marcus would react to the revelation that Della had, in her position as executive assistant to one of the company's vice presidents, discovered a trail of illegal money laundering for unsavory overseas groups and the gross misuse of government bailout funds. She couldn't tell him about how she'd smuggled out files over a period of two weeks, or about going to the FBI with what she'd uncovered, or about how they'd immediately put her into protective custody with the U.S. Marshals and moved her out of New York to keep her under wraps until she could appear before the grand jury. She couldn't tell him how she'd been in hiding for the past eleven months while the feds built their case.

And she for sure couldn't tell him about how, once the trial was over—and Geoffrey had just told her the grand jury was convening in two weeks—she was probably going to be placed in the Witness Security Program, for safe measure. Even though her life hadn't been threatened, and even though none of the crimes committed had been violent ones, being a whistle-blower wasn't exactly the most celebrated gig in the world. There was no way she'd ever find work in the financial world again.

And, well, even though it was unlikely, there was no guarantee there wouldn't be some other kind of retaliation against her. Some of the groups to which Whitworth and Stone had diverted funds had done some pretty terrible things in other parts of the world. It would be best for her to start over somewhere as a new person, with a new identity and a new life. A place where nobody knew her real name and where there was no chance she would ever be discovered.

A place completely removed from the spotlight Marcus so joyfully embraced in his own life. The last thing Della could afford was to have someone see her with him and recognize her from her former position. It would be even worse for her to be recognized after she'd given her testimony and put a lot of powerful people behind bars. At best, she would be a social pariah. At worst… Well, she didn't want to think about things like that.

Bottom line, there was no way this thing with Marcus could last beyond a weekend. He would never give up the big, showy lifestyle he loved. And she was a woman who had to avoid a big, showy life at all costs.

"Well, if Geoffrey isn't your…benefactor," Marcus said now, "then who is he? A relative?"

Stalling, she asked, "Why do you want to know? What difference does it make? Once the snow lets up, you and I are never going to—"

"I just want to know, Della."

"But why?"

"Maybe because you burst into tears after talking to the guy?"

Oh, right. That. That had kind of startled Della, too. But for some reason, during this morning's talk with Geoffrey, she had begun to feel keenly how truly alone she was. Geoffrey had been her only tie to the outside world for eleven months—at least until she met Marcus—and the conversations she had with him never lasted any longer than it took for her to check in every day and let him know she was okay. She always wanted to talk longer, since she never got to talk to anyone. Just to hear a human voice that wasn't coming from an electronic device. Every time, Geoffrey cut short the conversation because there was no reason to prolong it. Especially on weekends, he wanted to be with his family. Geoffrey always had things to do, places to go, people to see after he hung up. And Della always had to go back to the vast nothingness of waiting, all alone.

But this morning, after hanging up, she'd realized she *didn't* have to go back to being alone. This morning, she'd known Marcus was waiting for her. Someone who would talk to her. Someone who would share breakfast with her. Someone who would care for her. Be with her. Touch her. If only for a little while. And the thought that she would have such intimacy—even if it was only temporary and superficial—only made it worse to think about leaving it, leaving him, behind. Something about that was so intolerable. So bleak. So heartbreaking. Della simply hadn't been able to stop the tears from coming.

She felt the sting of tears threatening again and shoved the thought to the furthest, darkest corner of her brain. "He's not a relative, either," she said wearily.

When she didn't elaborate, Marcus asked, "Then how and why is he taking care of you?"

She expelled an impatient sound. "I don't guess you'd settle for 'It's complicated,' would you?"

He shook his head. "The directions for assembling a nuclear warhead are complicated," he told her. "Life? Not so much."

She managed a smile. "Trust me, Marcus. My life is currently *very* complicated."

"In what way?"

She couldn't tell him. She couldn't even hint. Maybe if he didn't have the job he had. Maybe if he wasn't a rich guy who didn't keep his finger on the pulse of the financial world. Maybe if he was just some average guy with an average job who didn't for a minute understand the workings of Wall Street...

She still couldn't tell him, she knew. So she stalled. "The place where I come from on the East Coast I had to leave a while back, because I—I got into some trouble there."

His expression wavered not at all. "You did something illegal?"

"No," she was quick to assure him. "Nothing like that. But I—I got caught up in something…not good… without intending to. So Geoffrey found me a place to live until things blow over. And I call him every day so he knows I'm okay."

"That doesn't sound complicated," Marcus said. "That sounds dangerous."

Della opened her mouth to contradict him, then realized she couldn't do that without lying. The chances of her being in danger were very small. The main reason the feds wanted to keep her under wraps was so no one at Whitworth and Stone would catch on to the fact that they were being investigated. And, too, to make sure Della didn't skip out on them after promising to give testimony.

"Not dangerous," she said. "They just want to be sure."

"And by *they,* you would mean…who?" Marcus asked. "The police?"

She shook her head, but didn't elaborate. It wasn't the police keeping an eye on her. Not technically. She was much further up the law enforcement ladder than that.

"Then who?"

"I can't tell you any more than that," she said. "I only said that much because I wanted you to know the truth about Geoffrey. I'm not…tied to him. Not that way."

Marcus hesitated a moment. "Are you…tied to anyone…that way?"

She should tell him yes. Make him think she was

involved with someone who meant a great deal to her. Maybe that would make it easier when the time came for them to part. If Marcus thought she was going home to another man, and if he thought she was shallow enough to have sex with him when she was involved with someone else, then it would be easier for him to put her in his past and keep her there.

If only she could do the same with him.

But instead of lying, her damnable honesty surfaced again. "There's no one," she said. "There hasn't been for a long time."

That, she supposed, was why she capitulated to Marcus so quickly and easily the night before. Because he was the first person she'd had face-to-face contact with for months. The first person who'd conversed with her. Who'd smiled at her. Who'd laughed with her. Who'd touched her. She'd gone too long without the most basic human need—the need to bond with someone else. Even if it was only over an article in a tabloid while waiting in line at the supermarket or sharing a few words while making change for another person at the Laundromat. People needed to be with other people in order to feel whole. Della hadn't had that for too long.

Marcus eyed her thoughtfully for another moment, then said, "So if it wasn't legal trouble, then what kind of trouble was it?"

"I can't tell you any more than I have, Marcus."

"Why not?"

"Because…it's complicated."

He dragged his chair around the table until it was directly facing hers, then sat close enough that their knees were touching. He took both of her hands in his.

"Look, there's a good chance I can help you out. I know a lot of people on the East Coast. Good friends. People I trust and who can pull strings. Some owe me favors. Others I know things about they'd rather not see made public so they'd be happy to grant me favors."

"I'm not sure those sound like friends to me."

"Maybe not. But I can still trust them to do what I tell them to. A lot of them are people with clout. They know people who know people who know people who can get things done."

And it was precisely that network of people who knew other people that was what Della was afraid of. Marcus might inadvertently tip her hand to the very people who were under investigation. His friends might be their friends, too. They were people like him—rich, powerful, enjoying an elevated social standing they didn't want to have compromised. They worked in the same industry. They were of the same tribe. Hell, he might not even want to help her if he found out what was at stake.

"You can't help," she said. "I appreciate the offer, Marcus, but you can't."

"How do you know?"

"I just do."

He studied her for another moment. "It's because you don't trust me. Because you just met me and don't know anything about me. But that doesn't have to be the case, Della. I—"

"It isn't that." And she was surprised to realize that was the truth. She did trust Marcus. In spite of having just met him. And she knew more about him after one night than she did about a lot of people she'd known in New York for years. But money made people do funny things. Lots of money made people do bad things. And billions of dollars… That made people do desperate things.

"There must be something I can do, Della," he insisted, his voice laced with something akin to pleading. "The thought of you being in trouble somehow…it isn't right."

Unable to help herself, she leaned forward and cupped his strong jaw in her hand. "You're a good guy, Marcus. And it's nice of you, wanting to help. But this is on me. Eventually, things will be better, but for now…"

She didn't finish. Mostly because, for now, she wanted to forget. She had another day and night to spend with Marcus, here in this hotel room where nothing from the outside could get to them. For now, she only wanted to think about that.

He covered her hand with his, then turned his face to place a soft kiss at the center of her palm. Warmth ebbed through her at the gesture. It was so sweet. So tender. So unlike their couplings of the night before.

"There must be something I can do to help," he said again. "Please, Della. Just tell me what to do."

She reached out with her other hand and threaded it through his hair, letting the silky tresses sift through her fingers before moving them to his forehead, his jaw, his mouth. "You can make love to me, again," she said softly. "You can hold me and touch me and say meaningless things that both of us know aren't true anywhere but here in this room. You can make me feel safe and warm and cherished. You can make me forget that there's anything in the world except the two of us. Do that for me and I'll—"

She stopped herself before saying *I'll love you forever*. Even though she was confident he would know it was hyperbole, it didn't feel like something she should put out there in the world.

He smiled, but there was something in the gesture that was a little hollow. His eyes were dark with wanting, however, when he reached for her and murmured, "Well, if you insist…"

Seven

Without hesitation, Marcus leaned forward and covered Della's mouth with his, dipping his hands into the deep V of her robe to curl his fingers over her bare shoulders as he deepened the kiss. Her skin was warm and fragrant from her recent shower, and the soft scent grew both stronger and more delicate as he slowly spread open the fabric of the garment. He traced the delicate line of her collarbone to the divot at the base of her throat, then his fingers stole around to her nape, spreading into the silk of her hair. It was still damp, and tangled around his fingers as if trying to trap his hand there forever. He wished they could stay embraced this way forever. He would never grow tired of touching her.

Della seemed to sense his thoughts, because her hands fell to the knot in her robe and untied it before she cupped his face in her palms. Spurred by her silent invitation, Marcus moved his hand lower, skimming the backs of his knuckles over the sensitive skin above her breasts before dragging his middle finger down the delicate valley between them. She gasped as he curved his fingers under one heavy breast and lifted it, then opened her mouth wider to invite him deep inside.

His last coherent thought was that he was responding to her the same way he had the night before, losing himself to her with a velocity and intensity that surpassed every other reaction, every other emotion, he had. The moment he touched her, everything else in the world ceased to exist. There was only heat and hunger, demand and desire, all of it commanding satisfaction.

Della seemed to understand that, too—or maybe she was feeling the same thing herself—because she was suddenly working feverishly at the sash of his robe, jerking it free so that she could dip her hands inside and explore him. Her fingers fumbled a bit as he gently began to knead her breast, but she recovered quickly, pushing his robe backward, over his shoulders and arms, spreading the fabric wider still. The next thing Marcus knew, she was on her knees in front of him, one hand curving over his taut thigh, the other moving on his hard shaft.

He nearly exploded at the contact, closing his eyes and sucking in a desperate breath as she gently palmed him. For long moments, she pleasured him that way, making his heart pound and his blood race until the rhythm of his passion roared in his ears. And when he felt her mouth close over him…

Oh, Della… Oh, baby…

When his fingers convulsed in her hair, she must have sensed how close he was to coming apart, because she stood and she took his hand in hers, then led him to the bed. When she pushed his robe completely from his shoulders and nudged him down to the mattress, he went willingly, watching with great interest as she shrugged out of her robe, too. She joined him in bed, but when she tried to face him, he cupped his hands over her shoulders, gently turned her around and positioned her on her hands and knees. Then he moved his hands to her hips and knelt behind her. He splayed his palms open on her back, skimming them up and down as he slowly entered her, then leaned forward until his chest was flush with her back. He caught her breasts in his hands and held them for a moment, thumbing her stiff nipples and eliciting a wild little sound from deep inside her. Then he withdrew himself slowly and thrust forward again. Hard.

She cried out at the depth of his penetration, curling her fingers into the fabric of the sheet. Marcus filled her again, even harder this time, eliciting a response from her that was hot, erotic and demanding. So what could Marcus do but obey her? He had never been with a woman who was so uninhibited about sex. Della both commanded and surrendered in ways no other woman ever had. She rode astride him, wrapped her legs around his waist when she was beneath him, demanded he take her kneeling and sitting and standing. When they finally surrendered to the climaxes that shook them simultaneously, she was bent over the chair where they had started as Marcus pummeled her from behind again. They came together, cried out their satisfaction together, rode out the waves of their orgasms together. Then, together, they relaxed and reined themselves in, and collapsed into the chair.

For long moments, they sat entwined, Marcus on the chair and Della in his lap, neither willing—or perhaps able—to say a word. Della opened her hand over the center of Marcus's chest, and he mimicked the gesture with her, noting how the rapid-fire beating of her heart kept time with his own. Gradually, it slowed along with his, too, until both of them were thumping along in happy, contented rhythm. At least, for now. Marcus suspected it wouldn't be long before their desires overtook them again.

But there had been something different in this coupling that hadn't been there before. He wasn't sure what it was or how it mattered, but it was there all the same. Yes, the sex had been hot, intense and carnal. Yes, they had both been consumed by an almost uncontrollable passion. Yes, they had said and done things they might not have said and done with other partners.

But there had been something else there that Marcus hadn't had with other partners, too. Not just a lack of inhibition, but a lack of fear. As if coming together with Della was simply a natural reaction to feelings he'd had for a very long time. He didn't know any other way to describe it, even though they'd known each other only a matter of hours. Sex with Della felt…right somehow. As if everything up until now had merely been a warm-up. *Della* felt right somehow. As if every woman before her had been practice. It meant something, he was sure of it. If he could only figure out what…

Marcus knew the moment he awoke that Della was gone. Even though it was still dark in the hotel room. Even though her fragrance still lingered on the pillow beside his own. Even though the sheets were still warm where she had lain. Maybe it had been the snick of the hotel room door closing behind her that woke him, he thought with surprising clarity for having just woken. Maybe if he hurried, he could still catch her before she made it to the elevator. Or if she had already disappeared into it, maybe he could hurry faster and catch her in the lobby before she made it out of the building.

But even as the thoughts raced through his head, he knew, too, that none of them were true. Because, somehow, he knew what had woken him wasn't a sound at all. What had woken him was the simple awareness, on some subconscious level, that Della was irretrievably gone and that he was irrevocably alone.

Alone, he marveled as he jackknifed up in the bed and palmed his eyes. It was a familiar condition, but it had never felt quite like this. It had never bothered Marcus to live alone or eat alone or work alone or do anything else alone. On the contrary, he'd always preferred his own company to that of others. Well, except for Charlotte, but that was because she had been a solitary creature herself. Marcus had never really felt as if he had that much in common with others, anyway. If he wanted companionship, it was easy to find it. There was always someone he could call or someplace he could go where, in a matter of minutes, he would be surrounded. Sometimes by friends, more often by acquaintances he pretended were friends, but the point was, he liked being alone.

He didn't like it this morning. Della's absence surrounded him like a rank, fetid carcass.

He rose and shrugged on his robe, knotting it around his waist as he moved to the window. In the sliver of moonlight that spilled through a slit in the curtains, he glimpsed a piece of paper lying on the table between the two chairs where he and Della had sat only hours ago.

Something hitched tight in his chest as he reached for it, because he thought it was a note from her. But it was the paper on which he'd written his numbers for her the day before. She'd left it behind. Because she'd wanted to make clear to him that she wouldn't be contacting him in the future.

She'd said she'd found trouble in New York. He couldn't imagine what kind of trouble a woman like her could be in. But if Della said she was in trouble, then she was in trouble. And if she'd said he couldn't help her...

Well, there she could be wrong.

Marcus crumpled the paper in his palm and tossed it onto the table, then pulled back the drape. The sky was black and crystal clear beyond, dotted with stars that winked like gemstones under theater lights. Uncaring of the bitter cold, he unlatched the window and shoved it open as far as it would go—which was barely wide enough for him to stick his head through—then gazed down onto Michigan Avenue. He'd never seen the street deserted before, regardless of the hour, but it was now, even though the snowplows had been through. People had yet to brave their way out into the remnants of the blizzard and probably wouldn't until after the sun rose.

For some reason, Marcus looked to his right and saw the red lights of a retreating car disappear around a corner some blocks up. Another light atop it indicated it was a taxi. Della's taxi. He knew that as well as he knew his own name.

As well as he knew her name, too.

Never had he been more grateful for his lack of decorum than he was in that moment. Had he not rifled through her purse, he would have nothing of her now save her first name. Well, that and the memory of the most unforgettable weekend he'd ever spent with anyone. Now there was another reason he wouldn't forget it. Because he knew where to find Della Hannan. Maybe not in Chicago, but he did in New York. And that alone was worth its weight in gold. Provided one knew the right people.

And Marcus definitely knew the right people.

His cheeks began to burn in the freezing temperature, so he closed the window and retreated into the room. He scooped up his jacket from the back of the chair as he passed it, then sat on the side of the bed and dug his phone out of the inside pocket. He and Della had switched off their phones shortly after entering the room and had promised to keep them off, and he had kept that promise—at least where his own phone was concerned. Now that their brief interlude was over, he switched it back on. A dozen voice mails awaited him. He ignored them all and went right to his contacts, scrolling through to the one he wanted. A private detective he'd used a number of times, but always only with regard to business. Nevertheless the man had an excellent reputation when it came to investigations of a personal nature, too. Just how excellent, Marcus was about to discover.

He punched the talk button, and after three rings, a voice on the other end answered. Answered with a filthy epithet, but then, that wasn't unexpected considering the source. Or the time of night.

"Damien, it's Marcus Fallon." He gave the other man a few seconds for the synapses in his brain to connect the dots.

"Right," Damien finally said. "Whattaya need?"

"I need your services for something a little different from what I normally hire you for."

"No problem."

"I have a name, a physical description and a former address in New York City. Can you find a person who's now living in Chicago with that?"

"Sure."

"Can you do it soon?"

"Depends."

"On what?" Marcus asked.

"On how bad the person wants to be found."

"How about on how bad *I* want the person found?"

It took another few seconds for more synapses to find their way to the meaning. "How much?" Damien asked.

Marcus relaxed. This was the thing he did best in the world. Well, other than the thing he and Della had spent the weekend doing. He started to turn on the bedside lamp, then remembered he would only see an empty room and changed his mind. "Tell you what," he said, "let's you and I negotiate a deal."

Della had been forced to part with a lot of things in her life. Her family, her friends and her home—such as they were—when she left the old neighborhood at eighteen. Jobs, offices and acquaintances as she'd climbed the professional ladder, moving from one part of Whitworth and Stone to another. An entire new life she'd built for herself in Manhattan. Soon she'd be parting with everything that had become familiar to her in Chicago.

But she didn't think any of those things had been as painful to part with as the crimson velvet Carolina Herrera gown and Dolce & Gabbana shoes, not to mention the Bulgari earrings and pendant and the black silk Valentino opera coat. Not because they were so beautiful and rich and expensive. But because they were the only mementos she had of the time she'd spent with Marcus.

The only physical mementos, at any rate, since she'd left behind the paper on which he'd recorded all of his phone numbers—something for which she was kicking herself now, even if she had memorized all of them. It would have been nice to have something he'd touched, something personal in his own handwriting.

And when had she turned into such a raging sentimentalist? Never in her life had she wanted a personal memento from anyone. Not even Egan Collingwood. That was probably significant, but she refused to think about how.

Besides, it wasn't as though she didn't have plenty of other reminders of Marcus, she thought as she watched Ava Brenner, the proprietress of Talk of the Town, write out a receipt for the return of the rentals. Della had her memories. Memories that would haunt her for the rest of her life. The way Marcus had traced his fingertips so seductively over the rim of his champagne glass when they were in the club. How his brown eyes had seemed to flash gold when he laughed. The way his jacket had felt and smelled as he draped it over her shoulders. How the snow had sparkled as it had fluttered around him on the terrace and came to rest against his dark hair. The way his voice had rumbled against her ear when he murmured such erotic promises during their lovemaking

But mostly, she would remember the way he looked lying asleep in their bed before she left him.

He'd been lying on his side facing the place where she

had been sleeping, his arm thrown across the mattress where she had lain—she'd awoken to find it draped over her. He'd been bathed in a slash of moonlight that tumbled through the window from the clear sky outside. His hair had been tousled from their final coupling, and his expression, for the first time since she met him, had been utterly, absolutely clear. He'd looked... happy. Content. Fulfilled. As if he'd learned the answer to some ancient question that no one else understood.

She'd tried to write him a note, had tried to capture in writing what she so desperately wanted to say to him. But when she'd realized what it was she wanted to say, she'd torn the paper into tiny pieces and let them fall like snowflakes into the tiny handbag that now lay on the counter between her and Ava. They had been silly, anyway, the feelings she'd begun to think she had for him. Impossible, too. Not only because she'd known him less than forty-eight hours. And not only because he was still carrying a torch for someone else. But also because Della wasn't the sort of woman to fall in love. Love was for dreamers and the deluded. And God knew she'd never been either of those.

"There," Ava said as she finished tallying everything. "If you'll sign here that we agree to agree that you returned everything safe and sound, I'll return the full amount of your damage deposit."

"But I'm late getting everything back," Della said. "I was supposed to be here at opening on Sunday. Not Monday."

Ava made a careless gesture with her hand. "I was supposed to be here Sunday, too. But Mother Nature had other ideas for all of us, didn't she?"

Boy, did she ever.

"So Monday morning is the next best thing," Ava continued. "I appreciate you being here so promptly."

Yeah, that was Della. Always perfect timing. Especially when it came to anything that would thoroughly disrupt her life. Had she been five minutes later meeting Egan on New Year's Eve, she would have missed seeing him with the woman she would learn was his wife. Had she been ten minutes later to the office on New Year's Day, she would have missed the memo to her boss that had set everything into motion. She would still be living her life blissfully unaware in New York. Even if she'd ultimately realized Egan was married, and even if she'd quit her job because of him, she would have found another position elsewhere on Wall Street in no time. She would still be picking up her morning coffee at Vijay's kiosk, would still be enjoying Saturdays in Central Park, would still have the occasional night at the Met when she could afford it.

And she never, ever, would have met Marcus.

She couldn't decide if that was a good thing or not. Traditional thinking said it was better to have loved and lost than never to have loved at all, but Della wondered. Maybe it was better to never know what you were missing. Not that she *loved* Marcus. But still…

"Did you enjoy *La Bohème,* Miss Hannan?" Ava asked, bringing Della's thoughts back to the present.

She smiled, only having to fake part of it. "It was wonderful," she said. "I can't remember the last time I enjoyed an evening so much." Or a night afterward, she added to herself. Or a day after that. Or a night after that.

"I've never been to the opera," Ava told her. "Never mind a red-carpet event like opening night. It must have been very exciting, rubbing shoulders with such refined company in a gorgeous setting like the Lyric with everyone dressed in their finest attire."

The announcement surprised Della, though she wasn't sure why. Certainly there were a lot of people out there, especially her age, which Ava seemed to be, who didn't care for opera enough to see it performed live. It was the red-carpet comment and the breathless quality of her voice when she talked about the refined company that didn't gibe. There was an unmistakable air of refinement and wealth about Ava that indicated she must move in the sort of social circle that would promote opera attendance and red-carpet events, never mind gorgeous settings and fine attire.

Both times Della had encountered Ava, the other woman had exuded elegance and good breeding, and had been extremely well put together in the sort of understated attire that only reinforced it. Today, she wore a perfectly tailored taupe suit with pearly buttons, her only jewelry glittering diamond studs in her ears—large enough and sparkly enough for Della to guess they alone cost a fortune. Her dark auburn hair was arranged in a flawless chignon at her nape, and her green eyes reflected both intelligence and sophistication.

Standing across the counter from her, Della was more aware than ever of her impoverished roots. Although she was dressed nicely enough in brown tweed trousers and an ivory cashmere sweater under her dark chocolate trench coat, she felt like more of an impostor than ever. Ava Brenner obviously came from the sort of old money background that Della had had to insinuate herself into—and still never really belonged in. She recognized all the signs, having been surrounded by people like Ava in her job.

Not for the first time, she wondered why the other

woman ran a shop like this. She was probably rich enough on her own to do nothing but be idly rich, but she'd been at the boutique late Saturday afternoon when Della picked up her clothes, and she was here bright and early Monday morning, too. For some reason, that made Della glance down at Ava's left hand—no wedding ring. No engagement ring, for that matter. She wondered if Ava had ever loved and lost and how she felt about it.

Della pushed the thought away. Women like Ava could pick and choose whomever they wanted for a mate. She was beautiful, smart, successful and chic. Once she set her sights on a man, he wouldn't stand a chance. He would love her forever and make her the center of his universe. No way would she settle for a one-night stand with a guy she'd never see again.

"Well," Ava said now as she counted out the last of Della's refund, "I hope you'll keep Talk of the Town in mind the next time you need to look your best."

Right. The next time Della would need to look her best would be when she appeared before the grand jury in two weeks. Somehow, though, she was pretty sure one of her suits from her old life would work just fine for that. But maybe in her new life...

She pushed that thought away, too. Her new life would be miles away from Chicago. And there was little chance she'd need to don haute couture for anything in it. It would be nothing but business attire, since she'd be doing little other than establishing herself in a new job, starting all over again from square one. It was going to be a long time before she was earning enough to recapture the sort of life she'd had in New York.

It would be even longer before she trusted any man enough to let him get close to her again.

That hadn't been the case with Marcus, a little voice

inside her head piped up. *You got close to him pretty fast. And you trusted him enough to have sex with him.*

But Marcus was different, Della assured the little voice. Marcus had been a one-night stand. It was easy to trust someone you knew you were never going to see again.

Seriously? the voice asked. *Is that the reason you want to go with?*

Um, yeah, Della told the voice.

Fine. But you're only kidding yourself, you know.

Shut up, voice.

"Be careful out there," Ava said, bringing Della's attention back around. "The snow may have stopped, but there are still some slick spots on the sidewalk and slush in the gutters and all kinds of things that could harm you."

Oh, Ava didn't need to tell Della that.

"Don't worry," she said. "I can take care of myself."

And she could, Della knew. She'd been doing it her entire life. That wasn't going to change simply because she had a new life to get under way. Especially since there wouldn't be any Marcuses in her future. Men like him only came along once in a lifetime—if even that often. No way would a man like that show up twice.

In two weeks, Della would be embarking on a second life. A life in which she'd be alone again. Alone still, really, since Egan had never actually been with her the way he could have—should have—been.

Only once in her life had Della really felt as if she was sharing that life—sharing herself—with someone else. And it was someone she would never—could never—see again.

Eight

Nine days after returning the red dress to Talk of the Town, Della was still struggling to go back to her usual routine. It felt like anything but routine now that she had memories of Marcus shouldering their way into her thoughts all the time. The safe house where the feds had placed her was what one would expect to find in middle-class, middle-income, Middle America: sturdy early American furnishings in neutral colors and synthetic fabrics, with white walls and artwork that might have been purchased at any yard sale in suburbia. The lack of personality on the house's part had only contributed to Della's feelings of entrapment during her time here, but that feeling was compounded in the wake of her separation from Marcus. The handful of days she had left here stretched before her like an oceanful of centuries.

And she was even more fearful now than she'd been

before about the uncertainty of her future. Before, she'd been prepared to face life on her own and had felt reasonably certain she would be able to manage. But now she knew what might have been under other, better circumstances. Wonderful. Life with Marcus would have been wonderful. Because he was wonderful. No other man would ever be able to hold a candle to him.

She sighed fitfully. There he was again, at the front of her thoughts. She told herself the only reason she thought him so wonderful was because she knew so little about him. Anyone could be wonderful for thirty-six hours in a small room with no one watching. The time she'd spent with him had been a fantasy. *He'd* been a fantasy. They'd both been playing the role of the phantom, perfect lover. Once free of the hotel room, he might be the same kind of man Egan had turned out to be.

How could she be so certain that Marcus hadn't lied about everything that weekend anyway? He'd said the woman he was waiting for was out of his life, but what if he'd only said that to further his seduction of Della? How could she expect him to have been completely open and honest about himself when she hadn't been open and honest about herself? Once she learned more about him, once she'd discovered what kind of person he really was…

But then, how could she do that when she would never see him again? When she didn't even know his last name? At this rate, he would always be a fantasy to her, and as time went on, he'd grow into an even more legendary lover and all-around great guy, and then she'd really never have a chance to fall in lo—ah, she meant—never have a chance to appreciate someone else she might be compatible with.

A way to counter that possibility came to her immediately, and it wasn't the first time the idea had crept into her brain. This time, it wasn't creeping, though. This time, it was stampeding like a herd of wild, trumpeting wildebeest. And those wildebeest were running right to the laptop in the bedroom.

Maybe she didn't know Marcus's last name. But she knew where he worked. Fallon Brothers. The company must employ thousands of people nationwide, but Marcus wasn't the most common name in the world, and she could narrow the search to Chicago. He'd said himself he was a fixture on a number of websites, so by doing an internet search of his first name and Fallon Brothers and the city of Chicago, she'd probably get a lot of hits. A lot of *notorious* hits. Maybe if she could see him on notorious sites, surrounded by notoriously beautiful women in notoriously compromising situations, she'd realize he wasn't the kind of man she needed in her life anyway. Maybe if she could see him in his natural state of debauchery, it would be easier to forget him.

What could it hurt? She would never see him again. He would never be able to find her, if he was even trying. In a matter of days, she would be swallowed up even deeper into the system with a new name, address and social security number. And then there would *really* be no way for him to find her.

As she folded herself onto the bed and fired up the laptop, Della's heart began to race, and her stomach erupted with nerves. She wasn't sure what was more exciting—the prospect of learning more about Marcus or the prospect of seeing his face again, even if it was just in an online photo.

She brought up the Google page and clicked on the

image option, then typed in the name *Marcus* and the word *Chicago,* along with the words *Fallon Brothers* in quotation marks. And in the blink of an eye—literally— she was staring at the first three rows of what the site told her was hundreds of images. Marcus was in every one of the first batch. And the second, third and fourth batches, too. As she scrolled down the page, she saw him in even more, sometimes alone, but more often with women. Lots of women. Lots of different women. All of them smiling. All of them clinging. All of them beautiful.

Only when Della moved her hand to run her finger over the mouse pad did she realize it was trembling. In fact, all of her was trembling. She had no idea why. Maybe because seeing Marcus online only reaffirmed that the weekend had really happened. That he really existed. That she had some link, however tenuous, to him. From now on, no matter where she was, or what she was doing, or who she was, she would still be able to find him. She would have physical photographs of him to go along with the insubstantial pictures in her mind. He wouldn't be ephemeral, as she had feared. He could still be with her forever.

Even if he wouldn't be with her forever.

She flexed her fingers to calm them and chose a photo of Marcus alone to move the mouse over. It wasn't one of the candid shots, but rather a posed, formal portrait that must have been one he'd had taken for professional reasons. It was probably from the Fallon Brothers website. When the cursor moved over it, the picture grew larger and added information, starting with a url, then the fact that it was a jpg—sized seventy-something by eighty-seven-something else—then, finally, a description that read Marcus Fallon, Chief Investment Officer, Fallon Brothers Chicago.

Della's hand began to tremble again, and her stomach pitched with nausea.

Marcus Fallon. He was a member of the Fallon family and one of the highest ranking executives in the company. She'd known he must be well-connected to the business. It didn't take seeing him in a place like the Windsor Club to know how well-paid he was or how many perks he must have enjoyed. But this... This went beyond well-connected. And it went way beyond well-paid with excellent perks. He was a descendent of some of the very people who had designed the way the country did business. His ancestors had been the equivalent to royalty in this capitalist society. As such, he was, for all intents and purposes, a prince.

So CinderDella's Prince Charming really was a prince. And she... Well, that would put her in the role of pauper, wouldn't it?

She recalled his assurances that he had friends with clout on the East Coast who might be able to help her out, and her stomach pitched again. Those friends were probably of equal rank to him in New York's financial district. Some of them might very well be officers of Whitworth and Stone. She wouldn't be surprised if some of his friends ended up behind bars because of her. Oh, yeah. He would have loved to help her once he learned what the nature of her "trouble" was. He would have been on the phone in no time flat, tipping off everyone he knew that might be at risk.

Any small hope that Della might have been harboring that she and Marcus still had a chance—and she was surprised to discover she had indeed been entertaining hope, and not such a small amount at that—was well and truly squashed at the realization. Once she gave her testimony to the grand jury, she would be an exile in the financial world. It didn't matter that she was bringing to light illegal activity that should be stopped and punished. No one on Wall Street was going to applaud her, and every door would slam in her face. People like Marcus—and Marcus himself—would want nothing to do with her. She would be bringing down some very powerful people. And other very powerful people didn't like it when that happened. Especially when it was a peasant doing the tearing down.

Unable to help herself, Della clicked on the link and found herself looking at a larger version of Marcus's photo, and it was indeed on the Fallon Brothers website. She read that he was the eldest great-grandson of one of Fallon Brothers' founding members who would be moving into his father's position as CEO in the not-too-distant future. She read about his hobbies and favorite pastimes—she already knew about opera, squash and port, but the sailing and polo came as something of a surprise—and about his education at the country's finest schools. All in all, it was a sanitized version of the Marcus she knew and wasn't particularly helpful. Once she got past the part about him being the crown prince of the Chicago financial kingdom, she meant.

So she went back to Google and began clicking on some of the other pictures she'd found. There was one of Marcus with a former Miss Illinois taken at a New Year's Eve party last year. That would have been right around the time Della's world was beginning to fall apart, but Marcus looked as if he didn't have a care in the world. Another photo showed him and a *very* generously endowed redhead at a fundraiser for a children's hospital. Yet another had him sitting on the deck of a high-rise with Lake Michigan in the background and a *very* generously endowed blonde in his lap. The next was a picture of him at some red-carpet event with a woman who looked very much like a certain Hollywood starlet who was known for appearing in public without underwear.

This was how she needed to remember him, Della told herself. In photos taken within months of each other in which he was with a different woman every time. She had to stop thinking of him as Prince Charming and start recognizing the fact that he was just another rich guy with a sense of entitlement who took advantage of everyone who crossed his path. His emotions ran as deep as a strand of hair, and he thought of little other than how to make his own life more enjoyable. He had probably stopped thinking about Della the moment he woke up and found her gone.

He wasn't Prince Charming from a fantastic castle in an enchanted land, she told herself again. He was a big, nasty toad from the toxic swamp of entitlement. The sooner she forgot about him, the better.

She told herself the same thing in a dozen different ways, every time she clicked on a new photograph. But her memories of him crowded out her admonitions. She remembered his smile and his tender touches, and the genuine sadness in his eyes when he had talked about the woman who hadn't been with him that night. That was the real Marcus Fallon, she knew. Maybe not Prince Charming. But not a toad, either.

She just hoped that, wherever he was, he was remembering her fondly, too.

Marcus sat in the study of his Lakeshore Drive penthouse, his black silk robe open over a pair of matching pajama bottoms, nursing a glass of port and sifting through a thin file of information that had been couriered to him that afternoon. Beyond the expansive picture window to his right, Lake Michigan was as inky black as the sky above it, dotted here and there with lights from commercial vessels in the usual shipping lanes that twinkled the same way the stars above them did.

He didn't much notice the vista, however, settled as he was in a boxy, overstuffed club chair that was bathed in the pale amber glow of a floor lamp beside it. Much of the room was amber, in fact, from the coppery fabric of the chair to the golds and browns of the area rug, to the bird's-eye maple paneling to the small, sculpted bronze originals displayed on the built-in shelves. Marcus liked the warm colors. They made him feel calm.

Usually.

Tonight, he felt anything but. Because the file he had thought would be stuffed with information about Della Louise Hannan of New York City contained little he couldn't have discovered by himself. That didn't, however, make what information was here any less interesting. Especially the part about her having worked at Whitworth and Stone, one of Wall Street's biggest—if not *the* biggest—powerhouses. Marcus knew more than a few people who worked there. And since Della's position as executive assistant to one of its executives would have had her moving in the upper echelon of the business, there was a small chance someone he knew there had at least made her acquaintance. Tomorrow, as soon as the business day started on the East Coast, he would make some phone calls.

Not that having any information about Della's time at

Whitworth and Stone would help him much now, since she hadn't worked at the brokerage house for nearly a year. In fact, Della Hannan had pretty much dropped off the face of the map in mid-January of this year and hadn't been seen or heard from since. The apartment where she had lived was now being rented by a married couple who had moved into it in March—and it had been advertised as being a "furnished apartment," because Della had left virtually all of her belongings behind, and her landlord had claimed them on the grounds she hadn't fulfilled the terms of her lease. She'd left her job as abruptly, had simply not come to work one day…or any day afterward.

What was even more troubling was that, in spite of her sudden disappearance, no one had reported her missing. Not a family member, not a friend, not a neighbor, not a lover, not her employer. There was no police report on file, no formal complaint from her landlord, nothing in her personnel file at Whitworth and Stone about why she may have stopped coming to work after more than a decade of not missing a single day.

There was, however, office chatter about why that may have happened. Word in her department was that Della had been dating an executive in another part of the business who had turned out to be married. Whether or not Della had known about his marital status was a bit murky. Either she had known and then been angry that the man refused to leave his wife, or she hadn't known and had left once she discovered the truth. In either event, her office affair seemed to be the reason everyone cited as to why she no longer worked at the company.

It was a reasonable enough explanation. It might even

offer a reason for why she had left New York. Except that she was a native New Yorker without family or friends in any other part of the country to whom she might turn for help. Except for the fact that she hadn't started working somewhere else. Except for the fact that there was no record of her having done *any*thing, *any*where, after January 16th. She hadn't applied for any jobs. Hadn't applied for a new driver's license in any state. Hadn't accessed her bank accounts or used her credit cards. Her cell phone service had been canceled due to her failure to pay, in spite of her having had a tidy sum in both a checking and a savings account, neither of which had been touched.

His thoughts halted there for a moment. Her cell phone. He recalled scrolling through her information at the hotel, all the photos and numbers she still had, even though she hadn't called any of them. Obviously she was using a different number now than the one that had been cut off, but why wasn't there a record of her having applied for a new number? Even if she'd requested it be unlisted, his man Damien should have been able to find out what it was. Why hadn't he?

And why had she had all her contacts from the old phone transferred to a new one, clearly wanting to hang on to them even if she wasn't using any of them? He spared a moment to give himself a good mental smack for not bringing up her number on her phone when he'd had it in his hand. Then he cut himself a little slack because he'd been in such a hurry and so preoccupied by the photos he'd discovered. Still, had he remembered to get her number, it really would have made things a lot easier.

He returned his attention to the P.I.'s report. Marcus might have begun to wonder whether or not the woman he'd met even *was* Della Hannan if it hadn't been for the photographs contained in the file along with the information. He had the picture from her ID badge at Whitworth and Stone, along with copies of photos from her high school yearbook and early driver's licenses. The woman he had met was definitely the same woman in those photos, but, as had been the case with the pictures on her phone, her hair was shorter and darker in all of them.

She'd changed her appearance after she disappeared, but not her name, and his contact hadn't found any evidence that she had any aliases. So there was little chance she was some con artist and a very good chance that everything she had told him about being in trouble was true. The file also had information about Della's early life, which also corroborated what she had told him. There was information about the two brothers she had said she had— one older, one younger. What she hadn't mentioned— probably because she hadn't wanted to dissuade him of his completely wrong ideas—was that she had come from a notoriously bad neighborhood and wasn't the product of wealthy society at all.

At the end of the file was a handwritten note from Damien. It was short and to the point:

> *The only time someone drops off the face of the planet like this, it's because they're in the hands of the feds. Or else they're trying to avoid the feds and are tapped into a network that makes that happen. I have a friend on the government payroll who owes me a favor. I'll let you know what he finds out.*

Marcus lifted his glass to his mouth. But the warm, mellow port did little to soothe the tumultuous thoughts tumbling in his head. So the trouble Della had found herself in in New York was criminal, after all. But which was it with her? Was she helping the authorities or hiding from them?

Who the hell was she? In a lot of ways, she seemed like a stranger to him now. But in another way, she felt even closer than she had been before.

But why and how had she disappeared so completely, not once but twice now? Because she had disappeared again. Damien hadn't been able to find a single clue that might indicate where she was living in Chicago, how long she had been here or when she was planning to leave. Another reason why the man had made the assumption he had in the note, Marcus was certain. Della herself had said she was in trouble. Whether she was helping or hiding, it must be something pretty bad for her to have made herself so invisible.

He closed the file and tipped his glass to his lips again but the glass was empty. He grimaced as he set both the file and the glass on the end table, then rose. He started to walk away, then stopped and went back. For the glass, he told himself. To put it in the dishwasher before he went to bed.

But he picked up the file, too, and opened it again. He took out the photo of Della that had been on her ID badge at Whitworth and Stone. She was the picture of businesslike gravity, unsmiling, wearing no makeup, her short, mannish hair combed back from her face. She looked nothing like she had during the time he'd spent with her. Even after she had washed off her makeup, she had still been beautiful. Even after the inconvenience of the snow, she had still been happy.

And so had he.

That was when Marcus began to understand his

obsession with finding her. Not because she was a mysterious woman in red he couldn't get out of his mind. But because the time he'd spent with her had marked the first time in his life he'd been truly happy. He wasn't sure of the why or when or how of it. He only knew that, with Della, he'd felt different. The same way Charlotte had entered his life when he was a teenager and guided him toward finding contentment with himself, Della had entered his life when he was an adult and guided him toward finding contentment with someone else.

That was what had always been missing before—the sharing. He had shared his life with Charlotte while she was alive, and that had made living it so much better. With Della, he had shared himself. And that made himself so much better. He had been grieving since Charlotte's death, not just for her, but for the emptiness in his life her absence had brought with it. Over the weekend he'd spent with Della, that emptiness had begun to fill again. The hole Charlotte's vacancy had left in his life had begun to close. The wound had begun to heal. With Della, Marcus had begun to feel again. And the feelings he had…

He started to tuck the photograph into the file, but halted. Instead, after taking his glass to the kitchen, he carried everything into his bedroom. He placed the picture of Della on his dresser, propping it up in front of a lamp there. Even if the woman in the photo didn't look much like the one he remembered, Marcus liked having her in his home. He liked that a lot.

Nine

Two nights after finding Marcus on the internet, Della was still feeling at loose ends about everything that had happened and everything left to come. The media frenzy she had feared would follow the announcement of the arrests at Whitworth and Stone had actually been fairly mild. Geoffrey had told her that wasn't surprising at this point, that when people were that rich and that powerful, it was easy for their attorneys to keep a tight rein on how much information was made available to the press. It would only be after the grand jury arraignment, when evidence was presented to support the charges, thereby making any arguments on the defense's part moot, that the media storm would break. Probably with the fury of a category five hurricane. Geoffrey had also assured her, though, that by the time that happened, Della would be safely ensconced in her new life elsewhere, hidden away from any repercussions.

Hidden away from everything.

But she was doing her best not to think about any of that yet. It was Friday night, the eve of her last weekend in Chicago. On Monday, she would be returning to New York. On Tuesday, she would make her first appearance before the grand jury. In a week, give or take, she would be ushered out of this life and into a new one.

One week. That was all Della Hannan had left. After that...

Oh, boy. She really needed a glass of wine.

She changed into her pajamas, poured herself a glass of pinot noir and grabbed a book that had arrived in that morning's mail. She was settling into a chair in the den when the doorbell of the safe house rang. To say the sound startled her was a bit of an understatement, since she jumped so hard, she knocked over her wine, spilling it over both the book and the snowflake print of her pajama shirt, leaving a ruby-red stain at the center of her chest in its wake.

No one had ever rung the doorbell of the safe house. Not even Geoffrey on those few occasions when he had been here. He always called first to tell her he was coming and at what time, and he gave a couple of quick raps and called out his name once he arrived.

She had no idea who was on the other side of the door now. Not Geoffrey, that was certain. It could be another marshal, or someone from the FBI or SEC who needed to brief her about her grand jury appearance next week. But Geoffrey would have let her know about something like that before he sent anyone over. And no such meeting would ever take place after 10:00 p.m. on a Friday night.

She wasn't sure whether she should sit tight and pretend no one was home, or go to the bedroom for her cell phone to call Geoffrey. Any movement she made might tip-off whoever was outside. Of course, it could just be someone who'd mistaken her address for another on the street. It could be someone delivering a pizza to the wrong house. It could be neighbor kids who thought it would be funny to play a joke on the weird neighbor lady who never left her house. It could be any of those things. It could.

But Della doubted it.

As silently as possible, she closed the book and set it and her half-empty wineglass on the side table, then rose carefully from the chair. The doorbell rang again as she was taking her first step toward the bedroom, setting off explosions of heat in her belly. She went as quickly as she could to the bedroom and grabbed her phone, punching the numbers to Geoffrey's home phone into it but not pushing the send button yet. If it *was* the pizza guy making a mistaken delivery, she didn't want to bother Geoffrey for nothing.

The doorbell rang a third time as she approached the living room, but this time, it was followed by a series of quick, rapid knocks. The front drapes were drawn, as they were every evening, and there were no lights turned on in that room. Della clasped her cell phone tightly in one hand as she came to a halt at the front door, then placed the other hand over the trio of light switches to the left of it. The one closest to her turned on an overly bright bug light on the porch, something that would temporarily blind whoever was out there if she flipped it on. For the moment, however, she only pressed her eye to the peephole to see who was on the other side

Oh, great. A dark, shadowy figure who could be almost anyone. That helped ever so much.

The dark, shadowy figure must have sensed her nearness or heard her approach, however, because as she was drawing back from the peephole, a voice called from the other side, "Della? Are you home? Let me in. We need to talk."

The sound of Marcus's deep voice startled her even more than the doorbell had. Her phone slipped from her fingers and clattered to the floor, her heart began to pound like a marathon runner's and her mind raced in a million different directions. How had he found her? Why was he here? If he'd found her, did someone else know she was here, too? Would his being here compromise the case? Would the feds go so far as to arrest Marcus to keep him under wraps, too?

What should she do?

"Della?" he called out again. "Are you there?"

How *had* he found her? *Why* had he found her? And if he knew her whereabouts, did he know about everything else that had happened, too?

What should she do?

Instead of panicking, however, a strange sort of calm suddenly settled over her, in spite of all the questions, in spite of her confusion, in spite of her fears and misgivings. Even though Della didn't know *what* to do, she knew, very well, what she *wanted* to do….

The chain was latched, as it always was, so, ignoring the phone on the floor, Della turned the three dead bolts on the door and opened it. It was still too dark on the other side for her to make out Marcus clearly, but the absence of light made her feel better. If she couldn't see him, he couldn't see her, either. But it wasn't because of vanity about being in wine-stained pajamas and no makeup or having her hair pulled back in a lopsided ponytail. It was because she knew Marcus couldn't see the real Della Hannan this way. She could still be the fantasy she hoped he remembered her as.

"Della?" he said again, evidently still not certain he'd found her.

All she could manage in response was, "Hi, Marcus."

His entire body seemed to relax at her greeting. "It's really you," he said softly.

The remark didn't invite a response, so Della said nothing. Truly, she had no idea what to say. If Marcus knew she was here, he must know why she was here, too. The marshals had kept her hidden for eleven months without any problems. Yet in less than two weeks, Marcus had managed to find her, without having anything more than her first name. He must know everything about what had happened at this point.

For a long moment, neither of them said a word, and neither moved a muscle. The cold winter wind whipped up behind him, sending his overcoat fluttering about his legs and his hair shuffling around his face. Even though she couldn't make out his features in the darkness, she remembered every elegant contour of his face—the rugged jawline, the patrician nose, the carved cheekbones. As the wind blew past him and against her, it brought his scent, too, the spicy, smoky one she recalled too well. Smelling him again, even one fleeting impression, filled her with desire and hunger and need. It was all she could do not to pull back the chain and throw the door open wide and welcome him into the house, into her life, into her.

But she couldn't do that. She wasn't the woman he thought she was. He might not be the man she'd thought him to be. And even if they could both be what the other wanted, in a matter of days, Della would be disappearing into another life Marcus couldn't be a part of. Her new life would be one into which she was retreating, one that would necessitate living quietly and unobtrusively. His life was one into which he would always go boldly and always live lavishly. And neither the twain could meet.

"Can I come in?" he asked.

"No," she said quickly.

"Della, please. We need to talk."

"We are talking."

"No, we're not. We're greeting each other."

"Then start talking."

He growled out an epithet. "It's cold. Let me in."

Well, he did have a point there, she conceded. Her sock-clad toes were already screaming that they were about to get frostbite. Not to mention her robe was in the other room.

Not to mention she really wanted to see him again. Up close and in good light. She wanted to stand near enough to feel his warmth. Near enough to inhale his scent. And she wanted to pretend again, just for a little while, as she had during their weekend together, that nothing in her life would ever be wrong again.

Unable to help herself, she pushed the door closed enough to unhook the chain, then pulled it open again. Strangely, Marcus didn't barrel immediately through and close it behind himself. Instead, he remained at the threshold, waiting for some cue from her.

Striving to lighten the mood, she said, "Unless you're a vampire, you don't need a formal invitation."

He hesitated a moment, then said, "I'd like to be invited anyway."

She remembered the night at the club, how he had joined her without asking first, and how he had taken the lead for everything after that. There had been no uncertainty in him that night two weeks ago. But tonight, it was as if he were as uncertain about everything as she was. For some reason, that made her feel a little less uncertain.

"Would you like to come in?" she asked quietly.

He nodded, then took a few steps forward. When she stepped out of the way to let him enter, her foot hit the cell phone on the floor and skittered it to the other side of the foyer. As Della stooped to pick it up, Marcus closed the door behind himself. In the dark room, she could still sense nothing of what he might be feeling or thinking, so she led him into the den. As she walked, she restlessly tugged the rubber band from her ponytail and did her best to fluff and tame her hair at the same time. There was nothing she could do about the wine-spattered pajamas, however, so she only crossed her arms over the stain as best she could and told herself the posture wasn't defensive.

Even if she was feeling a little defensive.

She gestured toward the sofa. "Have a seat," she said as she tucked herself into the chair.

But Marcus didn't sit. Instead, he stood with his hands shoved into his coat pockets, gazing at her.

He looked magnificent, different from the last time she had seen him, but somehow completely unchanged. In person, she'd seen him dressed only in the tuxedo and the bathrobe—one extreme to another—and this incarnation of him was somewhere in between. His trousers were casual and charcoal in color and paired with a bulky black sweater. Coupled with the dark coat and his dark hair, and having come in from the darkness the way he had, he still seemed as overwhelming as he had been the first time she saw him. But his eyes were anxious and smudged with faint purple crescents.

His hair was a bit shaggy, and his face wasn't closely shaved. His posture was both too tense and too fatigued, as if he were trapped in some state between the two. Or maybe both conditions had just overwhelmed him. All in all, he looked like a man who had been worrying about something—or perhaps someone—a lot.

When he didn't sit, Della automatically stood again. "Wine?" she asked. Her words were rushed and unsteady as she prattled on. "I just opened a bottle of pinot noir. It's good on a night like this. I'll get you a glass."

Without awaiting a reply, she grabbed her glass and headed into the kitchen to retrieve one for him, her mind racing once again with all the repercussions his arrival into her reality brought with it. Why, oh, why, had she let him in? Why hadn't she called Geoffrey the minute she heard a knock at the door? What if it hadn't been Marcus standing there?

When she turned to go back into the den, she saw him standing framed by the kitchen doorway. He'd removed his coat and ran a hand through his wind-tossed hair, but he didn't look any more settled than she felt. Crumbling under his scrutiny, Della looked away, then, leaving both glasses neglected on the counter, went to the table to fold herself into one of the chairs. Marcus pulled out the chair immediately next to hers and, after sitting down, scooted it in close enough so that his thigh was aligned with her own. For another long moment, neither of them spoke. Neither looked at the other. Neither moved. Finally, unable to stand the silence, Della took the initiative.

"How did you find me?"

He didn't say anything for a minute, only looked down at the table and began to restlessly trace the wood grain with his finger. All he said, though, was, "I'm well-connected."

"No one is that well-connected, Marcus. I've been here for eleven months without anyone knowing. All you had was my first name, and you managed to find me less than two weeks after we—"

She halted when she saw the stain of a blush darkening his cheek. It hadn't been there when he came in, so it couldn't be a result of the cold. That meant something she'd said had made him uncomfortable. He looked up at her when she stopped talking, then, when he saw her staring at him, his gaze ricocheted away again.

"Marcus, how *did* you find me knowing only my first name?"

Still, he avoided her gaze. "Yeah, about that. I, uh, I actually had more than your first name. I kind of took the liberty of going through your purse while you were in the shower, and I got your last name and your address in New York from your driver's license."

Della closed her eyes at that. How could she have been so careless? She never left the safe house without her driver's license, on the outside chance that if there was an accident of some kind, she could still be returned to the proper authorities. The thought of dying nameless bothered her almost as much as dying friendless. But Della had never expected anyone other than an emergency medical worker or law enforcement officer to see it. She knew enough to use cash instead of her credit cards to keep from being identified, and her phone was one Geoffrey had given her that couldn't be traced. But the personal ID thing...

The fact that she hadn't given it a thought while she was with Marcus was another indication of how much of her trust she had placed in him. Or perhaps misplaced, as the case may be.

"So I had more than your first name to give to...my contact," Marcus confessed.

"The address on my license isn't my address anymore," she told him. "I haven't lived in New York for almost a year."

"I know. But having even your most recent known address along with your full name gave my guy all the information he needed to track you down."

Della let that sink in for a minute. It had been that easy for someone to find her. But no one had. Geoffrey had told Della, too, that all of the defendants had been made aware during questioning and as charges were filed that there was a federal witness in custody who was willing to testify against all of them. And that there were documents this witness had smuggled out that corroborated every charge.

She hadn't slept or eaten much after hearing that, so anxious had she been about whether someone from Whitworth and Stone was trying to track down who the witness was and what information they had, putting together her disappearance with the timing of the investigation.

But no one had. Or, if they did, none had tried to locate her. Or, at least succeeded. Not until Marcus. Who, one would think, didn't have nearly as much at stake. Then she remembered that Marcus was a part of the world she had just punched a big hole in. Who said he wasn't here for the very reason she feared?

No, she immediately told herself. No way. In spite of everything, she still trusted him. In spite of everything, she still...cared for him.

When she trusted her voice again, she asked, "You hired someone to find me?"

"Yes," he acknowledged without hesitation.

"Why?"

This time, his response came less quickly. Finally, he told her, "Because I couldn't stand the thought of never seeing you again."

Something that had been knotted tight inside Della began to loosen and flow free at his words. Until she remembered how impossible it would be for them to be together.

He started to say something else, but she held up a hand to stop him. "How much do you know about my situation? I mean, if the person you hired to find me found me, he must have uncovered a lot of other information about me, too."

Marcus looked disappointed that she had changed the subject, but he replied, "I know you're in the custody of the U.S. Marshals. I know you're slated to be a material witness for a federal case. Beyond that, I didn't ask for details, except about where you were living now."

She shook her head. "I still can't believe you found me as easily as you did," she said, stalling. "Just what kind of system are the feds running, anyway?"

"It wasn't easy to find you," Marcus countered. "The P.I. I always use to get the information I need can usually get it for me within forty-eight hours."

"Even when it's federally protected?"

"Nothing is foolproof, Della. My guy used to be a highly placed operative on the government payroll before he went into business for himself. He can find things out others can't because he still has a lot of contacts in high places. In federal, state and city governments."

"He must cost a fortune," she muttered.

"He does."

She spared a moment to find enormous pleasure in the fact that Marcus would spend an exorbitant amount of money to find her, then sobered again when the impact of his discovery settled over her again.

"But even he couldn't work as fast as he usually does," he continued. "And I still didn't get everything I wanted."

She wasn't sure if Marcus was talking only about information in that statement, so she diverted to their original subject. But she did her best to be as vague as possible. She didn't want to say anything that might compromise the hearing next week. She couldn't stand the thought that everything she'd gone through over the last eleven months might end up being for nothing.

But then, without the last eleven months, she never would have had her weekend with Marcus, would she? So regardless of what did or didn't happen in the future, those tedious, anxious, interminable months could never have been for nothing.

"Look, Marcus, I can't give you any particulars about the case I'm involved in," she said. "I'm not even sure if your mere presence here right now is going to mess everything up or not. Suffice it to say that one day, I was doing my job and living my life and everything was as normal as it could be. The next day, I discovered something my employer was doing that was illegal, and I turned all the information I had over to the proper authorities. The next thing I knew, I was being told I couldn't go back to work, and that I was going to be placed into protective custody while the government took over the investigation. I was told it would only be for a couple of months. That was eleven months ago."

"And to explain your disappearance," Marcus said, "they concocted a story about you having an affair with a married man in another department."

Now it was Della's turn to blush and look away. "That wasn't concocted," she said softly. "And if you know that, then you *do* know something about my situation."

His expression changed then, turning contemplative, and he said nothing for a moment. Then his expression changed once more, this time to one of understanding. "Whitworth and Stone," he said. "That was your employer."

"Yes."

His lips parted fractionally, as if he were going to say something else, then closed again. For another moment, he studied her in silence, then he opened his mouth again. But, again, it took a moment before he spoke. "I read in the trades and the *Wall Street Journal* about the arrests. It was because of you, wasn't it?"

Her stomach knotted again, and she shook her head vehemently. "I can't say anything about it."

"You don't have to," he told her. "It didn't occur to me until now to put it all together. There just hasn't been that much in the news about what's really going on there. There was so little fanfare, in fact, that most of us figured the charges were bogus, just the government flexing its muscle to keep Wall Street in its place, or that it would turn out with one or two guys getting a slap on the wrist for some minor infractions. It never occurred to me that they'd actually make a federal case out of it."

Della said nothing, but couldn't pull her gaze away from his. The wheels were clearly spinning in his brain now, and he was obviously able to put way more than two and two together. A man like him, as highly placed as he was in the financial community, could fully appreciate how much was at stake here, and how much trouble a company like Whitworth and Stone could be in. A man like him would know exactly how important Della's role was in what was happening, and he would understand completely how devastating her impact would be.

He nodded slowly. "But the reason there hasn't been much media coverage is precisely because of how massive a case this is going to be. Executives that high up, with that much money and that many resources at their disposal—not to mention that much to lose—can afford the kind of lawyers who can keep things quiet, at least for a while."

Still, Della said nothing. Still, she couldn't look away.

"It never occurred to me to put those arrests together with your disappearance," Marcus said. "The married lover story made a lot more sense."

"I didn't know he was married," she said, finally relieved to be able to talk about something that wouldn't compromise the case. "I was supposed to meet him on New Year's Eve. Though after midnight because he said he had a professional dinner to attend. I arrived a little early and saw him kissing another woman good night before putting her into a cab. When I asked who she was, he informed me she was his wife, who he had no intention of leaving because, by the way, he also had three kids and his wife's family was so well-connected socially and financially, and he couldn't afford to lose those connections."

Marcus's expression then indicated the wheels were still turning in his head, though they might be going in a different direction now. "You disappeared in mid-January, meaning you must have uncovered the wrongdoing at Whitworth and Stone right before that."

"On New Year's Day," she said without thinking. But that wasn't compromising information, was it? Surely not.

Marcus nodded slowly, as if making more connections. "So you found out on New Year's Eve that the man you were seeing was married, and then, hours later, discovered that your employer was involved in matters that threatened national security."

"That's it in a nutshell, yeah."

"Sucky way to start the new year."

She wished she could laugh, then wondered if she would ever be able to find humor in anything again. "Yeah."

"You know, anyone else would have been devastated by either one of those things, but even after suffering both, you still had the presence of mind, and the courage, to do the right thing."

Della had never really looked at it like that. "I just did what anyone else in that position would do."

"No, you didn't," he said. "A lot of people would have walked away from both and wallowed in self-pity. Or they would have kept their mouths shut and not risked losing their job or their benefits or anything else that might mess up their life."

"Maybe…"

"Instead, you risked everything to make sure the people who were putting other people—strangers you didn't even know—in danger didn't get away with what they were doing."

"Yes."

He lifted a hand and started to reach for her, then hesitated, as if fearing how she would react. Reluctantly, without touching her, he dropped his hand to the table. "And you have to ask why I came looking for you."

Whatever was left of the knot inside her unraveled. In spite of that, she told him, "You shouldn't have come, Marcus."

"Why not?"

"Because I'm leaving Chicago in three days, and I'm not coming back."

"I know that was your plan before, but now—"

"Now, it's still the plan," she told him. "I can't stay here, Marcus."

"Why not?"

How did she say this without having it sound melodramatic and paranoid? Probably, she should simply spell it out. "Because after I give my testimony to the grand jury, I'm going to be one of the most hated people on Wall Street. No one's going to give me a job. The people I'm going to help put away have contacts everywhere. Not only in other brokerage houses, but in banks and all kinds of businesses. They have corporate America eating out of their hands. No one will hire me. Whistle-blowers might make for great movies and documentaries, but in the real world, their lives are shattered. They can't find work. They can't support their families. They lose everything."

He was still looking at her in a way that made clear he didn't understand what she was saying. So Della spelled it out further. "After this thing is over, the government is giving me a new ID. New name, new social security number, new history, new everything. They're going to move me someplace where I have a chance to start over again where no one will know me, and where there's no chance I'll be recognized. I'll be able to find a job doing something I love, something I'm good at. I won't be Della Hannan anymore."

Marcus sat back in his chair and inspected her openly now. "Then who will you be? Where will you go?"

"I don't know yet," she said. "But it won't be here."

"Why not here? It's as easy to start over in Chicago as anywhere else. Better. There's a vital financial community here. Where else are you going to go and find that? Go ahead and change your name and history. You'll still be Della. You'll still be the woman I met at Palumbo's. You'll still be the woman I spent the most amazing weekend of my life with. You'll still be the woman I—"

He halted before finishing, probably because Della had started shaking her head as soon as he finished his first sentence. "If I stay here, Marcus, I'll want to be with you."

He gaped at her. "And that's a problem?"

"Yes!" she cried. "Because you're so…" She recalled the adjective he'd used himself. "Notorious. You're all over the society pages and a regular fixture on a lot of celebrity websites. You said so yourself."

Now he closed his mouth. She was pretty sure he was starting to understand. But since she was still in spell-it-out mode, Della continued, "You live a big life, Marcus. It's what makes you happy. It's who you are. You like your notoriety. And I don't blame you," she hastened to add. "Big life suits you. You were born for the spotlight. But me…" She shrugged lightly. "I wasn't born for a big life. And now, more than ever, I need to be invisible. It's the only way I'll be able to rebuild my life. It's the only way I'll be able to get back everything I've lost."

"In other words, you don't want to be seen with me."

"I *can't* be seen with you," she corrected him. "What if someone recognizes me? What if, as I'm starting to get my groove back, someone in your world realizes who I really am? They could destroy everything I have." She swallowed hard against the anguish she felt threatening. "And they could hurt you, too. Doing what you do for a living, if you were seen consorting with the woman who brought down Whitworth and Stone, no one would ever trust you again. Then your life would be shattered, too. I can't let that happen to you. I can't be responsible for it."

"I'd never worry about something like that," he told her.

"I would always worry about it," she said. "It would never work out for us, Marcus," she said. "It would be a mistake for me to stay. That is just as well, because after Monday, I'll be gone."

He leaned forward in his chair, taking both of her hands in his. "No, Della, you can't. We need to talk more about—"

This time, when Marcus stopped speaking, it wasn't because he cut himself off. This time, it was because of a loud crash in the living room—which Della was pretty sure was the sound of the front door being broken in—followed by a wildly shouted, "Della, it's Geoffrey! Are you okay?"

And then, just like in the movies, everything turned to chaos.

Ten

Marcus sat on the sofa in Della's house—even though both obviously really belonged to Uncle Sam—and wondered when his life had morphed into a Quentin Tarantino film. One minute, he'd been sitting at the kitchen table trying to tell her how he felt about her, and the next, he had been face down on the linoleum with some guy's knee in the small of his back yelling that he should keep his hands where the guy could see them at all times.

At least the guy, whom Della had eventually been able to introduce as the federal marshal assigned to keep an eye on her, had taken off the handcuffs after shoving Marcus onto the sofa. Now, as he rubbed at his wrists and tried to crane his head around the man to see how Della was faring, the guy—who Marcus couldn't help thinking looked like an older version of Dwight Schrute, only not as well-dressed—leaned the same way he was trying to look, cutting off his view of Della. Again.

"Geoffrey, it's okay," Della said. Again.

Marcus had gathered from the frantic exchange between Della and the marshal only moments ago that before answering her front door, she had dialed Geoffrey's number without pressing the call button, and that when she dropped the phone on the floor, it had somehow performed that function anyway. Geoffrey had answered his phone after seeing Della's name attached to the caller ID and heard her talking to someone in the distance. Even though the conversation hadn't sounded threatening and she hadn't sound frightened, she wasn't supposed to be talking to *anyone,* so he had leaped into action and driven to the safe house to check on her. Then, when he mistook the wine stain on her shirt for blood...

Well, that was when the knee in Marcus's back had nearly broken his spine.

Now, however, all was well. The marshal was only looking at him as if he planned to cap him in both kneecaps with the sidearm he hadn't even had the decency to reholster. At least he wasn't pointing the weapon at Marcus anymore.

"Tell me one more time," Geoffrey said, "what the hell you think you're doing here."

Marcus had already told him that twice—as had Della—but Geoffrey didn't seem satisfied. This, okay, maybe Marcus could understand, since he hadn't been completely honest with the guy. But there was no way he was going to tell a total stranger he was here because he was in love with Della Hannan when he hadn't even told Della that yet.

"He's a friend," Della said. Again.

Marcus looked at Geoffrey to see if that would satisfy him. It clearly did not.

"I thought you didn't have any friends in Chicago," Geoffrey told Della. Still looking at Marcus.

When Della didn't reply right away, the marshal glanced over his shoulder in silent inquiry, then quickly returned his attention to Marcus. As if realizing his dilemma in not being able to see them both at the same time, Della moved to sit on the sofa, too. Marcus tried not to read too much into the fact that she crowded herself into the corner as far from him as she could get. But—call him an alarmist—the gesture wasn't exactly encouraging.

Della glanced at Geoffrey, then back at the floor, looking like a twelve-year-old who'd been caught with her first cigarette. "I met him two weeks ago," she said.

Geoffrey narrowed his eyes at her. "How could you have met him two weeks ago when you never leave the house?"

Della nibbled her lip nervously but said nothing.

"Della?" Geoffrey prodded.

"Yeah, about that," she said. She then launched into a long, winding, somewhat convoluted explanation about sneaking out of the safe house from time to time due to extreme cabin fever, then about some promise she'd made to herself as a child, then she spoke at length about opera in general and *La Bohème* in particular, then she backtracked to something about a little shop off Michigan Avenue and haute couture, then she moved on to dinner, then Marcus, and then—

And then she stopped abruptly. Probably, Marcus thought, because she'd gotten to the part about where the two of them checked into the Ambassador Hotel.

At that point, had Geoffrey been a character in an old-time novel, he was what would have been referred to as *apoplectic*. But his voice was level when he told Della, "I cannot believe you've been sneaking out of the house on a regular basis without letting me know where you were going."

"Only a few times," she said defensively. When she looked up and saw how sternly her caretaker was eyeing her, she amended, "Okay, six. But that's all. And if I'd told you, you wouldn't have let me go. I was always careful."

Geoffrey spent a few more minutes admonishing her like a child and making her look even guiltier, but there was little he said that Della—or Marcus—could take exception to.

That didn't, however, stop Marcus from taking exception. "Give it a rest, Geoffrey," he interrupted the man midsentence. "It's the feds' fault for keeping her cooped up here for eleven months."

Both Geoffrey and Della glared at him for that. Geoffrey's irritation Marcus could understand, but Della's?

"Don't make this worse than it already is," she told him. "Geoffrey's right. I shouldn't have left the safe house. Ever."

Something in the way she said it made Marcus think her reasoning had less to do with the fact that she'd broken the rules and more to do with the repercussions of her actions. He just hoped one of the repercussions in question wasn't having met—and spending a weekend with—him.

He opened his mouth to try and reassure her that the weekend the two of them had spent together had been anything but wrong, but Geoffrey jingled the handcuffs he was still holding and said, "Keep it up, Fallon, and you're going to find yourself in federal custody, too. Only it won't be a safe house you'll be going to."

Yeah, yeah, yeah, Marcus wanted to say. He knew his rights when it came to law enforcement. He watched network television.

"I only meant—"

"I don't care what you meant," Geoffrey admonished. "I really ought to take you into custody, at least until Della leaves town."

"But—"

"But since she'll vouch for you, and since, like she said, you're such a paragon of professionalism and a scion of the community—" there was no mistaking the sarcasm in his voice when he said that last part "—I'm going to let you go."

Marcus bit back the indignation he felt and forced himself to mutter a reasonably tempered, "Thank you."

"But you'll have to leave the premises now and not come back."

Okay, so much for the reasonable temper. "What? But you just said yourself that Della vouched for me, so what's the harm in—"

"I don't have to explain the harm again," Geoffrey stated emphatically. Then, to hammer it home, he added, "To either of you. Now maybe the physical threat to Della is minimal, but she's got a big job to do next week, and we can't have it messed up because she gets a little stir-crazy being cooped up."

Both Marcus and Della started to speak at once, but Geoffrey lifted a hand to stop them. When neither of them stopped, the marshal raised his voice louder than theirs and talked right over them.

"Here's what's going to happen," he said. "Fallon, you're going to go home and forget you ever saw Della Hannan here in Chicago."

"Oh, no I'm not," Marcus said. He didn't care how loud the other guy was talking.

"Yes. You are," Geoffrey countered. "And, Della." He turned his attention to her before Marcus had a chance to object again. "You're going to pack everything you brought with you to Chicago while I wait."

"What? But why?" Della sounded as annoyed as Marcus was.

"Because you're checking out of Chez Uncle Sam tonight," Geoffrey told her. "The safe house has been compromised. You can't stay here."

"But Marcus is the only one who knows—"

"The safe house has been compromised," Geoffrey repeated. "You can't stay here. Now go pack your bags. We'll find you somewhere else to stay for the next couple of nights—not that you're going to be let out of my sight, meaning I'll be missing my favorite nephew's bar mitzvah on Sunday, thank you very much—and then, Monday, you'll fly back to New York as scheduled."

For a moment, Marcus thought Della was going to fight the other man's edict. Her back went ramrod-straight, her eyes flashed with anger and her hands doubled into fists. Then, as quickly, her entire posture changed. Her shoulders rolled forward, her gaze dropped to the floor, her fingers uncurled.

"All right," she conceded softly. "I guess it's inevitable."

"And, Della," Geoffrey said, bringing her attention to him. "I want the cell phone that we gave you. You're not to have any contact with the outside world until after the grand jury hearing. And you're going to be assigned a twenty-four-hour escort in New York—no, *two* twenty-four-hour escorts in New York," he hastily corrected himself, "until the powers that be say it's okay to cut you loose into the program."

"The program?" Marcus asked.

Now Geoffrey turned to look at him. "WITSEC," he said. "The Witness Security Program. You might know it better as witness protection, thanks to our good buddies in Hollywood," he added with more sarcasm.

Marcus looked at Della. "Is that true?" he said.

She continued to study the floor as she replied. "Yes."

"You're going into the witness protection program?"

"I told you I had to start over somewhere new, Marcus, where no one would know me. Where I had a whole new identity."

"I know, but I thought…"

Now she did look at him. "You thought what?"

He struggled over his words. "I thought…I mean, I just figured… After everything that happened between you and me…" He halted, took a deep breath and released it slowly. "Witness protection means you'll never be able to contact anyone from your old life," he finally said. "It means I won't have any way to find you. Not even my guy with the contacts could find you there."

"What guy with the contacts?" Geoffrey asked, turning suspicious again.

Marcus ignored him. Della still looked at the floor.

"Della," he pleaded. "Don't do it."

"What guy with the contacts?" Geoffrey repeated. "If he knows how to get past government smoke-screens, we need to know about him."

"Then you can question me at home later." Marcus ground out the words without sparing the marshal a glance.

"Oh, we will, Mr. Fallon. We will."

Della remained silent.

Marcus knew there was no way he would be able to find her once she disappeared. It was obvious that Geoffrey's concern for her went beyond what a federal marshal would undertake. From the moment he'd crashed into the kitchen, there had been an unmistakable air of paternity about the guy. He was protecting Della the way he would protect a daughter. Marcus might as well be doing battle with a mama polar bear.

"Della," he said again, "please. You and I need to talk."

"Not tonight, you won't," Geoffrey assured him. Then, to Della, in a much gentler voice, he said, "Go pack your stuff. I'll call around and find another place for you. A place that's *safe,*" he said, looking back at Marcus, still obviously not trusting him.

Della lifted her head and looked at Marcus, her eyes brimming with tears. "I'm sorry," she told him. "I—I just…I can't—" She shook her head. "Goodbye, Marcus."

And then she was off the sofa and disappearing into the hallway. Unthinkingly, Marcus stood to follow her, but a heavy hand on his shoulder stopped him.

"Front door's that way," Geoffrey told him. "Use it."

Marcus didn't have much choice but to obey. He took two broad steps in that direction, but stopped to look down the hall. There was a light on in one of the bedrooms at the end, and he could see Della's shadow moving around in front of the lamplight. That was all she was to him now—a shadow. Just as he'd been before she came into his life, Marcus was back to being alone.

No, wait, he realized as the thought formed in his head. It wasn't like before at all. Because before, Marcus hadn't realized what he was missing. Before, he hadn't recognized the emptiness, because he'd been able to fill it with mind-numbing carousing and willing, if faceless, women. Before, Marcus had been able to delude himself that he had everything he could possibly ever want and that his life lacked absolutely nothing. Before, he had been able to pretend that he was happy and contented. But now...

Now he really did know what happiness and contentment were. Because those were the things he'd felt when he was with Della. Now he knew how full, how fun, how fantastic his life could be. Now he understood how much more enjoyable it was to share life with someone else. He realized that loving someone wasn't just something a person *did,* but how being in love was something a person *was.* Marcus was in love with Della, and that completed him as a human being. It was something that brought him greater joy, greater peace, than he ever could have imagined. With Della gone...

Well. He would still be in love with her. He would always be in love with her. But with her gone, so went a part of himself. A part she would always keep with her, but a part he would never have back. Not unless he had Della.

And Della would be someplace where the feds would make sure she was never found again.

Although the grand jury hearings lasted less than a week, they seemed even more interminable and emotionally draining than the eleven months Della had spent cooped up in Chicago. Because she was the only witness the federal prosecutors had, her testimony took up the majority of the time, and she spoke for hours every day, until she thought she would run out of voice and words and nerve. By the end of the proceedings, all she wanted was to escape into her new life where she would be left alone.

Until she remembered that being alone would mean, well, being alone. If only she could take Marcus with her…

But she couldn't do that. What made things more difficult was that, even after the grand jury hearing concluded, she still wouldn't be left alone—not yet. At some point, she would have to return to New York to repeat everything she'd said. Because the grand jury had been given an overwhelming amount of evidence against Whitworth and Stone and a number of its highest-placed executives. They would, without question, rule that the case go to trial. A trial that would involve the same star witness—her. Only then would she be able to slip back into her new anonymity. Only that time, it *would* be forever.

For some reason, the word *forever* made her think about Marcus. But then, nearly everything made her think about Marcus. Every time someone brought her a cup of coffee, she thought about him pouring one for her in the hotel. Whenever room service showed up with her dinner at the hotel where she was staying in New York, she thought of how Marcus had ordered such a breakfast feast for her. When she looked out over all the power suits in the courtroom, she thought of him. When she saw men in long overcoats on the streets of New York, she thought of him.

But worst of all, Friday evening, as she left the federal courthouse in New York City, dressed for the weather in a camel-hair coat and red scarf, mittens and hat, with an equally bundled-up marshal on each side of her, it started to snow. Maybe not as furiously as it had the night she met Marcus in Chicago, but seeing the sparkling white snowflakes tumbling out of the inky sky, Della was overwhelmed by memories of what had happened on the terrace of the Windsor Club, when she'd had the most incredible sexual experience of her life with a mysterious lover named Marcus.

Though he hadn't been a mystery for long. Della had gotten to know him pretty well during their time together, even better than she had realized. Over the time that had passed since their weekend together—and even more since they'd parted ways in Chicago—she had come to understand exactly how very well she did know Marcus, and how very deeply she'd come to feel for him. She couldn't pinpoint the moment when it had happened during their weekend together—maybe when he was wiping away her tears or pouring her a cup of coffee or tracing a finger lovingly over her naked shoulder—but she had fallen in love with Marcus. What had started as a sexual response had grown in mere hours to an emotional bond. She only wished she had admitted that to herself when she still had the chance to tell him.

She loved Marcus. Maybe she hadn't admitted it to herself at the time because the feeling was so new and unfamiliar to her. But it was that newness and unfamiliarity that finally made her realize she was in love. Being with Marcus had made her feel complete for the first time in her life. When she was with him, she'd felt as if she could handle anything. Everything that had been wrong in her life had suddenly seemed less likely to overtake her. She'd been less fearful when she was with Marcus. Less anxious. Less troubled. But most of all, with Marcus, she'd been happy. Since leaving him…

Since leaving him, nothing felt right. Even the snow falling down around her now didn't have the magic for her it would have had—that it did have—only a few weeks ago.

"Stop," she said to the two marshals as she paused halfway down the courthouse steps.

The man on her right, whose name was Willoughby, halted in his tracks, but the woman on her left, Carson, continued down two more steps, glancing right, then left, before turning to face Della.

"What's wrong?" Carson asked.

"Nothing. I just… It's snowing," she finally said, as if that should explain everything.

"So?"

"So I want to stand here for a minute and enjoy it." *Or at least try to.*

She heard Willoughby expel an irritated sigh, saw Carson roll her eyes. Della didn't care. She'd done a lot for her country this week. She'd sacrificed the past year of her life. The least her country could do was let her enjoy a minute in the snow.

She closed her eyes and tipped her head back, letting the icy flakes collect on her bare cheeks, nose and mouth. She sighed as she felt them melt one by one, only to be replaced by others. She heard the sound of a honking taxi, felt the bustle of people around her, inhaled the aroma of a passing bus. And she smiled. She loved the city. She didn't care what anyone said about noise and crowds and traffic. All those things only proved how alive the city was. She had grown up in this place. It was a part of her. No matter how badly it had treated her—as a child or as an adult—she couldn't imagine living anywhere else. She hoped, wherever her new life was, she would live in a big city again. Because maybe, just maybe, being surrounded by people—even if they were strangers—would help keep the loneliness at bay.

"Della."

Her eyes flew open at the sound of the familiar voice. The first thing she saw was Carson's back, because the woman had stepped in front of her. The second thing she saw was how Willoughby was reaching inside his open overcoat for what she knew would be a weapon. The third thing she saw was Marcus.

At first, she thought she was imagining him, because he looked so much as he had that night at the Windsor Club, dark and handsome and mysterious, surrounded by swirls of snow. The only difference was that he'd exchanged the tuxedo for a dark suit. That and the fact that he looked so very lost and alone.

"Marcus," she said softly. She covered Carson's shoulder with one hand as she curled the fingers of the other over Willoughby's arm. "It's okay," she told them both. "He's…a friend."

Carson didn't even turn around as she said, "Our orders, Ms. Hannan, are to—"

"I'll take full responsibility for anything that happens," Della said.

"That's not the problem," Carson told her. "The problem is—"

But Della didn't wait for her to finish. She strode away from the two marshals, down the steps of the courthouse, until she stood on the one above Marcus, facing him. It was only then that she realized he was holding a suitcase. He must have come here straight from the airport. He must have been following the court proceedings and knew that by today, they'd come to an end.

"Hi," she said softly.

"Hi," he replied just as quietly.

Neither of them said anything more for a moment. Marcus set his suitcase on the ground beside him and shoved his hands deep into his overcoat pockets. So Della took the initiative, raised her mittened hands to his shoulders, leaned forward and covered his mouth with hers. She told herself it was because she hadn't had a chance to kiss him goodbye. Not at the hotel, and not at the safe house. So this was what that would be. A chance to tell him goodbye properly.

Funny, though, how the moment her lips met his, it didn't feel like goodbye at all. Because the next thing she knew, Marcus was roping his arms around her waist and crushing her body against his, pulling her completely off the concrete. What had been frigid air surrounding her suddenly turned blistering, and heat exploded at her center, igniting every extremity. The memories of him that had tortured her all week evaporated, replaced by the impressions of his reality. She felt his arms around her waist again, the scruff of his beard against her cheek again, the solid strength of his shoulders beneath her hands again. She couldn't believe he was actually here.

Wait a minute. What was he doing here?

The thought made her pull away from him, but Marcus followed and captured her mouth with his again. Although he set her down on the step, he curved his hands over her hips to keep her there and kissed her more deeply still. She allowed herself to get lost in blissful sensations for another long moment. But when she heard the sound of not one, but two throats clearing not so indiscreetly behind her, she found the wherewithal to pull away from him again.

Marcus must have heard the marshals' reactions, too, because he didn't try to reclaim Della this time. He did, however, move to the same step she was on and loop an arm around her shoulders, then he pulled her close, as if he were afraid her guardians would try to take her from him again.

But neither marshal seemed eager to come between them. In fact, they were both smiling.

"He looks like more than…a friend," Carson said.

"Yeah, I don't have any…friends…like that," Willoughby agreed. "I don't think my wife would like it too much if I did."

Della felt Marcus relax beside her. But he still didn't loosen his hold on her. Not that she cared.

"Do you mind?" Della said to the two marshals. "Can I have a few minutes to talk to my…friend?"

Carson and Willoughby exchanged a wary look, then turned back to Della.

"I'm sorry, Ms. Hannan," Carson said, "but privacy is one thing a federal witness doesn't get much of. And you're not out of protective custody yet. If you want to talk to your…friend…it's going to have to be in front of me and Willoughby."

"It's okay, Della," Marcus said.

With one more pleading look aimed at her escorts— who both regretfully shook their heads in response— she turned to Marcus. He lifted a hand to her face to trace the line of her cheekbone, her nose, her jaw and her mouth. He didn't seem to be bothered by their audience. Then again, Della was so happy to see him, she didn't really care who saw them, either.

"I'm going to have to get used to this witness security thing sooner or later, anyway," Marcus said. "It might as well be now."

The remark puzzled her. "Why do you have to get used to it?"

He inhaled a deep breath and released it slowly, then dropped his hand from her face so that he could take her hand in his. When her mittens hindered his efforts, he gently tugged one off. Then he wove their fingers together and squeezed tight.

"I have to get used to it," he said, "because I'm going with you."

Her mouth fell open a bit at that. "What are you talking about?"

"I'm going with you."

She shook her head. "Marcus, that's crazy talk. You don't know what you're saying."

"I know exactly what I'm saying." He lifted her hand to his mouth and pressed a small kiss in the center of her palm. Then he said a third time, "I'm going with you."

"But you can't," she insisted. "You have a life in Chicago. A big life. A larger-than-life life. There are lots of people who will miss you if you disappear."

"None that matters as much as you," he told her.

"But your friends—"

"—are not particularly close ones," he finished for her. "They don't matter as much as you."

"Your family—"

"—is more of a corporate entity than a family," he assured her. "I've spent ninety percent of my life rebelling against them and the other ten percent taking advantage of them. We're not that close, either. They definitely don't matter as much as you."

"But your business. Your job is—"

"—mostly as a figurehead," he told her. "It especially doesn't matter as much as you." He gave her hand another gentle squeeze. "I don't do that much for Fallon Brothers as it is now, Della. Once I'm in charge, I'll do even less. I'll just make a lot more money for that lack of performance. Corporate America is kind of funny that way."

She latched on to the money thing. "Your money. You can't walk away from all that. It's—"

"—money," he concluded easily. "That's all. Just money. It doesn't even come close to mattering as much as you."

"That's all?" she echoed incredulously. "Marcus, that's a lot of money you're talking about. Millions of dollars."

He only smiled, tugged off her other mitten and took that hand in his, too, giving it a kiss identical to the other one. "Billions, actually," he said matter-of-factly.

All Della could manage in response to that was a soft squeak.

That only made Marcus laugh. "Della. I would think you, of all people, would understand how that much money can bring *a lot* of trouble into a person's life. It's not that hard to walk away from it."

"Oh, right," she sputtered. "Spoken like someone who's never had to go without money in his life."

"Della, there's more to life than money," he stated unequivocally. "The best things in life are free. Simple pleasures are the best. Money is the root of all evil."

She shook her head at him, but couldn't help smiling.

Probably because of the warm, gooey sensations meandering through her. "When did you open an unlimited account at Platitudes 'R' Us?" she asked.

"Actually," he said lightly, "the account is at words-to-live-by-dot-com. But you're right—it is an unlimited one." He leaned in close, moving his mouth to her ear. Very quietly, he whispered, "Besides, the woman I intend to spend the rest of my life with is adamant about rebuilding her career. She can take care of me. She loves me to distraction, after all."

The warm gooeyness inside her swirled into a river of sweet, sticky goodness. Unable to help herself, Della leaned forward to press her forehead against Marcus's shoulder. He looped his arms around her waist and settled his chin on the crown of her head.

"See there?" he said softly. "You do love me, don't you?"

She was amazed to hear an unmistakable uncertainty in his voice. "Yes," she whispered against the fabric of his coat.

Now he pressed a kiss to the crown of her head. "Good. Because I love you, too."

He loved her, too, Della thought. He loved her, too. He loved her, too. It was like a magic incantation in her brain, breaking all the evil spells of her old life and bestowing new ones in their wake. He loved her, too. He loved her, too.

"But, Marcus," she said softly, "there's so much more you should consider besides—"

"Della, there's *nothing* more to consider than you. I've had weeks to think about you and me, and you know what I figured out that was most significant?"

With her head still pressed against his chest—it felt so good to have it there—she asked, "What?"

"What was significant was that I didn't need weeks to think about it. I didn't even need days to think about it. I didn't need to think at all. I only needed to feel. And what I feel for you, Della…"

When he didn't finish, she tilted her head back to look at him. He was still smiling, but there was something in this one she hadn't seen in any of the others before. Peace. Contentment. Happiness. She recognized it, because with him here beside her, she felt all those things, too.

"What I feel for you is like nothing I've felt before in my life. And I like it, Della. I like it a lot. I want to feel this way forever." He dipped his head to hers and kissed her again. When he pulled back, he repeated resolutely, "So I'm coming with you."

Della didn't know why she kept wanting to object, but she couldn't quite keep herself from giving it one more shot. "But what if—"

Marcus lifted his hand to press his fingers lightly against her mouth. "It doesn't matter what if," he said. "Whatever happens, Della, we'll face it together. We'll *be* together. That's all that matters."

"But—"

"Shh," he said.

And then he dropped his fingers from her mouth to place a chaste kiss there instead. It was enough to quiet her voice if not quell her reservations. He was right, she told herself. It didn't matter what the future brought, as long as the two of them were together. She'd brought herself up from very humble beginnings and made a decent life for herself before everything went wrong at Whitworth and Stone. And she'd managed to make the best of a bad situation for eleven months in Chicago. The place from which she would be starting over again now was infinitely better than the places where she'd started off before. And this time, she wouldn't be embarking on the journey alone. This time, she would be with Marcus. And that made even the bleakest prospects tolerable.

He tucked a strand of dark blond hair behind her ear and leaned down until his mouth hovered just next to it. His warm breath on her cold skin sent a delicious shiver down her spine. Or maybe it was his simple nearness that did that. As he had with her mouth, he placed a small, soft kiss on her ear lobe. Then he pulled back far enough to murmur in a voice too soft for anyone but her to hear, "Besides. Thirty percent of my wealth is liquid and highly accessible. It's in conveniently numbered Swiss bank accounts, and I'll be able to get to it whenever I want. We won't starve, sweetheart. Trust me."

Meaning, she thought with a grin, that she would never have to settle for rented clothing again. A single, genuinely happy chuckle escaped her. But even this information didn't matter. It was as Marcus said, all that mattered was that the two of them would be together. Forever.

She looked at the suitcase by his feet. It was the size of one that could be carried onto a plane. There wasn't much that would fit in a bag that size.

"That's all you're bringing with you into our new life?" she asked.

He glanced down at the bag, then back at Della. "It's more than I need, really. Because everything I need is right here."

And then he kissed her again. And kissed her. And kissed her. And kissed her. In fact, he kissed her so long, and so many times, that only the appearance of

Carson and Willoughby on each side of them made him stop. Even at that, it took a moment for Della to remember her surroundings. But when she saw the two marshals smiling at her, she remembered all too well.

She'd completed what she'd come to New York to do. Now it was time to head into a new chapter of her life.

"Carson, Willoughby," she said to the two marshals. "Tell your boss there's been a slight change in my plan." She turned to Marcus and looped her arm through his. "Tell her I'm going to have one more piece of baggage than I'd planned."

And as baggage went, she thought, Marcus was the kind she would happily carry with her forever.

* * * * *

"A rich husband is all you need to keep the baby?"

She nodded. "For my family to see me as the perfect mother?" She gave a fake trilling laugh. "Oh, yes, a husband is the must-have accessory of the season. The richer, the better."

His lips quirked in a smile, his eyes crinkling at the corners, just a hint of cockiness. The expression gave her pause, because he wasn't laughing at her joke. No, she knew this look, too. It was his *I've solved the problem* look. "I think we've got that covered."

"Excuse me?"

"You said it yourself. All you need is a rich, successful husband."

For a moment she just stared blankly at him, unable to follow the abrupt twist the conversation had taken. "Right. A rich, successful husband. Which I don't have."

"But you could." He smiled fully now. Full smiles were rare for him. Usually they made her feel a little breathless. This one just made her nervous. "All you have to do is marry me."

Dear Reader,

I worked really hard last year. I'm not complaining, mind you…just mentioning it. Here's one of the weird things about me: when I'm writing a book, I can't read anyone else's books. I need to be completely in my own story. So last year, when I was working hard, I didn't read much.

Oh, man, I missed it.

So, over Christmas, when I took a break, I read, read, read. Seven books and some three thousand six hundred pages later, I finally feel like myself again. And I've decided I never again want to go so long without reading fiction.

So why am I sharing this with you? Shouldn't I instead be telling you all about the book you're about to read? (A sexy tycoon, a plucky heroine, an orphaned baby…there, now you know the highlights.) But I'm baring my soul about this because it just seems like you'll understand. After all, you're a reader, too. You know what joy it brings. You've felt the excitement that vibrates just beneath the surface of your day when you know you've got a great book waiting for you at home. I hope that this book brings you some small measure of the same pleasure that my holiday reading brought to me.

As always, thank you for letting me entertain you!

Emily McKay

THE TYCOON'S TEMPORARY BABY

BY
EMILY McKAY

Published in Great Britain 2012
by Mills & Boon, an imprint of Harlequin (UK) Limited,
Eton House, 18-24 Paradise Road, Richmond, Surrey TW9 1SR

© Emily McKaskle 2011

ISBN: 978 0 263 89115 7

51-0212

Harlequin (UK) policy is to use papers that are natural, renewable and
recyclable products and made from wood grown in sustainable forests. The
logging and manufacturing processes conform to the legal environmental
regulations of the country of origin.

Printed and bound in Spain
by Blackprint CPI, Barcelona

Emily McKay has been reading romance novels since she was eleven years old. Her first romance book came free. She has been reading and loving romance novels ever since. She lives in Texas with her geeky husband, her two kids and too many pets. Her debut novel, *Baby, Be Mine*, was a RITA® Award finalist for Best First Book and Best Short Contemporary. She was also a 2009 *RT Book Reviews* Career Achievement nominee for Series Romance. To learn more, visit her website at www. EmilyMcKay.com.

For Tracy and Shellee, two great friends and phenomenal writers. Ladies, thanks for making this so much fun. And to Ivy Adams, 'cause…well, you know.

One

Jonathon Bagdon just wanted his assistant to come home, damn it.

Wendy Leland had left seven days ago to attend a family funeral. In the time she'd been gone, his whole company had started falling apart. A major deal she'd been finessing had fallen through. He'd missed an important deadline because the first temp had erased his online calendar. The second temp had accidentally sent R&D's latest prototype to Beijing instead of Bangalore. The head of HR had threatened to quit twice. And no fewer than five women had run out of his office in tears.

As if all of that wasn't bad enough, the fourth temp had deep-fried the coffee maker. So he hadn't had a decent cup of coffee in three days. All in all, this was not his best moment.

Was it really too much to ask that at this particular time—when both of his business partners were out of town and when he was putting the finishing touches on the proposal for a crucial contract—that his assistant just come home?

Jonathon stared into his mug of instant coffee, contemplating whether he could ask Jeanell—the head of HR—to go out and buy a coffee maker, or if that would send her over the edge. Not that Jeanell was at the office yet. Most of the staff wandered in sometime around nine. It was barely seven.

Yes, he could have just gone out to buy himself a cup o' joe—or better yet, a new coffee maker—but with one deadline after another piling up, he just didn't have time for this crap. If Wendy had been here, a new coffee maker would have magically appeared. The same way the deal with Olson Inc. would have gone through without a hitch. When Wendy was here, things just worked. How was it that in the short five years she'd been the executive assistant here she'd become as crucial to the running of the company as he himself was?

Hell, if this past week was any indication, she was actually more important than he was. A sobering thought for a man who'd helped to build an empire out of nothing.

He knew only one thing, when Wendy did get back, he was going to do his damnedest to make sure she never left again.

Wendy Leland crept into the executive office of FMJ headquarters a little after seven. The motion sensor brought the lights up as she entered and she reached down to extend the canopy on the infant car seat she carried. Peyton, the tiny baby inside, frowned but remained asleep. She made a soft gurgling sound as Wendy lowered the car seat to a darkened corner behind her desk.

She rocked the seat gently until Peyton stilled, then Wendy dropped into her own swivel chair. Swallowing past the knot of dread in her throat, Wendy studied the office.

For five years, this had been the seat from which she'd surveyed her domain. She'd served as executive assistant for the three men who ran FMJ: Ford Langley, Matt Ballard and Jonathon Bagdon.

Her five years of Ivy League education made her perhaps a tad over-educated for the job. Or maybe not, since she hadn't procured an actual degree in any of her seven majors. Her family still thought she was wasting her talents. But the work was challenging and varied. She'd loved every minute of it. Nothing could have convinced her to leave FMJ.

Nothing, except the little bundle of joy asleep in the car seat.

When she'd left Palo Alto for Texas to attend her cousin Bitsy's funeral, she'd had no idea what awaited her. From the moment her mother called her to tell her that Bitsy had died in a motorcycle crash, the week had been one shock after another. She hadn't even known that Bitsy had a child. No one in the family had. Yet, now here Wendy was, guardian to an orphaned four-month-old baby. And gearing up for a custody battle of epic proportions. Peyton Morgan might as well have been dipped in gold the way the family was fighting over her. If Wendy wanted any chance of winning, she'd have to do the one thing she'd sworn she'd never do: move back to Texas. And that meant resigning from FMJ.

Only Bitsy could create this many problems from the grave.

Wendy gave a snort of laughter at the thought. Grief welled up in the wake of the humor. Squeezing her eyes shut, she pressed the heels of her hands against her eye sockets. Exhaustion had made her punchy, and if she gave in to her sorrow now, she might not stop crying for a month.

There would be time to grieve later. Right now, she had other things to take care of.

Wendy flicked on the desktop computer. Last night, she'd drafted the letter of resignation and then emailed it to herself. Of course, she could have sent it straight to Ford, Matt and Jonathon. She'd even spoken to Ford last night on the phone when he called to offer his condolences. Physically handing in the letter was a formality, but she wanted the closure that would come with printing it out, signing it and hand delivering it to Jonathon.

She owed him—or rather FMJ—that much at least. Before

her life became chaotic, she wanted to take this one moment to say goodbye to the Wendy she had been and to the life she'd lived in Palo Alto.

Beside her, the computer hummed to life with a familiarity that soothed her nerves. A few clicks later, she'd opened the letter and routed it to the printer. The buzz of the printer seemed to echo through the otherwise quiet office. No one else was here this early. No one but Jonathon, who worked a grueling schedule.

After signing the letter, she left it on her desk and crossed to the closed door that separated her office from theirs. A wave of regret washed over her. She pressed her palm flat to the door, and then with a sigh, dropped her forehead onto the wood just above her hand. The door was solid beneath her head. Sturdy. Dependable. And she felt herself leaning against it, needing all the strength she could borrow.

"You can hardly blame Wendy," Matt Ballard pointed out, a note of censure in his voice. At the moment, Matt was in the Caribbean, on his honeymoon. It was why they'd scheduled this conference call for so early. Matt's new wife, Claire, allowed him exactly one business call a day. "It's the first time in five years she's taken personal leave."

"I didn't say I blamed her—" Jonathon said into the phone, now sorry he'd called Matt at all. He'd had a legitimate reason for calling, but now it sounded as though he was just whining.

"When is she supposed to be back?" Matt asked.

"She was supposed to be back four days ago." She'd said she'd be in Texas two to three days, tops. After the funeral, she'd called from Texas to say she'd have to stay "a little longer." The lack of specificity made him nervous.

"Stop worrying," Matt told him. "We'll have plenty of time after Ford and I get back." As if it wasn't bad enough that Matt was on his honeymoon during this crisis, Ford and his family were also away, at their second home in New York City. "The proposal isn't due for nearly a month."

Yes. That was what bothered him. "Nearly a month" and "plenty of time" were about as imprecise as "a little longer." Jonathon was a man who liked precise numbers. If he was putting together an offer for a company worth millions, it mattered if the company was worth ten million or a hundred million. And even if he had nearly a month to work on the proposal, he wanted to know how long a little longer was.

Rather than take out his frustrations on his partner, Jonathon ended the phone call. This government contract was driving him crazy. Worse still was the fact that no one else seemed to be worried about it. For the past several years, research and development at FMJ had been perfecting smart grid meters, devices that could monitor and regulate a building's energy use. FMJ's system was more efficient and better designed than anything else on the market. Since they'd been using them at headquarters, they'd cut their electricity bills by thirty percent. This government contract would put FMJ's smart grid meters in every federal building in the country. The private sector would follow. Plus the meters would boost sales of other FMJ products. How could he not be excited about something that was going to cut energy consumption and make FMJ so much money?

Everything he'd been working for and planning for the past decade hinged on this one deal. It was the stepping-stone to FMJ's future. But first they had to actually get the contract.

Once he snapped his laptop closed, he heard a faint thump at the door. He wasn't optimistic enough to imagine the temp might come in this early. But did he even dare hope that Wendy had finally returned?

He pushed back his chair and strode across the oversize office he normally shared with Matt and Ford. When he opened the door, Wendy fell right into his arms.

Though unexpectedly falling through an open door seemed an apt metaphor for her life at the moment, nevertheless Wendy was surprised to find herself actually falling through the doorway. Jonathon's arms instantly wrapped around her, cradling her safely against his strong chest. One shoulder was pressed against him and her free hand automatically came up to the lapel of his suit jacket.

Suddenly she was aware of several things. The sharply crisp scent of his soap. The sheer breadth of his chest. And the clean, just-shaven line of his jaw, which was the first thing she saw when she looked up.

Normally, she did a decent job of ignoring it, but Jonathon Bagdon was the stuff of pure, girlish fantasies. He always looked on the verge of frowning, which lent his expression an air of thoughtful intensity. Though he rarely smiled, when he did, deep dimples creased his cheeks.

At just shy of six feet, he wasn't too tall, but his physique more than made up for what he lacked in height. He had a build more suited to barroom brawls than boardroom negotiations. He was strong and muscular. She'd never seen his naked chest, but he had a habit of shucking his suit jacket and rolling up the sleeves of his white dress shirt when he worked. Obviously she spent too much time looking at him. But until this moment, she'd never noticed he had a single mole on the underside of his perfectly square jaw.

Staring up into his green-brown eyes, she felt something unexpected pass between them. An awareness maybe. Some tension she'd never felt before. Or perhaps something she was too smart to let herself feel.

He swallowed. Fascinated, she watched the muscles of his throat shift mere inches from her face. She flattened her palm and pushed herself out of his arms.

She was all too aware of Jonathon's gaze following her every move. And even more aware that her outfit was inappropriate for work. He'd never seen her in jeans before. Certainly not topped with her favorite T-shirt, a retro Replacements concert T-shirt she'd bought online as her twenty-first birthday present to herself. It was old and ratty and she'd cut the neck out of it years ago. But somehow the rushed up behind him and practically threw herself in his path.

"I can explain!" She held up her hands in front of her as if warding off an attack.

"Explain what?" He dodged around her to look behind the desk. Her chair had been shifted to the side and where Wendy normally sat was an infant's car seat. And in that was a pale pink bundle.

He turned back to Wendy. "What is that?"

"That's a baby."

Jonathon's shock was palpable.

If she didn't know better, Wendy would have thought he'd never even seen a baby before. Though she imagined they were rare in his life, surely he had encountered at least one. After all, Ford had one himself. Jonathon must have been in the same room as his best friend's child at some point.

She dashed around him and squatted beside the car seat. She gave the back of it a gentle nudge but Peyton continued to fuss. Peyton's sleepy eyes flickered open, blinked and then focused on Wendy.

Something inside of Wendy tightened into a knot. A gut-level reaction to those bright blue eyes. Perhaps the only thing she'd ever felt that was actually stronger than that burst of attraction she'd felt for Jonathon just now.

Of course, she couldn't *have* Jonathon. She wasn't stupid enough to try. But for now, she did have Peyton. And she'd do anything in her power to keep her.

She unfastened the buckle strapping Peyton in and picked up the pink cotton bundle. Snuggling the baby close to her chest, she pressed her lips near Peyton's ear and made shushing noises. Then she drew in a breath scented like tear-free shampoo and pure love.

Suddenly feeling self-conscious, she looked up to find Jonathon watching her, a frown on his face.

She tried to smile but felt it wavering under the weight of her shifting emotions. "Jonathon, meet Peyton."

"Right," he said bracingly and he looked from her to the baby and then all around the room as if searching for the spaceship that must have dropped off this strange creature. "What is it doing in our office?"

"*She's* here because I brought her here." Which maybe hadn't been the smartest move, but she and Peyton had only gotten in the previous evening, after driving from Boulder, Colorado. With less than seventy-two hours of parenting experience under her belt, Wendy hadn't known what else to do with Peyton. "I didn't have anyone to watch her. And I don't think she's ready to be left with a stranger yet anyway. I mean, I'm strange enough, right? And—"

Jonathon cut her off. "Wendy, why do you have a baby?" His gaze dropped to her belly, suspicion lighting his gaze. "She's not...yours, is she?"

She was glad he'd cut her off, because she'd been babbling, but at the same time dreading the conversation to come, because he was not going to like what she had to say. Still, when she glanced down at the sixteen-pound baby, she had to laugh.

"No, I didn't go away for seven days and miraculously get pregnant, gestate and deliver a four-month-old. She's—" Her throat closed over the words, but she forced herself to say them. "She was my cousin's. Bitsy named me guardian. So she is mine now."

There was a long moment of silence during which Jonathon's expression was so blank, so unchanging she thought he might have suffered a stroke.

"I—" he began. Then he looked down at Peyton, his frown deepening. "Well—" He looked back at her and cocked his head to the side. "It turns out Jeanell was right. On-site childcare was a good idea. I'm sure she'll be just fine there."

Dread settled in Wendy's belly. As well as something else. Sorrow. Nostalgia maybe. She didn't want to leave FMJ. Even though she was just an assistant here, she'd never felt more at home anywhere else. Professionally or personally. Working at FMJ had given her purpose and direction. Something her family had never understood.

"I'm not going to bring Peyton to work," she began. And then decided there was no point in pussyfooting around this. "I'm not coming to work anymore. I came in today to resign."

Two

"Don't be ridiculous," Jonathon barked, too shocked to temper the edge of his words. "Nobody quits a job because they have a baby, much less because they inherited one."

Wendy rolled her eyes in exasperation. "That's not—" she started, but he held up a hand to cut her off.

"I know how stupid that sounded." This was why he needed Wendy. Why she was irreplaceable. Most of the time, he was too outspoken. Too blunt. Too brash. He had a long history of pissing off people who were easily offended. But not Wendy. Somehow, she managed to see past his mistakes and overlook his blunders.

The thought of trying to function without her here as his buffer made him panic. He wasn't about to lose her over a baby.

"FMJ has one of the highest-rated on-site child-care facilities in the area. There's no reason why you can't continue to work here."

"I can't work here because I have to move back to Texas."

As she spoke, she crossed to the supply closet in the corner. She moved a few things around inside and pulled out an empty cardboard box.

"Why on earth would you want to move to Texas?"

She shot him another one of those looks. "You know I'm from Texas, right?"

"Which is why I don't know why you'd want to move back there. I've never once heard you say anything nice about living there."

She bobbed her head as if in concession of the point. Then she shrugged. Rounding to the far side of the desk, she sank into the chair and opened her drawer. "It's complicated."

"I think I can keep up."

"There's a chance members of my family won't want me to raise Peyton. Unless I can convince them I'm the best mother for her, there'll be a custody battle."

"So? You don't think you can win the battle from here?"

"I don't think I can afford to fight it." Sifting through things in the drawer, she answered without looking up. She pulled out a handful of personal belongings and dropped them into the open box.

He watched her for a moment, barely comprehending her words and not understanding her actions at all. "What are you doing?"

She paused, glancing up. "Packing," she said as if stating the obvious. Then she looked back into the drawer and riffled through a few more things. "Ford called yesterday to offer his condolences. When I explained, he said not to worry about giving two-weeks' notice. That if I needed to just pack up and go, I should."

Forget twenty-two years of friendship. He was going to kill Ford.

The baby squirmed. Wendy jostled her knee to calm the little girl, all the while still digging in the drawer. "I swear I had another tube of lip gloss in here."

"Lip gloss?" She'd just pulled the rug out from under him.

If he'd had two weeks, maybe he could talk some sense into her. But no. His idiot of a partner had ripped that away too. And she was worried about lip gloss?

She must have heard the outrage in his voice, because her head snapped up. "It was my favorite color and they don't even make it anymore. And—" She slammed the drawer shut and yanked open another. "Oh, forget it."

"You can't quit."

She stood up, abandoning her task. "You think I want this? You think I want to move? Back to Texas? You think I want to leave a job I love? So that I can move home? I don't! But it's my only option."

"How will being unemployed in Texas solve anything?" he demanded.

"I…" Peyton squirmed again in her arms and let out a howl of protest. Wendy sighed, sank back into the chair and set it rocking with a pump of her leg. "I may not have mentioned it before, but my family has money."

She hadn't mentioned it. She'd never needed to.

People who grew up with money had an air about them. It wasn't snobbery. Not precisely. It was more a sense of confidence that came from always having the best of everything. It was the kind of thing you only noticed if you'd never had money and had spent your life trying to replicate that air of entitlement.

Besides, there was an innate elegance to Wendy that was in direct contrast to her elfin appearance and plucky verve. Yet somehow she pulled it off.

"From money?" he said dryly. "I never would have guessed."

Wendy seemed too distracted to notice his sarcasm. "My grandfather set up a trust for me. For all the grandkids, actually. I never claimed mine. The requirements seemed too ridiculous."

"And the requirements are?"

"I have to work for the family company and live within fifteen miles of my parents." She narrowed her eyes as if glaring at some unseen relative. Peyton let out another shriek of frustration and Wendy snapped back to the present. "So if I move home now—"

"You can claim the trust," he summed up. "You'd have enough money to hire a lawyer if it does come down to a custody battle."

"I'm hoping it won't come to that. My grandmother still controls the purse strings. The rest of the family will follow her wishes. Once she sees what a great mother I'm going to be, she'll back off and just let me raise Peyton." Wendy's jaw jutted forward in determination. "But if it does come to a custody battle, I want to be sure I have enough money to put up a good fight."

"I don't get it. You're doing all this for a cousin you barely knew? Someone you hadn't seen in years?"

Wendy's eyes misted over and for a second he thought that—dear God—she might actually start crying. She squeezed the baby close to her chest and planted a kiss on top of her head. Then she pinned him with a steady gaze brimming with resolution. "If something happened to Ford and Kitty, and they wanted you to take Ilsa, wouldn't you do whatever it took to honor their wishes?"

All he could do in response was shove his hands deep into his pockets and swallow a curse. Damn it, she was right.

He stared at the adorable tot on Wendy's lap, summing up his competition. He wasn't about to lose the best assistant he'd ever had. He didn't care how cute and helpless that baby was.

Peyton undoubtedly needed Wendy. But he needed her too.

Fighting the feeling of complete and utter doom—which, frankly, was a fight she'd been losing ever since the nanny had first handed her Peyton—Wendy glanced from the baby, to the open desk drawer and then to Jonathon.

She had so much to do, her mind couldn't focus on a single task. Or maybe it was lack of sleep. Or maybe just an attack of nerves brought on by the way Jonathon kept pacing from one side of the room to the other, pausing occasionally to glower in her direction.

When she'd first started work at FMJ, Jonathon had made her distinctly nervous. There was something about his combination of magnetic good looks, keen intelligence and ruthless ambition that made her overly aware of every molecule of her body. And every molecule of his body for that matter. She'd spent the first six months on edge, jumping every time he came in the room, nearly trembling under his gaze. It wasn't nerves precisely. More a kind of tingling anticipation. As if she were a gazelle who wanted to be eaten by the lion.

She'd forced herself to get over it.

And she'd thought she'd been successful. Only now that feeling was back. Either she could chalk it up to exhaustion and emotional vulnerability. Or she could be completely honest with herself. It *wasn't* nerves. It was sexual awareness. And now that she was about to walk out of his life forever, she wished she'd acted on it when she'd had the chance.

Forcing her mind away from that thought, she stared at the open desk drawer. The lip gloss was gone forever, just like any opportunity she might have had to explore a different kind of relationship with Jonathon. The best she could hope for now was to gather her few remaining possessions and make a run for it.

She had a Voldemort for President coffee mug in the bottom drawer, her Bose iPod dock, a tub of Just Fruit strawberries and in the very back, a bag of Ghirardelli chocolate caramels. Precious few possessions to be walking away with after five years, and the cardboard box dwarfed them. On the bright side, at least she'd only have to make one trip out to the car.

Balancing Peyton on her hip, she wedged the box under her arm only to find Jonathon blocking her route to the door.

"You can't go."

"Right. The car seat. I can't believe I forgot that." She turned back around, only to notice the diaper bag as well.

She blew out a breath. Okay. More than one trip after all.

"No," Jonathon said. "I'm not letting you quit."

Turning back around, she stared at him. "Not letting me? How can you not let me? If I quit, I quit."

"You're the best assistant I've ever had. I'm not going to lose you over something this…" He seemed to be searching for the least offensive word. "Frivolous."

She raised an eyebrow. "She's a child, not a frivolity. It's not like I'm running off to join the circus."

There was something unsettling about the quiet, assessing way he studied her. Then he said, "If keeping this baby is really so important to you, we'll hire a lawyer. We'll find the best lawyer in the country. We'll take care of it."

She felt her throat tighten, but refused to let the tears out of the floodgate. Oh, how tempting it was to accept his help. But the poor man had no idea what he was getting into.

"You should know, my family is extremely wealthy. If they fight this, they'll put considerable financial and political weight behind it."

"So?"

She blew out a long breath. The moment of reckoning. She always dreaded this. "Leland is my mother's maiden name. I legally took her name when I left college."

Jonathon didn't look impatient, the way some people did when she explained. That was one of the things she liked best about Jonathon. He reached conclusions quickly, but never judgments.

"My father's name—" Then she corrected herself. "My *real* last name is Morgan."

Most people, it took a couple of minutes for them to put together the name Morgan with wealth and political connections. She figured as smart as he was, it would take Jonathon about twenty seconds. It took him three.

"As far as I know, none of the banking Morgans live in Texas. That means you must be one of the Texas oil Morgans."

He didn't phrase it as a question. His tone had gone flat, his gaze distant.

"I am." She bit her lip, not bothering to hide her cringe. "I should have told you."

"No. Why would you have?" His expression was so blank, so unsurprised, so completely disinterested, that it was obvious, at least to her, that he cared deeply that she'd kept her true identity to herself. His calm, direct gaze met hers. "Then Senator Henry Morgan is…"

"My uncle." In the interest of full disclosure, she nodded to the baby gurgling happily on her hip. "Peyton's grandfather."

"Okay then." He stood with his hands propped on his hips, the jacket of his suit pushed back behind his hands. He often stood in that way and it always made her heart kick up a beat. The posture somehow emphasized the breadth of his shoulders and the narrowness of his waist all at the same time.

Despite his obvious disappointment, he immediately went into problem-solving mode. He stared at her blankly, then left the room abruptly. A moment later he returned with a copy of the *Wall Street Journal.* He flipped the paper open, folded it in half and held it out to her. "So, Elizabeth Morgan is your cousin. The baby's mother."

It was an article about her death. The first Wendy had seen. She didn't need to read it to know what it would say. It would be carefully crafted. Devoid of scandal. Bitsy may have been an embarrassment but Uncle Hank would have called in favors to make sure the article met with his approval. That was the way her uncle did business, whether he was running the country or running his family.

Jonathon frowned as he scanned the article. His eyes crinkled at the edges as his face settled into what she thought of as his problem-solving expression. But if he could figure a way out of this one, then he was smarter than even she thought he was.

"It says here she is survived by a brother and sister-in-law. Why don't they take the baby?"

"Exactly," she said grimly. "Why not? It's what every conservative in the country will be thinking. Those conservative voters made up a huge portion of Uncle Hank's constituents." And they weren't the only ones who had that question. It was no secret that their grandmother, Mema, didn't approve of modern families. In her mind, a family comprised a mother and a father. And possibly a dog. Mema would want Hank Jr. to take Peyton. And what Mema wanted was generally what the family did.

She may have been in her late eighties, but she was a wily old dame. More importantly, she still controlled the money.

"It's so frustrating," she admitted. "This wouldn't even be an issue if I had a husband I could trot out to appease my grandmother and Uncle Hank's constituents."

"You really think that's all you need?"

"For my family to see me as the perfect mother?" She gave a fake, trilling laugh. "Oh, yes, a husband is the must-have accessory of the season. The richer, the better. Optional add-ons are the enormous gas-guzzling SUV, the Junior League membership and the golden Lab."

"And it's really that simple?"

"Oh, sure. *That* simple. I'll just head over to the laboratory and whip up a successful husband out of spare computer parts. You run out to the morgue and steal a dead body I can reanimate and we'll be good."

His lips quirked in a smile, his eyes crinkling at the corners, just a hint of cockiness. The expression gave her pause, because he wasn't laughing at her joke. No, she knew this look too. It was his I've-solved-the-problem look. "I think we can do a little better than that."

"Excuse me?"

"You said it yourself. All you need is a rich, successful husband."

For a moment she just stared blankly at him, unable to follow the abrupt twist the conversation had taken. "Right. A rich, successful husband. Which I don't have."

"But you could." He smiled fully now. Full smiles were rare for him. Usually they made her feel a little breathless. This one just made her nervous. "All you have to do is marry me. I'll even buy you a dog."

Three

Having never before asked a woman to marry him, Jonathon wasn't quite sure what reaction he expected, but it wasn't Wendy's blank-faced confusion. Or maybe that was a perfectly normal reaction under the circumstances. After all, it wasn't every day a man proposed to his assistant for such transparently selfish reasons.

For a long moment, she merely stared at him, her blue-violet eyes wide, her perfect bow mouth gaping open in surprise.

She wasn't just surprised. She was disconcerted. His proposal had shocked her. Maybe even offended her. On some deeply intimate level, the thought of marriage to him horrified her.

Not that he could really blame her. Despite his wealth, he was no prize.

She was going to say no, and he couldn't let her do it.

He needed her. Quite desperately, if the past seven days had been any indication.

"I'm not proposing a romantic relationship," he reassured her, hoping to make his proposal seem as benign as possible.

"Obviously," she muttered. Still holding the baby in her arms, she sank to the edge of the desk. She dipped her head, nuzzling the tuft of dark hair on Peyton's head.

"This would be strictly a business arrangement." He argued more vehemently as he felt her slipping away. "We'll stay married as long as it takes to convince your family that we're suitable parents. We won't even have to live together. I'll grant you an annulment as soon as we've convinced them."

"No," she said softly.

He felt a pang in his chest at her response. Then he saw it. Her letter of resignation. Signed, dated and ready to be handed over. As official as an order for his execution.

This past week had been a premonition of his future without her. He could envision an endless parade of incompetent temps. Countless hours of interviewing assistants, all of whom would fail to live up to the precedent set by Wendy. This government contract would slip through his fingers, just as the Olson deal had. FMJ had lost millions on that one. Which was nothing compared to what they'd miss if they didn't secure this contract. He could feel the stepping-stone slipping out from under him, the future he'd planned out for the company dissolving before his very eyes.

Panic mounting, he kept talking. "If you're worried about sex, don't be. I certainly wouldn't expect to sleep with you."

Her gaze darted to his as she bolted to her feet. "No." Then she squeezed her eyes closed for an instant. "What I meant was…" She drew in a deep breath. "…a fast annulment wouldn't work."

Just as quickly, her eyes shifted away from his. In that moment, a powerful, unspoken message passed between them.

Not once in all the years they'd worked together had they talked about sex. They had shared countless other intimacies. Eaten meals late at night. Sat beside each other on long plane flights. He'd had her fall asleep with her head on his shoulder somewhere over the Atlantic Ocean. They had slept in hotel rooms with walls so thin he'd heard the sound of her rolling over in her bed. And yet despite all that, neither of them had ever broached the subject of sex.

But now that the word had been said aloud, it was there between them. The image of her, sprawled naked on a bed before him, was permanently lodged in his brain.

He found himself oddly pleased by the faint blush that crept into her cheeks as she couldn't quite meet his gaze.

"If we're going to do this—" she shot him a look from under her lashes as if she were trying to assess his commitment "—then we have to go all in."

He raised his eyebrows, speculatively. She wasn't saying no. She was making a counteroffer. He felt a grin split his face. Just when he thought he knew her, she always managed to surprise him.

"We can't get an annulment in three or even six months," she said. "My family will see right through that. In a year, maybe two, we'll have to get divorced. Simply pretend the marriage didn't work out."

"I see."

She shook her head. "I don't think you do. I'm committed to fighting for Peyton. I'll do whatever I have to. But I can't ask you to do the same."

"You're not asking," he pointed out. "I'm offering. And just so we're clear, I'm not doing this out of the goodness of my heart." The last thing he needed right now was her developing some starry-eyed notion about his motives. "I'm doing this to keep you working for FMJ. You're the best damn assistant I've ever had."

She threw up her hand to interrupt him. "This is ridiculous. Just hire another assistant. I'll even help you find one. There are plenty of other competent people in the city."

"But none of them are you. I need you," he argued. "None of them know the company the way you do. None of them would care about what FMJ does the way you do."

She seemed to be considering for a moment, then admitted, "Well, that's true."

"Besides. I don't have the time or energy to train someone new. My motives are very selfish."

"Trust me, I wasn't about to swoon from the romanticism of the moment." Her lips twisted in a wry smile. "I just want to make sure you know what you're getting into. If my family suspects what we're up to—"

"Then we'll convince them that our marriage has nothing to do with Peyton."

Her eyebrows shot up. "Convince them we're in love?"

"Exactly."

Wendy gave a snort of laughter. Baby Peyton squirmed in response. She turned her head and gave Jonathon a look of annoyance. If a baby could be annoyed. Obviously she wasn't going back to sleep. Pressing her tiny palms to Wendy's chest, she pushed away as if she wanted to be set free.

Wendy crossed to a diaper bag sitting on her desk. He hadn't even noticed it before, but when Wendy tried to unzip it with one hand, he moved to help her. He brushed her fingers aside and unzipped the bag. "What do you need?"

"The blanket. That pink one there. Spread it out on the floor."

Once the blanket was out, she situated the baby on her belly in the center of it.

The sight of a baby in the middle of FMJ's executive offices was so incongruous he could barely remember what they'd been talking about. Oh, right. She'd been snorting with laughter over the idea of them being in love. Nice to know he'd amused her.

"So you don't think we can convince your family we're romantically involved?"

Wendy was back at the diaper bag now, pulling out an array of brightly colored toys. "No offense, Jonathon, but in the five years I've been here, I don't think I've ever seen you romantically involved."

"That's ridiculous. I—"

She held up her hands to ward off his protests. "With anyone. Oh, I know you've dated *plenty* of women." She stressed "plenty" as if it was an insult. "But romance is not your strong suit."

Dropping to her knees, she strategically placed the toys in an arc in front of the baby. By now, Peyton had wedged herself up on her elbows.

"You think I can't be romantic?" he asked.

"I think you approach your love life with all the warmth and spontaneity of a long-term strategic planning committee."

"You're saying...what? That I'm a cold fish?" His voice came out tight and strained.

There was something very matter-of-fact about her tone. As if she were stating the obvious. As if it hadn't even occurred to her that this might insult him.

"Not really." She tilted her head to the side, her attention focused on Peyton. She nudged a stuffed elephant closer to the baby. He didn't know if the topic made her uncomfortable or if infant toys were really just that fascinating. "More that you keep your emotions tightly under control." Apparently satisfied with the arrangement of toys, she stood, dusting her hands off. "You're a dispassionate man. There's nothing wrong with—"

Okay, he'd had enough. He strode toward her, pulled her into his arms and kissed her.

He didn't know what pushed him over the edge. Whether it was her unending lecture about how dispassionate he was. Or the fact that ever since he'd said the word "sex" aloud a few minutes ago he hadn't been able to get it out of his head. Or maybe it was that tempting bit of shoulder her shirt kept exposing. Or hell, maybe it was even the hot-pink strap.

Whatever it was, his restraint snapped and he had to kiss her. And then, he couldn't stop.

Wendy had not seen it coming. One minute, she was trying to calm Peyton down, keep her distracted enough so she could keep talking to Jonathon. Because frankly, Wendy was having enough trouble concentrating on the logistics of the conversation without Peyton breaking out into all-out fussiness.

And then, a second later, her body was pressed against Jonathon's and his mouth was moving over hers in a kiss heaven made to knock her socks off.

One hand cradled her jaw, his fingertips rough against the sensitive skin of her cheek. The other was wrapped firmly around her waist, his hand strong against her back, pressing her so close to him she could feel the buttons of his shirt through the thin cotton of her T-shirt.

His kiss was completely unexpected. When he had crossed the room to her, the lines of his face taut, his expression so full of intent, it had never occurred to her that he was going kiss her.

Sure, in the past, she'd imagined what it might be like to kiss him. After all, they'd worked side by side for years. Just because she had a modicum of restraint didn't mean she was dead. Despite the pure perfection of his exterior, she'd always imagined that in the bedroom Jonathon was very much how he was in the boardroom. Analytical. Logical. In control. Dispassionate.

Holy guacamole, had she been wrong.

His lips didn't just kiss hers. They devoured her.

She felt his tongue in her mouth, stroking hers, coaxing a response, all but demanding she participate, until she found herself rising up onto her toes and wrapping her arms around his neck, brushing her palm against the bristle of soft hair on the back of his head.

The kiss was hot and endless. He tasted faintly of coffee and fresh minty toothpaste and deeply buried longing. He stirred feelings within her that she'd never even imagined. And she could just not get close enough to him.

He backed her up a step. And then another. She felt the

edge of her desk bump against the back of her legs. And still he pressed into her, bending her so her back arched.

An image flashed through her mind of him sweeping the desk clear, pressing her down onto her desk and taking her right there. The idea came to her so completely, it was as though it had been right there in the back of her mind for years. Just waiting for his kiss to pull it out of her.

There was no one else in the building. Why shouldn't they give in to this thing between them? She couldn't think of a single reason not to.

She still hadn't thought of one a moment later when he pulled his mouth from hers and stepped away. He cleared his throat, then tugged down the hem of his jacket to straighten it.

He left her aching for him. Missing the warmth of his body, even though he was only a foot away. Wishing she had some idea of why he'd kissed her. Why he'd stopped…

Peyton.

Oh, crap. Peyton!

Wendy looked past Jonathon to where Peyton still lay on her belly on the floor.

Holy guacamole, indeed! She'd been a mother for less than four days and she'd already abandoned her daughter on the floor to make out with her boss. Maybe her family was right. Maybe she really was unfit to be Peyton's mother.

Her gaze sought Jonathon. He'd crossed to the other side of the room so that Peyton lay between them like a landmine.

He ran a hand across his jaw, then shoved his hand deep in his pocket. She'd never seen him look quite so disconcerted. Though he still looked less shaken than she felt.

"Well," he began, then swallowed visibly. "I think we can both agree that if I need to I can convince your family that I am more than your boss."

"Yeah. I think so." Then she paused for a beat while his words sank in. *"That's* what this was about?" For a second, confusion swirled through her, muddling her thoughts even further. "You kissed me merely to make a point?"

"I—" He shrugged, apparently at a loss for words.

Indignation pushed past her embarrassment. "I was seconds away from dropping my panties to the floor and you were making a point?"

For an instant, his gaze fell to her feet as if imagining her panties lying there. He swallowed again as he dragged his gaze back to hers, then ran a hand down his face.

Well, at least she wasn't the only one whose world had been rocked.

"It seemed a prudent move," he said stiffly.

She nearly snorted her derision. Prudent? The kiss that had curled her toes all the way up to her kneecaps had seemed *prudent* to him?

"Oh, that is wrong in so many ways, I don't even know where to start."

He tried to interrupt her. "Actually—"

But she cut him off with a wag of her finger. "No, wait a second. I *do* know where to start. If you think offering to marry me for Peyton's sake gives you an all-access pass to this—" she waved her hand in front of her body "—then you have another think coming." He looked as if he might say something in protest, but she didn't give him a chance. "And secondly, you have no business kissing me merely to make a point."

And then—because she realized that was practically an invitation to kiss her for other reasons—she added, "In fact, you have no business kissing me at all. If we're going to do this pretend-marriage thing, we need to set some boundaries. And thirdly…well, I have no idea what thirdly is yet, but I'm sure it will come to me eventually."

For a long moment, Jonathon merely stared at her, one eyebrow slightly arched, his lips curved to just hint at his amusement. "Are you done?"

She clamped her lips together, painfully aware of how coo

and collected he seemed when she'd just been rambling like an idiot. A surefire sign that her emotional state was neither cool nor calm.

Maybe she was wrong about the kiss affecting him as much as it did her. And wouldn't that just suck. Didn't she have enough on her plate just now? This was so not the time for her to be nursing a crush on her boss. Or her husband.

When had her life gotten so complicated?

On the floor between them, Peyton wedged her tiny hands under her to push up onto her forearms. She let out an excited squeal of pride.

Right. This was when her life had gotten complicated. Approximately five days ago in her grandfather's study when the lawyer dropped Bitsy's will on her like a bomb.

Wendy let loose a sigh of frustration. "I'm sorry," she said. "None of this is your fault. I shouldn't take it out on you. I just—"

"I agree we need boundaries," he said abruptly, cutting her off before she could bumble further into the apology. His tone was stiff, as if he was searching for the most diplomatic way to broach the subject. "Keeping sex out of this is a good idea. However, kissing you now seemed prudent because we will have to kiss again at some point."

"We will?" she asked weakly, her gaze dropping to his mouth.

"Naturally."

She felt a curious heat stirring deep inside at the idea. He was going to kiss her again. Soon? She hoped so. Even if it was a very bad idea, she hoped so.

"If we're going to convince people we're in love and getting married, people will expect certain displays of affection."

"Oh, I hadn't thought…" Obviously, there was a lot she hadn't considered about this idea. She didn't know whether or not to be thankful that Jonathon's brain worked so much faster than her own. Was it a good thing he was around to consider things she hadn't? Or was it merely annoying to always be one step behind?

"The people who know us best will be hardest to convince. Luckily Ford and Matt will both be out of town for another few weeks. We'll have to get used to the idea ourselves before see them."

"Ford and Matt? Surely we don't need to lie to them?" Jonathon had been best friends with Ford and Matt since they were kids.

He leveled a steady gaze at her. There was no hesitation. No doubt. "Yes, we do. If your family decides to fight us on this, it could mean a court battle. I can't ask either of them to lie for us."

"Oh." Feeling suddenly weak, she sank back to the edge of the desk.

Of course they couldn't ask Ford and Matt to lie for them. In the five years she'd worked with FMJ, she'd served as executive assistant for all three men equally.

They worked so closely together they'd decided long ago it was easier to share one assistant among the three of them. Undoubtedly that was why they'd gone through so many assistants before she'd come along. Managing the schedules and needs of three such disparate men was no easy task. In short, she was a miracle worker.

If the thought of lying to them was this difficult for her, then how must Jonathon feel about the matter?

She propelled herself away from the desk and crossed to stand in front of him. Gazing up into his mossy-green eyes, she studied him. "This is a crazy and ridiculous plan. Are you sure you want to do this?"

His lips curved into a slight smile. His eyes lit with a reckless gleam as they crinkled at the corners, giving her the distinct impression that he was enjoying this. "Yeah. I'm sure. If there's one thing I know, it's how to make the strategic risk pay off."

The resolve in his gaze was as clear as the doubt probably

was in her own. Then she looked down at where Peyton lay on the floor. She scooped up the precious little girl and held her close. This moment felt profound. As though she and Jonathon were striking a bargain that was going to change all of their lives. It seemed only right that Peyton be a part of it as well.

"Okay," she said. "Let's do this."

Jonathon's face broke into a full grin. He gave a brisk nod then spun on his heel, moving toward his office as he started barking orders, back into full boss mode.

"First off, email Ford and Matt and schedule another teleconference for later in the day. Then call Judge Eckhart and see if he has time in his schedule to perform the ceremony next Friday. Clear my schedule and yours for the following two weeks."

Wendy was used to having Jonathon rattle off a to-do list like this. Even trying to juggle Peyton, she kept up pretty well. Until he got to the last item on the list.

"Wait a second. Clear our schedules? What are we going to be doing? And what about the government contract?"

"We'll work on that this week. And we'll have another couple of weeks after we get back. It'll be tight, but I have no doubt we'll get it done."

"Get back? Get back from where?"

He paused by his desk and looked up at her, that cocky smile still on his face. "From our honeymoon."

"Our honeymoon?" Surprise pitched her voice high.

"Don't get too excited. We're just going to Texas. If we're going to win this battle with your family, we need to go on the offensive. That means taking the fight to them."

Four

When Jonathon called her into the conference room the next morning, she was surprised to see Randy Zwack there. Randy had gone to college with Jonathon, Matt and Ford before going on to law school. He'd occasionally done work for FMJ, before they'd hired an intellectual property legal department, but that had been long before her time. She was more confused than surprised when she walked into the conference room and saw him there—looking more harried than usual.

Jonathon stood at the far end of the room, back to the door, staring out at the view of Palo Alto sprawling below. Randy sat dead in the center of the table, stacks of paper spread out before him. The lawyer looked up when she entered. He half stood and offered her a strained smile.

"Oh, good. You're here," he said as if he'd been waiting for her. "We can get started."

"Hi, Randy." She looked past him to Jonathon. When he turned around, she raised her eyebrows in question. "What's up?"

He frowned and with unusual hesitancy said, "I asked Randy here to draw up a prenuptial agreement for us." He held out a hand to ward off some protest he imagined she might make. "Don't worry. I trust his discretion."

"I'm not worried." In fact, delighted was more like it. "Calm down. I think a prenup is a fantastic idea."

"You do?" Randy looked surprised.

"Why wouldn't I?" She sat down in the chair opposite Randy. "I assume Jonathon told you why he's helping me?"

Randy gave a little nod, still looking suspicious.

"This is a marriage custom-made for a prenup."

"In the interest of full disclosure…" Randy ran a hand over his hair, which today looked disheveled, though it was normally meticulously styled to hide his growing bald spot. "This is not my area of expertise. I told Jonathon he should hire a good family lawyer, but—" Randy winced.

"But Jonathon can be very pig-headed."

"I was going to say determined."

No wonder the poor guy looked so disconcerted. Jonathon had obviously browbeat him into drawing up the prenup. And doing it on a very tight schedule, since Jonathon had proposed less than twenty-four hours ago.

"Don't worry." Wendy reached across the table and patted Randy's hand. "I'm sure you did great. It's all pretty cut-and-dry."

Jonathon took a few steps closer to loom over them from the end of the table. He'd shoved his hands into his pockets in that way she found so distracting.

This was the man who was going to be her husband. In less than a week. Her stomach tightened at the thought.

"Okay, let's see this puppy. It's just your standard prenup, right?"

Reaching for the stack of papers in front of Randy, she clapped her hands in a way that was overly cheerful, as if this was a big fake check from Publishers Clearinghouse. But neither man noticed. Randy was too busy sending Jonathon a pointed glance and Jonathon was too busy glaring Randy into intimidated silence. She looked from one man to the other.

"This *is* a standard prenup? Right?"

Jonathon cleared his throat and loomed some more.

"You have nothing to worry about. Any assets you bring to the marriage or inherit while married revert to you upon the absolution of the union." Randy flushed bright as he spoke. Just in case she'd seen through his obfuscation.

Ignoring Jonathon, she looked pointedly at Randy, waiting for him to cave. "That's not what I asked, now, is it?"

He cleared his throat. "You…um…have nothing to worry about."

"Yes, you said that already. What about him?" She nodded in Jonathon's direction.

"The prenup was written to my specification," Jonathon said tightly. "I'm satisfied."

Which was not the same thing at all.

Randy blushed all the way to his receding hairline, but refused to look at her. Jonathon, on the other hand, met her gaze without even flinching, which actually made her more nervous.

"Give me a minute." Neither man budged. "Alone. With the prenup." Still no movement from the united front. "Either you give me time to read it or you—" she pointed at Randy "—tell me what it is he doesn't want me to see."

Randy looked to Jonathon, who glowered at her for a second before granting a tight nod. Randy pulled her copy closer and flipped to a page midway through.

She scanned the paragraph, then read it aloud to give voice to her exasperation. "In the event of separation, annulment or divorce, the following premarital assets belonging to Jonathon Bagdon shall transfer to Gwendolyn Leland—the monetary value of twenty percent of all real property, tangible property, securities and cash owed by—"

She broke off in frustration, too stunned to continue. She glared at them both. "Whose idea was this ridiculous clause?"

Randy held up his hands. "Not mine." He sounded as offended as she was.

"But you *let* him include this? Are you insane?" She clenched and unclenched her fingers around the pen Randy had handed her as he gave a what-could-I-do shrug. She smiled tightly at him and said through clenched teeth, "Will you please give me a minute alone with my future husband?"

Randy skittered away like a death-row inmate given a pardon. She didn't blame him. Someone was going down. She wouldn't want to get caught in the crossfire either.

The second they were alone she asked, "Twenty percent? Twenty? Are you crazy?"

Jonathon at least had the good sense to try to sound placating. "Now, Wendy…"

"You know I'm not taking twenty percent!"

"After two years being married to me, you may think you've earned it."

She blew out a breath of exasperation. "I'm not taking. A penny. Of your money."

"Don't forget, California is a community property state. If you don't sign the prenup, you're entitled to half of anything I earn while we're together. For all you know that could be more than this twenty percent."

"What? Because you haven't been meeting your full potential before now?" He just scowled at her. "You know that has nothing to do with why I'm marrying you."

"I also know exactly how much money you make and that you'll have trouble supporting yourself and a child on that income."

"Lots of single-parent families get by on what I make," she pointed out.

"Maybe they do," he countered. "But you don't have to."

"So what? You're just going to give me all of that money? Did you somehow miss the conversation yesterday where I mentioned that I'm a Morgan? Trust me when I tell you, Jonathon, I will be fine."

His lips curved into the barest hint of a smile. "No. I didn't miss that, but I also know how damn stubborn you are. And I know that you're not going to ask your family for money. If you were the kind of person who would do that, you wouldn't be in this position to begin with."

Hmm. Good point. "But," she countered, "you thought you'd talk me into taking twenty percent of your assets?"

"No. I rather hoped you'd sign the prenup without noticing that part."

Well, that she could believe. He was just arrogant enough to think he could get away with a stunt like that.

"Even if I *had* signed the papers, I still wouldn't have taken the money. That's almost—" She struggled to do the math. Jonathon, no doubt, knew exactly how much that was, to the dime, at any given moment. "That's…tens of millions of dollars." Certainly more than the trust she'd never bothered to claim, which was a measly eight million. "I'm not taking that kind of money from you."

He shrugged dismissively. "It's a drop in the bucket."

"It's a fifth of the bucket. That's a lot of drops." She forced out a long. slow breath. Why was she angry? Why exactly?

She put voice to her thoughts as they came to her, not willing to give herself time to soften them. "Look, you've always been arrogant and controlling."

He raised his eyebrows. Probably in surprise that she'd say it aloud to him. He certainly couldn't be shocked by the idea.

"At work, it's fine," she continued. "You're my boss. But if we're going to get married, then the second we walk out that door each day—" she jabbed a finger toward the door "—you have to stop trying to control everything. Even if this isn't a real marriage."

"Wendy, I'm not—"

"But you are," she said, cutting him off. "Don't you get it? If I wanted to sit back and be taken care of for the rest of my life, I never would have left Texas. I *like* having to work for a living. I've been rich. I know that money alone won't make me happy. And I also know that being with someone who's always trying to control me will make me miserable. So either you back off, or we walk away from this now."

He stared at her a long time, his gaze hard-edged and steely. She didn't back down. She couldn't. Her gut told her that if she lost her foothold now, she wouldn't recover. Besides, she was far too used to intimidating glares from her father or uncle to do that. Eventually, she even smiled. "See. Your Jedi mind tricks don't work on me."

His lips twitched at her comment and finally, he gave a terse, reluctant nod, as if agreeing to keep his own money was an affront to his personal honor.

"There's something else you should know."

"Okay, hit me."

"In the event of my death, you and Peyton get it all." She opened her mouth to protest, but he raised a hand to cut her off. "I'm not budging on that one."

"What about your family?" As familiar as she was with his schedule, she knew he didn't see them often, but they did exist. "Surely you want them to have your fortune."

His eyes were dark and shuttered. His face nearly expressionless. "There are certain charitable organizations that I've already provided for. If I die while we're married, I want you to have the rest."

She studied him for a moment. Since this was the most she'd ever heard him say about his family—precisely nothing—she had to assume he was serious. Boy, and she thought her relationship with her family was screwed up. "Okay," she said softly. "Then we'll just have to take very good care of you for the next two years. Make sure you take your vitamins." She smiled at her own joke, but he didn't return the smile. "Now that that's settled, I'll go tell Randy he can do his job and protect his client."

She'd almost made it out the door when Jonathon's words stopped her.

"I don't want you to fall in love with me."

Hand already on the doorknob, she turned to face him, eyebrows raised. "Excuse me?"

His expression was so strained as to be nearly comical. "If we're going to be together a year or maybe two, I don't want you imagining that you've fallen in love with me."

Fighting back a chuckle, she searched his face, but saw no signs that he was joking. In fact, he looked so serious, it made her heart catch in her chest. She had to force a teasing smile. "Why? Because you're so charming and charismatic that I won't be able to be constantly in your company without falling in love?" He didn't smile at her, so she asked, "Is this a separate issue from the money or are the millions of dollars supposed to ease my heartache if I did fall in love with you?"

His lips twitched again, but she wasn't sure if it was with suppressed humor or irritation. "Separate issue. But I'm serious."

She could certainly see that. It made her uneasy, but she couldn't say why. It wasn't arrogance—his fear that she might fall in love with him. No, despite his natural confidence, she didn't see that in his gaze now. Instead, she saw only concern. For her.

"Let me guess. You're not the type of man who believes in love." She could imagine that all too easily. Jonathon may feel physical passion—he'd proven that clearly enough when he'd kissed her yesterday—but love was something else entirely.

But to her surprise, he shook his head. "Oh, I believe in love. I know exactly how crippling it can be. That's why I don't want you to imagine you've fallen in love with me."

"Okay," she said, torn between wanting to reassure him, without telling him outright that she had absolutely no intention of risking her heart. Finally, she made the only counteroffer she could think of. "Then don't fall in love with me either."

He studied her for a moment, slowly smiling.

Her chin bumped up a notch. "What? You think you're above falling in love with me? I'll have you know I'm very loveable." Arching an eyebrow, she said, "I'm cute. And plucky. Greater men than you have fallen in love with me."

"I'm sure they have."

"You think I'm joking?" she demanded, all fake belligerence.

"Not for a minute," Jonathon conceded. And the really pathetic things was, he was being honest. In this moment, watching her trying to cajole him into laughing, it was all too easy to imagine falling in love with her. Smart, funny, never taking herself too seriously. Wendy was the whole package. Men who wanted things like a wife and family were probably waiting in line for a woman like her. Too bad he wasn't one of them.

"Just don't forget why I'm doing this. This isn't a favor to you. This isn't because I'm a nice guy. Don't romanticize me. Don't forget, not even for a minute, why I'm here. Why I'm doing this."

She looked up at him, her eyes wide, her expression suddenly serious but a little bemused, as if she had no idea where he was going with this. "Remind me then. Why are you doing this?"

He was struck—not for the first time—that she wasn't merely cute, but truly beautiful. With her swoopy little button nose and her pixie dimples, her face had more than its share of cuteness. But she was also lovely, with her dark—almost violet—blue eyes and her luminous skin. Her beauty had an ephemeral quality to it. Like a woman in a Maxfield Parrish painting.

He was so struck by her beauty that for a second, he forgot her question. Forgot that he was trying to direct this conversation. To remind her that he wasn't some hero.

"I'm doing this for the same reason I've done everything else since I was eleven. I'm doing this because it serves my own goals. It serves FMJ."

She gave him an odd look, as something almost like pity flickered across her expression. "If you didn't want me to romanticize you, then maybe you shouldn't have tried to give me a big nasty chunk of your fortune. So I'm going to reserve the right to think you're not the heartless bastard you pretend to be."

"You have to believe me when I tell you that everything I've done for you was for my own benefit. Keeping you in California was the best thing for FMJ. Marrying you is the best thing for FMJ. That's the only reason I'm doing it."

Finally she nodded. "Okay. If you want to keep insisting you're so coldhearted, then I'll try to remind myself as often as possible. We'll start with the prenup, okay? We'll ask Randy to rewrite it so I have to pay you twenty percent of my money. How does that sound?" She smiled as she asked, but it looked strained.

"Wendy—" he started.

"At the very least, we'll put Randy out of his misery. We'll go with the bare-bones prenup. Everyone walks away with what they had when they came into the marriage."

He sighed. It wasn't what he wanted. Not by a long shot. But he was starting to realize that when it came to Wendy, he wasn't ever going to get what he wanted.

She paused at the door and looked over her shoulder, her forehead furrowed in thought. "The thing is, Jonathon, if you really were a heartless bastard, you wouldn't have warned me off."

Five

The next few days passed in a blur of planning and activity. Wendy often felt as if her life was moving at double time while she was stuck at half speed. She'd felt like that ever since she'd gotten that fateful call about Bitsy, less than two weeks before. Her shock and grief were finally beginning to recede into the background. Though she no longer faced the daunting challenge of moving back to Texas, agreeing to marry Jonathon had created even more turmoil in her life.

True to his word, Jonathon managed to cram in considerable work on the proposal for the government contract, delegating things he normally would have handled himself. Ford and Kitty flew home immediately with their daughter, Ilsa. Matt and Claire arrived a few days later, having cut short their honeymoon, something Wendy still felt bad about. Claire insisted that seventeen days in a tropical paradise was enough for anyone and that she wouldn't miss the wedding for anything. Her reassurances didn't make Wendy feel any less guilty.

The Sunday before the wedding, she was still half-asleep watching a rerun of *Dharma & Greg* wishing Peyton seemed half as drowsy. Jonathon had eventually convinced her that she should move into his house. Since they were planning on being married for a year or more, he pointed out that people were unlikely to believe they were truly in love if they weren't living together. The night before she'd pulled out her trusty suitcase and hoped to pack the bare essentials once Peyton fell asleep. If she could stay awake herself. She'd leave her other belongings for some later date.

She hadn't slept well since…well, since taking Peyton, and her exhaustion was creeping up on her. Frankly, it had been all she could do to drag herself out of bed this morning. The middle-of-the-night feedings were just not her thing. She was sitting on the sofa, blearily rocking back and forth, wondering if she could get Babies "R" Us to deliver a rocking chair by the end of the day, when the doorbell rang.

It was a bad sign that it took her so long to identify the noise.

She set the bottle down on the side table, stumbled to her feet and pried the door open, praying that no one on the other side would expect coherent conversation.

She frowned at the sight of Kitty and Claire. She'd only known Claire for seven months, but the concern lining the other woman's face was obvious in the crinkle between her brows. As if to distract from her frown, she thrust forward a pink bakery box with the Cutie Pies logo stamped on the top.

"We brought food!" Claire announced, her tone overly chipper. "We just flew in from Palo Verde this morning. I made this batch just before I left."

Claire owned a diner in the small town of Palo Verde, a couple of hours away. Jonathon, Ford and Matt had grown up in Palo Verde. If Claire had baked whatever was in the box, she couldn't wait to dive in. And if fate was kind at all, the box would be filled with the spicy, dark chocolate doughnuts that the diner was known for.

Kitty gave Wendy a once-over, then announced, "Since you're obviously too tired to invite us in, why not just step aside." She held out her hands. "Here, hand me the baby. You take the doughnuts. Please, eat some before I fight you for them."

Mutely, Wendy handed the fussy Peyton over to Kitty.

Kitty Langley was the kind of woman who looked as if she didn't have a maternal bone in her body. The jewelry-store-heiress-turned-jewelry-designer had lived in New York until falling in love with and marrying Ford the previous year. How that woman could look glamorous while cradling a baby in her arms, Wendy didn't know. But she did envy the skill, since she was pretty sure she herself looked as if she was recovering from the flu.

Wendy happily traded baby for doughnuts.

Though her arms ached from the hours of holding Peyton, the bone-deep weariness melted a bit as she sank her teeth into the dense buttermilk doughnut.

"I'm not sure why you came," she muttered past a mouthful of heaven. "But, frankly, I no longer care. You can hold me at gunpoint. Rob me. Even take the baby. Just leave the doughnuts and I'll be happy."

Kitty stifled a smile as she pressed her bright red lips to the crown of Peyton's head. "You're in that too-exhausted-to-be-tired stage, aren't you?"

After a few minutes of being held by Kitty, Peyton stopped fussing long enough to put her head down on Kitty's shoulder. And then there was silence. Peyton's eyes drifted closed and she exhaled a slow, shaky breath. Then her back settled into the gentle rhythm of sleep.

Tension seeped out of every pore in Wendy's body.

"Oh, thank goodness," she muttered.

Claire smiled wryly. "Did you get any sleep at all last night?"

"A couple of hours here and there," she admitted. "This caring for a baby gig is way harder than I expected."

"Oh, honey, you said a mouthful there." Kitty gave a low whistle, no doubt remembering her own new-to-mothering days. Walking with an exaggerated sway, Kitty crossed to the bassinet, so she could lay the baby down. "And at least I had seven months to get used to the idea."

The room fell silent as Kitty eased the sleeping Peyton down. Claire trotted off to the kitchen and returned a few minutes later with a steaming cup of coffee. "With cream and sugar," she said as she handed it over. "I assume all sane people take it that way."

Wendy took a grateful sip as Kitty asked, "Can we get you anything else? Something to eat maybe? I can't cook worth a damn, but Claire could McGyver a feast out of the barest cupboard."

Wendy didn't doubt it. "I think I'll save room for another doughnut."

"You sure?" Claire asked, in hushed tones so as not to wake the baby. "I could whip up an omelet. Or something else? I saw some nice Gouda in the fridge when I was foraging for cream." With a smile she added, "I could make you a grilled cheese sandwich so good you'll cry."

"No, thank you."

"You should try the grilled cheese," Kitty urged. "It's amazing."

"No, really. I'm okay." Wendy looked from Kitty to Claire, suddenly suspicious. "Why do I get the feeling I'm being plied with food for nefarious reasons?"

Kitty and Claire exchanged a look.

Wendy raised an eyebrow. "Come on, spill. What's up?"

Claire's cheeks reddened with what Wendy could only assume was guilt. Kitty played her cards closer to her chest. Her expression revealed nothing.

"Okay, obviously you have some bad news for me. Either that or you're going to try to get me to join a cult. Which is it?"

Claire bit down on her lip, her chin jutting out at a rebellious angle.

Kitty gave a little eye roll and sighed with obvious exasperation. "Fine," Kitty said, managing to flounce a bit while sitting almost perfectly still. "We're worried about Jonathon."

Wendy gave a little grunt of surprise and sat back against the sofa. "Worried? About Jonathon?"

"Whatever is going on between you and Jonathon," Claire began, "obviously has something to do with Peyton."

Wendy opened her mouth to protest, but Kitty didn't give her a chance.

"Jonathon wouldn't talk about it, so I assume you won't either. That's fine. But we're not idiots. Don't forget, you told Ford why you were resigning just twenty-four hours before you and Jonathon announced you were getting married. If I had to guess, I'd say you're pretending to be some happily married couple so your family will let you keep Peyton."

Well, so much for hiding the truth from their friends.

"As convoluted and bizarre as that seems," Kitty continued. "We're not going to try to stop you."

"We'll even play along," Claire added in. "Anything you need from us, you've got."

"But when you're off playing house together, just be very careful."

For a long moment, Wendy had no idea what to say. She turned away from their careful scrutiny and walked over to the bassinet where Peyton lay sleeping.

She thought about the conversation she'd had with Jonathon before they'd signed the prenup. Apparently, he wasn't the only one who thought she was in danger of falling in love with him. And here she'd thought she'd hid her attraction to him so well over the years. Was she really so transparent?

Glancing back at Kitty and Claire, she forced a perky smile. "Look, I admit Jonathon is a great guy. I've always thought so. But I know his dating history probably better than either one of you. I know he doesn't open up easily. I'm not going to make the mistake of falling in love with him."

Claire and Kitty exchanged nervous glances, seeming to have an entire conversation with just their eyebrows.

"What?" Wendy demanded after a second, crossing back to the sofa to get a better view of their unspoken exchange.

Claire kept her mouth shut.

But it was Kitty who admitted, "Actually, it's him we're worried about."

Wendy sank back to the sofa. "You're worried about Jonathon? Falling in love with me?"

Claire nodded.

"Not me falling in love with him, but him. Falling in love. With me."

Kitty gave an elegant wave of her hand. "Obviously we don't want to see you left brokenhearted either. But you're a smart woman. Very practical. We just assumed you can look out for yourself."

"But you're worried that Jonathon, the brilliant, analytical CFO is going to get his feelings hurt?" Wendy fought back a giggle.

"Well," Claire hedged. "Yes."

Wendy looked from one woman to the other, her amusement fading. "You're serious?"

They nodded.

"I know that Jonathon seems…" Claire trailed off, searching for the right word.

"Detached," Kitty provided. "Ruthless."

Claire glared her into silence. "You're not helping."

"Like a heartless bastard," Wendy offered quietly.

"Yes!" Kitty agreed.

"But he really isn't," Claire said quickly. "Don't forget, I've known him longer than you have."

Which was technically true. Claire had grown up in the same small town as Matt, Ford and Jonathon. "But you're younger than he is. You didn't even go to school together."

"We overlapped some," Claire argued. "And I've seen him in love. Senior year, he was…" she trailed off, apparently struggling to convey the full force of his emotion. "He was just head over heels in love. Crazy in love with this girl. He would have done anything for her."

"Who was she?" Wendy found herself asking.

Claire hesitated. "Just a girl at school. Kristi hadn't grown up in Palo Verde. Her parents were divorced and she moved there to live with her dad her sophomore year."

"And they dated?"

"A little." Then Claire shrugged. "I think mostly he just chased her. She flirted a lot. He was completely determined to win her over. Any grand gesture you can imagine an eighteen-year-old guy making, he made it. Flowers, jewelry. The whole nine yards."

Flowers and jewelry? She knew he didn't have a lot of money growing up. He'd once told her he'd started saving money for college when he was twelve. She couldn't even imagine the man she knew taking money out of his precious college fund to buy gifts. For a girlfriend.

"Once," Claire said, leaning forward and warming up to the story, "she told him that her mother always bought her birthday cake from the same bakery. She'd grown up in San Francisco. So for her birthday, the guys made a road trip out to San Francisco to buy her a cake. On a school day. They got in so much trouble." Claire chuckled for a second. Then seemed to realize how much she'd revealed about herself. Her blush returned as she sank back against the sofa.

"You were a little bit of a stalker, weren't you?" Kitty asked, grinning.

"I had a crush on Matt. That's all." Then she smiled smugly. "Besides, he eventually came around."

"I'll say." Kitty bumped her shoulder against Claire's in easy camaraderie.

"So what happened?" Wendy asked, unwilling to leave the thread of Jonathon's story dangling. "Why did they break up?"

"That's the thing." Claire gave a little shrug. "I'm not sure they were ever really together. And not long after the birthday cake thing, she moved back in with her mother. Jonathon was…"

"Heartbroken," Kitty supplied.

"No." Claire frowned thoughtfully. "He was just never the same." She gave her head a little shake, as if she was returning to the present. "But I know it's still there, buried inside of him. The capacity to love like that."

Claire and Kitty exchanged another one of those pointed glances and Wendy felt a stab of envy. This girl he'd loved, Kristi… Wendy had never been loved like that. Kitty and Claire, that's what they had with their husbands. But no one had ever felt that way about Wendy.

She pushed herself to her feet. "I don't think you have to worry. He doesn't love me. I'm sure of it." She forced a bright smile. "You can go home and rest assured that I'm not going to crush his delicate heart beneath my boot heel."

"It's not just you we're worried about." Kitty stood also and looked across the room to the bassinet. "What about Peyton?"

"What about Peyton?"

"Have you ever seen Jonathon with Ilsa?" Kitty asked.

"I—" Then she broke off. Remembering that she had, once, seen him holding Ilsa. Right after she'd been born, Wendy had brought flowers by and Jonathon had been there, an expression of pure wonder on his face as he held the baby.

She nodded, rubbing at her temple, trying to dispel the tension headache that was spiking through her head. When had this all gotten so complicated?

"He's fantastic with kids," Kitty was saying. "He adores Ilsa. He's been bugging us to have another one in fact."

"And if you are getting married just to fool your family," Claire said. "And he falls in love with you or that darling little girl, how do you think he's going to feel when you end the marriage?"

"I—" What could she say to that? She'd never imagined Jonathon might fall in love with her. The idea was preposterous. But Peyton? Yeah. She could imagine that. And if they

really were married for two years—it might take that long—
then he'd have plenty of time for Peyton to wrap him around
her tiny finger. She looked up at Kitty and Claire and found
them watching her expectantly. "All I can say, is that when...*if*
we get divorced, I wouldn't dream of keeping him away from
Peyton. If he wants to see her, that is. From this moment on,
I'll think of him as her father. Just as I think of myself as her
mother."

Jonathon as a father. The idea was...so foreign. So odd.
Yet, she knew in her heart that Kitty and Claire were right
to warn her. He was doing this amazing thing for her. She
didn't want him to get hurt because of it and she would do
everything in her power to make sure he didn't. She only
wished she was half as confident in her ability to protect
herself.

After a long moment, Kitty stood and gave a dramatic sigh.
"Very well, then. I suppose there's only one thing left to
do."

"What's that?" Wendy asked, hesitantly.

Kitty's face broke into a smile. "Welcome you to the family."

Six

The wedding itself went off with all the precision of a well-planned military maneuver. And it was just about as romantic. A small ceremony performed in a drab municipal office in downtown Palo Alto, it was over so quickly that Jonathon felt sure Claire and Matt wished they had stayed in Curaçao instead of making the trip back.

After that first kiss in her office had gotten so out of control, he didn't even dare cement the ceremony with more than a quick peck. So much for convincing their friends that they were in love. But no one in the office that day seemed surprised, least of all Wendy.

That evening, they swung by Wendy's apartment to pick up her suitcase and Peyton's few possessions before heading over to his house. They'd decided to keep her apartment for now. Her lease wasn't up for another few months, which would give her plenty of time to decide when she wanted to move into his house and what she wanted to keep in storage. When they arrived at his house, they discovered that Claire had made them dinner, and they found it waiting for them in the warming drawer of his kitchen.

He stood beside Wendy in the doorway to the kitchen, staring at the table with a fist clenching his heart. The table had been set with two of the elegant place settings his interior designer had bought seven years ago and which he'd never used. Long, thin tapers sat in the center of the table, a book of matches propped against the candle holder. In between the two chairs sat the new Svan high chair he'd had delivered. A bottle of unopened champagne sat chilling in a bucket opposite the high chair.

Wendy cleared her throat. "Um…" She hitched Peyton up on her hip. "I think I'll just…um…unpack a few of the bags first." Her gaze looked from the wine to him. "I'm not really hungry yet."

Before he could muster a response, she took the final suitcase from him and made a dash for the door. Probably a wise decision. Neither of them was ready yet for a intimate dinner. Let alone wine.

Three hours later, she still hadn't made it back down to eat. He'd sat at the table himself, eating in front of his laptop. Finally, he shut his laptop and went in search of Wendy. He found her upstairs in the room he'd set aside as a nursery.

He paused just outside the door. Leaning his shoulder against the doorjamb, for a long moment he simply watched her. The room had been painted pale pink. Butterflies fluttered across the walls and bunnies frolicked in the grass painted along the trim. A white crib sat in the corner under a mobile of more butterflies and flowers. Overall, the décor of the room was a little cloying in its sweetness, but the decorator had assured him that it was perfect for the new addition to his life. This evening, he barely noticed the butterflies, but rather focused his attention on the woman sitting in the rocking chair in the corner and the baby she held in her arms.

At some point, Wendy had changed out of the dress and into a pair of jeans and a white V-neck T-shirt. Peyton was asleep in her arms. Her eyes were closed, her head tilted back against the headrest of the rocking chair. Only the faint tensing of her calf as she occasionally nudged the chair into movement indicated that she wasn't asleep too.

He cleared his throat to let her know he was there.

Her head bobbed up. "Oh," she said, wiggling in the chair to reposition Peyton in her arms without waking her. "How long have you been there?"

"I just walked up."

She glanced down at the baby in her arms as Peyton stirred but didn't wake. "I suppose I should put her down," she whispered. "But I hate to do it. If she wakes up again…"

If the smudges of exhaustion under her eyes were any indication, Peyton wasn't the easiest of babies. No wonder given the upheaval in her young life.

"If she wakes back up," he found himself saying, "then I'll take over and you can get some sleep. You should go eat."

Wendy shook her head. "I can't ask you to do that. That's not why we got married."

There was almost a hint of accusation in her voice.

"Maybe not," he hedged. "But we are married now. And you obviously could use the sleep. At this point, I'm more rested than you are. A sleepless night won't hurt me, but a good night's sleep could do you a world of good."

"If she needs a bottle in the night—"

"Then I'll give it to her."

Wendy looked skeptical. "The bottles are downstairs. You just—"

"I saw you mixing the formula. I've got it."

"But—"

"Wendy, I'm one of five kids. I had a niece and two nephews before I graduated from high school. Peyton won't be the first baby I've ever fed."

"Oh." After a moment of hesitation, she stood and crossed to the crib.

As he'd told her, he knew his way around an infant. It

was so obvious to him that she did not. There was a sort of fearful hesitancy to the way she moved. As if she were afraid of breaking Peyton.

She lowered the baby into the crib then stood there for a long moment, her hand resting on Peyton before she moved back a step. She cringed as she raised the side of the bed and the hardware clattered. But Peyton slept on and Wendy slowly backed away.

She paused as she closed the door to unclip the baby monitor from her hip and turn it on, as if Peyton might start crying any second and Wendy would miss it now that she was out of sight. He couldn't help chuckling when she raised the monitor to her ear to listen more closely.

She shot him an annoyed look. "What?"

"You know you're only one room away. You could probably hear her cry without the monitor." When she looked as if she might comment, he reached out and carefully extracted it from her fingers. "Not that you're going to need this tonight anyway."

"I really don't mind staying up with her."

"The discussion is over."

She opened her mouth to respond, then snapped it shut, her lips twisting into a smile. "I guess I know you well enough to recognize that I'm-the-boss-and-what-I-say-goes tone."

"I have a tone that says all that?"

She snorted her derision. "Yeah. And don't pretend you don't know it." She took a step in the direction of the room at the end of the hall—the guest room she'd claimed for her own—then she paused. "You didn't have to do this, you know."

"Wendy, let's not have another discussion about my motives."

She took another step toward him, closing the distance between them and lowering her voice. "No. I'm not talking about the wedding. I'm talking about all this." She nodded her head in the direction of Peyton's room. "I mean the nursery. The crib. The rocking chair. It's all—"

"It's nothing."

She quirked an eyebrow. "Like the twenty percent nothing? Unless you were up all night hand-painting butterflies and daisies last night, I'm guessing you hired an interior decorator to come in and do this. In less than a week. That's not nothing."

"Kitty mentioned that all you had was a bassinet."

She smiled a slow, teasing smile. "And you knew that wasn't enough. Being such an expert on babies and everything."

He was struck once again by the idea that this was their wedding night. That if there wasn't a baby asleep in the next room, he might now be slowly lifting that sweater up over her head. He might be unhooking that hot-pink bra of hers and stripping her naked.

But of course, if there wasn't a baby asleep in the next room, then there wouldn't have been a wedding to begin with. Let alone a wedding night.

Suddenly she reached up and cupped his jaw in her hand. Her gaze was soft, her touch gentle. "Thanks for taking such good care of us."

For a solid heartbeat—maybe longer—his brain seemed to completely stop working. He couldn't remember all the reasons why touching her was such a bad idea. All he knew was how much he wanted her. Not just in bed, but here. Like this. Looking up at him as if he was a decent guy who deserved a woman like her.

Before he could give in to the temptation to let her go on thinking that, he grabbed her hand in his and gently pulled it away from his face. Backing up a step, he said, "You should go to bed. Catch up on that sleep you've been missing."

He even used his I'm-the-boss tone.

"Right." She gave a chipper little salute. "Got it, boss."

* * *

Wendy had been so sure she wouldn't be able to sleep. She'd been positive she'd find herself waking at every sound coming from Peyton's room. She feared that she'd lie awake in bed thinking about the moment in the hall. But instead of the sleepless night she expected, she woke ten hours later to sun streaming in her bedroom window, feeling more rested than she had in weeks. Then she bolted upright in bed as panic clogged her heart. She'd slept through the night. Which meant she'd slept through Peyton waking and needing her God only knew how many times.

Wendy dashed down the hall and into Peyton's room, skidding to a halt beside the crib. It was empty. Her heart doubled its already accelerated rate. Where could—

"Morning."

She spun around to see Jonathon seated in the rocking chair, Peyton nestled on his lap as he fed her a bottle. Wendy pressed a hand to her chest, blowing out a whoosh of air, willing her heart rate to slow.

"You have her," she muttered. "She's fine."

Jonathon gave her a once-over, his gaze lingering on the tank top and boxers she always slept in. Finally his eyes returned to hers. "What did you think had happened to her?"

Wendy tugged at the hem of the thin white cotton, resisting the urge to glance down to verify just how thin the tank top was. She doubted knowing would bring her comfort. Instead she crossed her arms over her chest. "I don't know," she admitted. "It's the first morning in…what, almost three weeks now, that she hasn't been the one to wake me. For all I knew, she'd been abducted by aliens. I panicked."

His lips curved in an amused smile. "Obviously."

For a second she was entranced by the transformation of his face. He had a smooth, charming smile he used at work. She thought of it as his client-wooing smile. He also had a wolfish grin. That was his I'm-about-to-devour-some-innocent-company expression.

Neither of those reached his eyes. Neither held any warmth.

But this slight, amused twist of his lips wrinkled the corners of his eyes, and it nearly took her breath away.

Before she could respond, or do something really stupid, like melt into a puddle at his feet, he continued. "Peyton and I have been up for hours now."

"I'm—"

"Don't apologize. I'd have woken you if she'd been any trouble."

Wendy's eyebrows shot up. When was Peyton not trouble? She fussed a lot. Wanted to be held constantly. Screamed anytime Wendy put her down. In general, made Wendy feel like a real winner as a parent.

"We got up a couple of hours ago," Jonathon was saying. He continued rocking as he spoke, looking down at Peyton the whole time. "She had her morning bottle. Then we made me some oatmeal. She sat on my lap while I read through some emails. She spit up a little on the office floor. Thank God for the plastic mat my chair sits on, right, Peyton?"

Oookay. Maybe that explained why his smile looked so different than his normal grin. Obviously, it was Jonathon who'd been abducted by aliens and replaced by some sort of pod person. The man before her bore no resemblance to the cold and calculating businessman she'd dealt with for the past five years.

Unfortunately, this new guy was way more appealing, which was so annoying.

Jonathon looked up at her, his expression clouding with concern. "Anything wrong?"

"No, I… Why?"

"You looked a little, faint or something."

"No. I'm…great. Fantastic. But hungry. That's it. I must be hungry."

"Okay." The concern lining his brow had taken on a decidedly skeptical gleam. As though he suspected she might need to spend a little time in a padded room. "Why not get dressed and grab yourself some breakfast. Peyton and I will be fine here."

As if to signal her assent, Peyton blinked up at him with wide blue eyes, then gave the bottle a particularly vigorous suck before sighing and allowing her eyes to drift closed. She looked for all the world like a baby completely happy and at peace.

Emotion choked Wendy's throat, something that felt unpleasantly like envy. She'd worked her butt off for that baby over the past few weeks, turned her life upside down, prepared to battle her family to the end. And yet Peyton had never once looked up at her with dreamy contentment. Then again, Jonathon always had been quick to win over the ladies.

Wendy sighed. "I wish she was half as peaceful in my arms as she is with you."

"Why do you say that?"

Because if growing up a Morgan had taught her anything, it was that the best way to deal with negative emotions was to voice them aloud. Get them out into the open rather than letting them simmer. Still, admitting such a feeling was unpleasant, so she softened her words with a diffident shrug. "She seems to fight me constantly. Makes me wonder if—" Wendy blew out a breath. "I don't know, if she knows something I don't. If she knows I don't have what it takes to be a good mother."

When she looked back at Jonathon, his smile was still there, but the humor in his eyes had dimmed to understanding.

"The thing about dealing with babies—" he gently pulled the bottle nipple from Peyton's mouth, then maneuvered her so her belly rested against his shoulder "—it's about five percent instinct and ninety-five percent experience. Plus, they're very intuitive—that's all they've got. So if you're nervous, she'll pick up on it and she'll be nervous too."

Jonathon gave Peyton's back several thumps. After about the tenth, she burped without even opening her eyes.

"How'd you do that? I can never get her to burp."

"Like I said. It's experience. If she's been a difficult baby so far, it's not because she has you pegged as a bad parent. You just don't know all the tricks yet. Besides, she's been through a lot in her short life."

Was it really that simple? Time would heal all wounds? Watching Peyton sleep on Jonathon's shoulder, Wendy certainly hoped so. But she couldn't help worrying if there was more to it than that. That there were deficiencies no amount of experience could compensate for. After all, she'd never be Peyton's real mother.

Almost as if he could read her mind, Jonathon added, "Give her some time. Give yourself some time too." Then Jonathon let out a bark of laughter. "Jeez, I sound like Dr. Phil."

She laughed along with him, despite the lump of sorrow burrowing into her chest. "Don't worry. I won't tell anyone at work."

"Thanks."

A moment of silence stretched between them. She should leave. Take advantage of Peyton's sleep to go shower or something. Yet she found her feet rooted to the ground as she watched him rocking the tiny infant.

"Why aren't you a father?" she asked, almost before she realized she meant to say it.

He arched an eyebrow.

Heat crept into her cheeks. "I mean, clearly you're great with kids. It seems like a no-brainer that you should have some of your own."

"I get frustrated enough trying to get Matt to clean up his third of the office."

"I'm serious."

"So am I. I've never had any desire to be a father." His tone was harsh, leaving no room for doubt. The touchy-feely portion of their discussion was over. "She should be asleep for a couple of hours at least. You should take advantage of it and get some breakfast."

"Thanks. I will."

She left the room without looking back, but with his words still echoing in her mind. He'd never wanted to be a father. Yet he'd just signed up for a two-year gig. She'd assumed when he asked her to marry him that he wouldn't be playing an active role in raising Peyton. But less than twenty-four hours in and he'd cared for Peyton more than she had.

He was going to an awful lot of trouble to keep her around. She could only hope she was half as good an assistant as he thought she was. Because she was certainly going to need to earn her keep.

Since he'd insisted repeatedly that he didn't need her, she wandered down to the kitchen for breakfast. She'd never even stepped into his house before last night. It wasn't quite what she'd expected. Like Matt, a few years before, Jonathon had bought one of the ridiculously expensive craftsman houses in Old Palo Alto. Though the homes were aging and modest, the neighborhood was one of the more expensive in the country. The interior of Jonathon's house had been renovated to its early-20th-century glory with meticulous detail. The furniture was a collection of authentic Mission antiques and clean-lined Japanese pieces that complemented them. She found the kitchen surprisingly well stocked. Not in the mood to cook anything, she rummaged through his pantry until she found a box of Pop-Tarts. She eyed them warily for a second—because Jonathon so did not seem like the Frosted Strawberry Pop-Tart type—then snagged a package and headed back upstairs.

She took a leisurely shower, nibbling on the pastry as she dressed. Jonathon had never been one of those men who didn't know how to ask for help. If he'd needed her before now, he would have woken her up. She'd gotten enough phone calls at six o'clock in the morning over the years to know that. Whatever he was doing with Peyton, he didn't need her immediately. Confident that Peyton must still be asleep, she took the time to linger over her grooming in a way she hadn't in the past couple of weeks. She did things like brush her hair. Floss her teeth. And put on ChapStick.

The rest had done wonders for her. Not only had she finally gotten a decent night's sleep, but obviously Jonathon had handled Peyton with perfect competence. Just as he'd said he would. That one small thing renewed her faith in this whole endeavor.

They had a week before they left for Texas. Which was more than enough time for them to settle into enough of a routine to fool her parents and family about their relationship. Jonathon obviously knew enough about babies that he'd be able to help her over the rough spots she was sure to encounter.

They'd spend a quick weekend in Texas convincing her family that they were Peyton's perfect guardians. Then they'd head back to Palo Alto and their lives would return to normal. Or as normal as they could be since she and Jonathon were now married and living together. All in all, life seemed damn good.

Once she'd verified that Peyton wasn't asleep in the nursery, she headed downstairs. She was about halfway down the stairs when she heard voices. Trepidation tripped along her nerves as she paused, head tilted to better hear the conversation coming from the kitchen.

Heart pounding, she made her way there. It could be Ford or Matt. Or a neighbor. Or… Then she heard it. Just outside the swinging door leading into the kitchen. A deep Texas twang.

"We would have come earlier if you'd given us more warning that y'all were fixin' to get married."

She squeezed her eyes closed, fighting back a burst of panic as she blew out a long breath. Then she shoved open the door and walked into the kitchen. To face her family.

Seven

Having lived his entire life in the northern half of California, Jonathon had weathered his share of earthquakes. He'd long ago gotten over whatever fear he might have had of them. But there were plenty of other act-of-God weather systems that scared the crap out of him. Tornadoes. Hurricanes. Tsunamis.

Anything that would swoop in and level an entire coastal plain deserved a healthy dose of respectful fear.

Clearly, Wendy's family fell into that category.

About ten minutes after Wendy had disappeared to take a shower, her family had arrived on his doorstep in a tidal wave of hearty handshakes, welcoming slaps and tearful hugs. It was a bit overwhelming, given that he'd never met any of them and would have had no idea who they were if he hadn't recognized her uncle, Big Hank, from the news clips he'd seen of the senator. And before Jonathon knew it, Wendy's parents, Tim and Marion, had swept into the house, followed by Big Hank, carefully lending an arm to the infamous Mema.

Jonathon had barely recovered from the stinging clap on

the arm from Big Hank, when he faced down Mema. After Wendy's description, he'd half expected an old battleship of a woman. Instead, Mema was thin and stooped, fragile in appearance despite the strength of will that seemed to radiate from her.

A hush fell over the other members of the family as she shook his hand and appraised him. She had the wizened appearance of a woman who had lived hard and buried too many loved ones, but who was not yet ready to release her control over the rest of her clan.

She eyed him up and down. "Well, at least you're real."

"You doubted it?" he asked.

She sniffed indignantly. "I wouldn't put it past Gwen to invent a husband just to defy me."

"I assure you, ma'am. I'm real."

"As for what kind of father you'll be for my great-granddaughter, that we'll have to see about." Then her steely gaze narrowed with sharp perception and raked over Jonathon a second time. Finally she gave a little nod. "I've never had much use for overly handsome men. But then, neither has my Gwen, so I suppose there must be more to you than good looks."

He offered a wry smile. "I should hope so."

It was almost thirty minutes later when Wendy came down. The guarded look on her face as she walked through the door told him she'd heard them before entering the kitchen.

She was greeted with hugs that lasted longer and more joyful tears than he would have expected, given the way she'd described the strained relationship she shared with her family. Throughout it all, she kept a careful eye on Peyton, who was currently being held by Wendy's mother, as if Wendy expected that any moment the family might escape with the baby.

"What are y'all doing here?" she asked when she was finally able to get a word in edgewise.

He suppressed a smile. In five years, he'd never heard a

hint of the Texas accent her family all sported. But three minutes in their company and she was slipping into *y'alls*.

"Oh, honey," her mother cooed, her voice all sugary sweet. "Of course we would come for your wedding. If we'd had enough warning, we would have been here." She shook her head, tears brimming in her eyes. "I can't believe I missed the wedding of my only daughter."

"I did tell you a week ago we were getting married. If you'd really wanted to come, you could have."

"But Big Hank had the jet in D.C.," her mother bemoaned, "and we had to wait until he could fit the trip into his schedule."

Jonathon felt a pang of regret, but Wendy muttered, "I'm glad to know you found the idea of flying commercial more repugnant than the prospect of missing my wedding."

Tim's head snapped up. "Young lady, you'll speak respectfully to your mother."

"Or what?" Wendy asked, anger creeping into her voice. "You'll cut off my allowance? The woman has missed almost every major event in my life since I was ten. And those that she showed up for, she criticized endlessly. I think she'll live."

"Gwen—" her mother started to protest.

Then Mema cleared her throat and both Wendy and her mother fell silent. Their heads swiveled to face her.

"In the wake of our Bitsy's recent and tragic death, it is time for you to put aside your past differences." She stared them both down. Mother and daughter both dropped their gazes. "Now, the flight from Texas was long and I'd like to clean up before resting a bit before lunch." She turned to Jonathon. "I assume all the bedrooms are on the second floor?"

"They are," he said, not sure what she was getting at.

"Very well, then. I noticed an office just off the foyer. I'll sleep there. I don't do stairs well. Big Hank, please arrange for a bed to be delivered before evening. In the meantime, I'll rest on the sofa there."

Jonathon watched in amazement as a senior U.S. senator practically leaped to help his mother out of the kitchen. A moment later, Wendy's father had been sent out to the limo to instruct the driver where to bring the bags, and her mother had retreated to the nursery "to get reacquainted with her great-niece."

The second Jonathon and Wendy were all alone, she practically threw up her hands. "Why didn't you come get me the second they arrived?"

"You were dressing. I told them they could wait until you came down."

She tilted her head, studying him as if he were some foreign life form she'd never seen before. "You stood up to them?"

Ah. So that's what had her so puzzled. "Yes. I stood up to them. Do people not normally do that?"

She gave a bemused chuckle. "No. People don't normally do that." Shaking her head, she started carrying coffee cups from the kitchen table to the sink. Almost under her breath, she said, "I once dated a guy whose parents were lifelong members of Greenpeace. He'd spent every summer since he was ten on boats protesting whaling in Japan. He'd marched on Washington forty-four times before he was twenty. He'd been a vegan since he was three. Within thirty minutes of meeting my family, he was eating barbeque and smoking cigars out on the back porch with Big Hank." Shaking her head, she started rinsing out coffee cups and loading them into the dishwasher. "Within a week, he'd accepted a job working for my dad."

Jonathon studied the tense lines of her back. Her tone had been sad, but resigned. "The guy sounds like an idiot."

"No. He was very smart. The last I heard, Jed was VP of marketing for Morgan Oil. And Daddy would never promote anyone that high up who wasn't brilliant."

Jonathon gently turned her away from the sink and tipped

her chin up to look at him. "That's not the kind of idiot I mean."

Her gaze met his, confusion in her eyes for a minute. Then her gaze cleared as she realized his meaning. Pink tinged her cheeks and pulled away from his touch. Tucking her hair back behind her ear she swallowed. "Thank you. For standing up to them, I mean. For everything."

"You're welcome."

She gave a bitter laugh. "You say that now. But you don't actually know what you've gotten yourself into." She looked pointedly at the kitchen door through which her family had left not long before. "This nonsense with them sweeping down on us unannounced? Inviting themselves to stay here? Ordering a bed for Mema to sleep on? This is all just the beginning. It'll only get worse."

"Of course it will," he stated as blandly as he could. "You think I didn't know that the second I opened the door?"

"I…I don't know. I guess… Most people don't see them for what they are."

"Try to have a little faith in me," he chided.

"I'm just warning you. My dad and Uncle Hank will woo you with their good ol' boy charm. And just when you think that you're their buddy and they're nothing more than simple roughnecks, they'll use that keen intelligence of theirs to manipulate you. And if they can't control you, they'll try to squash you."

"Consider me warned." He nodded. "Coming here was obviously a power play. They think they have the upper hand because they've chosen the time and location of the showdown. They're trying to establish themselves as the decision makers in the relationship. What about your mother? She seems harmless enough."

"Um, no." Wendy thought about it. Of all the family members, her relationship with her mother was the most complicated. There were times when she actually liked her mother. Of course, she loved all of them, but her mother she actually liked. But she'd never understood her. And her mother had her moments of being just as vicious as Uncle Hank. "In all those scuba-diving trips you take, you ever been in the water with a jellyfish?"

"Several times. They sting like hell."

"Exactly. They look delicate and frail, but they have more than enough defenses. That's my mother in a nutshell. She can play the victim, but she's as smart as—" That's when it hit her. "Oh, crap."

"What?"

"The bedroom!" She leaped to her feet and dashed for the stairs.

Jonathon snagged her arm on the way past. "What?"

She whispered, just in case anyone was close enough to hear, "The guest bedroom. Where I slept last night."

He continued to stare blankly at her. Seriously? Mr. Genius couldn't figure this out?

She lowered her voice to a hiss. "Last night. On our wedding night. I slept in the guest bedroom." She resisted the urge to bop him on the forehead. "And now my mother is upstairs with Peyton. And if she sees the guest bedroom, she'll realize we didn't sleep together last night."

This time, she didn't wait around to see if his sluggish brain had started working at normal speed. Instead, she pulled her arm from his hand and made a break for the stairs. He was hot on her heels as she took the stairs two at a time.

She stopped at the top, breathing rapidly through her mouth and she looked around for her parents. A long gallery hall ran from the top of the stairs to the guest room at the end. They'd have to pass the nursery to get there.

Crap, crap and double crap.

This was going to be tricky. She crept down the hall, praying that Jonathon would walk as softly. Or head back downstairs if he couldn't.

She tiptoed right up to the doorway and pressed herself

against the wall, listening. She heard the faint, steady creak, creak of a rocking chair.

If her mom was sitting in the chair rocking Peyton, there was a good chance Wendy could sneak past to the guest bedroom, make the bed and sneak out with anyone being the wiser. Or more importantly, becoming suspicious.

Slinking past the door, she heard two things that would have stopped her in her tracks if she hadn't been in such a desperate hurry. The first was Jonathon's heavy footfall behind her. The next was her father's voice from within the nursery.

She glanced through the open door, but saw no one. Maybe they'd make it. But when she heard the rocking chair still, she grabbed Jonathon's hand and made a dash for it.

If her parents heard them and followed, she and Jonathon would never have time to actually make the bed. Certainly not neatly enough to put her father off the scent.

And this wasn't the day to leave up to fate.

Pulling Jonathon into the room after her, turning him so his back was to the door, she flashed him a wry smile. "Sorry about this."

"About what?"

She only had an instant to appreciate how charming he looked with that bemused expression on his face before she launched herself at him. They both tumbled backward onto the bed in a tangle of arms and legs. He might have gasped with surprise. She didn't have a chance to notice, as she pressed her mouth to his and kissed him.

The second Jonathon felt Wendy's mouth on his, he gave up trying to figure out what she was doing. She'd been babbling about the bedroom one minute and kissing him like a woman overwhelmed by desire the next. A smart man knew when to hold his questions for later.

Instead, he wrapped his hand around the back of her head and deepened the kiss. Her lips moved over his in sensual abandon, her tongue stroking against his in the kind of soul-deep kiss that made a man forget everything except the burning need to possess.

Desire pounded through him, heating his blood and tightening his groin. He fought against the desperate need to strip her naked and plow into her. A need that had been building within him for what seemed like years. Hell, probably had been years. As desperately as he wanted her, he didn't want this. This frantic, rapid rush of sex without fulfillment.

He wanted more. He wanted all of her.

Rolling her over onto her back, he took control of the kiss. Her hand had started pulling his shirt out from his waistband. If her hot little hand so much as touched his bare chest, he'd lose the last shreds of his control. So he grabbed both her hands in his and pulled them over her head, pinning them there. She let out a low groan, arching her back off the bed.

Yes. This was what he wanted: her, on the brink. As desperate and needy as he felt.

He slowed the kiss down, exploring every sweet corner of her mouth. Loving her sleepy flavor, the faint hint of coffee. The smooth heat of her tongue against his. Her hips bucked against his as she ground the vee between her legs against the length of his erection. Even through the multiple layers of her clothes, he could feel the heat of her.

But it wasn't enough. Merely kissing her would never be enough. Not when there was so much of her body left to explore. That silken shoulder that had been tempting him for so long. That tender swath of skin along her collarbone. The hollow at the base of her throat. The glimpse of her belly he sometimes saw when she rose up on her toes to get a fresh ream of printer paper.

His hand sought the hem of her shirt. He slipped his hand up to her rib cage, relishing how incredibly soft her skin was. He felt the edge of her bra and hesitated. He'd waited years to touch her naked skin. His hand damn near trembled at the prospect.

But was this really what he wanted? A quick grope in the guest bedroom when her family was just down the hall?

No, he wanted her naked. Laid out before him like a feast. He wanted hours. Days.

He wanted—

Jonathon's head jerked up as he pulled back from Wendy and sent her a piercing look.

Her family was just down the hall. What the hell had she been—

A sound came from the doorway. A man clearing his voice.

Jonathon whipped his head around and saw Wendy's parents standing in the doorway. Her mom, a perfect, older version of Wendy, stood with her hands propped on her hips, but the teasing smile on her lips softened any reproach in her gaze. Wendy's father, on the other hand, looked ready to throttle him.

With good reason.

The man had just caught him groping his daughter like a desperate teenager.

Wendy's dad growled—actually growled—with displeasure and took a step toward him. Wendy's mother grabbed her husband by the arm. Though the petite woman couldn't possibly have had the strength to stop the man in his tracks, her touch still gave him pause.

"Wendy, your father and I will be waiting for you in the hall. Why don't you come out in a minute when you've had a chance to get yourselves…under control."

A moment later the guest bedroom door closed.

Jonathon rolled off Wendy, planted his feet firmly on the ground and dropped his head into his waiting hands.

What a mess.

Wendy's parents—waiting in the hall with her dad looking as if he wanted to chew his ass out—were the least of his worries. Whatever criticism they'd deliver he'd take.

None of it would come even close to the talking to he was going to give himself. He'd completely lost control. For several moments there, he'd forgotten where they were. Forgotten that she wasn't really his to take whenever he wanted. Forgotten that this was merely a sham.

Worse still, she hadn't. Clearly, she'd manipulated the situation—manipulated him—all so that her family wouldn't notice the fact that she'd obviously slept in the guest room. And it hadn't even occurred to him that that's what she had been doing.

He drew in several deep breaths, but barely felt calmer. The scent of her was heavy in the air, and with every breath she only seemed to fill more of the room, rather than less. That faint pepperminty smell that was uniquely her. His very hands seemed steeped in her.

He sat fully up, looking over his shoulder. She'd scrambled back into the corner of the bed, pressed against the headboard. She looked almost afraid of him. He didn't blame her. His control felt too shaky just now to offer her any reassurances.

She bit down on her lip as she tucked a strand of hair behind her ear. It was a ridiculous effort, fixing that one strand of hair when the rest were still so mussed.

"I—" she started to say, then cleared her throat. "Boy, that was close."

Not trusting himself to say anything just yet, he merely raised one eyebrow. Apparently she had no idea just how close that had been. Just how lucky she was that her parents had walked in, since he'd been about three minutes away from taking her right there.

"I—I'm sorry," she stammered. "I couldn't think of any other way to distract them from the bed."

He pushed himself to his feet. "I doubt your parents noticed the bed."

She scrambled up onto her knees. "No. I mean, that was the idea, right?"

He gave a tight little nod, hating her a little bit in that

moment. Or at least hating that she was still thinking coherently when he'd lost the ability. "Yeah," he said as blandly as he could manage. "Apparently it was."

"I—" She climbed off the bed, coming to stand right beside him. "I'm sorry."

He was struck suddenly by how petite she was. Standing flat-footed beside him, the top of her head barely reached his chin. And yet, she never seemed small. She had more than enough personality to fill a woman half a foot taller. And more than enough strength of will to stand up to him.

He hadn't been able to face her father without embarrassing himself a few minutes ago, but her endless stream of excuses certainly killed the mood. She hadn't been as affected by the kiss as he had. Fine. But she could damn well stop harping on it.

"Stop apologizing," he ordered. "We all make mistakes. I'm just not used to making such stupid ones."

She opened her mouth as if to say something, but snapped it shut again when he brusquely smoothed down her hair. Then, since he couldn't seem to keep his hands off her, he pressed one quick kiss to her forehead. "Let's go face your parents."

Eight

Some things are embarrassing no matter what your age. Having your father stare down your boyfriend is one of them.

At seventeen, she and her boyfriend had been caught necking in the back of his truck. The make-out session had been bad enough. Worse still was the fact that her date had been high. Her father wasn't very forgiving of that sort of thing. Never mind that she hadn't known it at the time. She'd gotten reamed. He'd had the poor boy arrested. And had her hauled in and tested for drug use just to make a point. Was it any wonder the next year when she went to college she'd picked one thousands of miles away?

She'd always assumed that would be the low point of her boyfriend/father debacles. But this—oddly enough—felt worse.

Maybe it was because Devin—or had it been Drake?—had been carefully chosen for his many red-flag qualities. He'd been guy number twenty-six in her ongoing teenage quest to piss off her parents.

As she followed Jonathon into the hall, she held her breath, half afraid of the argument to come and half relieved to be escaping Jonathon's one-on-one scrutiny.

Her parents were waiting for them in the hall. Her mother sent a wan smile, a hint of apology in her eyes. Her father, on the other hand, looked as if he could happily strangle Jonathon with his bare hands. Which was saying something, because Wendy had always figured it her father was going to murder someone, as a lifelong hunter and a member of the NRA, he would opt for a gun rather than sheer brute force.

Even with Devin—or was it Derek?—her father hadn't seemed this mad. Normally, she knew how to handle her parents. Twenty-three solid years of pushing their buttons made her an expert at undoing the damage. But just now, she was drawing a blank. Every brain cell she had was still stuttering with the memory of that soul-searing kiss.

He could have taken her right there, with her parents on the other side of the door, and she would have been okay with that. More than okay. She would have been begging for more.

Not a good thought, that one.

Since she could barely put a single coherent thought together, she was infinitely thankful that Jonathon seemed to be recovering more quickly than she was.

He draped an arm over her shoulder in a possessive, but nonsexual way. Giving her parents a distant nod, he said, "Mr. and Mrs. Morgan, I'm sorry you saw that."

"Oh, no need to apologize—" her mother began.

"You're sorry we *saw* that." Her father talked over her mother. "Or you're sorry you *did* it?" His tone was as ice-cold as his reproof. "Because to my way of thinking, a man who loves his wife doesn't fool around with her in the middle of the morning when her family is in the house and the child they hope to rear is in the next room."

"Dad!"

"Now, Tim—"

Jonathon held up a hand, stopping both her protest and

her mother's. He drew out the moment just long enough for everyone to know he wasn't about to just kowtow to her father's bullying. "And to my way of thinking, a family that respects their daughter doesn't show up on her doorstep unannounced."

Her mother opened her mouth, looked ready to say something, then pressed her lips into a tight line and stomped off down the stairs.

Wendy's father continued to glare at Jonathon. Jonathon did a damn fine job of glaring back.

"If you think making my wife cry will endear you to me," her father said through gritted teeth, "then you're sorely mistaken."

Wendy wanted to protest. Those hadn't been tears in her mother's eyes. Just anger. But Jonathon didn't give her a chance to point it out.

"The same goes for you. Sir," Jonathon bit out. But apparently he couldn't leave well enough alone. Because a second later he stepped closer to her father and said, "And I'll have you know, that before she agreed to marry me, I never once so much as touched your daughter at work. I have the greatest respect for her intelligence. And her decisions. I'm not sure you can say the same."

Both men seemed to expand to fill their anger. Any second now, they would either start bumping their chests together like roosters or one of them would throw the first punch.

She figured they were equally matched. Her father was a solid six-five, and a barrel-chested two hundred and fifty pounds. Plus, he'd worked on rigs alongside roughnecks in his youth. Jonathon, on the other hand, had grown up poor, spent a few weeks in juvie, and had two older brothers, both of whom had criminal records. She figured he could probably handle himself.

She looked from one man to the other. Neither of them seemed to be willing to budge. Finally, she just shook her head. "I'm going to go talk to Mom. You two, sort this out."

She gave Jonathon's arm a little squeeze, willing him to see her apology in her eyes. Then, as she walked passed her dad, she laid a hand on his arm. "Dad, I'm not seventeen anymore. And if Jonathon was planning on besmirching my honor or whatever it is you're worried about, then he probably wouldn't have married me. Give him a chance. You have no idea how good a guy he is."

She went down the stairs, half expecting her father and Jonathon to come tumbling down after her in a jumble of brawling arms and legs. And she tried to tell herself that if they did, it wasn't any of her business.

Peyton was apparently asleep again, because a stream of lullabies could be heard through the baby monitor sitting on the kitchen counter. Her mother was doing what most Texas women do when they're upset. Cooking.

Wendy gave a bark of disbelieving laughter.

Her mother's head jerked up, her eyes still sharp with annoyance. She had a hand towel slung over her shoulder, paring knife in her hand and a chicken defrosting in the prep sink.

She gave a sniff of disapproval before returning to the task at hand, dicing celery.

Wendy bumped her hip against the edge of the island that stretched the length of the kitchen. That honed black granite was like the river of difference that always divided them. Her mother on one side: cooking to suppress the emotions she couldn't voice. Wendy on the other: baffled at her mother's ability to soldier on in silence for so many years.

"You might as well just say it," her mother snapped without looking up from the celery.

"I didn't say anything," Wendy protested.

"But you were thinking it. You always did think louder than most people shout."

Wendy blew out a breath. "Fine. It's just…" Anything she said, her mother would take as a criticism. There was probably no way around that. "You're alone in the kitchen for less than five minutes and you start cooking?"

Her mother arched a disdainful brow. "Someone has to feed everyone. You know Mema isn't going to want to go out to eat. God only knows what the food is like up here."

Wendy laughed in disbelief. "Trust me. There are plenty of restaurants in Palo Alto that are just fine. Even by your standards. And we're a thirty-minute drive to San Francisco, where they have some of the best restaurants in the world. I think on the food front, we're okay. And if Mema doesn't want to go out, there are probably two dozen restaurants that would deliver."

Naturally, having food delivered wasn't something that would have occurred to her mother. Back in Texas, all of the Morgans lived within a few miles of each other, in various houses spread over the old Morgan homestead, deep in the big piney woods of East Texas. Sure you could have food catered out there, but not delivered. As a kid, Wendy used to bribe the pizza delivery guys with hundred-dollar tips, but that only worked on slow nights.

Her mom sighed. "I've already—"

"Right. You've already started defrosting the chicken." Here her mother was, making chicken and dumplings. Wendy could barely identify the fridge, given that it was paneled to match the cabinetry. She walked down the island, so she stood just opposite her mother. "Give me a knife and I'll get started on the carrots."

Her mother crossed to a drawer, pulled out a vegetable peeler and knife, then pulled a cutting board from a lower cabinet. A few seconds of silence later and Wendy was at work across from her mom.

Her mother had always been a curious mix of homespun Texas farmwife and old oil money. Wendy's maternal grandparents had been hardscrabble farmers before striking oil on their land in the sixties. Having lived through the dustbowl of the fifties, and despite marrying into a family of old money and big oil, her mother had never quite shaken off the farm dirt. It was one of the things Wendy loved best about her mom.

"You used to love to help me in the kitchen," her mother said suddenly.

Wendy couldn't tell if there was more than nostalgia in her voice. "You used to let me," she reminded her mother. She paused for a second, considering the carrot under her knife. "But you never really needed me there. I stopped wanting to help when I realized that whatever I did wasn't going to be good enough."

Her mother's hand stilled and she looked up. "Is that what you think?"

Wendy continued slicing the carrots for a few minutes in silence, enjoying the way the knife slid through the fibrous vegetable. As she chopped, she felt some of her anger dissipating. Maybe there was something to this cooking-when-you're-upset thing.

"Momma, nothing I've ever done has been good enough for this family." She gave a satisfying slice to a carrot. "Not my lack of interest in social climbing. Not my unfocused college education." She chopped another carrot to bits. "And certainly not my job at FMJ."

"Well," her mother said, wiping her hands on the towel. "Now that you've landed Jonathon—"

"No, Momma." Wendy slammed the knife down. "My job at FMJ had nothing to do with landing a husband. If all I wanted was a rich husband, you could have arranged that for me as soon as I was of age." Picking the knife back up, she sliced through a carrot with a smooth, even motion. Keep it smooth. Keep it calm. "I work at FMJ because it's a company I believe in. And because I enjoy my work. That's enough for me. And for once in my life, I'd like for it to be enough for you and Daddy."

"Honey, if it seems like I've been trying to fix you your entire life, it's because I know how hard it is to not quite fit in with this family. I know how hard this world of wealth and privilege can be to people who are different. I didn't want that for you."

"Momma, I'm never going to fit into this world. I'm just not. Your constant browbeating has never done anything except make me feel worse about it."

Her mother blanched and turned away to dab delicately at her eyes, all the while making unmistakable sniffling noises. "I had no idea."

Wendy had seen her mother bury emotions often enough to recognize this for the show it so obviously was.

"Oh, Momma." Wendy rolled her eyes. "Of course you did. You just figured you were stronger than I was and that eventually you'd win. You never counted on me being just as strong willed as you are."

After a few minutes of silence, she said softly, "I'm sorry, Mom."

Her mother didn't pretend to misunderstand. "Apology accepted."

"I really do wish you'd been here for the wedding. I guess I should have made sure you knew that."

Her mom slapped the knife down onto the counter. "You *guess?*"

"Yes," she said slowly, putting a little more force into the chopping. "I *guess* I should have."

"I am your mother. Is it so wrong for me to wish you'd wanted me here enough to—"

"Oh, this is so typical," she said. "Why should I have to beg you to come to my wedding? I've lived in California for over five years. When I first moved here, I invited y'all out to visit all the time. You never came. No one in the family has shown any interest in my life or my work until now. But now that baby Peyton is here, you've descended like a plague of locusts and—"

"My land," her mother said, cutting her off, her hands

going to her hips. "And you wonder why we didn't want to come before now, when you talk about us like that."

Wendy just shook her head. Once again, she'd managed to offend and horrify her mother. Somehow, her mother always ended up as the bridge between Wendy and the rest of the Morgans. The mediator pulled in both directions, satisfying no one.

"Look, I didn't mean it like that. Obviously I don't think you're a locust. Or a plague."

"Well, then, how did you mean it?"

"It's just—" Bracing her hands on either side of the cutting board, she let her head drop while she collected her thoughts. She stared at the neat little carrot circles. They were nearly all uniform. Only a few slices stood out. The bits too bumpy or misshapen. The pieces that didn't fit.

All her life, she'd felt like that. The imperfect bit that no one wanted and no one knew what to do with. Until she'd gone to work for FMJ. And there, finally, she'd fit in.

Her mother just shook her head, sweeping up the pile of diced celery and dumping it in the pot. "You're always so eager to believe the worst of us."

"That's not true."

"It most certainly is. All your life, you've been rebellious just for the sake of rebellion. Every choice you've made since the day you turned fifteen has been designed to irritate your father and grandmother. And now this."

"What's that supposed to mean?"

"Remember when you were fifteen and you and Bitsy bought those home-perm kits and gave yourselves home perms four days before picture day at the school?"

She did remember. Of course she did. Bitsy had ended up with nice, bouncy curls. But she'd been bald for months while her hair grew back out. Her father had been so mad his face had turned beet-red and her mother had run off to the bathroom for a dose of his blood-pressure medicine.

That had not been her finest moment.

"Or the time you wanted to go to Mexico with that boyfriend of yours. When we told you no, you went anyway."

"You didn't have to have the guy arrested," she said weakly. She couldn't muster any real indignation.

"And you should have told him you were only sixteen."

Also, not her proudest moment.

"And don't try to say we were being overprotective. No sane parent lets their sixteen-year-old daughter leave the country with a boy they barely know."

"Look, Mom, I'm sorry. I'm sorry I was such a difficult teenager. I'm sorry I never lived up to your expectations. But that has nothing to do with who I am now."

"Doesn't it?" Her mom swept up the carrots Wendy had been chopping and dumped them into the pot, lumpy, misshapen bits and all. She added a drizzle of oil in the pan and cranked up the heat. "You've rushed into this marriage with this man we've never even met—"

There was a note of censure in her voice that Wendy just couldn't let pass. "This man that I've worked with for years. If you've never met him, it's because you never came out to visit."

Her mother planted both her hands on the counter between them and leaned forward. "Jonathon seems like a very nice man. But if you married him solely to annoy us then—"

"Oh, Marian, don't be so suspicious."

Wendy spun around toward the kitchen door to see her father and Jonathon standing just inside. She and her mother had been so intent on their own conversation that neither of them had heard them enter.

The two men had obviously come to an understanding about the argument upstairs. Her father had his arm slung over Jonathon's shoulders as if they were old buddies. The smile on his face was downright smug.

Jonathon looked less comfortable. In fact, he rather looked

like he'd swallowed something nasty. Slowly his gaze shifted from her mother to her. Obviously, he heard everything her mother said to her. And he didn't like it.

Nine

"I'm sure," Wendy's father was saying, "that our little Gwen here has grown out of her rebellions."

Jonathon swallowed the tight knot of dread in his throat. "Mrs. Morgan, I assure you—"

But Wendy's mother sent both of them withering glares and he was smart enough to shut up when a woman wielding a butcher knife sent him a look like that.

Wendy pointed the tip of her own knife in her father's direction. "You stay out of this." For the first time in years she felt as though she and her mother were actually talking. She wasn't about to let her father muck it up.

Turning her gaze back to her mother, she continued as if the men hadn't entered at all. "I'm not a rebellious teenager anymore. I'm a grown woman. With a job I love. I may not have married the next political golden boy and I may not be VP of Twiddling My Thumbs at Morgan Oil, but I'm successful in my own right. And a lot of people would be proud to have me as their daughter."

"It's not that we're not proud," her mother began. "But—"

"Of course there's a but. There's always a but."

Her mother ignored her interruption, slicing to the point of the matter as easily as she sliced through the joints in the chicken. "But you've always delighted in rebelling against your father at every turn. If I thought for a minute that marrying Jonathon and raising Peyton was truly what you wanted—"

"It is."

"—and not just another one of your rebellions then I would support you wholeheartedly."

Wendy threw up her hands. "Then support me!"

"But I know how you are. If Mema or Big Hank, let alone your daddy, announced that the sky is blue, the very next morning you'd run out and join a research committee to scientifically prove that it's not."

"You make me sound completely illogical." Wendy shook her head as if she didn't even know how to defend herself against her mother's accusations. "It's like you haven't heard anything I just said."

"Well, you tell me whether or not this is just rebellion." Her mom propped her fists on her hips. "Everyone in this family thinks Hank Jr. and Helen should raise Peyton, except you. Do you have any logical reason why you're so darned determined to raise this baby?"

Jonathon had had enough. He stepped away from her father. Pulling Wendy back against his chest, he said calmly, "I believe that's the point, isn't it? Everyone in the family except for Wendy. And Bitsy. Since Bitsy didn't want her brother raising her daughter, shouldn't that be enough for everyone?"

Marian snapped her mouth closed, narrowing her gaze and setting her jaw at a determined angle. He'd seen that look often enough on Wendy.

"You didn't know Bitsy," she said to him, obviously making an effort to moderate her tone. "Bitsy was never happy if she wasn't stirring up trouble. I don't like to speak ill of the dead, but has it occurred to either of you that naming

Wendy guardian might just have been her way of creating conflict from beyond the grave?"

He felt Wendy pulling away from him, tensing to speak. He tugged her back soundly against him and said, "I may not have known Bitsy. But I know Wendy. I know she's going to make a wonderful mother."

Her mom studied him for a second, apparently searching for signs of his conviction. Finally, she nodded. "Hank Jr.'s wife, Helen, sees that baby as little more than a crawling, crying dollar sign. Peyton is a fast ticket to a bigger chunk of Mema's estate. Helen will fight you for that baby."

"Helen has three boys of her own that she's done a crappy job raising," Wendy pointed out. "If she hadn't shipped those boys off to boarding school the second they were old enough to go, maybe I'd see things differently."

"Just be prepared. Helen's like a bulldog with a bone when money's involved."

"That may be true," Jonathon said. "But Helen isn't here now. And we have all weekend to convince Mema that we'll be the best parents for Peyton."

Her mother harrumphed. "Don't think Helen hasn't figured that out as well. Mark my words, girly, you might be glad we came to visit you here instead of waiting for you to come to us. This might be your only chance alone with Mema to convince her that you and Jonathon are the happy, loving couple you want us all to believe."

There were few things that terrified Jonathon. He thought of himself as a reasonable and logical man. Irrational fears were for small children. Not adults.

At nineteen, he'd spent a solid hour in the dorm room of a buddy, holding the guy's pet tarantula in his hand to get himself over his fear of spiders. At twenty-three, about the time he'd made his first million, he'd spent three weeks in Australia learning how to scuba dive. That trip had served the joint purpose of getting him over his irrational fear of sharks and his equally irrational fear that FMJ would go under if he wasn't available 24/7.

He now took annual diving vacations. After the first, he'd stayed closer to home.

He was a man who faced his fears and conquered them.

Which didn't entirely explain why at nearly midnight on Saturday, he was still sitting in the kitchen sipping twenty-year-old scotch with Wendy's father and uncle. He'd been there for hours, listening to them tell stories about Texas politics and—as her father colorfully called it—"life in the oil patch."

Her family was entertaining, to say the least. And that was the sole reason he hadn't headed to bed much earlier. This had nothing to do with the fact that Wendy was now sleeping in his bed.

He'd been dreading sleeping in the same bed, but that was unavoidable now. As if that wasn't bad enough, now he couldn't get her mother's words out of his head.

After reminding Wendy over and over again that his own motives were selfish, why did it bother him to think that hers might not be so pure? He didn't know. All he knew was that he hated the idea that their marriage was just one more rebellion in a long line of self-destructive behaviors. Worse still was the idea that she'd quickly lose interest in him once the tactic failed to shock her parents.

If she offered herself to him, he wouldn't be able to resist. Even knowing what he did now, the temptation would be too sweet.

To his chagrin, he actually felt a spike of panic when her uncle stood, tossed back the last of his drink and said, "Jonathon, I appreciate the hospitality—and the scotch—but I know I'll regret it tomorrow if I drink any more."

Wendy's dad stood as well. "Marian is gonna have my hide tomorrow as it is."

Jonathon held up the decanter toward Wendy's father. "Are you sure I can't offer you another?"

"Well…"

But Hank slapped his brother on the arm in a jovial way. "We're keeping him from his bride."

"Don't remind me," her father grumbled.

"No man should have to entertain a couple of old blowhards when he has a lovely new wife to warm his bed."

Jonathon nearly smiled at that, despite himself. He liked Wendy's family far more than he wanted to admit. He knew she found them overbearing and pretentious, but there was something about their combination of good-ol'-boy charm and keen intelligence that appealed to him.

Besides, the longer he kept them here, shooting bull until all hours of the night, the greater the chance that Wendy would be fast asleep by the time he got up to the bedroom.

However, before he could even offer them yet another drink, Wendy's father and uncle were stumbling arm in arm up the stairs to the guest bedrooms where they were staying. He winced as they banged into the antique sideboard his decorator had foolishly put outside his office. And then cringed as her father cursed loudly at the thing. Maybe he should consider himself lucky that all of their fumbling didn't wake Mema.

He waited until they vanished down the upstairs hall before he followed, turning off lights as he went. That afternoon, he and Wendy's father had moved Peyton's crib from the nursery to the master bedroom. Ironic, since it had only just arrived in the past week. They'd moved the spare mattress up from the garage and now the guest-bedroom-turned-nursery was once again a guest bedroom. Throughout the process, Wendy kept insisting that her family should just book rooms at one of the many hotels in town. Mema had looked scandalized. Marian had looked offended. And Wendy had eventually caved.

And so, after thirteen years of living completely by himself, he now had six additional people under the roof. Maybe he should buy a bigger house. One with more bedrooms. Though a dozen bedrooms wouldn't have saved him from this. When the family of your new wife was visiting, they all expected you to share a room with her. There was just no way around that.

After putting it off as long as he could, he finally bit the bullet and let himself into the master bedroom. The room he'd be sharing with Wendy. His wife.

Despite his numerous prayers, she wasn't asleep.

She sat up in the bed, her back propped against the enormous square pillows his decorator had purchased—personally he'd never been able to stand the damn things and wasn't entirely sure why he continued to pile them on the bed every morning.

Peyton was asleep on Wendy's chest, her tiny fist curled near her face so that she sucked on one knuckle. Wendy was on his side of the bed. The bedside lamp was on and in her other hand, she held a Kindle.

He glanced at the bedside table. Scratch that, she held his Kindle.

She looked up as he closed the door behind him. Try as he might, he couldn't force himself to walk into the room more than a step or two.

Wendy smiled sheepishly. "Sorry to steal your Kindle," she whispered. "She fell asleep here and I didn't want to risk waking her by digging around for my own book."

She was dressed in a white tank top and Teenage Mutant Ninja Turtle boxer shorts. Her legs were stretched out in front of her. How a woman as short as she was had ended up with legs that long was a mystery, but damn, they seemed to stretch for miles.

Her skin was creamy white, her legs lightly muscled, ending in perfect, petite feet. And her toenails were painted a sassy iridescent purple. He had to force his attention away from her bare legs, but couldn't make his gaze move all the way up to her face. He got caught on her arms, which were just as bare as her legs and somehow nearly as erotic.

In all those years that they'd worked together, he hadn't

ever seen her in something sleeveless. Her upper arms were just like the rest of her. Small and lean, but lightly muscled. Unexpectedly strong.

There was something so intimate about the sight of her holding Peyton on her chest, dressed for bed. In *his* bed.

His muscles practically twitched with the need to cross the room and pull her into his arms. To do all kinds of wicked things to her body. Or maybe to just sit on the bed next to her and watch her sleep.

That thought—the idea that he'd be content without even touching her—that was the thought that scared the crap out of him. Physically wanting her, he could handle that. He'd been fighting his desire for her for years. He always won that battle. But this new urge to just be with her. He didn't even want to know what the hell that was about.

Suddenly his master bedroom seemed way too small.

That new house he was going to buy—the one with a dozen guest bedrooms—apparently the master would need to be four times bigger. He was going to have to move out to Portola Valley to find a house big enough.

"You're mad, aren't you?" Wendy asked.

He dragged his gaze up to her face. She was frowning in that cute way she did, biting down on her lower lip in a half frown, half sheepish grin. He walked closer so that he didn't have to speak louder than a whisper. "Why?" he asked.

"You're mad that I borrowed your Kindle." She flicked the button on the side to turn it off. "I didn't even think. That was a horrible invasion of your privacy."

He wanted to stand here watching her sleep and she was worried that reading from his Kindle was an invasion of his privacy. She had no idea.

"It's okay. No big deal."

"Are you sure?" Despite the whisper, her voice sounded high and nervous. "Because you look really annoyed."

If anything, he probably looked as though he was trying

not to kiss her. Good to know she interpreted that as annoyed. "It's just a Kindle. Not a big deal."

Then he crossed automatically to his side of the bed. The side she was sitting on. He took off his watch and set it on the valet tray on the bedside table. The familiarity of the action calmed his nerves. Of course, normally there wasn't an empty baby bottle beside the lamp, but still...

"Did you have trouble getting her to fall sleep?" he asked as he pulled off his college ring and dropped it beside the watch. Then he hesitated at the simple gold band on his left hand. Since he'd slept in Peyton's nursery last night, he'd had both rings and the watch on all night. This was the first time he'd taken off the wedding ring.

"No." Wendy rubbed at her eyes a little before arching her back into a stretch. "I think she's finally getting used to the new feeding schedule. I woke her at eleven for that bottle and she went right back to sleep...."

Jonathon looked up when he heard her voice trail off. Like him, she was staring at the ring on his hand. Her gaze darted to his and held it for a second. He watched, entranced, as she nervously licked her lips. Something hot and unspoken passed between them, once again stirring that need to kiss her. To mark her as his own. To bend her back over the bed and plow into her.

Thank God, Peyton was asleep on her chest, keeping him from doing anything too stupid.

He yanked the ring off his finger and dropped it onto the tray beside his watch and his class ring.

Her gaze dropped to where his watch and rings lay on the nightstand. Then it snapped up to his face again. She gave another one of those wobbly, anxious smiles. "I'm on your side of the bed, aren't I?"

"It's fine."

"No, I'll move. Just give me a second." Bracing an arm at Peyton's back, she half sat up, then hesitated. Peyton squirmed and Wendy's frown deepened.

"Just lie her down in the center. She can sleep there."

"You sure?"

"Absolutely." Was it wrong that he was scheming to get Peyton in the bed between them? A little devious maybe, but not wrong. He wouldn't make a move on Wendy as long as Peyton was in the same room. But having her in the bed was a stroke of genius. Better than an icy shower, he was sure. And less conspicuous. Besides, he even had sound scientific reasoning in his corner. "I've been reading this book on—"

"Attachment parenting?" she asked as she waggled the Kindle. "I've been stalking your Kindle, remember?"

That playful, suggestive tone of hers was like a kick in the gut. Maybe he'd still need that cold shower. "I should just sleep on the floor."

"Don't be ridiculous."

She leaned over and rolled Peyton from her chest to the center of the bed. Then came up onto her hands and knees to climb over the still sleeping baby. The thin cotton of her boxer shorts clung enticingly to her bottom and his groin tightened in response to the sight.

She had no idea just how far from ridiculous he was being. This was him at his most practical.

Hell, forget the floor. He'd just sleep in the shower. With the cold water on.

"I don't mind."

"Well, I do," she said, tossing the pillows on that side of the bed onto the floor—the side that from this moment on would always be *her* side of the bed. "When I think of all the things you've done for me in the past few weeks…"

"Don't make me into some kind of hero. You know why I married you." The problem was he was no longer sure *he* knew why he'd done it. "My motives weren't altruistic."

At least that was true.

She flashed him a smile that was a little bit sad. "I know. But neither are mine. And I'm not about to kick you out of bed."

Ten

"Not about to kick you out of your *own* bed," she corrected, a blush tinting her cheeks.

As if she wasn't irresistible already.

He wanted to argue about the sleeping arrangements. Dear God, he did. But he couldn't logically make an argument for sleeping in the tub. Besides, he'd doubt he'd fit.

"Oh, I get it," she said with teasing concern. "You're embarrassed about your body."

Clearly she was trying to hide her own embarrassment. "Wendy—"

"You're probably all pasty white under those dress shirts, huh?" She clucked her tongue in sympathy. "Maybe you put on a few extra pounds over the holidays? Is that it? Is that why you're standing there like a statue, refusing to get undressed?"

He wasn't about to tell why he really wasn't getting undressed. If she hadn't figured out how thin her tank top was and how much that turned him on, then he wasn't going to be the one to tell her.

"Hey, I won't even look," she teased, making a great show of rolling over to face the wall. "Now I can't see you. You can even turn out the light if you want."

Rolling his eyes at her silliness, he reached over and turned off the lamp before starting on his buttons.

"I guess you made peace with my dad," she said after a minute.

"I guess so," he admitted, slipping off his shirt and tossing it vaguely in the direction of a nearby chair. He toed off his shoes and socks. "He's not such a bad guy."

"No." Her voice was small in the darkness. "He's not. Everyone comes around eventually."

He hesitated before unbuttoning his jeans. He hadn't slept in anything other than his underwear since college. He didn't even own a pair of pajama bottoms. First thing in the morning, he was buying a pair. No, twenty pair. Maybe thirty just to be safe.

A moment later he lay down so close to the edge of the bed that his left shoulder hung off the side. His awkward position was still not uncomfortable enough to block out the scent of her on his pillow. It smelled warm and feminine and faintly of peppermint.

He lay there stiffly, eyes resolutely closed, keenly aware that she too was still awake. He searched for something to say. "I never knew you liked the Teenage Mutant Ninja Turtles."

Damn, was he smooth or what?

He heard her roll over in the dark and prop herself up on her elbow. "Doesn't everyone?"

He turned just his head to look at her, but found himself eye to eye with Peyton. Her tiny face was seven inches from his. Her lips pursed as she dreamed about eating. He remembered his niece doing that, from all those long years ago when he used to help feed his sister's kids. Lacey would be in college now. He felt a powerful punch of longing. The kind he normally kept buried deep inside. To push it back down, he rolled up onto his elbow to look at Wendy.

At least he understood the longing he felt when he looked at her. Pure sexual desire. He got that. He could control it—at least, he thought he could. God knew, he'd controlled it so far. But this unfamiliar longing to reconnect with his family? That was new and terrifying territory.

He doubled his pillow under his head, allowing him to look over Peyton to where Wendy lay. She'd moved the night-light in from the nursery, a glowing hippo that cast the room in pink light and made Wendy's skin look nearly iridescent. When he looked back up at her eyes, her gaze darted away from his, as if she was all too aware of the desire pulsing through his veins.

He could see she was about to lie back down, so he said, "No, not everyone loves Teenage Mutant Ninja Turtles. Most people don't even know they were a witty and subversive comic book before becoming a fairly cheesy movie marketed to kids."

She gave a playful shrug, smiling, either because the topic amused her or because she was relieved he'd stopped looking at her like something he wanted to lick clean, he couldn't tell which.

"That's me, I guess." She imitated his hushed tone, obviously no more willing to wake Peyton than he was. "A fan of things witty and subversive."

"Yeah, I get that. What I don't get is how I never knew it until now."

"Oh." She gave another shrug, this one self-effacing.

"For five years, you've dressed like the consummate, bland executive assistant." Whispering in the dark as if this made the conversation far more intimate than the topic was. "Bland clothing in a neutral palate. Demure hair. Now I find out you've been hiding a love of violet nail polish and eighties indie punk rock." He nodded toward her boxers. "Not to mention the Turtles."

She frowned. "Punk rock?"

"The Replacements T-shirt you had on the other day."

"You recognized them?" She gave him a pointed once-over. "And yet you don't seem like a fan of eighties alternative."

"I'm a fan of Google. And you couldn't possibly have been old enough to attend the concert where that T-shirt was sold."

"I'm a fan of eBay. And of defying expectations."

"Which brings me back to my original question. Why didn't I know this about you?"

She paused, seeming to consider the question for a long time. Then she sank back and stared at the ceiling. He watched her, lying there with her eyes open as she gazed into the dark, long enough that he thought she wasn't going to answer at all.

Finally she said softly, "Working at FMJ..." Her shoulders gave a twitch, as if she was shrugging off her pensive mood. "I guess it's been the ultimate rebellion for me. When you're from an old oil family, what's worse than working for a company that's made their money in green energy."

"We do a lot of other things too," he pointed out.

"Well, sure." She rolled back to face him. "But even then, it's all about innovation and change. My family is all about tradition. Maybe when I was working for FMJ, I never felt like I needed to rebel."

He felt his heart stutter as he heard her slip. *When I was working for FMJ,* she'd said. Not *now that I am working for FMJ,* but *when I was.* But she didn't seem to notice, so he let it pass without comment.

"Working at FMJ," she continued, her voice almost dreamy, "I felt like I had direction. Purpose. I didn't need to define myself by dying my hair blue or getting my navel pierced or getting a tattoo."

The image of her naked belly flashed through his mind. The thought of a tiny diamond belly-button ring took his mind into dangerous territory.

"A tattoo?" He was immediately sorry he asked. Please let it be somewhere completely innocuous, like her...nope.

He couldn't think of a single body part on Wendy that didn't seem sexy.

She gave a little chuckle. "One of my more painful rebellions." Then—please God, strike him dead now—she lifted the hem of her white tank top to reveal her hip and the delicate flower that bloomed there.

He clenched his fist to keep from reaching out to touch it. For a second, every synapse in his brain stopped firing. Thought was impossible. Then they all fired at once. A thousand comments went through his brain. Finally, he cleared his throat and forced out the most innocent of them. "That doesn't look like it was done in a parlor."

As lovely as it was, the lines were not crisp. The colors weren't bright.

Wendy chuckled. "Mine was done by a boyfriend." She held up her hands as if to ward off his criticism. "Don't worry, his tools were all scrupulously sterilized and I've been tested since then for all the nasty things you can get if they hadn't been." She gave the tattoo a little pat and then tugged her hem back down. "I was eighteen, had just finished my freshman year at Dartmouth and I wanted to study abroad. My parents refused and made me come home and intern at Morgan Oil. So I dated a former gang member who'd served time in county."

Jonathon had to swallow back the shot of fear that jumped through his veins. She'd obviously survived. She was here now, healthy and safe, but the thought of her dating that guy made his blood boil.

He unclenched his jaw long enough to say, "And you wonder why your parents worry about you."

She gave a nervous chuckle. "Joe was actually a really nice guy. Besides, after spending the weekend with my family—"

"Let me guess, now he works for Morgan Oil? Interns for your uncle in Washington?"

"No. Even better. He went on to write a book about how to leave the gang life behind. He teaches gang intervention throughout Houston and travels all over the U.S. working with police departments."

"You sound almost proud," he commented.

She cocked her head and seemed to think about it. "I guess I am proud of Joe. He turned his life around." Then she gave a little laugh. "Maybe my family should start a self-help program."

"Tell me something. What's with all the cautionary tales?"

"What do you mean?"

"This is the second boyfriend you've told me about whose life was changed by meeting your parents."

"I'm just warning you." Her tone was suddenly serious. "This is what they do. They'll find your weakness—or your strength or whatever—and they use it to drive you away from me."

"No," he said. "That's what they've done in the past. That's not what they're going to do to me."

"Don't be so sure of that." She looked at him, her expression resigned. "Can you honestly tell me you haven't considered how helpful my uncle could be in securing that government contract?"

"That contract has nothing to do with this."

"Not yet. But they're doing it already."

"I don't—"

"You were up late drinking scotch with my dad and uncle, weren't you?"

"How—"

"I can smell it on your breath. And you don't drink scotch."

"How do you know that I don't drink scotch?"

"You never drink hard liquor." Her tone had grown distant. "Never. You keep very expensive brands on hand at the office—and I assume here—for associates who do drink. You read *Wine Spectator* magazine, and can always order a fabulous bottle of wine. You don't mind reds and will drink white, if that's what your companion is having, but you don't really like either. You prefer ice-cold beer. Even then, you never have more than two a night."

He leaned back slightly, unnerved that she knew so much about his taste. "What else do you know about me?"

"I know that anyone who has such strict rules for themselves about alcohol, probably has a parent who drinks. I'd guess your father—"

"It was my mother."

"—but that would just be a guess."

"You have any other theories?"

Between them Peyton stirred. He reached out a hand to place on Peyton's belly to calm her. Wendy reached out at the same time and their fingers brushed. Wendy hesitated, then linked her fingers through his.

"I didn't say it to make a point. I'm just…" She brushed her thumb back and forth over his. "There's something about my family that makes people want to impress them. It's made you want to impress them, or you wouldn't have bent your no-hard-liquor rule."

"My mom did drink," he said slowly. "'Functioning alcoholic' is the term people use now. You have any other old wounds you want to poke?"

The second the words left his mouth, he squeezed his eyes shut.

Christ, he sounded like a jerk.

He opened his eyes, shoving up on his elbow to look at her. He fully expected to see a stung expression on her face. Instead, she just gave his hand a squeeze and sent him a sad smile.

"I'm sorry," he admitted.

"Don't apologize. I got a little carried away with the armchair psychology." She was silent for a minute and he could hear the gears in her brain turning. "But since you mentioned it…"

"Okay, hit me with it. What horribly invasive question are

you going to ask next? You want to know my deepest fear? Clowns. How much I'm actually worth? About—"

"Actually I wanted to know about Kristi."

He fell silent.

"She was your—"

"I know who you mean."

He didn't say anything for a long time, all but praying she'd let it drop. She shifted in the bed beside him. Fidgeting, but saying nothing. She wasn't going to let it drop, and if he didn't respond soon, she'd think Kristi was a bigger deal than she had been.

"She was just someone I knew in high school. Who told you about her?"

He wanted to know who to kill. He hoped it wasn't Matt or Ford, because murdering one of his business partners would probably be the end of FMJ.

"Claire," Wendy answered.

Well, crap. He couldn't very well kill a woman. Especially when she'd just married his best friend.

"Don't be mad at her," Wendy continued. "I practically begged for information."

"Why on earth would you beg for information about my old high school girlfriend?"

"I dunno." She rolled over, but with his eyes squeezed shut, he couldn't tell if she was rolling toward him or away from him. "As dead set as you are against love...well, no one feels that way unless they've been hurt."

"What did Claire tell you about Kristi?"

She didn't answer right away. "Just that you were crazy about her. And she left."

She'd paused long enough for him to know she'd been fabricating her answer. Condensing it down to the barest details.

But in his mind, he could all too easily imagine the longer version. The real version. The one where he made a complete ass of himself over Kristi. Where he handed her his whole heart…and did nothing but scare her away.

"And?" he prodded.

"I figured…she must have been the one."

"And that's what you surmised from Claire's story? That Kristi was the one to break my heart?"

"Am I wrong?"

What exactly was he supposed to say to that? Kristi *had* broken his heart. But he'd only been eighteen. "That was a lifetime ago."

"What happened with her? What really happened?"

He forced his eyes open and tried to sound casual. "You're the armchair psychologist. What do you think happened?"

She tilted her head to the side, considering. "I think that you, Jonathon Bagdon, are a pretty intense guy."

He looked up at her. In the dark of the room, her skin was luminous. Her eyes were so dark they looked almost purple. She was so beautiful, it made his heart ache. As well as plenty of other parts of him.

Damn, but he wanted her. Not just her body. But all of her.

Thinking of her comment, all he could was mutter, "You have no idea."

"The way I see it, I'm a grown woman. Someone who's used to dealing with strong personalities. And there are times when even I'm a little overwhelmed by you. So this girl— Kristi?—she probably didn't have a chance. I'm guessing you falling in love with her must have scared the hell out of her."

"Yeah. That's about it." He let his eyes drift closed again. "This thing between us," he began, but then corrected himself, "this physical thing between us, it's pretty intense."

"Yes, it is," she agreed softly. He opened his eyes to see her still sitting up, looking down at him. The look in her eyes made heat churn through his body, but it was her words that made his heart pound. "I'm not scared of you, Jonathon."

"Maybe you should be."

She tilted her head, studying him in the pink glow of the

hippo. Indeed, she looked more aroused than frightened. "Maybe."

"Scratch that. You should definitely be afraid. If you knew half the things I want to do to you…"

She arched a brow, her expression a little curious, a little challenging. "You think you're the only one with pent-up desire and an active imagination?"

Was she purposefully trying to destroy any chance he had of getting some sleep? Ever again?

"I think," he answered her, "there's a damn good chance you underestimate how sexy you look in a tank top." It was hard to tell in the pink light, but he could have sworn she blushed. He couldn't stop himself from going on. "And I also think you underestimate just how hard it is for me to keep my hands off you."

Her chest rose as she sucked in a deep breath, highlighting all the wonderful things that tank top of hers did.

"You think you're the only person this is hard for?" she asked.

"I think I'm the only one who's a big enough jerk to wait until there was an innocent baby here in the bed between us, just to guarantee I'd keep my hands off you."

She gnawed on her lip for a second then, looking secretly pleased with herself. He squeezed his eyes shut, blocking out the image of her and that sexy bow mouth of hers.

He felt the bed shift as she lay back down. Then, so softly he thought he might have imagined it, she said, "Don't be so sure about that."

Eleven

She'd fallen asleep with her body fairly throbbing with un-fulfilled sexual tension and she woke up alone. The feeling of jittery anticipation stayed with her as she headed for the bathroom and dug through the suitcases she'd left in Jonathon's closet the day before. She quickly pulled on an oversize gossamer shirt and a pair of black leggings and headed downstairs to search out food and her family.

She walked into the kitchen just in time for her mother to pile her plate high with the last batch of buttermilk pancakes. Peyton was gurgling happily in the high chair beside the table, being cooed to by Mema. The kitchen was as warm and as welcoming as a Hallmark special. The tangy scent of pancakes mingled with the bitter zing of the coffee to stir long-forgotten memories of her childhood. She swallowed back a pang of loneliness and regret. She'd chosen to leave Texas and to distance herself from her family. That didn't mean she didn't miss them.

But with all that was going on in the kitchen, there was one thing that was missing. Jonathon.

Or to be more precise, three things: Jonathon, her father and Big Hank.

She didn't notice at first, so caught up as she was in the pancake-scented time machine. But she paused, that first bite halfway to her mouth, and listened with her head cocked toward the kitchen door, mentally reviewing the walk down the stairs.

She set down the fork, heavenly bite uneaten. "Okay, where'd you send them?"

Mema's back stiffened. "Why would you assume I'd sent them anywhere?"

Wendy shoved the bite of pancakes into her mouth and chewed out her frustration. "Well, they're not here, are they? That means you've sent them off somewhere. Either so you can ply him for information. Or me, I suppose."

Her mother and grandmother exchanged a look that made her very nervous. She forked off another bite and crammed it in. Weren't carbs supposed to be calming? So why didn't she feel any more relaxed?

She felt a niggling of fear creep up her spine. If she was honest with herself, she knew why she didn't feel any calmer. When a pride of lions went hunting, they'd separate the weaker members of the pack from the rest to make it easier to pick them off.

Jonathon had just been separated from the herd.

"Where did they go?" she asked, feigning a calmness the pancakes hadn't provided.

"Seriously, it's nothing nefarious. Jonathon offered to show them FMJ's headquarters. It's not like they've taken him out back to beat him or anything."

No. Maybe it wasn't like that. But she feared how buddy-buddy they'd be when they got back.

She and Jonathon had only been married for two days and already her family was driving a wedge between them.

* * *

It was no easy task slipping out of the house when her mother and grandmother were there hovering. In the end, she lied. She wasn't proud of it, but she did it.

I just want to run out to the grocery store for a few things, she'd said. *Diapers. New formula. Oh, right. There are several cans in the pantry. But Peyton's been so fussy I want to try a different brand.*

Who knew motherhood would provide such ample opportunity for lying?

"I think between the two of us, Mema and I have raised enough children to muddle through," her mother had said as Wendy headed for the door.

Wendy took the grocery store at a mad dash, storming the unfamiliar baby aisle as if it were the target of a shock-and-awe military campaign. She raked into her cart five different varieties of formula and enough diapers to keep Peyton dry until college. Then, back in the car, she retraced her path, bypassing Jonathon's street and heading for FMJ's headquarters.

Stopped at a light—mentally urging it to change more quickly—she took one brief minute to question her motives. Why was she so worried? What was the worst that would happen?

A few hours alone with her family wouldn't convince Jonathon to revamp his entire life, write a tell-all and travel the country on the lecture circuit. After a single night of tossing back scotch with her uncle, he wasn't going to quit FMJ and accept a position at Morgan Oil. Or worse, run for office.

But none of that logic slowed the pounding of her heart. Nor did it dry out her damp palms.

She so desperately wanted to believe that Jonathon was different than every other guy she'd ever dated. But what if he wasn't?

He had to know how influential her uncle was within the

government. One word from Big Hank and that contract they'd been working on could be a done deal. All Jonathon had to do was sell her uncle on the idea.

And when it came to FMJ's proprietary technology, no one was a better salesman than Jonathon. If he had the chance to schmooze her uncle, he'd be a fool not to take it. She'd just hoped he wouldn't have a chance.

By the time she swiped her security card at the campus gate, she was twitchy with anxiety. Part of her wanted to just drive. Not back to his house, not even back to hers, but just drive. She'd had a friend once who hopped in her car and drove to Cabo San Lucas every time life got messy. It was a twenty-eight-hour drive from Palo Alto. By tomorrow afternoon, Wendy could be sipping tequila on the beach. But none of her problems would go away. And then she'd be drunk or hungover and two thousand miles from them. That hardly seemed like the perfect solution. Twenty-seven years of rational decision-making wouldn't let her go the Shawshank route.

She scurried into the front office, dropped her purse on the desk and sank into her chair. The simple familiarity of the actions settled her nerves. How crazy was it that the faint scent of ozone coming off all the computer equipment in the other room could be so calming?

Maybe her family was right and she was a nut for loving this job so much, but she couldn't help it. Everything felt right in the world when she sat behind this desk.

She knew it was an illusion. If she went down to the R&D lab, she'd find Jonathon there with her father and uncle. And she just wasn't ready to see that yet. Apparently, she'd run across town for nothing.

Letting out a sigh, she crossed her arms on the desktop and dropped her head into the cradle of her elbows. Then she heard a faint sound coming from the back office that Ford, Matt and Jonathon shared. She stilled instantly, listening. Slowly she stood and crossed to the door, giving it a nudge so it swung inward.

Jonathon stood behind his desk along the west wall. She was unused to seeing him in casual clothes, and couldn't help admiring how good he looked in a simple cotton T-shirt and jeans. Though his laptop was out on his desk, it wasn't open. There was a manila file in his hand.

"Oh," she murmured as he looked up. "It's you."

His lips twitched. "Who'd you expect?"

"I…" She paused, momentarily stumped. Finally, she admitted, "I thought you were downstairs in the R&D lab. With my father and Big Hank."

"Nope." He frowned, obviously puzzling through why she would have thought that. "We ran into Matt. He offered to show them around."

"Oh." Relief flooded her. He wasn't off schmoozing her family. He hadn't fallen under their spell.

"Why'd you come in?" he asked.

"Oh, well I…" Not wanting to admit she suspected him of underhanded business tactics, she made a vague gesture toward her office. "Same as you. Wanted to catch up on some work."

Suddenly, now that her fears about Jonathon had been dispelled, another emotion came rushing into the void left by them: desire. Or maybe it had been there all along, right under the surface, waiting for an excuse to rise to the top, as it always did.

"Right." He nodded. "Since I figure we won't be in tomorrow we might as well—"

"Why won't you be in tomorrow?" she asked, without really listening for the answer, because her mind was back in the bedroom, the night before, hearing him confess how much he wanted her. And she was remembering how he'd looked in the light of that ridiculous pink hippo, the bedsheet pulled only to his waist, the muscles of his chest so clearly defined despite the dim lighting.

"Your family. They'll still be here then."

"So? What does that have to do with your work?"

"While they're here, our first priority is convincing them we're a happy couple. We can't do that if we're not together."

"But work—" she protested.

"Can wait for a few days."

Work? Wait? Who was this guy?

Whoever he was, she didn't like it. Not one bit. She was going to have a hard enough time sleeping in the same bed with him for the next week. She'd been counting on their time at the office to return to normalcy. Now more than ever, she needed him to be the hard, analytical boss she was used to.

Her mind was still reeling from that little bomb when Jonathon said, "Since we're both here, why don't you go grab your computer and we'll try to get some work done?"

"The thing is, Jonathon, I—"

Then she broke off abruptly. Because what could she really say? He was waiting, expectantly. Looking so handsome it made her heart ache. "The thing is, I don't know if I can do this."

"Do what?"

"Slip so easily between the work me and the me that has to pretend to be your wife. I don't know why it seems so easy for you, but—"

"You think this is easy for me?"

"Well. Yes. You barely seem aware that at this time yesterday you were kissing me. Or that last night we slept in the same bed." She paused, waiting for him to say something. Though his gaze darkened, he didn't comment and suddenly she felt ridiculous for saying these things aloud. "Which is fine, I mean, this is my problem. I'll figure it out. But I think I just need to get out of here for a couple of hours. Get my head on straight."

Maybe that trip to Cabo wasn't such a bad idea after all.

She turned and had made it most of the way to the door when he grabbed her arm and turned her around. She barely caught her balance when he pulled her roughly against him and kissed her.

Twelve

His mouth was hot and firm on hers. It only took a second for her to lose herself in the sensation of being kissed by him. No, not just kissed, devoured. She felt completely swept away by it. By him. By the sensation of his hand gently cupping her jaw. By his arm at her back, pressing her body to his. The feel of his lips as they moved over hers in a hundred delicate kisses.

"This is not easy," he pulled back just long enough to say. And then he kissed her again. "It's never been easy." Another kiss. "Not once in five years." And another kiss. "Not once has it been easy." And another. "To stay away from you."

And then his tongue was in her mouth, seducing her with long, slow strokes, stirring heat in her body. Making her all but tremble with need. She felt as though her skin was overheated. Tingly and antsy. As if she was on fire. Her nipples prickled, demanding to be touched and she arched against him, pressing her breasts to his chest, desperate for some kind of contact. And still it wasn't enough.

Wrapping her arms around him, she twined her fingers into his hair and pulled him back just enough to ask, "Then why did you stay away?"

He gazed down at her, his eyes foggy with lust. "I don't know."

And for the life of her, she didn't know either. Honest to God, she couldn't think of one damn reason why they shouldn't be together. It had nothing to do with Peyton or the marriage. Nothing to do with her family or the rebellious tendencies she'd thought were long dead. This was about them. It had always been about them. And now that she was kissing him—now that his hands were all over her, making her tremble—she couldn't think of any reason why they should stay apart. When it was so obvious that they were meant to be together.

His lips moved from her mouth down to her neck, leaving a delicate trail of red-hot nibbles. She arched into his lips, all but praying he'd move lower and take her breast into his mouth.

"Oh, Jonathon," she murmured. "Please…"

She wasn't sure what exactly she was pleading for. Not when there were so many things she wanted him to do to her. So many places on her body she wanted him to touch and explore. All she knew was she wanted more. All of him.

Then abruptly, he let go of her and stepped away. Her body sagged with mounting desire, her legs limp and barely able to hold her up.

Thank goodness, she didn't need to support her own weight for long. His hand grasped her bottom, lifted her firmly against him and she automatically wrapped her legs around his waist. The position was perfect. Exquisite. As if her body had been precisely designed to wrap around his.

Her leggings were thin enough that she could feel the denim of his jeans through the delicate fabric. She felt every seam, every ridge. The hard line of his erection beneath his zipper pressed against the very center of her. She rocked her hips, increasing the pressure against her core, sending fissures of pleasure rocketing through her body.

He groaned low in his throat, still kissing her. Then he pulled his mouth away from hers. "You're killing me here."

She grinned, brimming with pure feminine pride. "Am I?" she asked, shifting her hips again, delighting in tormenting him. But the sensation was too divine and she shuddered as well.

He muttered a curse that was half exasperation, half pride. "I shouldn't do this," he muttered. "I should be stronger than this, but I can't…" He nipped at her neck in a primal, animal-istic sort of way that sent a shower of pleasure radiating across her skin. "I can't stay away any longer."

A second later, she felt him bump against the edge of his desk. He lowered her slowly down the length of his body. She didn't have even a moment to miss his warmth or the pressure against her sensitive skin, because he reached under the hem of her shirt and hooked his thumbs under the waistband of her tights and pulled them down her legs in one smooth movement, stripping away her panties as he did so.

She kicked off her shoes as she stepped out of her leggings, naked from the waist down. Her shirt hit her mid-thigh, but the fabric was gossamer thin and left her feeling scandalously exposed. Standing in her boss's office, half-naked, trembling with desire.

He stepped back to look at her. The heat in his gaze made her skin prickle. Suddenly she was very aware of her hardened nipples pressing against the thin cotton of her bra. Of the moisture between her legs and the cool air on her thighs.

A feeling of vulnerability started to creep in under the heat of desire. Then she looked up and saw the expression on Jonathon's face. It was part dumbstruck awe and part reverent glee. Like a little boy standing in front of a Christmas tree, staring at the presents, wondering which one was his.

She brought her hands to the buttons running down the front of her shirt. Then flicked them free, one by one. His gaze stayed glued to the progression of her hands. He didn't move an inch. Except for his hands, which slowly curled into fists. As if it was all he could do not to reach for her and rip the shirt off her body himself. As if she was his deepest fantasy come to life.

For all she knew, maybe she was.

She wanted to think so. Needed to believe it. Because he was certainly hers.

It wasn't a fantasy she'd consciously entertained. Never something she dwelled on. Nevertheless, the idea of being with Jonathon, of seeing exactly this expression in his gaze… it had always been there. Right beneath the surface of her thoughts. Niggling at the edge of her awareness. She'd pushed it aside countless times. But now she pulled it from the depths of her mind and let it out into the light of day.

She wanted this. For years she'd wanted this. And now he was about to be hers.

Her hands reached the last button. She slipped it free of the buttonhole, letting the shirt fall open.

With a sweep of his arm, Jonathon knocked everything off his desk except for the blotter. Then he set her down carefully on the desk.

"You can't imagine the times I thought about doing this." He pressed a hot kiss to her neck as he nudged her shirt off one shoulder. "Every day." He nipped at her collarbone, sending hot spikes of desire radiating down through her chest. "I pictured you sitting here." His fingers popped open the front closure of her bra and peeled back the cups to reveal her bare breasts. "Right on my desk." Her bra dropped off and she arched her back as he trailed the tip of one finger from her collarbone down to her nipple. "Completely naked."

With a groan he dropped to his knees in front of her. As if he could no longer resist the temptation she presented. He parted her thighs, moved her bottom right to the edge of the desk and placed his mouth at the very core of her.

He devoured her in tantalizing licks. She dropped back

onto her elbows, her eyes almost closed as wave after wave
of pleasure washed over her. He was patient and thorough.

The pleasure was so intense that her eyes nearly rolled back
in her head, but she couldn't make herself look away from the
sight of his head between her legs, his close-cropped dark hair
in such sharp contrast to her pale, quivering thighs.

Just when she thought she couldn't take it anymore, he
focused his relentless attention on the tiny bundle of nerves
so central to her pleasure, stroke after stroke, until she could
hardly catch her breath. Then she felt his hand at her entrance.
One finger, then two, plunged into her. She dropped onto her
back, arching off the desk. As her climax crashed over her,
she cried his name.

It felt like more than five years. Maybe his whole life he'd
been waiting to see her like this. Spread out before him on the
very desk that had so often been between them. She was the
most delectable treat he'd ever sampled. Hot and moist with
desire. Trembling from the aftereffects of a climax. His name
still a whisper on her lips.

Now, here she was. Just like he'd always wanted. And he
couldn't find a damn condom.

He had them here. Somewhere in the desk. Because he'd
known for years how much he wanted her. And that some
day he might act on it. Hell, there had been no "might" about
it. With only the slightest hint of interest from her, he'd have
acted on it. She needn't have stripped naked for him here in
his office, though that certainly had been a dream come true.

And now he couldn't find the damn things.

He pulled one drawer out completely, dumping the contents
on the floor. And then he did the same with the next drawer.
And the next. Finally he found them, just when he thought
the sight of her might make him come in his pants, just when
his erection was twitching with the need to be inside of her.

When she saw what he'd been looking for, she was as
eager as he was. He ripped open the package with trembling

fingers, even as she unbuttoned his jeans and shoved them down around his hips. Then a second later, he was inside of her, her legs spread wide, her arms outstretched as she leveraged herself against the desk. Her hips bucked off the surface as he plowed into her over and over again. The feel of her body clenching around him was exquisite. The taste of her, still on his lips, was divine. But it was the sound of her cries of pleasure that sent his own climax rocketing through his body.

He knew in that moment, that he wanted her—just like this—forever. And that scared the hell out of him.

As soon as Wendy was able to move again, she sat up, pressing her face against his chest and wrapping her arms around him. She breathed in the musky scent of him. Relished the feeling of his taut muscles beneath her fingers and of his warm skin beneath her cheek. She wanted to sit like this forever, wrapped around him. Clinging to him. Her body still thrumming with pleasure. The feeling of complete and utter contentment cocooning her from the rest of the world.

But the world was out there and it wouldn't stay away forever. So when he stepped out of her embrace, she let him go, when what she really wanted to do was hold on fast.

She moved slowly, pulling her bra back on and then her shirt. Her fingers were still fumbling with the buttons when he spoke.

"This can't happen again."

Her head whipped up and she stared at him. He'd turned away from her, but she could read the tension in his back as he zipped up his jeans. "Why not?"

"It's not a good idea." His voice was terse.

She felt that tension like a solid wall between them. She could feel him building it up. One brick at a time. One brick with each word. Part of her screamed that this wasn't the time for an argument. That the more they talked about it, the higher the wall would become, but she just couldn't let it go. It wasn't in her nature to back down from a fight.

"Not good for whom?" she asked.

"For anyone." He paused, then turned back to face her. His gaze drifted to her shirt, which hung open, her fingers having stilled midway up on their progress. "I'm afraid it'll be bad for you."

"Um, then you weren't paying attention," she said snarkily as she hopped off the desk. "Because that was extremely good for me."

She was naked from the waist down. True, her shirt was long enough that it hit her mid-thigh, but she still felt extremely exposed. Twenty minutes ago, before he'd rocked her world off its axis, that had been a good feeling. Now, not so much.

She swiped her tights off the ground, uncomfortably aware of how his gaze followed her every movement.

"Exactly. And good sex is addictive. You'll have a problem with that."

That cool, clinical tone of his made her blood pressure creep up. How the hell did he sound so calm? So rational?

"What kind of problem am I supposed to have with this… this extremely addictive sex?" And damn it, her tights were inside out. She rammed her hand down one of the legs, trying to snag the ankle hem so she could right them, but anger made her clumsy.

"I just don't think it's a good idea. It's not good for Peyton."

Watching Wendy's frustration grow as she wrestled with her tights, Jonathon wondered if perhaps he should have taken a different route.

"We're her parents now," she snapped, clearly exasperated. "I can't see how it would possibly hurt her for us to sleep together."

"You can't?" Why did she have to be so strongheaded?

Why couldn't she just make it easier on both of them and agree with him for once?

"No. I can't. In fact, since we agreed that this marriage could last up to two years, I actually think it's a good idea."

"Then you haven't thought it through."

Of course, nothing was ever that easy. Not with Wendy.

One of the things that made her such a great assistant was that she never hesitated to give her opinion. No mindless agreeing for her. If she had a better idea, she said so. If she spotted a problem he'd overlooked, she pointed it out. Unfortunately, right now, it made her a pain in the ass.

Because what he really wanted—no, damn it, what he needed—was for her to stop talking about sex.

"Okay, maybe I didn't think it through." Finally—thank God—she got her tights right side out and stepped into them. "But now that I am, I don't know that I see a downside. Two years is a long time. And—" She broke off, appearing to grit her teeth before spitting out her next words. "And I'm not going to tell you that you can't see other people while we're married."

"Wendy—"

"No. Just let me say this, okay?" She swallowed visibly, not quite meeting his gaze, though he could tell she was mustering the gumption to do so. "I'm not going to forbid you from…doing what you need to do. But goodness knows, I'm not going to be registering on eHarmony anytime soon. So, maybe it's not a bad idea to—"

"What?" he asked. "To hook up anytime either one of us has an itch?"

She rolled her eyes. "What is wrong with you? Are you purposefully being the biggest jerk in history for a reason?"

"What is wrong with *me*? What's wrong with *you*?" He swept a hand toward his desk, as if displaying the destruction they'd done. "Five minutes ago we were having sex on that desk and now you're talking about me being with another woman? How is that normal?"

This had to be the most awkward conversation in his entire

life. And considering that he sometimes talked to complete strangers about their finances, that was saying something.

She looked stricken by his words. Not for the first time either. She gave a little rapid blink, her eyes not quite reaching his gaze, and then swallowed. "I'm trying to be logical here. Two years is a long time and—"

"And you don't think I can keep my zipper up?"

Her gaze snapped to his face. "Let's just say, given that I've had a front-row seat to your dating practices for the past five years, I'm skeptical."

"Trust me. I can keep my zipper up."

She gave him a searing once-over. "All evidence to the contrary."

He gave her an icy, wolfish smile. "Is that really a stone you want to throw?"

"What do you want me to say? That I'm so impressed by your monkish fortitude?"

What *did* he want her to say?

He wanted her to say that she didn't want anyone else. That she wanted only him. And that she wanted him for some reason other than he was going to be convenient for the next two years.

"Okay, you want the truth? I don't think we should sleep together again, even if it means two years of celibacy. For both of us. I don't want you to get hurt, and you're too emotionally involved already."

"I'm too emotionally involved?" she scoffed, her voice dripping with sarcasm, but he could see the flash of pain in her gaze and knew he'd nailed it on the head. "*I* am? That's funny, because I wasn't the one just now who couldn't stop talking about how much I wanted this for the past five years. About how desperately I needed this."

Of course it would come back to that. He'd sounded like a lovesick fool. But neither of them would benefit from imagining he was some romanticized hero.

"Right," he said, bitterness seeping into his voice. "I talked about how I wanted your body. How much I wanted you physically. Not how much I loved you." As he spoke, the tear that had been clinging to her lashes, finally gave up its battle and dropped down onto her velvety cheek. He gently brushed it off with his thumb, then held it up as evidence. "And I'm not the one crying now."

"You bastard. I can't believe you said that." She stepped back, putting some distance between them. "And you're wrong about one thing. I won't be begging to sleep with you again anytime soon. Not now."

She stormed off, but made it only as far as the office door before turning around. Propping her fists on her hips, she said, "I need to know now. Are you in or out?"

"What?"

"Are you in or are you out? Do you still want to do this, or are you wigging out on me?"

"I'm in," he said slowly. Undoubtedly deeper in than he should be.

"Are you sure? Because two years is a long time. And I'd rather know now if you're having second thoughts."

"I said I'm in."

"Good. My family wants to meet yours. They're planning a reception for us. We leave for Palo Verde on Friday."

She didn't wait for his reply. It probably wouldn't have occurred to her that two years without sex wasn't nearly as off-putting as the idea of going to visit his family. A second later he heard the door to her office slam as she stormed out.

All alone in the office, he sank into his desk chair. Everything that had once been on his desk now lay scattered on the floor as well as the contents of three drawers. Years of keeping his life meticulously under control, of keeping his emotions neatly compartmentalized, and he'd blown it all in one reckless act.

He propped his elbows on his desk and dropped his head into his hands, ignoring the fact that his own cheeks felt suspiciously damp.

Thirteen

She wanted to stab him on her way out. There were several things in the office sharp enough to leave a nice puncture wound without being fatal. She took it as sign of great personal development that she didn't use any of them.

Then she sat in her car for several long minutes trying to hash out her feelings. Retrace her steps. Figure out where she'd gone wrong. In the end the only conclusion she could reach left her deeply unsatisfied.

Jonathon was right. She *was* too emotionally involved. She was up-to-her-tonsils-and-sinking-fast emotionally involved. Damn it.

Worse still, she couldn't follow her first instinct, which was to run like a rabbit and hole up somewhere until she sorted through her emotions. No, with her family here, watching her like a hawk… Or maybe a pride of ravenous lions was a better analogy? Whatever hungry predator they were, she couldn't bolt. They'd attack at the first sign of weakness. She had to remember what was important. Keeping Peyton.

Then she thought of what she'd seen just yesterday morning. Jonathon sitting in the rocking chair with Peyton cradled in his arms. He may not know it yet, but she wasn't the only one who was emotionally involved.

He may not care about her—beyond her body, which he was obviously rather fond of—but he did care about Peyton.

Whether or not he wanted to admit it, he was a good father. He was a better father than he was a husband. Well, she could live with that. For the time being, she had to.

The days before the trip to Palo Verde passed quickly. Jonathon insisted she take the time off to visit with her family. Which seemed counterintuitive to her since the whole point of the marriage was to keep her at work. But every time she brought it up, he just stared at her stiffly and reminded her that taking off work to bond with Peyton would go a long way toward convincing them that she would be a good mother. He assured her that they still had plenty of time to work on the contract proposal. He, however, went stalwartly into work alone. He never again mentioned taking time off himself to play the part of the loving husband. Apparently—after they'd had sex at the office—that would have strained even his resolve. She assumed that when he said she should spend time with her family, what he really meant was that she should spend time with anyone other than him.

Truth be told, she let him put her off over and over, because she wanted to avoid the office too. She wasn't ready to be in the office where he'd made love to her with such abandon. Scratch that. Made love to *her body* with such abandon. And she damn sure wasn't ready to see him sitting behind the desk, working as if nothing had ever happened.

So she spent the days playing tour guide to her family. Mema was determined to hate everything about California and Big Hank flew back to Texas for the week, but her parents seemed to actually enjoy the time she spent with them. Even more shocking, she enjoyed it too.

She assumed that would change by the end of the week, when Big Hank, Hank Jr. and Helen would arrive. Helen had insisted on planning the wedding reception Mema had suggested the Morgans host. Without even leaving Texas, Helen had arranged a venue, invited guests and booked lodgings for the Morgans, which was no small feat to accomplish in just a few days' time. Whenever Wendy offered help, she was firmly rebuffed. Helen had even located and invited Jonathon's family. Though, apparently, only his older sister, Marie, had returned Helen's phone calls.

Wendy could hardly blame Jonathon's family. By the end of the week, she was sick of talking to Helen. The only thing worse than dealing with her was dealing with Jonathon.

At the end of each day, he'd arrive home and she'd have to—once again—pretend to be a loving wife. With the tension between them as strong as it was, she doubted she fooled anyone. Jonathon, however, did a bang-up job. She could barely turn around without having him there to touch her. To wrap his arm around her shoulder and drop a careless kiss on her forehead.

The nights were the worst. She could make it all the way through the day, she could even pretend in front of her parents, but her stomach knotted every time they closed and locked the bedroom door. She didn't know if her family found it odd for them to be locking the door, but she didn't dare risk having them walk in unannounced and seeing his pallet at the foot of the bed, where he'd been sleeping. The closest they came to communicating was the moment each night when she threw the pillow at him. Unfortunately, he always caught it. Damn him.

And before she knew it, it was Thursday. The week had slipped by and they'd be driving out to Palo Verde in the morning.

She lay there in the dark, unable to sleep and staring at the ceiling, irritated by the rhythm of his slow, even breathing from the foot of the bed. Thirty minutes passed. Then another twenty. Then she heard him roll over and sigh.

"Are you still awake?" she whispered in the dark.

"Of course. I'm on the floor and you're tossing and turning so much it sounds like a bounce house over there."

She bolted upright and snapped on the bedside lamp. "Would you just get into bed."

He blinked up at her, wedging his elbows under him. "Turn off the light. Try to get some sleep."

"I'd be able to sleep better if I didn't know you were uncomfortable sleeping on the floor."

He lay back down and stared up at the ceiling. "It's not that bad."

"It's two blankets and a pillow. It can't be good. You'll be safe sleeping in the bed. I'm not going to attack you or anything."

"It's just better if we limit our contact as much as possible. I'm trying to be noble here."

"Yeah." She snorted, falling back onto the bed. "I think that ship sailed the day we had sex on your desk."

"You're going to wake up Peyton."

Even though Big Hank had left, they'd decided to keep Peyton's crib in their room. She'd slept so much better when she was only a few inches away from them.

And though she knew Jonathon had a point—winning the argument wasn't worth waking Peyton, who would want to be fed in a few hours anyway—it only irritated her more. She yanked her pillow out from under her head and threw it at him. There was a satisfying whump as it landed on his torso.

"I already have a pillow."

"I know. I just wanted to throw something at you."

"Very mature."

"I know." Smiling, she snapped off the light.

He brought the pillow back to her, standing next to her side of the bed in the dark and holding it out to her. "I don't need it.'

"Keep it. Maybe it'll make the floor a little less uncomfortable."

"Wendy—" he growled.

"I'm trying to be *noble*."

"Fine," he snapped and went back to lie down.

It was wrong how pleased she was by the irritation in his voice. He may act as if he was completely indifferent to her, but she was still able to get under his skin. That shouldn't make her happy. But it did.

A few minutes later, she fell asleep smiling. And woke up in the morning with the pillow under her head.

At eighteen, Jonathon had left Palo Verde with $5,168.36 in his checking account—all earmarked for living expenses. His only other possessions were a partial scholarship to Stanford, two suitcases, a desk lamp, a used laptop, a backpack and a veritable mountain of student loans. He'd hitched a ride from their hometown to the coast in Matt's BMW. Jonathon hadn't been back since.

Palo Verde was a small but historic town on the highway between Sacramento and Lake Tahoe. When he'd left in the mid-nineties, it was only just beginning to climb out of the economic slump that had cursed it since the gold rush ended more than a hundred years before. Now Sacramento had grown enough—and was expensive enough—for people to commute from Palo Verde. On a purely intellectual level, Jonathon supposed Palo Verde wasn't such a bad place to live. The town had a certain charm to it. Not the sort that any teenage boy would appreciate, but surely plenty of people liked musty old buildings and the gently rolling foothills of the Sierra Nevada mountains.

Nevertheless, during the drive Jonathon practically itched to turn the car around and get the hell out of there. If someone had asked him a month ago, he'd have sworn that nothing short of the coming apocalypse would have enticed him back to Palo Verde. Maybe not even that. If the world was coming to an end, why would he go there?

As they entered Palo Verde, with Peyton safely nestled in her car seat in the backseat, and Wendy beside him in the front, Jonathon clenched his hands so tightly around the steering wheel that he feared he might snap it in half. Sure, it was unlikely, but if anything was going to imbue him with Incredible Hulk-like powers, it would be this.

Wendy's family was in the rented minivan behind them on the highway. She sat with her iPhone, carefully dictating directions from the GPS map, as if he hadn't spent the first eighteen years of his life trapped in this God-forsaken hell-hole.

"Okay," she said in a half whisper since Peyton was asleep. "It looks like this road will merge with Main Street just ahead."

"I know."

She ignored him. "And then, a couple of miles into town Cutie Pies will be on your left."

"I know."

"It looks like there's parking on the street, but according to Claire's email, it fills up pretty quickly, so if we don't get a spot, we should circle around to the back of—"

"I. Know."

Wendy dropped the phone in her lap and held up her hands. "Hey, I'm just doing my part as navigator."

"I grew up here." He blew out a slow breath, prying the fingers of his left hand off the steering wheel and giving them a flex. "I don't need a navigator."

"Things can change a lot in fifteen years."

He didn't need her to tell him that. He was a completely different man than the boy who'd left town straight out of high school. He'd always thought it odd that spending his whole life wanting to escape from Palo Verde, he'd end up living in a city with such a similar name. Of course, Palo Alto was a completely different kind of town. The bustling

ntellectual hotbed of technological development. A city with
many brilliant, very rich men. And he was one of them. So
here was no reason at all that just breathing Palo Verde air
should stir all his rebellious instincts. Yet it did.

It made him twitchy with energy and shortened his already
strained temper. As if she sensed his mood—not that he was
doing a great job of hiding it or anything—Wendy reached
out a hand and gave his leg a stroke that she probably meant
to be soothing. "It's just been a while since you've been back.
was trying to help."

He could feel the heat of her hand through the fabric of
his jeans and it made his thigh muscles twitch. Instantly, he
knew what he really wanted. The one thing that would expel
all the anger and tension roiling inside of him. Sex. Good,
clean, emotionless sex would do the trick. He could skip the
drive through town to Cutie Pies and head up to the hairpin
turns of Rock Creek Road, pull off into the trees, tug Wendy
onto his lap and screw her right here in the front seat.

It was a good plan if he ignored the baby sleeping in the
back of the car. It'd be even better if he didn't know emotionless sex was impossible with Wendy.

And then there was the minivan full of in-laws behind
them. And the wedding reception Wendy's helpful cousins
had planned for them.

He took little pleasure in knowing that once the wedding
reception was over, he could leave Palo Verde and never look
back. It didn't even help knowing that tomorrow Matt, Claire,
Ford, Kitty and Ilsa would arrive for the reception. Having
his best friends and their families there would make things
better, but only a little bit. Before he could get through that
reception tomorrow night, he still had lunch at Cuties Pies—
that part wouldn't be bad. But he'd begun to wish he'd refused
to come into town the day before the reception. Two whole
days in his hometown was way too long.

It meant a lot of time dreading meeting with his family. Oh,
he knew it was unavoidable. That was—after all—the sole

purpose in having a wedding reception in Palo Verde. But he certainly didn't relish the idea.

In short. It sucked. The whole situation sucked.

He'd been acting like an ass ever since they'd had sex in his office. Of course, he didn't need Wendy's faux armchair psychology degree to figure out why. He was pushing her away every chance he got. Now if he could just get her to actually *go* away. So far, she wasn't budging.

He knew there were infinite explanations for the tenacity with which she clung to their relationship. The very fact that she was desperate enough to marry him in the first place was testament to that. With her family hovering nearby for the past week, she couldn't very well boot him out the door. And then there were those defiant urges of hers. She'd said it herself. For a woman from an old oil family, a man who made his money from green technology was the ultimate rebellion.

He'd been trying all week to distance himself emotionally from her, and he'd only made things more awkward. Since actively driving her away didn't seem to be working, it was time to own up to his mistakes. "I'm sorry. I just—"

"You're sorry?" She laughed. "Why on earth are you sorry? It's not your family who's bullied us into this stupid reception. I'm the one who should be apologizing."

"No, I've been acting like a jerk."

"No argument there," she muttered.

"And it's been worse for the past couple of days. I just—" Why was this so hard to say aloud? "I just don't look forward to having you meet them."

"Them?" she asked, her brow furrowing in confusion.

"My family."

"Why? Because my family's so great? With the manipulation and the backstabbing?"

"But they're…" he let the sentence trail off, realizing how it would sound.

"They're what?" When he didn't answer, she arched a

brow. "They're rich. That's what you were going to say, isn't it? You think wealth excuses bad behavior? Well, it doesn't."

"That's not what I meant."

"Then what are you afraid of? Do you think I'm going to think less of you once I meet your family? Once I see firsthand that you grew up in poverty?"

There was enough indignation in her voice that he knew better than to say yes. That's exactly what he was afraid of.

As he pulled the car to a stop at a light, she shifted in the seat so she half faced him. "Be forewarned, I don't care about your past or where you came from, but the rest of my family might. And Helen is a real piece of work. If she thinks she can make you look bad by yanking the skeletons out of your closet, she'll do it. Just remember, no matter what she says, the fact that you come from a poor family doesn't make you less worthy in my eyes. It makes you more worthy. Yes, my family is wealthy, but so what? I didn't have to work for any of that money. You've worked for every penny you have. In my book, that says a lot."

Listening to her words loosened some of the anxiety in his chest. He could almost believe that she was right. And that where he came from made him a better man.

Almost. But not quite.

Fourteen

She'd heard a lot about Cutie Pies, but most of it had been from Matt. Considering that his wife owned the place, she'd expected all the praise to be exaggerated, but was pleased to find that it wasn't. It was a classic small-town diner on main street. It could have been found in any town in the United States. But rather than the standard greasy-spoon fare, the food was fresh, tasty and unique. However, at lunch, none of that made up for the tension hovering over the table like a dense, poisonous gas.

The atmosphere—compliments of Helen—was largely due to the fact that she'd invited Jonathon's sisters and brothers to the lunch without mentioning it to him or to her.

What had promised to be a stressful meal anyway was made even worse by Helen's interference. They arrived at the restaurant to find Helen and Hank Jr. out in front. Helen—always a picture of moneyed, blond sophistication—looked horribly out of place in the homey diner. She gave air kisses to everyone, then linked arms with Mema and sashayed through

he front door, the chime over her head tinkling, ringing the
death knell of any hope Wendy had that this visit would go
smoothly.

"I tried to call from the jet to reserve a table," Helen was
saying, "but apparently, this little place doesn't even take
reservations."

Wendy surveyed the restaurant with its simple red uphol-
stered booths and gleaming bar stools. "It's a diner," she said
dryly. "Of course it doesn't take reservations."

The interior of Cutie Pies was clean but worn, the staff
friendly but unsophisticated. Wendy instantly loved it.
Helen—who would turn up her nose at anything just to show
she could—offered strained smiles, as though it was a horrible
burden to be forced to eat in such a place. She didn't bother to
hide it when she pulled an antiseptic wipe from her Gucci bag
and gave the table a quick scrubbing before letting anyone sit
down.

Then before anyone even had a chance to look over a menu,
she hopped back up, standing behind Hank Jr. and talking as
though she were hosting an elaborate dinner party.

"H.J. and I just want to thank y'all for coming for this
reception we're throwing for our little Gwen."

Jonathon leaned close and whispered, "*Their* little Gwen?"

Wendy shot him a surprised look at the obvious amusement
in his voice. Apparently poking fun at Helen's extravagant
efforts to stay in the spotlight was enough to dissolve the tension between them.

Secretly pleased, she whispered back, "Fair warning—if
you ever call me 'your little Gwen,' I'm stabbing you in the
leg with a pickle fork."

Peyton sat in a high chair between them, happily gurgling
away on a ring of rubber keys. Jonathon smiled and their
eyes met over Peyton's head. For that moment—with Helen
spewing utter nonsense at the end of the table, surrounded
by her family with all their ridiculous eccentricities—she felt
a bone-deep connection to Jonathon. Somehow, being with

him made all of this—this weird family stuff she was having
to deal with—seem more manageable. Yes, her family was
overbearing, controlling, borderline obsessive. But for the first
time, she felt strong enough to handle it. Because he was here
with her.

That's when it hit her. She loved him.

This newfound feeling of being at peace with her family—
hell, with the whole world—was due to him. Having him in
her corner made her believe that she was capable of anything.

Wendy shook her head, rattled by the sudden—and damn
scary—insight. At the head of the table, Helen said something
that she must have intended to be funny, because she gave a
tittering laugh. Peyton let out a loud squawk of protest. To
calm her down, Wendy reached a hand over to pat her on
the back. From the other side, Jonathon did the same and
their hands touched. For an instant, they both stilled. Then
Jonathon brushed his thumb across the back of her hand. Such
a simple gesture, but the first time he'd voluntarily touched
her since they'd had sex at the office.

A feeling of calm swept over her. They were going to be
all right. Sure, they'd have some tough times ahead, but they
could work through them. She was pretty sure. She tried to
keep her smile to herself, but didn't quite manage it.

But then she glanced at Jonathon and realized he'd gone
stone still. His gaze was pinned to a woman by the door. She
was dressed simply in worn jeans and a T-shirt. Her hair was
long and dark, with an inch-thick gray streak arcing over her
forehead. She looked both earthy and beautiful. And her eyes
were the exact same shade as Jonathon's.

"Oh, good!" Helen clapped her hands. "You must be
Jonathon's sister, Mary. It's nice to meet after all the emails
exchanged."

"Marie," the woman said, her gaze sweeping over the
cluster of tables that now dominated Cutie Pies.

"I was afraid no one from Jonathon's family would make
it." Helen made a grand show of bustling over to Marie.

She hesitated, as if trying to figure out how to give Marie a welcoming hug without actually touching the other woman. She settled on giving an air kiss in the vicinity of Marie's cheek. "Welcome to the family."

Marie arched a brow, practically sneering her derision.

Wendy liked her instantly.

Unfortunately, it was obvious that Jonathon did not feel the same way.

Marie had never liked rich people. Of course, under these circumstances, Jonathon couldn't blame her. Helen was pretentious and obnoxious. She clearly thought she was better than Marie—probably better than everyone in the whole town—and she didn't bother to hide it.

Jonathon wasn't surprised that after all these years, Marie could still get her nose bent out of shape so easily. He also wasn't surprised that she was the only one in his family who would bother to show up. Family was everything to Marie. Even for family that had long ago deserted her.

Still it was obvious she didn't want to be there, in everything from the way she ordered nothing but tea, to the generous space she managed to wedge between her seat and the others near her.

Helen seemed doggedly determined to ignore the tension that hung over the table.

"So, Marie," Helen said brightly. "Tell us what you do."

Marie shot an annoyed look at Jonathon, as if he was somehow to blame for the inquisition. "I stay at home with my kids."

"Oh," was all Helen could say.

"What, you don't think that's real work?"

"No. I—" Helen fumbled for an answer. Jonathon couldn't help but enjoy her discomfort. After all, she had it coming. "I stay at home with my children myself. I know what a big job it is."

Beside him, Wendy snorted into her iced tea, trying to hide

her laughter and keep from spewing her drink. Hadn't Wendy said Helen's kids went to boarding school?

Wendy stepped in to rescue Helen before she made an even bigger ass of herself. "Marie, will more of Jonathon's family be able to make it to the reception tomorrow? We'd love to meet his parents."

Marie shot him a confused frown. "Our dad died when Jonathon was in high school."

He felt, rather than saw, the stillness sweep over Wendy. "Oh. I'm sorry to hear that."

He should have told her. Of course he should have. But it wasn't the kind of thing that came up in normal conversation and he'd never particularly wanted to talk about it with anyone.

"Cancer," Marie said. "Probably from all those chemical pesticides."

"Oh," Helen said, trying to smooth over the awkward pause. "Is your family in agriculture?"

"Our dad worked in the apple orchards, if that's what you mean, but I wouldn't fancy it up by saying he was in agriculture."

"I see." Helen managed to sound almost sympathetic, but the faint glimmer of satisfaction in her eyes ruined the effect. "And your mother?"

"She lives in Tucson now, with her sister."

"And are there other siblings?" Helen asked.

Beside him, Wendy stared sightlessly down at her plate. He could practically read her mind. All the things he hadn't told her about his family were coming back to bite him on the ass. And there wasn't a damn thing he could do about it. He couldn't very well call a time-out, pull her back into the kitchen and pour out his whole miserable life's story. Even if he was the kind of the guy who would do that.

Before Marie could answer, Jonathon cut in. "Enough, Marie." Marie sharpened her gaze into a glare and looked as if she wanted to respond, but he didn't let her. "Enough acting defensive. If you're mad at me for not visiting more often or whatever, fine. We'll talk about it later." He turned his gaze on Helen next. "And enough from you too."

Helen looked as if she'd been slapped. He suspected that it was rare for anyone to put her in her place. "I never—"

"If you want to know about my family, ask me. Chances are, none of us are going to meet with your approval. My father worked in the orchards. My mother checked groceries. There are a lot of babies born out of wedlock. A sprinkling of jail time, but no felons. On the bright side, all of my nieces and nephews who are old enough have graduated from high school and most of them have gone to college. On scholarship. Not many families can say that. All in all, we're mostly just hardworking people you'd look down your nose at." He swept his gaze from Helen to the rest of the table. "Any other questions?"

No one spoke. After several seconds of silence, he pushed his chair back and said, "Wendy, why don't you grab Peyton and we'll go check into the hotel."

He dropped some cash by the register on the way out and waited for her on the sidewalk.

The second he left Cutie Pies, he knew it was a mistake. People like Helen were emotional vultures. Once she saw his vulnerabilities, she'd be circling overhead until something else brought him down. Then she'd pick over his carcass.

There was a bench out on the sidewalk, just a few steps away from the door to the diner, but still out of view of the interior. He sank to the bench and propped his head in his hands.

"That was brilliant, by the way."

He looked up to see Wendy standing there, Peyton on her hip, purse slung over her shoulder.

"That was stupid," he replied.

"No. Brilliant. Helen needs to have someone stand up to her occasionally. She puts on airs too often. If she knew how much Mema hated it, she wouldn't do it." Wendy gave a sly grin. "Which, I suppose is why I've never told her that Mema hates it."

"It was still stupid." He stood, rolling his shoulders to release some of the tension there.

"No, I agree with Wendy," came a voice near the door.

Jonathon looked around Wendy to see Marie standing just behind Wendy. "You know how I feel about putting people in their place."

"Yes, I do. I'm just not sure the patented Bagdon method of dealing with things is the way to go."

"What?" Marie asked. "The old beat-the-crap-out-of-someone-until-they-agree-with-you wouldn't work on her?"

He chuckled, despite himself.

"Look," Marie said, taking a step closer and giving him a little pat on the cheek. "It was good to see you. Even if it meant putting up with Ms. Snooty-pants in there."

Marie turned and headed down the block.

"Wait!" Wendy called out. "Won't we see you tomorrow at the reception?"

Marie sent her an amused look. "No offense, but no Bagdon is going to set foot in the country club. It's just not going to happen."

"But—"

"Sorry. It was nice to meet you."

Wendy watched Marie walk away for a second before thrusting Peyton into Jonathon's arms and rushing after her. "Then where should we have it?"

"Excuse me?" Marie stopped and looked at Wendy as if she'd grown another head.

"Forget Helen and her stupid ideas about a wedding reception. The only point in actually having a reception— and having it in Palo Verde—is so that I can meet Jonathon's family. If none of them will come to the country club, then I would like to know where we should have the party so that his family will come."

Marie looked warily at Jonathon, undoubtedly trying to figure out if Wendy was serious. All he could do was shrug. After all, he couldn't very well tell either woman that the last thing he wanted was to see his family again, let alone introduce them to his new wife.

"Isn't the party tomorrow night?" Marie asked. "You won't be able to plan a new party in twenty-four hours."

Wendy just grinned. She nodded toward him. "I keep FMJ organized and running. This will be a breeze."

Marie looked from Wendy to him and then back again, but she still looked doubtful. "Okay. If you want…" Marie got a shifty look in her eyes, one he remembered all too well from his childhood. She'd always had a knack for pushing boundaries and his gut told him that just now she was going to see how far she could push Wendy. "You should have it at my house."

"Marie—" he warned.

"I can't ask you to do that," Wendy said, cutting him off. "It's too much of an imposition."

"Or…" Marie said archly, "you think my house won't be nice enough."

He watched Wendy carefully, curious whether she'd pick up on Marie's subtle manipulation.

"No, no!" Wendy began. "That's not what I meant."

But Marie ruined whatever advantage she might have had by letting just a hint of smug satisfaction creep into her smile.

Wendy caught it. For the briefest second, she looked puzzled, but she recovered quickly. "I'm sure your house is lovely. What time would you like us to be there?" She didn't give Marie a chance to answer, but linked arms with the other woman and began walking toward the back parking lot, where Marie had been headed before Wendy had stopped her.

Jonathon had little choice but, with Peyton in his arms, to fall into step behind the two women and observe the battle of wills from what he hoped was a safe distance.

"Do you want me to try to find a caterer?" Wendy asked.

"A caterer?" Marie said the word as if it was a curse.

Jonathon would bet she'd never had a catered meal in her life.

"No, you're right," Wendy responded. "If Jonathon's family would be offended by the ostentation of the country club, then a caterer wouldn't be good either. We'll just show up with food, if you don't mind us using your kitchen. My mother is an excellent cook. And my father and Big Hank make some of the best barbecue in the state. Texas, that is." She flashed a bright smile. "Of course, we'll have to arrive early for that. Say, seven?"

"In the morning?" Marie squeaked. "You might as well stay with us overnight."

Wendy pretended not to hear the sarcasm in Marie's voice. "Jonathon and I would love that! We'll come over as soon as we get the rest of my family settled at the hotel. I assume Jonathon knows where the house is?"

Marie looked as though she'd been sideswiped by a fast-moving vehicle. "It's the house he grew up in."

Marie stopped in front of an old Ford. The car was worn, with a dented bumper and enough scratches that it looked as if it had been mauled by a lion. There were booster seats in the back and toys littering the floorboard.

"Great! We'll get my family settled at the hotel and see you in a few hours." Wendy launched herself at Marie and gave her a hug. "I've always wanted a sister."

Wendy stood beside him, her arm around his waist and her head resting on his shoulder while they watched the flabbergasted Marie back out of the parking lot and drive away.

As soon as the car was out of sight, Wendy straightened and sent him an exasperated look as she took Peyton back from him. "You should have warned me how things were between you and your siblings."

He shrugged. "You were the one who's been so sure you know me."

She considered his words and then nodded. "Okay. Fair enough." She studied him, her head cocked to the side, her expression pensive. "Do you ever see them at all?"

Instead of answering, he asked a question of his own. "You realize, don't you, that Marie didn't really invite us to stay with her?"

Wendy scoffed. "Of course I do. I'm not an idiot. But I'm not going to let her believe that we think she's not good enough."

"The last time I saw it, the house I grew up in was a total dump. It *isn't* good enough. Certainly not for your family."

"Let me worry about what's good enough for my family. Helen may be a fool, but…" She exhaled a long, slow breath. "Well, they're certainly difficult, but they know when to keep their mouths shut. And don't forget, Big Hank has been in politics for twenty years now. You don't get as far as he has without appreciating the hardworking middle class."

"But—"

Wendy cut him off. "Come on, we don't have time to debate it. We've got an impromptu wedding reception to plan."

She turned and headed back to the restaurant, but he snagged her arm as she passed. "What exactly is it you think you're doing here?"

She arched an eyebrow. "Isn't it obvious?"

"Unfortunately, it is. You think you're going to repair my relationship with my family."

She shrugged. "Well, somebody has to."

"No." He dropped her arm and shoved his hands deep into his pockets. "No one has to do it at all. My relationship with my sisters and brothers is nobody's business but mine. Stay out of it."

"I'm not going to." She said it so simply, only a hint of condescension in her voice. "This is your family. I'm not going to stay out. You obviously regret how strained your relationship with them is. Someone has to bridge the gap."

"And what exactly is it you think you're going to gain by doing this for me? You want me to be thankful? You want me to drop down onto my knees in gratitude? What do you expect?"

A tiny frown creased her brow, as if she didn't understand the question. "I expect you to be happy."

"Mending the rift between me and my family isn't going to make me happy."

"Are you sure?" She cupped his jaw with her hand, her blue-violet eyes gazing up into his with such compassion it nearly took his breath away. "Because you want to know what I think? I think you've never forgiven yourself for walking away from them. I think, when you left to form FMJ, you never looked back and that you've always regretted it."

"If I did walk away from them and never looked back, maybe it's because I don't want them in my life. Did that ever occur to you? Maybe I'm just a selfish enough bastard that I want to enjoy my wealth and success without any reminders around of where I came from."

"I don't believe that."

"You don't have to believe it for it to be true."

"You know what I *do* believe? I believe you don't have any idea how to bridge the gap between you, so you just let it stand."

He didn't know what to say, didn't know how to convince her that she was spinning fantasies about him that just weren't true. And whatever words he might have used to convince her got choked in his throat anyway. So he said nothing and let her continue talking.

"I've seen you with Peyton. I know how good you are with her. How caring. And I know you must have felt that same way about your family. Your real family. I think you haven't married and had kids of your own because it's your way of punishing yourself for abandoning them. That's the real reason you wanted to marry me. By marrying me, you could lie to yourself about your motives, but you'd still have the family you've always wanted."

"That's bull." He said it with more conviction than he felt. "I married you because FMJ fell apart without you. But don't think that the freedom you have in running FMJ's office extends to meddling in my personal life."

"What personal life?" she scoffed. "That's the point, isn't it? That's why none of your romantic relationships last longer than a financial quarter and why Matt and Ford are your only friends."

He wasn't even going to dignify that with a response. Instead, he stalked toward her until she backed up a step and then another. "I'm going to make this real simple for you. Back off."

"No."

"No?" He stopped, flabbergasted by her gall. "What do you mean, no?"

"I mean, no, I'm not going to back off."

"Why the hell do you even care about this?"

"Because we're married now. And I care about you." She crossed her arms over her chest, bumping up her chin as if she was challenging him to argue with her. "There. I said it. I care about you and I want you to be happy. I don't think this—this thing where you cut yourself off from everyone is going to make you happy. So I'm going to do everything in my power to fix it." She took a step closer to him and gave his chest a firm poke. "And unless you want to fire me, admit to everyone that our marriage was a ruse and give me an annulment right now, there's not a damn thing you can do about it."

With that, she turned on her heel and marched away, back around the corner to Main Street and back to her family waiting for them in Cutie Pies. Where presumably she'd announce her plan to move the wedding reception to Marie's house. All in the interest of repairing familial bonds.

Ah, crap.

This marriage thing was ending up to be much more work than he'd anticipated.

Fifteen

Jonathon did not want to spend the afternoon becoming reacquainted with his big, sprawling mess of a family.

He did not want to spend the night in the tiny, three-bedroom, two-bathroom tract house where he'd grown up.

Hell, he didn't even want to leave the comfort of Palo Verde's one luxury hotel. Luxury being a somewhat fluid term. In this case, meaning historic, not decrepit and possessing a well-stocked bar.

After lunch, he'd drawn out the afternoon as much as possible, his annoyance with Helen surpassed only by his aversion to spending more time with his own family. So he showed Wendy's family around town, lingering over checking them into the hotel. Anything to avoid bringing Wendy to his sister's house.

Which was why he was now hiding out in the bar, waiting for Wendy to walk her grandmother back to her room.

He sat there, the ice-cold Anchor Steam almost untouched

in front of him, considering his options for getting out of sleeping on his sister's living-room floor on a blow-up bed.

While the place may or may not be quite the dump it had been when he was growing up, it was still smaller than his sister's five kids needed. And for some reason he'd never understood, his sister doggedly clung to the damn thing. While he didn't keep in touch with any of his siblings, he kept tabs on them and their finances. He didn't want to be involved in their lives, but he didn't want any of them out on the street either. And he'd made sure his sister could afford better if she wanted it. Apparently she didn't.

Now he wished he'd given up on being subtle and respecting her pride and had just bought her a damn mansion. Hell, maybe it wasn't too late. What were the chances he could find a twenty-four-hour Realtor?

He took one last swig of beer and then pushed away from the mostly full bottle. Before he could even stand up, Big Hank sauntered in.

"Thank God, you're here." Big Hank pulled back a chair for himself without waiting for an invitation.

"Is something wrong?" Jonathon asked, poising to head for the door if there was.

"No, no," Hank muttered. The big man pulled off his cowboy hat and settled it onto one of his knees. "I just hate to drink alone." Then he laughed as if he'd told the funniest joke.

Jonathon smiled, humoring the older man until the waitress could come over to take his drink order. For the first few minutes, while they were waiting, Hank spun his particular brand of good-ol'-boy charm.

Jonathon was too wise to underestimate him. Instead he said little and mostly listened to one over-the-top story after another. He knew better than to take the stories seriously. But also knew that every word out his mouth could be the truth. With a guy like Big Hank, just about anything was possible.

Just as Jonathon was finishing his beer and about to make his excuses, Hank settled back, stretched an arm along the back of his side of the booth and said, "But enough about me." If the past thirty minutes were any indication, he wasn't a man who could ever say enough about himself. "I want to talk to you about Gwen."

Something in his tone gave Jonathon pause. "What about her?"

Hank gave the ice in his scotch glass a little swirl. "When you left the restaurant today, Mema sent me to find you. I overheard your conversation in the parking lot."

Which could mean almost anything, depending on how much of the conversation Hank had heard. "And?"

"And I know your marriage is a sham."

"And?" Jonathon asked again.

"You know what I think? I think Gwen put you up to this. I think she's trying to worm her way into Mema's good graces, so she can avoid a custody battle." Hank chuckled, raising his glass as if in toast to Wendy's ingenuity. "What I couldn't figure out at first was how she roped you into going along with her." Hank gestured with the glass he held in his hand. "You're a smart man. I doubt you'd get involved with this scheme of hers unless it benefited you."

"I love Wendy," Jonathon said, the rehearsed words sounding flat on his tongue.

"No," Hank muttered. "I don't think you do."

Jonathon leaned forward, propping his elbows on the table. "You can't prove I don't love her."

Hank took a gulp of his drink and gave his head a sharp shake of his head. "I think she convinced you that a marriage to her would benefit FMJ. I think that's how she got you to marry her."

"She didn't *get* me to marry her. I proposed."

Hank studied him for a moment, then his lips twisted in a sly smile. "FMJ does some extraordinary work."

The sudden change of topic gave Jonathon only a moment's pause. "What's your point?"

"I know you're putting together a big proposal for the

Department of Energy. Those smart-grid meters of yours are mighty interesting. Matt said if y'all win this government contract, every government building in the country will be retrofitted with one of those meters. Could save the nation millions in electric bills."

"Matt wasn't supposed to show you the smart-grid meters."

"He got a little overenthusiastic. And I found them mighty interesting."

"And let me guess, if I do something you want, you'll make sure FMJ gets that contract?"

"No. Certainly not. That would be nepotism." He scoffed as though the idea were repugnant. Then added, "But what I could do is make sure that the FMJ doesn't get the contract."

"And what do I need to do in return?"

"Get an annulment. Send Wendy home with her family."

"No," Jonathon said without even considering an answer.

"Just think about all those smart-grid meters of yours," Hank said, his voice taking on a slick and oily quality. "All those fantastic widgets of yours. Sitting in a warehouse, doing nothing."

"You're threatening me."

Hank smiled. "More to the point, I'm threatening FMJ. Make no mistake about it. If you walk away from this marriage, I can make fabulous things happen for you and for FMJ."

"But only if I walk away. From Wendy and from Peyton."

"Exactly."

"Just tell me this. Why? Why go to all the trouble to blacklist me over one tiny baby. Wendy thinks it's all about the money. But I don't believe that. Did Mema put you up to this?"

"No. All she really wants is for Wendy to visit more often. She'd be happy with a promise to bring Peyton to Texas every once in a while."

"So why not just let Wendy raise her?"

Big Hank pinned him with a steely stare. "Now don't get me wrong, boy. I have a lot of respect for your Gwen. It takes some *cojones* to stand up for yourself in this family. And your Gwen certainly has a pair. Probably bigger than Hank Jr.— though Helen could give her a run for her money. The thing about Helen, at least I know how to control her. She always follows the money. But Gwen…Gwen's a loose cannon. She doesn't give a damn about the money."

Jonathon thought about Wendy and knew that her uncle was right, about the money at least. She didn't care about it. She cared about the baby. After a minute, Jonathon looked up to find Big Hank studying him. "What about me?" he asked.

Hank studied him shrewdly. "You're a businessman first and foremost. You haven't spent the last thirteen years of your life building a company from the ground up just to throw it away over a baby. Or even over a woman. You'll do what's right by FMJ."

Jonathon pretended to think about it. Mostly because Big Hank would never take seriously someone who would turn down his deal without considering it. Then he shook his head, chuckling a little under his breath. "You know, she said you'd do this."

Big Hank smirked. "Do what?"

"She said that her family always found a way to twist what someone wants. Turn it against them. Or rather turn them against her."

For a second, Big Hank looked as though he might deny the accusation. Then he just shrugged his shoulders and owned up to it. "Most of the time, she's made it easy. Wendy always dated men who were weaker than she was." Big Hank gave Jonathon a slow and assessing look. "But not you, son."

"No. Not me." He scraped a line of condensation off his beer bottle. "So tell me something. From what I understand, you tried to control your daughter, Bitsy, and in the end you only drove her away. So why are you trying to do the same thing to Peyton?"

"Why did the scorpion sting the turtle? It's in my nature.

And people don't really change, no matter how they wish they could."

Jonathon pushed back his chair. "Well, sir, with all due respect, I've lived my whole life in Northern California. And I don't understand homespun analogies about scorpions. Never seen a scorpion in my life."

"Is that your way of telling me you're not going to take me up on my offer?"

"I suppose it is."

Big Hank arched a skeptical brow. "You fancy yourself in love with Gwen? You think you're going to impress her by turning me down?"

For one overly long instant, time seemed to stop. As if everything in his body came to a complete and utter standstill, but the rest of the world kept turning and slammed against him with full force.

Love? Was he in love with Wendy?

The idea was preposterous. Ludicrous.

And yet...

He shook his head, partly in answer to Big Hank's question and partly to dispel the very idea before it could take root in his mind. "No. I don't think this will impress her. I don't plan on her ever finding out about your offer."

"You know my offer goes both ways. I could guarantee you get the contract. I could make sure every government building in the country uses one of your smart-grid meters. Hell, I could get one in every house built in the next decade. Or I can guarantee that FMJ never sees another drop of government money. Not on this project. Not on any project. Ever."

"You make it sound so tempting. Would you like a swivel chair to sit in and fluffy white cat to stroke while you repeat it?"

For a second, shock registered on Big Hank's pudgy features. Then he burst out laughing. "You know, Jonathon, I like you. It's a shame you're not going to be my nephew-in-law."

"I'm not going to accept your offer."

"Not yet. But you will eventually. You'll sit down and think about it. Do the math—which won't take you very long, if what Gwen says about you is true. Once you realize how much money I'm talking about, you'll come around. No woman is worth that much money."

The truth was, he'd already been doing the math. Calculations had started running through his mind the second Big Hank had spoken. "Maybe you're right. Maybe no woman is worth that. But where you're wrong is in thinking that Wendy is the reason I'm saying no." Big Hank's gaze narrowed, but he didn't interrupt. "This thing you do, this good-ol'-boy manipulation, this under-the-table way of doing business—" Jonathon gave his head a shake. "It isn't FMJ's style. We do things out in the open. We win contracts because our products are the best on the market, not because we have connections. FMJ's an honorable company. We don't make the kind of deals you're talking about."

Big Hank leveled a shrewd look at him. "That may be FMJ's policy. But I've done my research on you. The kind of background you have makes a man hungry for success. If there's one thing my twenty-five years in politics has taught me, it's that there's not much an ambitious man won't do if you offer him the right incentives."

"I suspect you're right. About me. But I'm only one-third of FMJ. And you're wasting your time."

And with that, Jonathon turned and left.

He only wished he knew what drove him away: the fear that Big Hank was right and he really had made that decision for Wendy's sake, or the fear that if Big Hank kept talking, eventually Jonathon would cave. Either way, he figured he was pretty much screwed.

Sixteen

Knowing what she knew about Jonathon's childhood, Wendy half expected the house Jonathon grew up in to be a decrepit shack. But Marie's house was just an average tract house, in a neighborhood that may have been on the low end of middle class. Though small, the house was obviously well cared for, with a neat, flower-edged lawn in front. Bicycles and toys littered the yard, a testament to the number of kids who lived there.

Jonathon parked his Lexus out in front. He studied the house, his expression grim, his hands tight on the steering wheel.

To lighten the mood, she said, "Oh, you're right. This place is horrible. A real dump. Maybe we should go get our hepatitis C shots before going in."

He glared at her. "It was worse when I was a kid."

"Everything always is." She could all too easily imagine how hard an impoverished childhood would have been on Jonathon, with his stubborn pride and his desperate need to control everything. She gave his thigh a pat. "Come on, let's go in."

She hopped out of the car, knowing he'd follow along if she forged ahead. By the time she'd removed the bucket car seat from the back, he was there to take it from her, but the tight line of his lips hadn't softened at all.

"Think about it like this…whatever happens, they can't be any worse than my family is." She meant to make a joke of it, but the oddest expression crossed his face. She frowned. "What?"

"Nothing." He shook his head, gripped the car seat a little tighter and headed across the street. "Let's get this over with."

"Great attitude, by the way," she muttered under her breath. But he ignored her, trudging up toward the house with such determination that she had to jog a few steps to catch up with him.

A moment later, the door was being opened by a lovely young woman. Wendy guessed she was in her early twenties. She had Marie's dark glossy hair and the Bagdon green eyes. There was only a moment's hesitancy in her expression before she threw her arms around Jonathon. "Uncle Jonny! It's so good to see you!"

Shock registered on Jonathon's face, then slowly, he wrapped his free arm around her back. "Hey, Lacey."

Lacey pulled herself out of his arms and gave him a once-over. Nodding in apparent approval, she said, "You haven't changed a bit." Jonathon looked as if he wanted to disagree, but she didn't give him a chance. Instead she moved on to Wendy, giving her a hug that was just as enthusiastic. "You must be Wendy. Welcome to the family."

Then she darted off into the house, calling out, "They're here! Momma, why didn't you tell us she was so cute?"

Jonathon—looking shell-shocked—just stood there for a moment. So Wendy pushed past him to enter the house. "You coming, Jonny?"

His gaze narrowed. "Shut up," he muttered, but his tone

was playful, which she figured was the best she could hope for under the circumstances.

Wendy met so many people in the next hour, she quickly lost track of them. There was Lacey, the oldest of Marie's three kids. Or was it four? Then there were two additional step-kids as well. Neither of Jonathon's brothers had come— though Marie insisted she was still working on them and hoped they would be there for the big reception the next afternoon. His other sister came by and brought three of her four kids. Even Lacey's boyfriend was there.

Everyone greeted her warmly and oohed and aahed over Peyton. But Jonathon spent most of the evening standing stiffly in the corner, giving monosyllabic responses any time someone talked to him and looking deeply uncomfortable.

Photo albums were brought out and pizza was ordered. Someone brought soda and beer. Someone else brought cupcakes. Wendy could see why none of them would have wanted to go to a party at the country club and she was glad Marie had spoken up and told them so.

She was talking to Marie's husband, Mark, when Lacey came up and coaxed Peyton out of her arms. "I have to cuddle with babies whenever I can," she explained. "Mom's forbidden me to get pregnant until I'm at least three years out of college."

"Useful rule."

Lacey, however, was already ignoring Wendy in favor of rubbing her nose against Peyton's.

Wendy glanced around the busy living room and noticed that Jonathon was nowhere to be seen. She asked around and finally, one of the many children huddled around the video games being played on the TV yelled over his shoulder that Jonathon had gone out into the backyard.

She grabbed a sweater that was draped over one of the kitchen chairs by the back door on her way out into the darkened backyard. Slipping her arms into the sweater, she shivered as she waited for her eyes to adjust. The night air was cool against her skin. The unfamiliar landscaping cast deep shadows over the lawn. She skirted the furniture scattered around the tiny patio and stepped out onto the grass. In the light from the half-moon overhead she could barely see Jonathon.

Picking her away across the lawn around horseshoe sets and toy dump trucks, she crossed to where he stood beside a sapling tree.

He turned as she approached, studying her in the moonlight.

"Are they really so bad you had to come out here to escape?" she teased.

"I wanted to see if it was still here." He nodded toward the tree. "I planted an acorn here on the day we buried my dad. I picked it up from the lawn at the cemetery."

Though the tree was taller than he was, it still looked gangly and young. "That tree couldn't be more than ten years old."

"Almost twenty years now," he said softly. "Trees grow more slowly than people do."

She nodded, but looking at him, wondered if that was true. Sometimes, it felt as if people didn't grow at all. "I don't know about that," she admitted. "Here I am at twenty-seven, making the same mistakes I made at seventeen." She let out a dry bark of laughter. "And at seven."

"You sure about that?" he asked. "You seem to be getting along with your family pretty well these days."

"Maybe." She shrugged. "My mom said something the other day that surprised me. She said the reason Mema is so against single mothers is—"

"Because she was a single mother herself," Jonathon finished the sentence for her.

She shot him a surprised look. "How did you...?"

"Your Uncle Hank's father died in Korea. He was just six months old. She didn't marry your grandfather for another two years."

"And you know this…how, exactly?"

He raised his hand. "Fan of Google. Remember?"

"You researched my uncle?"

"Well, your family. There's a Wikipedia article on the Morgans. You're sort of a footnote."

"We live in a weird world." She just shook her head, wrapping her arms more tightly around her body. "I never thought to Google myself. If I had, I guess I would have known that about Mema and Uncle Hank's father."

"You didn't know?"

"It was only vaguely familiar. I must have heard it years ago and forgotten. I've never even heard Mema mention her first husband. And when Papa was alive he treated Uncle Hank and Dad like they were both his children. He set up trusts for all of us grandkids. Just like Hank Jr. and Bitsy were his own." She felt tears prickling her eyes, and blinked them back.

It had been so long since she'd thought about her Papa. He filtered through her thoughts nearly every day, but she didn't often take out the memories and dust them off.

"He used to love having the whole family together," she said, suddenly wanting to share those memories with Jonathon. "He loved the holidays most. When all the grandkids were running around. He'd have adored Peyton."

For the first time, it occurred to her that maybe the tenets of her trust hadn't been designed to control and manipulate her. Maybe he'd just wanted all the family to stay together forever. How disappointed he'd be.

Of course, he'd never met Helen. He probably wouldn't want to be around her either.

Still, the thought of Papa's disappointment snatched her breath away and she found herself shivering again.

Jonathon must have noticed. He unzipped his windbreaker and pulled her close so her back brushed against his chest. Then he wrapped the edges of the jacket around her, enveloping her in his warmth.

She leaned her head back against his shoulder, looking at the tree he'd planted so long ago, marveling that he'd planted a single acorn and it had actually grown into something. Not something big yet, but with the potential to someday be massive and strong.

"Tell me something, Wendy," he murmured, his voice close to her ear. "If there was a way for you to keep Peyton without being married to me, without moving back to Texas, would you do it?"

Everything inside of her went dead still at his question.

She squeezed her eyes shut again. This time, not to shut in tears but to block out her dread. She knew every modulation of his voice. The question wasn't pure speculation. She knew if she could see his face, he'd be wearing his I-solved-the-problem expression. Was he wondering—as she was—if this greater understanding of Mema could be used to convince her that Wendy was a suitable mother, with or without a husband?

"No," she admitted softly. Barely a whisper. She was not even sure she wanted him to hear it.

But he did hear it. She felt it in the faint stiffening of his muscles.

And a moment later, he stepped back from her and held out his hand. Nodding toward the house, he said, "It's almost Peyton's bedtime."

She let him lead her back across the lawn and into the boisterously cheerful company of his family. Although she smiled brightly as everyone said goodbye and started heading home, she couldn't dislodge the lump of dread in her throat.

She'd admitted to him that she'd stay married no matter what, but he had—rather obviously—not done the same. And she couldn't help wondering, did he fully realize what she'd admitted? Did he know that she was already in love with him?

By the time Jonathon followed Wendy back into the house, Marie had noticed how sleepy Peyton looked and was beginning to shuttle people out the door. Wendy stood stiffly to the side, seeing people off. The bright smile on her face didn't quite reach her eyes. He wasn't sure what he'd done to upset her, but it was obvious that he'd made a mess of things.

Finally Marie showed Jonathon and Wendy to one of the bedrooms. There were bunk beds along one wall and—just as Jonathon had predicted—a blow-up bed on the floor. Marie had pulled a Pack 'n Play out of the attic and wedged it between the head of the bed and the room's only dresser. Toys had been piled up on the lower bunk bed to clear space on the floor for the blowup bed, which barely fit as it was. Unless one of them wanted to sleep on the top bunk, they'd be in the same bed tonight.

As soon as they were alone, Jonathon asked, "You sure you don't want to head back to the hotel?"

"I've stayed in worse," she said, her tone determinedly cheerful as she lay Peyton down on the bed and started to change her clothes.

He arched a brow. "Really?"

"Yes, really. I took a year off college to backpack around Europe." She dug through the suitcase and pulled out the pink footie pajamas Peyton liked. "I've even stayed worse places on FMJ's dime."

"I doubt that."

"Then you've obviously forgotten that hotel in Tokyo." With Peyton sitting on her lap, she began the complicated wiggle-and-giggle of dressing a squirming child. "The rooms were the size of shower stalls and the beds were too short even for me."

"I must have blocked it out."

"Yeah. I bet." She chuckled as she rolled Peyton onto her back to work on the snaps, leaning down to give the baby a raspberry on the belly. Peyton let out a sleepy squeal, kicking her arms and legs. Wendy zipped the pj's up and patted Peyton on the belly.

It was an action so intrinsically mothering it made his

breath catch in his throat. He knew in that instant that she was going to be okay. She and Peyton may have gotten off to a rough start, but they were going to be just fine. With or without him. He knew something else as well. He should tell her the truth about her uncle. Tell her what Mema really wanted.

It was such a simple solution. And if he told her, she wouldn't need him anymore.

She looked up to find him studying them and she frowned. "What?"

He gave his head a little shake. "Nothing. You're just getting good at that."

"Yep, that's me. Nearly a month of mothering under my belt and I've mastered the art of zerbert delivery."

"No. I mean it. You're going to be a good mother."

Despite the compliment, her frown deepened. She sat cross-legged on the center of the bed, her expression pensive as she picked up Peyton and set her on her knee.

The air between them was thick with all the things that had gone unsaid, but before he could say anything, she hobbled up, setting Peyton on her hip.

"Peyton and I are good here." She snagged the bottle she'd prepared earlier and gave it waggle. "We're all set. Maybe you should go hang out with your family for a while. While I get her to sleep, I mean."

"No. I—"

"I insist." She gave his shoulder a gentle shove. Then for effect, she rubbed her finger along her brow as if she was warding off a headache. "This weekend has been really hard on me. I just want a few minutes alone with Peyton."

He saw right through the ruse, but he didn't call her on it. Maybe she needed time alone. Maybe she just needed time away from him.

He left the room, all too aware that he hadn't told her about her uncle. Nor had he mentioned that she probably didn't need to stay married to him in order to keep Peyton. He hadn't told her yet. And he wasn't going to.

Seventeen

Wendy had no more answers when she woke up than when she'd fallen asleep. And to make matters worse—after more than a week of waking at the crack of dawn and hightailing it out of the room, this was the morning Jonathon decided to sleep in. So she woke to find herself draped across his body, her head resting on his chest, her left knee nestled against the hard length of his erection.

There was a moment when she didn't quite remember where she was. When all her sleep brain could process was the unbelievable feeling of total contentment.

That moment passed in a flash the instant she felt him move. She shot off the bed.

Or rather rolled to the edge, only to feel the bed give way beneath her weight. She sank to the floor and tried to stand, but the bunk beds were in the way. She clung to the upper bed's railing, the lower bed bumping her legs as she inched her way to a spot of open floor space.

"Morning," Jonathon muttered.

She stilled, then looked over her shoulder. He was awake, watching her awkward progress. "Um, hey." His gaze dropped to her bottom. Suddenly aware of the cool air on the cheeks of her buttocks, she gave the hem of her boxers a tug. "Good morning."

He just smiled, looking awfully smug. The jerk.

She finally reached the foot of the bed where there was about a four-inch gap between it and the wall. She shuffled around until she reached the dresser.

"I'm just going to—"

She didn't even finish the sentence. She just grabbed her clothes and ran for it.

Ten minutes later, out of her skimpy pajamas, clothed in as many layers as she could scrounge and determined to buy a pair of long johns to sleep in from now on, she made her way to the kitchen and the divine scent of freshly brewing coffee.

She found Lacey there, a cup of steaming coffee at her own elbow as she greased up a waffle iron. The younger woman smiled brightly. "Hope you're ready for the patented Bagdon Banana Chocolate Chip Waffles. You're a fan, right?"

Some wise person had left an empty coffee cup beside the coffee maker and Wendy poured herself a cup. "Of waffles? Sure."

"Not just waffles. These are the Banana Chocolate Chip Waffles. His signature dish."

Feeling unable to follow the discussion without caffeine, Wendy took a generous gulp. Whatever criticisms Jonathon might have had about his family, they brewed damn good coffee. Which in her book, about put them on the level with the gods.

A moment later, her brain caught up with the conversation. "Whose signature dish?"

Lacey, who was in the process of pouring a ladleful of batter onto the hot iron, looked up. "Jonathon's." She sprinkled chocolate chips across the top. "He has made them for you, right?" Lacey closed the lid, then pegged Wendy with her gaze.

"Um…no."

"Oh." The waffle iron released a fizzle of steam. A frown creased Lacey's forehead. "He used to make them all the time for me. He taught me how."

Caught off guard by the girl's wistful tone, Wendy was torn. The girl looked as though a cherished childhood memory had just been stolen. But Wendy couldn't exactly tell Lacey the truth. And for all she knew, Jonathon actually made waffles for all of his real girlfriends. He'd just never made them for his fake wife.

"Maybe," Wendy supplied, "he doesn't make them now because they remind him too much of you."

She couldn't imagine the Jonathon she knew behaving in such a sentimental manner, but the girl might fall for it.

Sure enough, Lacey's lips curved into a smile and she nodded slowly. "Yeah. That sounds like him."

"It does?" Wendy tried to hide her surprise behind a sip of coffee. "I mean, it does. Definitely."

The waffle iron beeped and Lacey bent down as she lifted the lid. Wielding a spatula with surgical precision, she pried the waffle free and flipped it onto a plate. She put on the finishing touches with a flick of a butter knife and drizzle of syrup, then held the plate out to Wendy. "Ta da!"

Wendy took the plate. Lacey stood there, her gaze darting from the waffle to Wendy and back like an overeager puppy.

"Now?" Wendy asked. "Shouldn't I wait until everyone else is here?"

"Nope. First come, first served, and you eat them while they're hot." As she poured the next waffle, Lacey flashed a wicked grin that reminded Wendy of Jonathon. "House rules."

Imagine that. House rules about waffle eating. Or, for that matter, house rules about anything food related that weren't restrictive and oppressive.

"Are you going to try it?" Lacey asked, her forehead starting to furrow again.

"Just taking a moment to enjoy house rules about food that aren't designed to inspire guilt or shame. I think I'm in heaven."

"And you haven't even eaten the waffle yet."

Since Lacey was still watching her expectantly, Wendy forked off a bite and popped it into her mouth. The sweet buttery banana contrasted nicely with the dark bittersweet chocolate. The waffle itself was light enough to melt on her tongue. Her eyes drifted closed in bliss.

Even though Wendy hadn't said anything, beside her, Lacey said, "I know. Right?"

"Divine," Wendy enthused before taking another bite. If Jonathon *did* make these for his real girlfriends, that went a long way toward explaining why they put up with his emotional distance for as long as they usually did. These waffles plus fantastic sex, and what girl would care if her boyfriend was a jerk?

Somehow depressed by the thought, Wendy took her waffle and wandered over to the table. She scooted the chair back with her foot and sat, stuffing another bite into her mouth with a fervor that had more to do with therapeutic stress release than with hunger.

A moment later, Lacey joined her, a waffle of her own on her plate, the waffle iron temporarily off since no one else was waiting for one.

They ate for a few minutes in silence.

Lacey gave a sigh of deep contentment. "Uncle Jonny used to make these for me when I was little. Mom worked at the Giddey-up Gas on weekend mornings."

"You must have been…what? Six or seven?"

"I was eight when he went off to college."

Went off to college and walked away from his family completely. As far as she knew, he hadn't seen a single family member since then. Okay, she could get walking away from the no-good mother who had been more interested in raising a bottle than raising a family. But walking away from his siblings? She'd wanted a brother or sister her whole life. So that was a grayer area. But walking away from an eight-year-old niece? A little girl he'd made waffles for every morning for years? Who did that?

Had it been hard? Had he ever looked back? Ever wondered about the family he'd left behind?

"And you haven't seen him since?" Wendy had to ask, even though in her heart she knew the answer to the question.

"Not really." Lacey shrugged, though her expression was more thoughtful than sad.

"What do you mean, *not really?*" Most of the time, she knew Jonathon's schedule better than her own. If he'd been within fifty miles of Palo Verde in the last five years, she would have known about it.

"I mean, sure, he never visits." Lacey spoke around a mouthful of waffle. "But it's not like we don't all know he's out there. Keeping an eye on us."

"Keeping an *eye* on you?" Wendy asked.

"Sure. Just watching out for us, you know?"

No. Wendy didn't know. She didn't have the faintest clue what Lacey was talking about. Luckily Lacey was a babbler and kept talking.

"Just little stuff mostly." She rolled her shoulder in a shrug. "Though sometimes it was big stuff. It used to make Mom so mad."

"What kind of stuff?"

"Like, oh, I don't know. I guess it started with the lab at school."

"Uh-huh," Wendy said encouragingly.

"That was about ten years ago. I won the regional science fair, but we didn't have the cash for me to go to the state competition. The newspaper ran this article about a fundraiser we were doing at school to raise money for it. Then—bam— anonymous donor steps in to cover the costs. The next year, the school district science labs were completely remodeled—middle school, all the way up to high school."

Lacey forked off another bite of her waffle, while Wendy poked listlessly at hers.

"I used to think that we were just incredibly, unbelievably lucky."

"What do you mean?"

"Well, like the science lab. I needed money and it magically appears. Or the time when Mom was out of work—this was before she got married—and this frozen-food delivery truck broke down right outside our house. The driver begged us to take the food inside to our own freezer before it went bad. Stuff like that happened all the time."

"And you think Jonathon was responsible?"

"Well, sure. Who else could it be? It's always made Mom so mad, but I kind of like it. It's nice knowing he's out there, keeping an eye out for us."

"Why does it make your Mom mad?"

"Because she always says it'd be nicer to have her brother back."

It was so like him. He wanted to help. Always wanted to be the hero, but never wanted the credit for it. He never wanted to be beholden to anyone. Never wanted to risk having someone know he was a decent guy beneath the mantle of corporate greed he wore. And he never let anyone close enough to see the man he really was underneath.

No wonder it pissed off Marie. Hell, it pissed her off.

"He finally wore Mom down," Lacey was saying. "I think it was the scholarship that did it."

"There's a scholarship?" Wendy asked, then instantly realized how stupid that sounded. With Jonathon's fervor for education, *of course* there would be scholarship.

Lacey nodded. "Ten top science students in the high school get a full ride to the university of their choice as long as they major in a science or engineering program."

"Naturally."

How had she not known about any of this?

She had thought she had her thumb in every pie on his plate, but here was this one element of his life that she'd never glimpsed until now.

He'd told her he'd cut himself off from his family entirely. Claimed that he had nothing to do with them anymore. And yet now she found out he'd been meddling in their lives for years. Not bad meddling, just…from a distance.

Which was the way he did everything. God forbid he let anyone get truly close.

"Hey. Yoowoo?"

Wendy looked up to see Lacey waving her fork back and forth in front of Wendy's face. Apparently she'd been caught drifting off into what-the-hell-have-I-got-myself-into land. "Oh. Sorry. I was just lost in thought."

Lacey smirked. "Obviously. No one lets waffles this good go uneaten without good reason."

Well, at least confidence ran in the family.

"I was just…wondering what to think about all this."

"All what?"

"The generosity. The altruism."

"Really?" Lacey's expression turned shrewd and assessing. "Because if I was with a guy like that, it would be one of the things I loved most about him."

"Well, sure. It would have been. If I'd known about it." She gave her waffle a particularly savage poke.

"Oh, no." Lacey had gone pale. "I've made you doubt him."

"Lacey—"

"This is my fault." She shoved back her chair, stood up and waggled her hands frantically. "He's finally met someone he can be happy with, and I have to go and screw it up."

"This isn't your fault." Wendy jumped to her feet and grabbed Lacey's hands before she could knock herself out with one of them. "If this is anyone's fault, it's his. He's the one who's emotionally unavailable."

"No!" Lacey interrupted. "He's totally available! I promise! He's just…shy!"

Wendy paused, staring at Lacey with raised eyebrows. "Shy? You think Jonathon is *shy?*"

"Okay," Lacey admitted. "Not shy. He just doesn't talk about his feelings much."

"Or at all."

"But I know he has them. I know he does. He just doesn't talk about them. I mean, not to you. But he does to Peyton," Lacey blurted out, trying to be helpful.

And here she'd thought her eyebrows couldn't go any higher. "He talks to Peyton? About his feelings?"

Sure, he was good with Peyton. Great with her as a matter of fact, but Wendy couldn't actually imagine him pouring his heart out to her.

"Yes, he does!" Lacey's words flew out in a garbled rush. "Last night, I woke up around one and I went to the kitchen for a glass of water, but before I got there, I heard him talking to Peyton. He was holding her on his lap and giving her a bottle and he told her that she was worth more to him than a hundred peppermint Pop Rocks."

Lacey stopped, her eyes wide and hopeful. As if what she'd said was supposed to convince Wendy. Or make sense.

"Um…it is possible you were dreaming?"

"No. This definitely happened."

"Jonathon told Peyton she was worth more to him than *peppermint Pop Rocks?*"

Lacey frowned. "I guess that's strange, huh?"

"A little." She didn't think they even made peppermint Pop Rocks.

"Okay, maybe I heard wrong. I didn't want to interrupt, so I snuck back to bed."

Wendy dropped Lacey's hands, her mind suddenly whirling. "Peppermint Pop Rocks" made no sense. But "government contracts" did. That sounded more like it.

Wendy fished her phone out of her back pocket and pulled

up her mother's number. After a few seconds of ringing, her mother answered. "Hey, Mom, are you at breakfast yet?" She rolled her eyes as her mother answered. "Yes, I know it's early. I need to talk to Uncle Hank. Put him on. Right now."

Eighteen

She ended the call after only a few minutes. It didn't take long for her to verify what she already suspected. Then she made a beeline for the guest bedroom where they'd slept last night, dodging two kids jumping gleefully on a blow-up bed in the living room. Neither Jonathon nor Peyton were in the guest bedroom. But the door to the master bedroom was open, and when she glanced inside, she saw Peyton gurgling happily on the bed as Natalie, one of Jonathon's teenage nieces, dangled a toy over her.

"Honey," she asked, struggling to keep the simmering anger out of her voice. "Do you know where Jonathon is?" It was a struggle to keep her voice light.

The teenager looked up. "He asked me to watch Peyton while he took a shower."

"Thanks."

Wendy spun on her heel and stalked out into the hall to the bathroom. She gave the door a tap, and waited only until she heard him say, "Just a minute." She slipped through the door without waiting for an invitation.

"What the—"

"We need to talk."

She shut the door behind her, looking up just in time to see him grabbing a towel to cover himself. Behind him the shower was already on, pumping steam out into the room. Despite her anger, she felt her gaze clinging to the sight of his naked chest. Logically, after a week of sleeping in the same room with him, she should have started developing a Jonathon immunity. But instead, the sight of him affected her even more strongly. All that bare skin. Lightly tanned. The muscles that were defined, but not pronounced. The towel slung low across his waist as he tucked it in. It was all very, very…she drew in a slow breath…just very masculine. And distracting.

She forced her gaze up to his eyes, only to find him grinning at her. As if he could read every salacious thought in her head.

"Do you need something?" he asked in a low voice.

His arrogance brought her anger back to her in full force.

Yeah. She needed something. She needed to take his ego down a couple of notches. And then she needed some answers.

"Did my uncle try to blackmail you?"

Every muscle in Jonathon's body tensed. At least, every muscle she could see. Which was a lot of them.

Despite that, he kept his expression carefully schooled. If he hadn't been nearly naked, she might not have realized how strong his reaction was.

"Who have you been talking to?" he asked.

"Just answer my question."

He opened his mouth, clearly debating what to say.

Then there was a knock on the door.

"Give me a minute," he snapped, and she wasn't sure if he was speaking to her or to the person knocking.

"I have to go pee-pee and someone's in the other bath-room," came a small voice from the other side of the door.

Jonathon glared at her as if this was her fault.

She shrugged and mouthed the name "Sara."

Jonathon nodded her to the door in a get-out gesture.

Wendy shook her head.

"I need to go really, really bad!"

Little wonder since just a few minutes ago she'd seen the girl jumping on the bed.

"I don't think I can hold it!"

They could hear the thump-thump-thump of the girl bouncing up and down.

Wendy toed off her shoes and socks and kicked them near the wastepaper basket. Jonathon arched an eyebrow in question, but she ignored him as she pulled back the shower curtain and stepped into the steaming shower. The last thing she saw before she pulled the curtain closed was the expression of pure exasperation on his face. As if this was all terribly beneath him.

"Come on in," she heard him say. "But be fast."

"Ugh. Uncle Jonny, you're naked!" she heard the girl say.

"I was about to get in the shower," he said, his tone far dryer than Wendy now was. Even pressing herself toward the back wall, the spray kicked up onto the legs of her jeans.

"Aren't you going to go?" she heard Jonathon ask.

"Not while you're watching!" the girl whined.

"I'll turn around." Wendy heard the impatience in Jona-thon's voice.

"Just get in the shower. And don't listen!" There was a moment of silence, during which Wendy imagined Jonathon mustering his patience. "Go!"

She saw Jonathon's fingers wrap around the edge of the shower curtain. She stepped under the showerhead to make room for him. An instant later, he pulled back the curtain and stepped in, towel still slung low across his hips.

The water slashed down, wetting her hair and clothes.

She was drenched within moments. Jonathon raked his gaze over her, his expression dark. She felt his stare like a touch, searingly hot and disconcerting. A shiver ran down her spine and she tried to tell herself that her damp clothes had made her cold, but she knew that was a lie. She wasn't cold at all. How could she be when Jonathon was so close? And nearly naked? He looked her up and down, making her painfully aware of her clothes clinging to her skin and of her nipples hardened against the silk of her bra. Desire mingled with her anger in a potent mix that made her head spin.

From the other side of the curtain, she could hear Sara moving in the bathroom. Then the girl started singing "The Ants Go Marching." Jonathon arched an eyebrow at Wendy and suddenly the mood shifted, and she barely suppressed a giggle. The toilet flushed. The water ran colder for a few seconds, making Wendy shiver for real. Then the sink ran. A moment later the bathroom door opened and closed.

Suddenly, they were alone. In the shower. She was drenched and he was nearly naked.

This seemed like a very bad idea.

"Now," he said, his tone tight and controlled, "will you please get out of the bathroom? Let me finish my shower. In peace."

"No." The word left her mouth before she could even fully process his request. But the instant she said it, she knew it was the right response. "I'm not leaving. Not until you answer me. Did my uncle blackmail you into getting an annulment?"

"No. Now get out."

"But—"

"Get out. Now. Or I can't be responsible for my actions."

"I'm not leaving until you explain—"

He didn't even give her a chance to finish her sentence, but pulled her to him and crushed her mouth with a kiss.

Her hands shoved uselessly at his shoulders even as her hips bumped eagerly against his. Her mouth opened under his assault, her tongue stroking his, savoring the taste of his hunger. Of his impatience. Every instinct she had screamed at her, but she could hardly distinguish her warring desires. She wanted him. She didn't want to want him. Her body desired him, but every shred of common sense she had warned her to stay away. He could bring her body enormous pleasure, but he'd surely crush her heart.

But when he touched her like this, she simply didn't care.

His kiss was deep and needy, as if he were trying to consume her. His hands seemed to be everywhere at once, meddling with the water coursing over her body in a chorus of stimulation. He touched her hair, her neck, her breasts. Teased the sensitive skin of her waist and massaged her nipples through her bra. Then under her bra. He peeled off her shirt and bra and they fell to the floor of the shower in a sodden lump. Then he was caressing her again. It was as if he was trying to absorb her very essence through his hands. As if he was binding her to him.

Or maybe that was just her, projecting her own emotions onto him. Because she couldn't stop touching him. Couldn't keep her hands from exploring all that glorious naked skin. Her fingers trembled with need as she reached for the towel. But stopped herself just in time. Instead, she flattened her palm against his chest and pushed.

"Stop," she said.

He stilled instantly, pulling back from her. She sank against the wall of the shower, her breath coming in ragged breaths.

This was the problem with their relationship. Physically, they were a perfect match. And if that was enough for her, then...this would be enough for her.

If all she wanted was fantastic sex, then it wouldn't matter to her that Jonathon had prevaricated about her uncle. If all she wanted was a husband to satisfy her family, then Jonathon would still be the perfect man. But she wanted more than that now. She wanted all of him.

Shaken to her very core, she reached over and turned off the water. She yanked back the curtain and grabbed a towel off the rack. Giving her hair a quick rub, she climbed out of the shower.

She looked over her shoulder and saw that he'd turned his back to her. He stood with his arm braced against the wall, resting his head on his forearm. As if he was struggled for control. Yeah, well, she felt the same.

"Why'd you lie?" she asked.

He looked up, turning around. "What?"

It was an effort for her to keep from looking down, but she managed it. "About my uncle. Why'd you lie about him black-mailing you?"

"I didn't." He grabbed a towel as well and scrubbed it down his face.

"I talked to my uncle. I know the truth."

For an instant, surprise flickered across his face, but he hid it well. "Then you know that he didn't blackmail me. He made the offer. I refused. That's not blackmail. That's attempted blackmail."

She stared at him blankly and after a moment all she could do was let out a bark of laughter. "That is just like you to try to get off on a technicality."

"You're mad at me about this?" The confusion in his voice was real. "What good would it do you to know that your uncle is a jackass?"

"I already knew that." She fished her shirt off the floor of the tub and gave it a vicious twist to wring out the water. "What good does it do you to try to hide it from me?"

"I was just—"

"Trying to protect me?" she finished for him as she pulled the shirt over her head. "Yeah. I get that. But you've got to stop doing me favors. Because it's not helping things at all."

"I don't know what you mean."

"Of course you don't." She gave a sharp, bitter laugh. She shook her head. He may be brilliant when it came to money, but when it came to emotions, he was an idiot. "I now know why you've been so determined to make this work. I just don't think you understand it yet."

"What are you even talking about?"

"You walked away from your family when you were so young and you still haven't found a way back to them. And you haven't made peace with that either."

"What does my family have to do with any of this?"

"You love kids. You'd be a great dad, but you don't feel worthy of having a family of your own. Not when you walked away from your family. So Peyton and I, we're consolation prizes. You get to have a family, but you get to lie to yourself and pretend you're doing it for FMJ or to protect me."

"You're wrong."

"I don't think I am. You're just so out of touch with what you really want, that you don't even recognize what's going on. Think about it, why did you marry me in the first place?"

"So you could keep custody of Peyton."

"No, that's why I married you. Not why you married me. You asked me to marry you, because it was supposed to be best for FMJ. I was going to leave and you were trying to protect the company. But somewhere along the way, you lost track of that. The company is supposed to come first for you."

His jaw tightened and his gaze drew dark. "It's not supposed to come before my wife."

"No. I'm your assistant. Before I was your wife, I was just the incredibly efficient, supremely organized, very best assistant you've ever had. That's why you married me. Because it was best for FMJ." She cupped his jaw in her hand and gently tilted his face down so he met her gaze. "I'm going to make this easy for you. Your loyalties lie with FMJ. With Ford and Matt. That's where they've always been. That's okay."

"Stop it!" He barked the order, jerking away from her hand. "It's not your decision to make."

She felt her lips curving in a bittersweet smile. "You really think it matters to my uncle which of us capitulates? Hell, he'll probably be glad it was me who broke."

"Is that what you're doing? You're giving in to your uncle?" There was a sneer of scorn in his voice, but she knew the pain it hid.

"If I accept my uncle's bargain for you, you get that government contract. FMJ wins."

She kept her voice calm and reasonable, even though her emotions were tearing her apart.

"I am not—" he growled "—going to sacrifice our marriage just so FMJ can win some stupid government contract."

"No. But I'm going to. You're not the only one who loves this company. I believe in it. And I believe you're going to continue to do great things with it, even if I'm not there. So don't disappointment me, okay?"

"That's it?" Jonathon asked, outrage pouring through him. "You're just going to walk away?"

"It's what I should have done to begin with."

"No. I don't believe that. I don't believe *you* believe that." She didn't even look at him as she straightened her sopping-wet shirt. Didn't even meet his gaze. And for the first time since this ridiculous conversation started, he considered the possibility that she was actually going to do it. That she was really going to walk out the door and leave him.

He grabbed her by the arm and turned her to face him. "If you really want to leave me, then fine. I can live with that. But don't lie to me and tell me you're doing it because it's what's best for FMJ. Don't lie to yourself either."

"Okay, you want the truth? Here it is—I know how important this deal is to you and I can't let you throw it away. Not for me. If I did, you'd only end up resenting me someday. And I couldn't stand that."

Then he said the one thing he thought might make a difference. "Don't forget, we've slept together. That annulment won't be so easy to get now. And I'm not going to make it easy for you to walk away from me."

She looked at him, meeting his gaze directly. There was something so sad in her eyes that his heart actually contracted a bit as she looked at him. Her lips curved into a smile that held no humor, but brimmed with warmth and sorrow. "It was never going to be easy to walk away from you. I knew that all along."

And with that, she left the room, her clothes dripping water in her wake. For what must have been a full minute, he stared after her, shocked that she'd actually done it, even though she'd said she would.

Then he slung a dry towel around his waist and ran after her, following the drops of water like a little trail of breadcrumbs. He dashed through the family room, barely aware of the curious gazes that followed his half-naked progress through the house. Then he stopped and ran back to the guest room where he and Wendy had slept the previous night. Natalie sat alone on the bed, looking confused.

"Did she take Peyton?" he demanded.

"Yeah." Natalie gave a confused shrug. "She ran in here, grabbed the baby and the suitcase and ran out. Where is she—"

He didn't wait to hear the rest of her question, but dashed back through the house. He heard adult laughter and one of his nieces ask, "Mommy, why is he naked?"

He made it out onto the front lawn in time to see Wendy close the backseat door and then climb into the driver's seat. The towel slipped as he ran for the car. Holding the drooping ends of the towel in one hand, he banged on the window with the other. But she didn't stop or even slow down. And a second later, he was left standing on the street. In a towel.

And since she'd taken his car, he had no way to get home.

Scratch that. Since she'd left and was taking Peyton with her, he no longer had a home.

Nineteen

Jonathon stood there in the road for a long time, watching the corner around which his Lexus had just disappeared.

He might have stood there all day, shock pinning him to the ground, if his sister hadn't walked out in the street to stand beside him. Arms crossed over her chest, she looked him up and down. "Wow, you really effed that up, didn't you?"

He shot her a look of annoyance. "After all these years, how is it that you're still this irritating?"

She grinned. "I'm a big sister. It's our moral obligation to point it out when you make a colossal mistake."

"Thanks," he muttered dryly. "Very helpful."

Glancing back at the house, he realized that Marie's brood—all five kids, plus the husband—had poured out onto the lawn after them. In fact, they'd even attracted the attention of a few neighbors. Little wonder. How often did you see a guy in nothing but a towel running after a car?

He turned around and headed back to the house. Marie fell into step beside him. "What are you going to do?"

"What do you think I'm going to do?"

Marie smiled. "The brother I remember would chase her down and win her back."

He nodded, hoping he looked more confident than he felt. "I'm going to need to borrow your car."

"Borrow?" Lacey laughed. "No way. You think we're going to let you do this all on your own?"

"I did hope," he admitted in exasperation. But when had his family ever done what he wanted them to do?

"Too bad," Mark said. "This is the most entertaining thing that's happened since that toy company's truck crashed on our corner and all the kids on the block got free toys the week before Christmas."

Wendy briefly considered skipping the hotel and driving straight back to her apartment in Palo Alto. After confronting Jonathon, the last thing she wanted was to see her own family. However she still needed to convince Mema she was the best mother for Peyton and abandoning them without a word in Palo Verde would do little to help her cause. And since she wasn't going to have that rich husband in her favor anymore, she figured she needed all the help she could get.

Besides, she had unfinished business with her uncle.

The historic Ellington House hotel sat in the middle of town, on Main Street, a block or two from Cutie Pies. She nabbed one of the parking spots on the street. She dug around in the suitcase and pulled out a dry shirt and jeans. It was tricky changing in the car without drawing attention to herself, but she managed it. Plus it gave her time to muster her courage, before she extracted Peyton from the car seat and headed into the hotel.

When she'd called her mom earlier, her entire family had just met for breakfast on the terrace of the hotel's dining room. If she was lucky, they'd be just finishing up and she could get this all over at once.

Striding with purpose, she carried Peyton through the

lobby and up the stairs to the second-story dining room. On another day, the hotel's elegance and meticulous restoration might have impressed her. As it was, she barely noticed the velvet-trimmed antiques and heavy oak furnishings.

Instead, she made a beeline for the double doors leading onto the patio. That was where she found them, sitting at a long table overlooking Main Street. Mema was at one end, Uncle Hank at the other. Her parents, Hank Jr. and Helen scattered in between. They all looked at ease among the fine china and sterling teapots, the poached eggs and hollandaise sauces. The meal was so perfectly her family.

No homemade banana chocolate-chip waffles here. Just elegant dining and a steely determination to ignore the tension simmering beneath the surface. This would be her life from now on.

She dreaded this with every fiber of her being. Yet it was still preferable to the life she was walking away from. She knew how important FMJ was to Jonathon. Its success had always been his first priority. She couldn't knowingly ruin all he'd planned for the company.

If she did, she'd be stuck on the sidelines in her own family, Jonathon's heart forever just out of her reach.

She stopped at Mema's end of the table. Peyton still propped on her hip, Wendy said, to the table in general, "Okay. You win."

Uncle Hank's face split in a wide grin. Helen's eyes lit up as if someone had just offered to sprinkle full-carat diamonds on her plate as a garnish. Hank Jr. just looked bored, as he had ever since setting foot in California.

Her mother and father exchanged worried looks. Looks that seemed—for once—to reveal actual concern for her. Maybe there would be an upside to this debacle after all. Her heart would be broken into a thousand pieces, but maybe the pieces her parents had broken years ago would start to heal. It gave her hope that maybe the parts Jonathon had broken would someday heal as well.

Mema dabbed at her mouth with her napkin, then nodded to a spare chair at another table. "Well, Gwen, since you've interrupted our meal yet again, you might as well pull up a chair and explain yourself." Then she shot an annoyed look at Helen. "Helen, dear, please try to contain your glee."

Somehow despite the situation, Wendy felt herself smiling. Funny how her overbearing family wasn't quite so unbearable now that she was an adult in her own right. Now that she was coming to them on her own terms.

Her father jumped up to pull a chair over for her and Wendy seated herself between her mother and her grandmother. Surveying the table, she felt oddly at peace about her decision. Yes, this would be her life from now on. Sometimes.

She would inevitably have to deal with them and so would Peyton. But this wouldn't have to be their only life. The two of them, together, could find their own way as a family. They could endure hollandaise sauce every once in a while, as long as they had banana chocolate-chip waffles most of the time.

Pinning her uncle with her gaze, she started with, "I fully expect you to honor the deal you offered Jonathon."

His grin widened only slightly. "Why, certainly."

Then she turned to her parents. "Mama, Daddy," she began. "I'd like to finally accept—"

But before she could tell them she'd like to take the job at Morgan Oil, the door to the terrace swung open behind her. Mentally cursing the wait staff for interrupting her big moment of capitulation, she turned in her seat to send them away.

Only it wasn't some overeager busboy. It was Jonathon. Along with what—at first glance—appeared to be every Bagdon in the county.

She jolted to her feet. "What the—"

"I'm not letting you go," he said unceremoniously.

For the first time since she'd known him, Jonathon looked decidedly disheveled, if that was possible for a man who kept his hair trimmed into such neat submission. He was dressed in jeans and a rumpled denim work shirt open over—bizarrely enough—a T-shirt, for some rap group, which was obviously too tight.

Clutching Peyton tighter to her chest, she tried her damnedest to glare him down. "I'm not having this discussion here."

"Then you shouldn't have rushed off." He quirked his eyebrow. "If you want, we can drive back over to my sister's and finish the conversation in the shower."

Helen gave an indignant huff, but beside her Hank Jr. sniggered. Then there was the unmistakable whack of someone getting kicked under the table followed by his grunt of pain. Wendy glanced over her shoulder to see Mema smiling faintly.

"My dear, since there is now no hope of us finishing our breakfast in peace, you should at least hear him out."

"Okay." She eyed him suspiciously. "Start talking."

But before he could say a word, Lacey darted between them and held out her hands. "Let me take Peyton. I have the feeling you're going to want your arms free before this is over."

"She's fine here," Wendy said stubbornly.

"Oh, for goodness' sake, Wendy," muttered her mother, standing. "If anyone is going to take Peyton, it should be me." Her mother practically wrestled the baby out of Wendy's arms.

With nothing to hold, Wendy wrapped her arms around her chest. "Go ahead," she said to Jonathon.

He opened his mouth, then snapped it shut again, casting a wary glance at the crowd around them, her family on one side, his family blocking the only door back into the hotel. He grabbed her arm and navigated her around the few empty tables to the far corner of the terrace.

"I want another chance to make this work. You and I are good together."

"Good together in bed?" she asked softly. "I'm not going

to argue that. Good together at work? Absolutely. But I want more than that." She swallowed. "I need more than that."

Jonathon scrapped a hand over his short hair, his mouth pressed into a straight line as he seemed to be mustering his words. He studied her face, looking for what, she wasn't sure.

Refusing to meet his gaze, her eyes dropped again to the absurd T-shirt. Frustrated that he claimed to want to talk, but still wasn't talking, she asked, "And why on earth are you wearing that T-shirt?"

"That's mine!" called a voice from near the door, shattering the illusion of privacy.

She looked around Jonathon's shoulder to see Lacey's younger brother Thomas holding up a hand.

Jonathon rolled his eyes in obvious exasperation. "You took our suitcase. I didn't have any clothes other than the jeans."

"Oh." She cringed. "Sorry. I didn't mean to leave you with nothing—"

"Then don't leave me with nothing," he interjected. "Don't you get it? If you leave at all, you leave me with nothing."

The tightness in her chest loosened a little. "Go on," she prodded.

"I don't know, maybe your wacky theory about me leaving my family is right. Maybe I have never forgiven myself for walking away from my family. And maybe that's why I haven't married before now. But that's not why I married you."

She finally let herself meet his gaze. The naked emotion she saw there stripped her breath away. But just seeing it wasn't enough. She needed to hear it. She needed him to say it aloud. "Okay, then. Why did you marry me?"

"Why do you think I married you?" he countered.

"If it was enough for me to just intuit how you feel about me, then we wouldn't have a problem. But it's not enough. I need to hear the words. From you. I need you to say it aloud." Frustrated, she reached up and cupped his jaw in her hands, forcing him to look her in the eyes. "Whatever you feel, it isn't going to scare me off."

"I love you, Wendy. I think I've always loved you." His lips curved into a smile. "That may not scare you, but it scares the crap out of me. Because I don't know what I'd do if you left me."

She bit down on her lip, trying to hold back the tears of joy threatening to spill over. "Better," she said finally. "Go on," she coaxed.

"Okay." He blew out a rough breath. "The way I see it, you can't leave me without voiding the terms of the prenup."

Her eyebrows shot up. "Huh?"

"You were the one who said that when the marriage ends, we each walk away with everything we had when we started. But if you left now, you'd walk away with my heart."

Someone behind them groaned. Then Thomas called out, "Dude, I hope that sounded cooler in your head. 'Cause that was lame."

Jonathon's eyes drifted closed for an instant and he gave a nod of chagrin. "It actually did sound cooler in my head."

"I thought it sounded great!" Lacey called out.

Wendy threaded her fingers through Jonathon's hair and pulled his mouth down to hers. Just before his lips touched hers, she admitted, "I thought it sounded pretty good too."

His mouth was warm and moist over hers. The kiss sweet and gentle. Full of love. Full of potential.

When he lifted his head, she said, "I love you, Jonathon Bagdon. If this scares you, then you're not alone. Because it terrifies me too. Everything about it. But I figured, at least we're not alone in it."

He flashed her one of those rare smiles that squeezed her heart and didn't let go. "I love you, Gwendolyn Leland Morgan Bagdon. Will you marry me?" Then he grinned and added, "Again."

She flung her arms around him and whispered a yes into his ear. Then added, "You know I prefer just the simple Wendy Bagdon."

She glanced around Jonathon's shoulder to see Lacey

giving her a big thumbs-up. Thomas was still shaking his head, as though the uncle he barely knew had been a huge disappointment. Marie had leaned her back against her husband's chest and he'd wrapped an arm around her. They were both grinning widely.

Wendy's own family looked less exuberant. Uncle Hank was scowling. Hank Jr. had pulled out his BlackBerry and was checking his messages. Helen had her arms crossed over her chest, looking about ten seconds away from a meltdown. But her mother was smiling and as Wendy watched, her father gave her mother's hand a squeeze. Even Mema seemed—almost—to be smiling.

Wendy nodded in her uncle's direction and whispered to Jonathon. "What about the government contract?"

He scoffed. "Who cares? One decision isn't going to change the course of FMJ's future. One government contract won or lost isn't going to make or break the company."

"It's a lot of money."

"And we're a diverse company. We'll be fine."

"You're sure?" she asked, because she hated to think he might regret the decision down the road.

By way of answering, he grabbed her hand and pulled her back over to the table where her family still sat.

He draped an arm over her shoulder and pulled her against his chest. "Henry," he began formally. "If you'd like, we can negotiate visitation rights for you, but only if you back off." He shifted his gaze to Helen. "If anyone in this family wants to fight for Peyton, then bring it on. Just know that we're going to fight for her. We have every intention of winning. No matter how much it costs. And if you do bring this fight to our doorstep, when you lose, you won't ever see Peyton or Wendy again."

Before Uncle Hank could say anything, Mema pushed back her chair and stood slowly. "I don't think we need to worry about that. Though I do expect to see both my granddaughter and my great-granddaughter more often now that she's settled down."

"We can do that." Jonathon nodded formally. Then he gave Wendy's shoulder a squeeze. "Now, if you'll excuse us, I'm going to take my bride and my daughter and we're going to go have breakfast." He glanced down at her. "How does a doughnut from Cutie Pies sound?"

"Perfect."

She didn't mention the banana chocolate-chip waffles. That seemed like a lifetime ago anyway.

They walked the few blocks to Cutie Pies with Jonathon's family trailing behind. They'd almost reached the restaurant, when Wendy asked, "When did you realize you loved me?"

He stopped walking and looked down at her. "I think I've always loved you." Then he laughed. "You didn't really think I asked you to marry me just to keep you from quitting, did you?"

"Yeah," she admitted. "I did."

"Come on, nobody's that good of an assistant."

She socked him in the arm. "Excuse me, but yes I am!"

"You are an amazing assistant." He dropped a kiss onto her forehead. "But you're an even better wife."

* * * * *

Read on for a sneak preview of Carol Marinelli's
PUTTING ALICE BACK TOGETHER!

Hugh hired bikes!

You know that saying: 'It's like riding a bike, you never forget'?

I'd never learnt in the first place.

I never got past training wheels.

'You've got limited upper-body strength?' He stopped and looked at me.

I had been explaining to him as I wobbled along and tried to stay up that I really had no centre of balance. I mean *really* had no centre of balance. And when we decided, fairly quickly, that a bike ride along the Yarra perhaps, after all, wasn't the best activity (he'd kept insisting I'd be fine once I was on, that you never forget), I threw in too my other disability. I told him about my limited upper-body strength, just in case he took me to an indoor rock-climbing centre next. I'd honestly forgotten he was a doctor, and he seemed worried, like I'd had a mini-stroke in the past or had mild cerebral palsy or something.

'God, Alice, I'm sorry—you should have said. What happened?'

And then I had had to tell him that it was a self-diagnosis. 'Well, I could never get up the ropes at the gym at school.' We were pushing our bikes back. 'I can't blow-dry the back of my hair…' He started laughing.

Not like Lisa who was laughing at me—he was just laughing and so was I. We got a full refund because we'd only been on our bikes ten minutes, but I hadn't failed. If anything, we were getting on better.

And better.

We went to St Kilda to the lovely bitty shops and I found these miniature Russian dolls. They were tiny, made of tin or something, the biggest no bigger than my thumbnail. Every time we opened them, there was another tiny one, and then another, all reds and yellows and greens.

They were divine.

We were facing each other, looking down at the palm of my hand, and our heads touched.

If I put my hand up now, I can feel where our heads touched.

I remember that moment.

I remember it a lot.

Our heads connected for a second and it was alchemic; it was as if our minds kissed hello.

I just have to touch my head, just there at the very spot and I can, whenever I want to, relive that moment.

So many times I do.

'Get them.' Hugh said, and I would have, except that little bit of tin cost more than a hundred dollars and, though that usually wouldn't have stopped me, I wasn't about to have my card declined in front of him.

I put them back.

'Nope.' I gave him a smile. 'Gotta stop the impulse

spending.'

We had lunch.

Out on the pavement and I can't remember what we ate, I just remember being happy. Actually, I can remember: I had Caesar salad because it was the lowest carb thing I could find. We drank water and I *do* remember not giving it a thought.

I was just thirsty.

And happy.

He went to the loo and I chatted to a girl at the next table, just chatted away. Hugh was gone for ages and I was glad I hadn't demanded Dan from the universe, because I would have been worried about how long he was taking.

Do I go on about the universe too much? I don't know, but what I do know is that something *was* looking out for me, helping me to be my best, not to **** this up as I usually do. You see, we walked on the beach, we went for another coffee and by that time it was evening and we went home and he gave me a present.

Those Russian dolls.

I held them in my palm, and it was the nicest thing he could have done for me.

They are absolutely my favourite thing and I've just stopped to look at them now. I've just stopped to take them apart and then put them all back together again and I can still feel the wonder I felt on that day.

He was the only man who had bought something for me, I mean something truly special. Something beautiful, something thoughtful, something just for me.

MILLS & BOON® Book Club *2 Free Stories!*

Get your free stories now at
www.millsandboon.co.uk/freebookoffer

Or fill in the form below and post it back to us

THE MILLS & BOON® BOOK CLUB™—HERE'S HOW IT WORKS: Accepting your free stories places you under no obligation to buy anything. You may keep the stories and return the despatch note marked 'Cancel'. If we do not hear from you, about a month later we'll send you 2 Desire™ 2-in-1 books priced at £5.30* each. There is no extra charge for post and packaging. You may cancel at any time, otherwise we will send you 4 stories a month which you may purchase or return to us—the choice is yours. *Terms and prices subject to change without notice. Offer valid in UK only. Applicants must be 18 or over. Offer expires 31st July 2012. **For full terms and conditions, please go to www.millsandboon.co.uk**

Mrs/Miss/Ms/Mr (please circle)

First Name

Surname

Address

Postcode

E-mail

Send this completed page to: Mills & Boon Book Club, Free Book Offer, FREEPOST NAT 10298, Richmond, Surrey, TW9 1BR

Find out more at
www.millsandboon.co.uk/freebookoffer

Visit us Online

0112/D2XEA

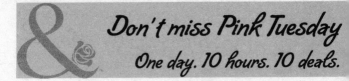

Don't miss Pink Tuesday
One day. 10 hours. 10 deals.

PINK TUESDAY IS COMING!

10 hours...10 unmissable deals!

This Valentine's Day we will be bringing you fantastic offers across a range of our titles—each hour, on the hour!

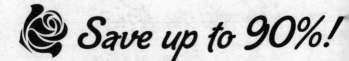

Save up to 90%!

Pink Tuesday starts
9am Tuesday 14th February

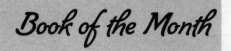

   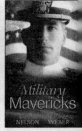